The Genesis Modification

Peter Kruger

Steinkrug

ISBN: 0 9540977 1 8

Steinkrug Publications Ltd
20 Leaden Hill Orwell
Royston Herts SG8 5QH
www.steinkrug.com

Printed and bound by Antony Rowe Limited, Eastbourne

Monday 16th April 2001

West Farm Way, a tree-lined country lane, cut across the rainswept fields bordered by the triangle of roads which joined the Fenland market towns of Wisbech, Littleport and Downham. This was not the obvious place to trap a passing criminal. True, some motorists, returning to Downham from the Three Holes public house, preferred this quiet route if they were over the alcohol limit. But the patrol car, half-hidden by a tall hedgerow, had been parked at the eastern end of the lane in the village of Nordelph long before closing time, and it was now an hour since last orders were called in the Three Holes.

For one of the occupants of the car, Sergeant Bryant, crime in West Norfolk had become predictably dull. Pieces of theatre were played out by a familiar band of actors: noisy youths who loitered at village bus stops on summer evenings; who fought with each other or carried out minor acts of vandalism — apprentice outlaws who sprayed graffiti on buildings or, on rare occasions, stole a car. Most of these bit players would leave the stage early, for a more mundane role in front of the television with the wife and kids. Those who persisted roamed the local industrial estates, gnawing like rats at the doors of factories. For meagre reward they set off burglar alarms, broke windows, terrified shopkeepers, injured petrol station attendants and dumped burnt-out vans and cars in fields and ditches.

There were, of course, guest stars. The long, dark roads aided a fast and undetected escape back to the Midlands and London for house burglars and hare coursers. But that night a different band of strolling players was to put on a show — one in which Bryant would have a starring role.

No cars had passed for an hour. Bryant's partner, Constable Parnell, suggested waiting another ten minutes, then moving on. Bryant did not answer. Five minutes later the radio controller's voice filled the car. "Report of a disturbance in a field at the Littleport road end of West Farm Lane. Are you still in place?"

Bryant picked up the radio microphone. "Yes, we're still here. Should arrive on the scene in five minutes." Parnell started the car, put it in gear and set off. The wheels slithered across the lane, shedding the mud they had collected from the verge, and ploughed through the deep puddles at the side of the road. Water swished

1

through the wheel arches, sounding like tearing cloth. Parnell felt the steering wheel tug at his hands. The car's headlights threw ghostlike reflections up into the overhanging willow trees. Bryant indicated with his hand that Parnell should slow down. At the next bend a minibus was parked some five metres down one of the small tracks which led off the lane into the darkness of the overcast Fen landscape.

"Not exactly well hidden," said Parnell, applying the brakes and bringing the car to a halt.

Bryant got out of the car. The bus had Green Alliance stickers on the windows and the rear door was unlocked. He climbed onto the bank of the ditch which ran along the edge of the track. The air was warm and damp, and the sound of switchbills slashing oilseed rape carried through the mist. In the car, Parnell was asking the controller to check the registration of the minibus.

Bryant returned and took the microphone from Parnell. "Could we have some back-up? There are about ten to fifteen people destroying crops. I suggest you get a unit with some dogs to approach West Farm Lane along the track which leads off the Littleport road to the south of our current position." He was just about to replace the microphone, but changed his mind. "Did the person who reported this say they were waiting at the scene?"

There was a delay before the controller replied. "It was a call from a mobile phone. They said they were driving past and saw some people in a field. That's all we've got, except that the field is owned by a farmer called Whiteside."

Bryant looked puzzled. He turned to Parnell. "I think there's someone a little way down the track, watching the bus."

"What makes you think that?"

"The bus isn't locked. Perhaps he was supposed to wait in it but has wandered off."

"Call of nature, you mean?"

"Perhaps."

Parnell sat and thought for a while, then said under his breath, "Not very clever — the bus being so obvious. They were bound to get caught, weren't they?"

Bryant laughed, then sighed. "That's the general idea. Get arrested and make their speeches in court for the media. Martyrs for the cause. God knows."

Thirty minutes later the radio controller confirmed that the second unit was in place. The two policemen got out of the car and switched on their torches. Parnell, striding down the track towards the sound of the switchbills, was glad of the opportunity to stretch his legs. Being over six foot tall, he found the cramped panda car uncomfortable. Bryant, being shorter, struggled to keep up. "Can you hear something?" he whispered. "Someone on the other side of that hedge?"

Parnell shone his torch around at waist level, then shook his head.

After forty metres, the track opened onto a field of rape. The pair pointed their torches to the ground and moved slowly through the opening. Bryant became aware of a shape moving on his right. Before he could turn, a wooden club smashed into his face. Overcome by a sickening dizziness, he collapsed, face downwards.

Bryant could hear a voice in the distance. The voice belonged to Parnell, who was leaning over him and calling for assistance on the radio. The odour of damp oilseed rape — a smell like that of rotting cabbage — filled his left nostril, while the right one dripped blood onto the ground. Now there were other sounds: voices, dogs barking and, from the top of the track, the roar of the minibus's engine as it drove away.

Bryant could feel his face begin to swell into the distorted mass of flesh which, two days later, was reproduced in lurid colour on the front pages of the tabloid newspapers, under headlines like 'Green Thugs Strike' and 'Time to Show the Greens the Red Card'.

By the following weekend Bryant had recovered enough to sit up in his bed and speak to the Agriculture Minister, who came to visit him in Cambridge's Addenbrooke's Hospital. However, in the media his face remained a smashed and bloody mess, and it appeared on a regular basis — even in the broadsheets. *The Times'* headline asked, 'Why has the Green Movement Resorted to Violence?'

Bryant's broken face made its final appearance in *The Guardian* — beside those of Green Alliance members convicted of criminal damage, in what had become known as 'the Whiteside Farm attack'. No-one was convicted of the actual attack on Bryant, who returned to work ten months later. He often complained of headaches and blurred vision, which were still troubling him when he died, seven years later, of sinusitis.

1

Friday 16th August 2041

"Did you hear me?" the young woman asked, raising her voice slightly. "I've just found a body. Now, are you going to do something about it or not?"

Private Simon Leftwich had heard the woman but gave her no more than a cursory glance. Fearing that the approach was an attempt to distract him, he slowly released the safety catch of his gun. He surveyed the top end of Oxford Street, then Park Lane and the edge of Hyde Park. Except for a few cyclists and pedestrians, they were all deserted. Finally he turned his attention to the woman. "Tell the police about it," he snapped nervously.

"You are the police," she replied.

"Army. London Regiment."

"Same thing."

It was not the same thing. The police did not spend all day standing guard outside restaurants, on bridges and in railway stations. Simon had made the mistake of not being able to suggest a skill or area of expertise he would be interested in pursuing when he finished technical college. So, at the age of seventeen, he was drafted into the army. That was nine months ago, and since then he had been through six months of basic training, before being allocated to the London Regiment as a guard.

As trouble was virtually unheard of in the city centre, boredom (which set in between mealtimes) was the only negative aspect of guarding this restaurant. He was not stuck out in some overgrown part of the suburbs. The Centre Point headquarters at the other end of Oxford Street was almost in view, and there were plenty of other soldiers passing by. Simon's worst assignment had been Waterloo station — anywhere near the river or the border with the East End was bad news. In six months they would ask him, again, if he wanted to learn a skill, and he would make damn sure he had thought of something by then.

It was the woman's East End accent, and the rumour that something major was going to happen today, which made Simon edgy. He took out his radio and flicked the switch. "Sir! Private Leftwich. Marble Arch. There's a situation here."

4

The mid-morning sun streamed into the control room on the top floor of Centre Point. Ross Smith, controller of London Central region, was surveying the horizon through binoculars while drinking tea from a gold-rimmed cup. He should have been studying the buildings beneath the window but a fire to the south had caught his attention. Ross had served with the South London Militia, which had been formed to protect the Afro-Caribbean residents from attack during the food shortages. However, during the epidemics it had been decided to evacuate the south. Those who survived in suburbs such as Croydon and Sutton had, in 2009, been evacuated through Southwark and Brixton. A year later Merton and Lewisham had been abandoned, and finally Ross came north with the remaining population of Brixton and Lambeth. Resettlement north of the river was seen as the only way of keeping London's population dense enough for the city to remain viable. It also avoided the sort of racial conflicts which had torn apart US cities like New York and Chicago. South of the Thames, only the houses around Waterloo station were safe enough to live in. This area, and a corridor of land along which the Eurostar trains travelled to the Channel Tunnel, was heavily guarded by the army.

Smoke rose from the area to the south of Brixton where Ross had lived as a child. The mixture of blue and white smoke meant the fire was being fuelled by a combination of dried vegetation and wood. Vegetation choked streets and gardens, and the wood was what remained of the roofs and flooring of abandoned and decaying houses. Most fires started spontaneously. Winter saw streets split open by the frost, and spring brought new crops of grasses and weeds, growing from the cracks. Each year the cracks themselves grew, and once-busy streets and pavements would eventually be full of trees and bushes. In the summer the vegetation was scorched by the sun. Soon there was enough dried material to fuel large fires — which raged, unchecked, for days. Each spring the cityscape would become greener as new vegetation grew up around and in the shells of buildings. Ross watched as, bit by bit, his childhood home sank into a bubbling green swamp of flora.

The radio on the desk crackled into life. Replacing the gold-rimmed teacup on its saucer and putting down his binoculars, Ross picked up the microphone. "What sort of situation?"

Leftwich's explanation broke the tension which had been

building up in the control room during the morning. "A body. That's novel. We don't see many of those, do we?" Ross said into the microphone, then turned and smiled at the other controllers. "Tell her to talk to the police."

Leftwich's voice came back over the radio, his sentences punctuated by the sound of the irate woman. Ross moved away from his desk to get a good view down Oxford Street.

Jack Patterson, commander of the London Regiment, had also overheard the conversation. He avoided the temptation to seek some visual fix on Leftwich's situation and kept his eyes on Ross. "Do you think it's a diversion?" he asked.

Ross shrugged. "Can't be sure yet, but the woman has an East London accent."

Patterson picked up the phone on Ross's desk and pressed one of the buttons. "Ted, Jack here. Seen anything odd on any of your screens?" He paused to listen. "Well, there may be something starting up. Probably a good idea to keep a special eye on the river, the East End border posts and the stations."

Putting the phone down, Patterson turned and addressed the room in general. "Right! Call everyone who is guarding anything other than a restaurant and make sure they're awake." He turned back to Ross. "Get the lad to relay this woman's name and address — and the place where she found this 'body' — then I'll pass it on to Police Liaison and get shot of it," adding, as an afterthought, "Perhaps the police will tell us more about this 'something big' they keep on about." He walked across the room to the east-facing window.

If something big was about to happen, it would probably start in the East. The sadness which Patterson always felt when looking out over the East End returned. Most of the controllers he knew had either been transferred into the army, when the militias and neighbourhood defence units were disbanded, or had been recruited in the last ten years. But the commander of the London Division had served in the army for thirty years, having volunteered before the famine and the epidemics.

Patterson believed Britain should not have sunk to this level. He blamed the Socialists for being too naive to realise people would tear each other apart for the last lorry-load of tinned beans rather than wait calmly for farmers to produce alternatives. He was bitter because the King — whom, in theory, he still served — vacillated and put his faith in the people's goodwill and patience, both of which ran out as soon as the supermarket shelves emptied.

6

He was angry because David Fairchild, leader of the UK Green Alliance and now effectively a dictator, had used anarchists and foreign powers to gain power himself.

If there had not been the confusion and anarchy — caused by food riots, the looting of warehouses, and the hijacking of any lorry or train that looked as though it might be carrying food — things *might* have been different. If the government had asked the army to prevent the ransacking of the countryside and the pillaging of hospitals, then perhaps (just perhaps) there wouldn't have been the epidemics.

The decision to let the army step in where the police had failed came to late. Even then, woolly-minded liberals thought it was worth giving people, who were behaving like animals, a fair trial. In those days the only way to deal with criminals was there and then - on the spot. But, by the time politicians realised that, the epidemics (everything from TB to food poisoning) were cutting a large enough swathe through the population to make executions virtually unnecessary.

It was from this same east-facing window of Centre Point that Patterson, then just a corporal, had seen two German Airforce Tornado fighter bombers closing in on their target. The planes, from the only operational air force left in Europe, were given the go-ahead to destroy Canary Wharf Tower. The tower was being used as a headquarters and command post by the East End Rebels, a loose alliance of anarchist and terrorist groups. The army had been pressing for some time for a clampdown on anarchists. The then socialist government also wanted the army to act, but the Green Party, who held the balance of power, voted against it. The bombing of the tower had taken place within months of the Green Party gaining absolute power. A cynic might suspect that a deal had been struck between the Greens and the army. He might think that the anarchists were merely being used by the Greens to weaken the Socialists. Shortly after the bombing, the army secured control of all eastern access points to the M25 London orbital motorway. Supplies of fresh food to the East End were cut off. A year later the rail route to the Channel Tunnel was re-opened and secured. By then, floods of refugees had streamed through border posts that had been set up at river crossings and along the old A11 road.

Today there are still dissenting elements in the rapidly decaying East End, but the bulk of the population has relocated to the fingers of settlements that push out to the north and west, into the undergrowth that becomes harder to penetrate each year. Settlement takes place along transport routes that, in most cases, are the sections of the underground that run near or on the surface. The route to Heathrow airport is still open and people occupy houses around the stations along the old District and Piccadilly lines. West Ruislip marks London's most north-westerly point; beyond, there are just a few dairy and chicken farms. To the north, the city boundary is the M25 itself, with viable communities in Barnet, Southgate and Enfield.

The fire Ross was watching was one of three burning just inside the city limits. Despite several overnight thunderstorms, the dried undergrowth had been alight for most of the week. The fire's location had been worked out by correlating reports from patrols on the M25 with observations from Centre Point. If fire moved close to an inhabited area, warnings were issued to local unit commanders. They, in turn, mobilised volunteer fire and rescue squads — an event which became rarer with each passing year.

Patterson left the window and descended the three flights of stairs to the office of the Police Liaison team. The size of London's remaining population, and the fact that the capital was still the seat of a government of sorts, gave Patterson more influence than commanders of other metropolitan areas, such as Manchester, Glasgow and Birmingham. He even had more clout than commanders in the rural areas, who were generally more favoured by the Green Alliance government. All the same, he felt he, and the army, were not trusted. The current alert was a case in point: he was hearing about it third-hand in the form of rumours and requests for extra guards.

Patterson hesitated when he reached the door of the Police Liaison office. He retraced his steps along the corridor and entered a door from which the nameplate had been removed. A weasel-faced youth with tightly curled blond hair peered over the top of a computer monitor. Patterson leant over the intelligence officer's desk and whispered: "Dennis, I'm just taking this along to Police Liaison." He handed over Ross's piece of paper. "It might be an idea if some of your people dropped in there before Plod arrives. Just in case someone on our side has been a bit naughty." Patterson watched as Dennis typed the details into the computer. "And Dennis," he added, snatching back the piece of paper, "tell them to put gloves on before they touch anything."

Standing behind the Police Liaison duty officer, Patterson could hear the usual banter and buck-passing that was part and parcel of any contact with the Metropolitan Police.

"No, we can't deal with it ourselves. It's a dead body. It's not going to get up and cause a riot, rob a restaurant or threaten food distribution. You know the rules." The slim grey haired woman was hunched over her desk, doodling around Ross's notes on the piece of paper. She listened, with obvious lack of interest, to the excuses and pleading coming from the telephone, then she picked up the paper and started to read out the address slowly.

"Adelphi, Hotel, Leinster Street, L-e-i-n-s-t-e-r, Street. Got that? A dead body, male, shot. Shot in the head. Off Bayswater Road. It was reported by a Miss Caroline Tate. No. Tate, T-a-t-e." The policeman, at the other end of the phone, repeated the last word, then made one last attempt to get the army to deal with it themselves.

"No we can't just take the body and bury it in the park," the woman said indignantly. She turned and looked at Patterson, then shouted down the phone: "Take it to the incinerator? What do you think we are? A refuse service? Anyway, there's one other thing. This body has got an American passport."

*

In the Army Liaison section of the Home Office the young police constable took his feet off the desk and lurched forward in his chair. "An American? Hang on a minute while I get a pencil and take some details"

The response was a loud shriek, which caused the policeman to move the receiver away from his ear. "No, that's right," he said, "I wasn't writing it down." A stream of abuse poured out of the phone. Eventually, when he felt it was safe to do so, he continued the conversation. "Well, I thought that, as we are very, *very* busy at the moment... No I'm not being patronising... I don't think using that sort of language is helpful. As I was saying, it's obvious that, in this heat, the hotel owner would have to get rid of the body as soon as possible. Now, if you had said from the start that the person was American, that would have made a difference."

The constable scribbled down the details on his notepad. "Well, thanks for the information, and sorry for the mix-up.

Anything we can do for you at the moment?" he asked, then listened as the woman relayed Commander Patterson's enquiry.

"Yes, we've heard there's something big in the pipeline. Beyond that, I can't say." Then, to make amends for the irritation he had caused, he added, "We haven't been put on a full alert or anything. No leave cancelled. My guess is, it isn't anything directly affecting the London area, but that's only a guess."

The woman thanked him. Putting down the phone, the policeman crossed the corridor to the Deputy Commissioner's office.

*

"Dead American. Hotel in Bayswater. Shot." He feigned indifference, and was about to drop the note into the in-tray when Deputy Commissioner Stephen Langford stopped him.

"Don't put it there. Take it downstairs to Mike Allchurch." Then, easing himself out of his chair, Langford grabbed the note. "Second thoughts. Take it myself. Could do with the exercise."

Langford's sixty-four years showed in his face and his gait. The bags under his hooded, bloodshot eyes bore witness to years of sleepless nights. Thinning grey hair — brushed back from his narrow, lined forehead — and a slow shuffling walk both betrayed the battering his mind and body had endured. For most of his career this professional policeman had tried to maintain order in times when the rule of law had been ignored by politicians, the army and the population at large.

The Deputy's office was on the tenth floor of the Home Office and commanded an impressive view of what was left of London's skyline and the area around the Houses of Parliament. Buildings belonging to the banks and financial institutions in the City were no longer occupied. Falling panes of glass and cladding meant whole streets had had to be sealed off. The police and the army used some of the remaining, taller, buildings. Apart from the lifts, Centre Point, the Home Office and the Post Office Tower were well maintained.

The Metropolitan Police, who should have been housed in New Scotland Yard, had been relocated to the Home Office during the troubles. Once there, they came under party control. While the party also exerted some control over regional police forces, it was the Metropolitan Police who (despite their claims of impartiality) were regarded as the Greens' own private security arm.

All the old ministries — such as Health, Education, and Industry —were housed in existing government buildings in Victoria Street. The exception was the Ministry of Agriculture, which was located in Great George Street, next to Parliament Square.

The Houses of Parliament contained only the offices of UKGA party members. The debating chambers, although they had been preserved, were never used. The transformation from democracy to a one-party state with a multitude of new laws — some of them conflicting because they had been created by anonymous *ad hoc* committees all acting independently — was one of Langford's biggest headaches. His sleepless nights were due, in part, to the knowledge that people were imprisoned, had even been executed, for infringing some obscure regulation; to the realisation that much of the law was fluid, and based on the whim of a party member whose opinion happened to be flavour of the week.

*

Mike Allchurch saw the door at the end of the corridor open. "Dead man walking," he thought when he saw Langford. He wondered why, when so many seemingly fit people had died, the Deputy, who was so visibly run down, had not been laid low by disease. Perhaps some inner force, or hidden motivation, was driving his crippled frame.

"Mike," mumbled Langford as he entered the office, his trembling hand clutching the piece of paper, "just got this from Army Liaison."

Mike glanced at the scribbled note, and was going to suggest it wasn't worth bothering about.

"American. The chap's an American," said Langford, his voice trailing away into a whisper. "We had better take a look, just in case..." Without waiting for a reply, he turned and drifted, ghostlike, out of the office and back down the corridor.

Mike took a second, more detailed, look at the note. He turned to his assistant, who was thumbing through a pile of papers and occasionally tapping at the keyboard of a computer. "Enjoying that?"

Brian Tyler, aged twenty-three, clean-shaven, with short brown hair and a broad, bony face, looked up and scowled. Without answering, he picked up another sheet of paper, ran his finger down it and tapped at the keyboard again.

"Just thought you might want a break," Mike said, holding out the note.

Brian took the piece of paper and read it. Then, standing up, he began to walk across to the wall map of Central London.

"It's within four miles," snapped Mike, before Brian had got anywhere near the map.

"Oh no, sir!" Brian pleaded.

"Oh yes! You know the rule."

"Any journey," they both recited together, "of less than four miles is, unless it is deemed an emergency, to be made without the aid of motorised transport."

"And this is not an emergency," added Mike. "Still, nice day for a bike ride round the park."

Brian reached into his desk drawer, took out a mobile phone and pressed one of the buttons. The phone in front of Mike rang, but stopped before he could answer it.

"Sorry. Just testing the battery." Brian dropped the phone into the rucksack he had picked up from beside his desk.

Mike sighed and shook his head.

Brian threw the rucksack over his shoulder and walked to the door. "Bet it was suicide. Ten euros says it's suicide."

"Go on. Get on with it," Mike said.

But Brian did not go. "This American comes over here thinking we've got plenty to eat, decent houses, hospitals and everything. Then finds out what it's really like and — bang! — shoots himself. Tell you what, five euros says it's suicide."

"No. And don't go up there with preconceived ideas. Just write down what you see. Get the body disposed of. Then come back."

"Go on. Five euros."

"No. I'm not betting."

"All right. My five says it's suicide — your one euro says it isn't"

"No. Final. Now go and get on with it."

"Your loss if I'm wrong." Brian's voice echoed back up the corridor.

*

Mike returned to the set of documents he had been working on before Langford interrupted him. Unlike the Deputy, he had not chosen policing as a profession. Thirty-six years ago he had been a graduate trainee with a firm of consultants, advising the retail industry on security. But thirty years ago the retail industry had ceased to exist. Both his parents died of malnutrition, as had so many other old people. He himself had been in a Ukrainian work camp when they died. A year after his return, food poisoning had taken both his wife and his daughter. Somewhere amongst all the loss Mike's own life had stopped. He remarried, of course. It was not a time when living alone was an option. Just as the inhabitants of the suburbs regrouped and resettled in order to keep communities viable, so individuals sought new partners to guarantee their family's survival. The whole of London could be viewed as one vast marriage of convenience. This did not mean that his marriage was an unhappy one. He and Linda spent most of their free time together; they ate and slept together and took care of each other's children.

Mike took a page from a fat, loose-leaf file. A copy of the same page was displayed on a computer screen. The file was a comprehensive list of the laws currently enforceable in the Greater London Area — or, as Langford called it, the 'Not So' Greater London Area. Britain was under martial law, but martial law in name only, as neither of the two other bodies of law — criminal and civil — had been suspended. This combination of laws was a by-product of various power struggles between politicians, vigilantes and the army.

In the main, martial law concerned itself with the distribution and storage of food. It also extended into areas such as assembly, civil order, and arms control. Criminal law dealt with the use of vehicles, immigration and the relocation of citizens, as well as with crimes against the person and against property other than food. Civil law, administered by district councils, dealt with housing and land rights, and also with the 'community education and responsibility programme'.

There was overlap, for example when someone stole a watch from a diner in a restaurant, or a van containing food. As most people arrested by the army claimed they had only broken a criminal — or even a civil — law, it had been decided to amalgamate the three sections. Arrest, trial and punishment could in theory be carried out by the army, the police or the district councils — regardless of which law had been broken. In fact, as Mike was both a policemen and a member of his district council, he could claim both civil and criminal jurisdiction. This had only been possible since the abolition of the death penalty. Many offences covered by martial law had been capital ones, whereas only a few of the crimes covered by criminal law — and none of those covered by civil law — had carried the death sentence.

Mike was dealing with the section of law covering the disposal of corpses. As the death rate had fallen dramatically since 2010, when these laws had first been drafted, most of the section had become irrelevant.

It was over ten years since he had looked at section ML 800.210. He had made the mistake then of not realising that, owing to staff shortages, the co-ordination committee (who assigned the law-amendment tasks) consisted of just two clerks. The clerks merely collated the returned sections and drafted any new regulations required. This turning of the law on its head had become apparent when, flippantly, Mike added a new law. His law stated that anyone found guilty of wasting potential agricultural land by decorating graves with flowers could be punished with a custodial sentence. Not only had the law been incorporated without question; a corresponding regulation was created. Since then, Mike had spent a number of embarrassing evenings listening to this law being derided. Fellow members of West Ruislip District Council Enforcement Committee would mutter, under their breath, that only an idiot would dream up such a regulation. Tearful old ladies were dragged in front of the committee, only to be given a conditional discharge. Nevertheless the regulation did increase interest in ornamental cabbages.

The regulations would have been regarded, in any other times, as both callous and comical. When a death was reported, the deceased's S-Card (food ration card) number had to be surrendered in exchange for a metal dog-tag with the S-Card number stamped on it. The dog-tag had to be attached to the body. 'The recommended means of disposal is cremation — Important — Do not attempt to do this yourself.' But, in the early days, people did. They put members of their family into old cars and set them alight. The alternative was to have their loved ones taken away and thrown into an incinerator, together with dead cattle, stray dogs and offal. If you had the land, you could bury the body yourself, but only if the burial required no more than five hours' labour. And 'Disposing of a body in a river or reservoir is punishable by death'.

Mike struck out the regulation relating to flowers and amended the concomitant law. Mercifully, detecting minor infringements of disposal regulations was difficult, if not impossible. Apart from spectacular home cremations, few people were caught and even fewer convicted. As far as Mike was concerned, punishing people at a time of grief was inherently unjust, and in some cases counter-productive. Sending a doctor and his wife to a penal farm merely aggravated the shortage of medical staff in London. And the soldier who executed a man on the spot, for trying to throw a body into the Thames, merely created another body to dispose of.

All references to execution and custodial sentences for first offences, with the exception of disposal in water, were deleted. Since the law had been drafted, attitudes to death had changed. The sheer number of bodies to be disposed of — in some weeks up to thirty thousand in the London area alone — meant that there was little time for sentiment. The modern funeral was about as ceremonial as the delivery of an old mattress to a domestic waste collection centre. Perhaps this explained why Brian and the rest of his generation had such a relaxed attitude to death. Death was no longer a private affair. It was no longer hidden away in back bedrooms or behind curtains in hospital wards. It was something the younger generation had grown up with. They had looked after dying parents, prepared their brothers and sisters for incineration and stepped over bodies in the street.

*

The telephone rang. It was Brian. "Sir, you had better come and have a look at this."

"Why?"

"Well, it was murder. Shame you didn't have that bet, isn't it?"

"I'm not coming up there just for you to gloat. Take some statements, sort the body out and come back. I'll see you..."

"No, sir. I think you should come." Brian hesitated, then added, "I don't want to talk about it over the phone. Just come."

"OK, OK. I'll be there in half an hour."

"Five euros says it will take you forty minutes."

Mike was tempted to accept the challenge, but didn't. Replacing the handset, then shutting down the computer, he debated whether to take his rucksack, and eventually decided that Brian would have everything that might be needed.

Four flights of stairs later, Mike was standing at the back of the building. Under the watchful eye of an armed police guard, he took a bicycle out of the rack. After riding the bicycle for some 10 metres, it became obvious the seat was set too high. He returned to the rack and selected another bicycle. It was better: he stood, and pushed hard on the pedals to propel himself up the ramp leading to the street.

"Legs shrunk again, have they?" The guard laughed as he raised the barrier.

"I'm wearing them out running up and down those bloody stairs," Mike shouted, over his shoulder.

*

The fresh, warm summer air rushed past his face as he rode along Queen Anne's Gate to St James's Park. It was only recently that cycling through London had been any fun at all. Up to a year ago, a choking blue haze, generated by the fires in the suburbs, had made travelling any distance an arduous and even (for asthmatics) perilous undertaking. Today there was no smoke. On Constitution Hill a group of young men were using wooden frames to herd pigs into the back of a cattle lorry. An older man, a shotgun slung over his shoulder, was hurling abuse at the boys as the squealing animals darted across the road. On the pavement, three carcasses lay in pools of blood.

Mike dismounted and approached the group warily, attempting not to startle the few pigs the young men had managed to trap.

"What a bunch of idiots! Sometimes I think it would be better to stick *them* in the lorry," said the old man.

"That the last of them?" asked Mike.

"Yep. All gone. These will be taken up to Harrow today, then that's it."

"I thought they were going to Hampstead."

"No. A change of plan. Harrow."

"They won't last long there."

"I told them that." The old man dragged the cap off his bald head and wiped his brow. "I told them, poachers will have the lot. Still, they'll find out."

A large pig crashed into a wooden frame, sending one of the boys sprawling onto the road. The rest of the pigs rushed into the thick undergrowth of Green Park. "Bloody idiots!" the old man shouted, grabbing the shotgun and going after the pigs. "At this rate we'll be eating bacon sandwiches from now till bloody Christmas!"

Mike remounted his bicycle and continued, on past Hyde Park Corner and into Park Lane. He smiled to himself as he imagined the meetings, which must have dragged on into the night at the Ministry of Agriculture, to resolve the long-standing problem of the Green Park pigs. On gaining power in 2008, the third year of the food shortages, the UKGA were concerned that they appeared to be an urban-based government forcing agricultural policies onto rural communities. With the King's help, a small mixed farm was set up in Hyde Park, opposite the headquarters of the UKGA in Park Lane. Wheat, barley and potatoes were grown inside the park. Flocks of sheep and herds of cows grazed the grass on the perimeter. The King had stocked the park with the animals from a number of farms on the royal estates — including one hundred pigs. Although the farm did raise the morale of Londoners (who could see that Britain might now be capable, despite rumours to the contrary, of producing enough food for everyone), it obviously produced only a small fraction of the food Londoners needed, even on the near-starvation diet of the time. In terms of convincing rural Britain that the government understood the people's plight, the farm was not a great success and, because food shortages had eased, the park was being returned to grass. Owing to chronic shortages of labour and fuel, however, the sheep and cows were retained as an alternative to mowing the grass.

The pigs had become an embarrassment for the UKGA. It was not good for a political party that promoted a healthy vegetarian diet to have porkers running around just metres from their headquarters. It was decided to move the pigs along the road to Hyde Park Corner. Breaking through the temporary fencing there, the pigs made their escape: groups of them were rounded up as far away as Piccadilly and Trafalgar Square, but the majority of the animals disappeared into the overgrown thicket of Green Park and resisted all attempts to remove them. It was decided to combine the clearance of Green Park with the recapture of the pigs. The task was assigned to the staff and pupils of Hertfordshire Agricultural College, with some input from the army. The army, and the civil servants in the Ministry of Agriculture, suggested that the best place for the pigs would be Hampstead Heath. This was overruled by the UKGA, who plumped for Harrow. Harrow was a poachers' paradise: the military presence was minimal, because the London Division thought it was too far away from the City, and the Middlesex Division were reluctant to operate inside the M25 boundary. Mike suspected that the UKGA were hoping the poachers would save them the embarrassment of having to act as butchers. However, judging by the gunfire he could hear behind him, things were not going to plan.

The ground floor of the UKGA headquarters had once been a car showroom. Behind a large plate-glass window were pictures of rolling fields, wind farms and smiling agricultural workers. There was no picture of David Fairchild, leader of the party. Fairchild's dislike of personality cults meant that the only reference to him was an announcement of his appointment for a second four-year term as European Minister of Agriculture.

At Marble Arch a small van, the first motorised vehicle he had encountered since setting out from the office, took Mike by surprise. It rushed past him and disappeared down a ramp into a large underground car park. The car park was used as a government commercial vehicle repair and storage depot. A restricted range of nearly two thousand cars had been collected from around the city for use as specialised transport. It looked, so Brian had told him, like a museum.

Mike turned off Bayswater Road into a wide street flanked by Victorian houses. Balconies with rust-stained and weathered iron railings, threatening to collapse onto the marble steps below at any moment, were supported by crumbling grey columns. The further down the street Mike rode, the less habitable the houses appeared to be. After forty-five metres the street ended prematurely where a small tree and a collection of bushes emerged from a large crack in the road. To his right were the remains of a shop. Its windows had once been boarded up, but the wood was now rotting in heaps on the pavement, leaving gaping rectangles in the facade.

The words 'Adelphi Hotel' had been neatly painted on a piece of wood that was once the back of an old cupboard or wardrobe. The home-made sign was tied to the railings outside what was now the second-last house on the left-hand side of a truncated Leinster Street.

The sun had bleached the colour from the hotel's front door, but the glass was still intact. Inside, in the lobby, Mike's footsteps echoed on a tiled floor which still bore traces of glue from the carpet that had once covered it. The air felt cool and damp. The smell of polish masked another smell, hard to identify, perhaps decaying wood or rotting fabric. Mike thought the air was sufficiently unhealthy to warrant the wearing of a face mask.

Behind the reception desk, a short grey-haired man sat staring into space. He had ruddy cheeks and a bulbous nose with broken veins. Without introducing himself he stood up and, walking towards the stairs, beckoned Mike to follow.

At the top of the first flight of stairs the man stopped. "You're the young policeman's boss." He gripped Mike's arm. "Now, look. I'm an old man. I don't want any trouble. No trouble. Right?" But for the fear in the old man's face, the outburst could have been interpreted as a threat.

They continued the climb until the stairs gave onto a large stone-tiled landing. A grime-covered window overlooked a small garden. The garden was paved, except for a raised flowerbed overgrown with weeds and grass. There was a lift on the other side of the landing; pressing the buttons confirmed it was no longer in use. Voices echoed from a corridor that led off the landing. At the end of this corridor was a window, half boarded up with wood from the same piece of furniture as the hotel sign. Leaning on the sill of the window, Brian was standing next to a young woman, who was holding a mobile phone. She pressed a button, then held the phone to her ear.

"It's got a recall button," Brian explained to her. "Press it and it dials the last number I called."

She pressed the button. "Oh yeah!" she squealed excitedly, holding the phone to her ear. "But no-one's answering, are they?"

Mike could imagine the phone ringing in his empty office.

When he took the phone away from the girl, Brian held it carefully, as though frightened it had been contaminated. Dropping the phone into his rucksack, he acknowledged Mike's presence but said nothing. He merely pointed to the open doorway, through which light was flooding into the corridor. Then, easing himself away from the windowsill, and with broken glass crunching under his feet, he followed Mike into the room.

The room overlooked Leinster Street. It contained one single bed, an armchair with its back to the window and a low table in front of it, an antique chair without varnish or polish, and a writing desk. On the desk, there was a telephone, and a lamp with no flex. A large area of floor was less faded than the rest, having once been covered by a second single bed which had since been removed and replaced with a dressing table and mirror. In the armchair, the body of a man — in his late fifties or early sixties, in Mike's estimation — sat facing the door. The left side of the man's head was intact, there was a small red mark in front of his left ear, and a rivulet of blood had run down his cheek and onto the collar of his white shirt, before congealing. But the right side of his head (or the largest part of it) lay, with its curly grey hair still attached, on top of the dressing table. Blood had sprayed over the mirror and the wall above it, the droplets decreasing in size the further up the wall they had landed. At the point where a bullet had left a neat hole in the plaster, the drops were so small they were almost invisible.

The man's arms hung down on either side of the chair. The left hand was still clutching a revolver.

On the low table in front of the seated body lay a thin, leather-covered box-style briefcase. Mike pulled the chair out from the desk, sat down and spun the briefcase round so that the handle and clasps faced him. Just as he was about to press the catches, Brian knocked his hands away and sprung open the case himself. Mike noticed that Brian was wearing a pair of white cotton gloves and was embarrassed by his own stupidity.

Inside the case lay a yellowing English newspaper and an American passport. The passport was in the name of Toby Troxley. Brian opened it and Mike could see some resemblance between the photograph and the lifeless face staring at him. Brian pointed with a pencil to the name in the passport, then to a paragraph on the front page of the *Wisbech Echo*: 'Yesterday fifteen people were given sentences ranging from six months to two years for their part in the violent attack, at Whiteside Farm, which left Police Sergeant Bryant struggling for his life. The longest sentence was handed out to David Fairchild, head of the UKGA, the group claiming responsibility for the destruction of eight other GM crop trials. Although no-one has been charged with the attack on Sergeant Bryant, the federal authorities in the US have been asked to help trace Toby Troxley. Troxley disappeared after he was remanded on bail by Norwich Crown Court.'

Mike sat back and thought for a moment, then turned to Brian. "Yes, you were right to call me," he said in a muffled voice.

Brian cupped his hand to his ear. "Sorry, sir?"

Mike slid the mask from his mouth, but was not going to repeat himself. "This is complicated, isn't it?"

Brian disliked 'complicated'. It meant writing things down, remembering things, looking things up, reading things, and (in this case) lugging a body around rather than handing it over to a disposal team. As if he could read Brian's thoughts, Mike said, "Suppose we'd better get this chap back for an autopsy."

Without his mask on, Mike could taste the foul air inside the room. He felt thirsty and was tempted to ask the girl for some water, but decided against it after noticing the dust-covered glass on the writing desk. "Brian, I left in a bit of a hurry and forgot my things. Any chance of a drink of water?"

"No problem," said Brian, plunging his hand into his rucksack and pulling out a bottle.

Mike unscrewed the cap of the bottle. As he gulped down two mouthfuls of the lukewarm water, he watched Brian crouch down beside the body and place a pencil next to the bloody patch on the left-hand side of the head. He tilted the pencil until it lined up with the bullet hole in the wall. Brian then slowly and steadily moved the pencil closer to the head. "Sticking a pencil through his ear is hardly a substitute for an autopsy," said Mike.

Brian snatched the pencil away from the head and sprang to his feet. "No, sir. Sorry." He paused for a moment, then screwed up his nose. "It's getting a bit thick in here. I'll open the window."

The girl stepped forward and shouted, but it was too late. As soon as Brian released the catches, the sash window crashed to the bottom of the frame, sending a shower of broken glass into the room.

"That's what happened to the one at the end of the corridor," she said.

"Now the flies will get in." Mike sighed, and after screwing the top back on the water bottle handed it back to Brian. "Pop across the road, there's a good lad, and get a van and driver to take this body back. See if you can get something with a refrigerator in it."

Brian moved quickly to the door. As he did so, Mike called out. "Let's have your phone and I'll warn Hutchinson we have a customer for him."

"Sorry, sir. Battery's flat."

"That's what you get for playing around instead of using it properly." Mike held out his hand. "Let's have your paper and pencil then. I'll ask this young lady some questions."

*

Mike sat for a moment watching the shadows of the leaves on the tree outside dance backwards and forwards across the wall. He turned in the chair. The girl was leaning in the doorway staring at the body. Mike beckoned to her, then pointed to the bed. "Not the first body you have ever seen, is it?"

"No, sir." The woman sat down on the bed. She had long black hair which was well combed, piercing blue eyes and a slightly lined face which led Mike to estimate her age as somewhere between twenty-five and thirty. In fact, she was only twenty.

Mike turned himself and the chair around to face the woman.

"Your name?"

"Tate. Caroline Tate, sir."

"You can drop the 'sir', Caroline."

"OK, s..."

"Give me your S-Card number."

The girl reached into her pocket and took out the card, which entitled her to three meals a day at any restaurant. She read off the numbers: "Zero three, twelve, nineteen, twenty-seven, thirty-three, thirty-six and forty-eight."

Mike wrote down the sequence of numbers. "You're from the East End. Seen lots of dead people there, I should think."

"One or two."

"The man who runs the hotel, who is he?"

"My father."

"Your mother?"

"My mother has gone."

Often it was impossible to determine, during casual conversation, whether the friend or relative being discussed had died ten years ago or had merely left the room. This was a society that, in the absence of any belief in the afterlife, was condemned to think of the dead in the present tense.

Once images of children with distended bellies, brushing flies from their faces as they shuffled through the streets of some half-forgotten war-torn city, were confined to television news programmes. Viewers had been implored to care by smartly dressed correspondents who did not give a damn.

Then famine and disease crept up into the Northern Hemisphere. Perhaps tired of experiencing them third-hand, we invited them into the developed world. Soon we too were stepping over bodies in the street. People spent weekends burying, or preparing for cremation, the victims of famine, disease, or a soldier's bullet. Families and neighbourhoods disappeared and workforces were decimated. The loss was so immense that those who survived were unable to translate the victims into the past tense. Relatives never 'died'; they had just 'gone' or become dead.

"So your mother went. Is that when you moved out of the East End, Caroline?"

"Yes, it was."

"When was that?"

"Four years ago. We used to run a bed and breakfast in Woolwich, so they gave us this place when we came across."

"So you've seen plenty of people shot. Did you see this person shot?" He watched for a reaction, but there was none.

Caroline looked at the body. "Na, I was asleep. And anyway there was a thunderstorm, wasn't there?"

Mike smiled. "I don't know. I was asleep as well." There was still no reaction. None of the usual venom or sarcastic banter which he had come to expect from East Enders.

"Seems a funny place for a person from America to end up. How do you think he knew about the Adelphi?"

"We've got a website."

"Oh. And what is a website?"

"Some sort of computer system." Caroline wriggled uneasily on the bed.

"Ah, yes. Did he book using this 'website' thing?"

"No. He just turned up. Look..." She was about to stand up.

"Just a couple more things. Did he say what he was doing in London?"

"No, he didn't say much."

"Any phone calls?"

She glanced nervously at her father, who was now standing in the doorway. "Not that I know of."

"Can I see the register?"

"I'm sorry, we don't have a register."

The father made as if to come into the room. "Sir, I don't want any trouble." But before he had taken more than a couple of steps the girl stood up, intercepted him, and guided him back into the corridor.

"My father is finding all this very worrying. Would it be all right if we answered the rest of your questions later?"

Mike stood up to follow the couple, but by the time he had reached the landing they were already half way down the stairs. Unlike the rest of the window frames, those on the landing were metal. Mike released the catches — just touching them made him feel he needed to wash his hands. He pushed one of the windows open and leant out to breathe in some fresh air. There he waited, gazing down at the garden and considering the old man's words: 'I don't want any trouble.'

*

Half an hour later the front door slammed and the voices of Brian and the driver echoed up the stairwell. Mike could hear that some sort of wager, concerning the day's big event, was being negotiated. Possible outcomes included running the underground twenty-fours a day and the re-opening of trade links with America.

The driver, heavily built and with close-cropped brown hair, was wearing oil-stained trousers and a torn grey tee-shirt. His right forearm bore the scars from a series of burns. "Strewth!" he said, on seeing the body. Regaining his composure, he turned to Mike. "Still easier to get hold of a gun than a bottle of aspirin then?"

The body's head was wrapped in a bed sheet. Brian collected as many skull fragments as possible from the dressing table and dropped them into a pillowcase. Into a second pillowcase went the briefcase and the contents of Troxley's pockets. The first pillowcase he folded and laid in the lap of the body; the second he handed to Mike. Rigor mortis had frozen the body in a sitting position, and Brian needed all his strength to stop it tumbling down the stairs and taking with it the driver, who was supporting it from below.

Brian and the driver were discussing the relative merits of living in Kensington or Earls Court until, at the window where Mike had been standing earlier, they had to stop for a rest. Breathing heavily and wiping the sweat from his brow, Brian looked down into the garden below. "Silly old sod. 'I don't want any trouble.' Huh! Why didn't he just bury the body out there and save *everybody* a lot of trouble?"

Mike held the front door open and guided the sitting body, and the two red-faced bearers, out onto the marble steps. Having had his back to the road, it was only when they were all outside that he saw the van.

"An ice-cream van!" he exclaimed.

Brian shrugged. "It's got a fridge, sir."

Mike was speechless. In a state of disbelief he sat on the steps and watched as Brian and the driver manoeuvred the body through the rear door of the van. Once inside, their muffled voices debated whether to sit the body on a box or put it in the refrigerator. Eventually, after a brief countdown, there was a dull thud and the van rocked. The rear door opened again. Brian stepped down into the road. "Ready, sir!" he shouted to Mike, as he threw the two bicycles into the back of the van.

The driver had eased himself into the front seat and started the engine. Brian walked round to the passenger door. It was obvious to Mike that Brian had already decided which of them was riding in the back. "There's a box to sit on in there, sir," Brian said as he climbed in. Without making himself sound childish there was little Mike could do. He squeezed past the bicycles and looked around for something to hold on to. The only rigid, and readily accessible, 'handle' was the lower half of Troxley's legs, which were sticking out of the top of the refrigerator at right angles. Mike, sitting on the wooden box, grabbed one of Troxley's ankles. The engine roared, and the van bumped and rocked its way down the street and into Bayswater Road.

As the van approached Marble Arch the driver began talking Brian through the controls and switches on the dashboard. "Lights, dipped and full beam. Windscreen wipers." Lights flashed and the wipers juddered across the dry windscreen. "Now listen to this!" At the flick of a switch, a speaker somewhere above their heads burst into life.

"What's that tune?" Brian asked Mike.

"It's 'Greensleeves'," replied Mike, struggling to stay on the box as the van negotiated the Park Lane exit of the Marble Arch roundabout. Flailing around with his free arm, he made a desperate attempt to find something else to hold on to.

Brian turned back to the driver. "Now there's a coincidence. I voted Green in the last election."

"So did I," the driver sneered.

"Probably will next time."

"Yep, I was thinking I might as well." This time the driver laughed.

"Another amazing coincidence," Brian murmured.

Perhaps Mike was being oversensitive, but he regarded Brian's cynical view of Britain's one-party state as a personal insult. Amongst the younger generation, it was popular to mock Ivan and the Green Party. They also seemed to blame the older generation for the present political situation. On the other hand, they showed little inclination to do anything about it. Even students — especially students — were models of conformity. Mike leaned forward to attract Brian's attention. "I'll tell you what really is a coincidence," he said. "We're now driving past the headquarters of the UKGA."

The driver hit the switch on the dashboard and the tune was strangled in mid-chord.

"Oops!" said Brian, looking out at the building before turning his attention once more to the interior of the cab. Pulling down the sun visor, he took out a dust-covered and discoloured wad of folded papers. He opened it out and studied the first sheet for a while. "Sir, what was a 'chocolate chip sundae'?"

Mike sighed. "As it turned out, it was a good way of giving kids salmonella," he said, with an air of resignation.

"One pound, twenty-nine pence. What would that be in euros?"

"One euro and twenty-nine cents."

"Oh yes, of course." Brian scrutinised the rest of the sheet, then worked his way through the remainder of the wad before refolding the papers and tucking them back behind the visor.

The security guard walked over to meet the van as it came to a halt in front of the barrier. He studied the faded pictures of ice creams, then poked his head through the window. "Giving up police work, Mike?"

"Chance would be a fine thing." Mike got up from the box and passed his ID card to the guard.

The barrier was lifted and the van drove down the ramp, eventually coming to rest outside the goods entrance at the back of the building. The entire Forensic Science Division now consisted of just three laboratories within the Home Office itself. Two medical examiners, Dr. Hutchinson and his assistant, carried out all crime-related autopsies within the London area. Most medical staff trained in forensic pathology worked in hospitals, but *they* concentrated on deaths from natural (rather than unnatural) causes. It was not unheard of for a pathologist, on discovering that a patient had died as the result of some criminal act, to declare the cause of death 'irrelevant' and send the body straight to an incinerator. Hutchinson's time too was at a premium and he was reluctant to carry out a post-mortem if, at the end of it, there was only a remote chance of an arrest.

At Brian's suggestion, the driver leant on the van's horn. They waited for someone to open the large doors that led into the laboratories' loading area. After two minutes, Brian flicked the switch on the dashboard: the sound of 'Greensleeves' echoed around the car park. A face appeared briefly at a first-floor window. Moments later, one of the large doors to the loading bay opened, and a wiry man with neatly parted grey hair strode towards the van. His steps were quick and precise, and his white coat flapped behind him.

"Laughing-boy Tyler. I might have guessed it was you." He rubbed his chin and stared at the van. Brian eased himself out of the passenger seat and appeared at the side window. Kicking one of the tyres, Dr. Hutchinson looked up at Brian. "Given up the idea of ever being a policeman, have you, laddie?"

Brian leaned out and smiled. "Well, what'll it be, Dr. Hutchinson? We've got giant cornets, plain cornets, chocolate nut sundaes, ice lollies — strawberry, orange, lemon...?"

"Yes, yes, very funny — and I suppose you know there's a new psychiatric unit up at the Central Middlesex Hospital?"

"Not interested in a lolly?" Stepping back, Brian revealed the body. "Well, how about an iced cadaver — with a strawberry-coloured topping?"

Hutchinson stared at the two legs and a head protruding from the refrigerator. "I'll tell you something for nothing, sonny. It's going to be a lot harder to get that out of there than it was to get it in." He turned and walked back to the doors, sliding the second one open.

Mike had removed the bicycles from the back of the van by the time the assistant pathologist arrived with a trolley. As Hutchinson had predicted, Brian and the driver struggled to lift Troxley in the confined space available. Eventually the assistant (who, with Mike, had been watching their performance) intervened. He slid his arms under the body and managed to stop it falling back into the refrigerator — as it had done during the three previous attempts to extract it.

Troxley's body was seated upright on the trolley; the pillowcase containing skull fragments was laid in his lap. Brian caught the assistant by the arm as he started to push the trolley away. "Can you tell Hutch not to touch the gun any more than necessary, and to send it upstairs for fingerprinting when he gets it out of the guy's hand?"

The assistant smiled. "Do you want to tell the Doctor yourself?"

"Er, no thanks," Brian said, slinging his rucksack over his shoulder and picking up the second pillowcase. He walked across to the driver. There was a short exchange, which Mike assumed was another wager being struck. The driver restarted the van. It roared, in first gear, back up the ramp to the barrier.

"Sam's arranging a trip for me in a fire engine this weekend," said Brian.

Mike pretended not to be particularly interested. "You really ought to start acting responsibly. You're a commander's assistant. It's about time you thought about your career and stopped horsing around," he muttered under his breath as he returned his bicycle to the rack.

27

Brian had no illusions about his career. 'Commander's assistant' was not 'assistant commander'. It sounded good as a title, but he was no nearer than any other policeman at the Home Office to being an actual commander. He was an assistant *to* a commander, and this particular one was an ex-security officer from a long-defunct supermarket chain. If anyone really thought Brian could do the Commander's job he would be given it, and this ageing ex-store detective would be put out to grass.

*

The second-floor forensic lab specialised in fingerprints, chemical analysis and photography. Once inside, Brian put on his white cotton gloves again while Mike held open the pillowcase.

A short middle-aged woman with blonde hair and wire-rimmed spectacles emerged from the back of the silent, and almost deserted, laboratory. "I hope it's not something you want in a hurry, Brian."

Mike felt irritated that the woman had ignored him and spoken to Brian. His irritation gave way to embarrassment as the conversation progressed.

Brian reached into the pillowcase, took out the briefcase and laid it on the white work surface of the laboratory bench. He then took the mobile phone from his rucksack and laid it next to the briefcase. "There's a fingerprint on the recall button of my phone. Can you see if there are any matches on the items in the briefcase?"

The woman reached forward, and with the tips of her fingers flicked open the catches on the case, then gently lifted the lid. "Maybe I can get something off the passport, perhaps the newspaper as well."

"It would be nice to have something this afternoon."

"No chance, Brian. Try Monday."

"What about the newspaper? Any chance of getting that back today?"

"I'll try. But can't promise."

Brian started to leave, then remembered Troxley's pistol. "Oh. Hutch is trying to get a gun out the hand of a body downstairs. I asked him to send it up to you when he's done."

"Definitely Monday in that case. Have a good weekend — and you, Mr. Allchurch."

Mike's morale was sinking fast, but Brian made no reference to the use of his phone to collect fingerprints, or to Mike's comment about running down the battery. "Lunch, sir?"

"Yes, good idea," replied Mike sheepishly.

*

Across Queen Anne's Gate from the Home Office was one of the largest Ivan's restaurants in London. Rather than the single guard assigned to most restaurants, the Victoria Ivan's had two guards at all times — and a third during the peak periods of breakfast and lunch.

The Ivan's Restaurant chain had been founded in 2010. It replaced the disastrous emergency soup kitchens that had been set up during the famines of 2003 to 2006 and were responsible for thousands of deaths during the great epidemics. With the arrival of the government-controlled Ivan's all private food preparation, storage and consumption was banned. In the last five years there had been a relaxation of the regulation concerning drinks. It was now permitted, using bottled water only, to brew tea and coffee outside Ivan's. Both had to be drunk black: milk was still not available for consumption outside a restaurant.

Ivan's provided every citizen with breakfast, lunch and dinner, free of charge. The total guaranteed calorific value of all three meals was enough to keep the average person from starving. However, the actual calorific value was far in excess of the minimum guarantee. No-one aged under twenty-five could remember it falling as low as the guaranteed level, but the high incidence of rickets amongst people aged thirty and over showed that, in the early days, a balanced diet had been difficult to obtain, especially during the winter months.

A person's entitlement to food varied according to their age, their employment and their state of health. Non-manual workers received a 'basic meal' and manual workers a 'basic meal plus'. Pregnant women and children were entitled to a 'basic meal extra', and those recovering from illness or an operation a 'basic meal medical'.

Each restaurant consisted of three areas. In the foyer were the card machines and their operators. The visitor handed their S-Card — a card pre-marked with their identification number — to an operator, who fed it into an electronic terminal. The diner's identification number was transmitted via an X25 telecommunications link to a central control room within the Ministry of Health. The number was fed into a database containing the person's medical and employment details. When the S-Card number had been cleared, a signal was sent back to the terminal instructing it to issue a badge: green for 'basic', blue for 'basic plus', yellow for 'extra' or white for a 'medical' meal. There was also a red badge, issued to diners who were suffering from any potentially contagious diseases, such as tuberculosis. After collecting their badges, most diners moved through to the main dining area. Those who had been issued with red badges made their way to a segregated dining hall.

Once in the food hall, the diner collected a stainless-steel tray, with compartments for the main and dessert courses and a recess for a stainless-steel soup bowl. Food was served from large heated trays and vats by kitchen staff who also collected the diner's badge. Waiters collected empty trays; they also delivered bottled water to the tables.

Face masks were worn by all staff in the 'red' dining room and by the terminal-operators and the armed guards in the foyer. Diners were advised to wear face masks until they were in the main dining area, although people had recently stopped doing so. The Victoria Ivan's had an impersonal and sometimes menacing feel to it. The rapid throughput of a large number of diners meant that it was not an easy place to meet people. The chance of sitting next to the same person two days running was slight. The waiters, terminal-operators and kitchen staff carried alarms in order to alert, as necessary, the armed guards in the foyer and outside. The restaurants in residential areas tended to be more relaxed: staff, and even some guards, were willing to enter into conversation.

Large-screen televisions were mounted in each corner of the dining room. They broadcast current news during the day and variety shows, films and soap operas in the evening. As the television was impossible to hear at mealtimes, a number of small printed news-sheets, headed *The Guardian* — 'Do Not Remove', were left on the tables.

The tremendous noise of stainless-steel trays and utensils made conversation difficult.

"So what do you think?" shouted Brian.

"I think it should be passed over to Park Lane."

"The Party? Why's that?"

"Because it involves Fairchild. Because it presents no immediate risk to public order."

Brian picked up the soup bowl and drank down the last drops, then pushed the rest of his bread roll into his mouth "But it's a murder."

"Sorry?"

Brian swallowed the bread. "Murder."

"Oh yes," replied Mike, using what was left of his roll to mop up the rest of his soup. This intrigued Brian as much as Brian's eating habits astonished Mike. "The thing is, we've rarely solved a murder and probably won't solve this one. We haven't got the time or the resources. But, as it looks like a threat to their leader, the party's security division will be able to throw everything they've got at it."

Brian shrugged and started shovelling the Soya and potatoes into his mouth. "Suppose so." He reached into his pocket and retrieved a handkerchief, wiped his mouth and continued: "The girl did it."

"Rubbish! If it was either of them, it was the father."

"If he was her father."

"Of course he was."

Brian shrugged again and looked around the restaurant. A person five tables away recognised him and held up four fingers, then three. Brian held up one finger, then eight. There was a burst of laughter from the other table. "He was a nervous wreck and she was as steady as a rock."

"So?"

"Well, whatever *he* had been through, *she* had come out of it in pretty good shape. And then there was her accent."

A tall youth tapped Brian on the shoulder. "Brian! All right?" he shouted. "Ten euros says it's quiche, five it's bacon roly-poly."

Brian looked up at the youth. "What with pigs lying all over the street for everyone to see, do you think they're going to get away with just spreading a bit of bacon on an egg pie? It's pork chops by Sunday and one bacon-and-egg breakfast."

"What? Here? In veggie paradise?" exclaimed the youth, surprised.

"No. Marble Arch, Earls Court, South Ken."

"How much then?"

"Five euros, bacon and egg. Eight, pork chops — and you're on for the quiche and roly-poly."

The youth signalled back to the other table. The group of young men and women laughed again. Raising his thumb, then looking at Brian, one of the men pushed the end of his nose up with his finger and made a noise like a pig. The rest of the table joined in, but stopped abruptly when they realised they were attracting attention.

Mike looked across to where they were sitting. "You know, years back, a policeman might have taken that the wrong way."

"Oh yeah, man! Like, the pigs, they were really bad! Know what I mean?" aped Brian.

"Yes, something like that," sighed Mike. "Glad to see you're up to date up with your history evening classes."

Brian realised that Mike was about to slide into one his nostalgic moods and quickly returned to their previous conversation. "Her accent. Now, if I was from the East End — and had been this side of the river for as long as she said she had — I would have got rid of that accent; or at least hidden it a bit. But her accent was fresh, idioms and all. It was like..." Brian paused, picked up the last piece of an apple pie and wiped it around the dessert section of the tray to gather up the last of the custard. He then pushed the pie into his mouth, chewed briefly, and swallowed. "God! Lugging bodies about does give you an appetite! I bet that driver, Sam, got a 'basic plus' lunch."

"It was like *what*?" asked Mike.

"It was like she was putting it on. And then there was the mobile phone."

"What about it?" Mike asked, with some embarrassment.

"Well, when I said it had a recall button she went straight for it. No 'Where's that then?' or messing about. Straight for it." Brian gulped down a cup of tea.

The waiter approached the table and picked up the empty trays. He dropped them into the tank of hot water that was an integral part of the trolley he was pushing "Any water?" he asked.

"Two bottles, please," Brian replied.

"Only one for me, thanks," said Mike.

Three bottles of water stood on the cleared table. The standard, returnable, half-litre bottle was used for everything from water to beer and orange juice. The waiter continued down the row of tables, collecting trays and empty bowls. When the tank on his trolley was full he wheeled it into the kitchen, where the semi-soaked items were removed and rinsed.

Brian and Mike put the bottles in their pockets, walked out into the silence of Queen Anne's Gate and returned to the office. As they started to climb the fourth flight of stairs, Brian stopped. "I'm just going to see how Amanda is getting on."

"She said Monday," Mike called out. But it was too late, and Brian had gone.

Mike switched on his computer and logged in to the London Police Network — a bulletin board contributed to, and accessed by, all divisions in the London area. As the network was not secure, it was mostly used for help with missing persons and trivial problems. Playing on the Police Network and tidying his desk were just two possible ways of coasting downhill to the weekend. Both were preferable to law reforms.

'Wolves Again' caught his eye. He clicked on it and read the message. Residents in North London had been reporting the sound of wolves; the North London Division were requesting help. Mike typed in a reply, pointing out that the problem had also occurred in West London. He suggested that Percival at the Natural History Museum would be only too pleased to confirm there were no wolves within three hundred kilometres of London. The sounds were merely children playing about. He pondered over this for a minute or so, then proposed that notices warning that wolves would be shot by the army should be posted in the area. After considering the implications of what he had just typed, he deleted it.

*

Brian entered the office, holding the newspaper found in Troxley's briefcase. "Finished with this, at least!" he exclaimed, sitting down at his desk and studying the front page.

"Shall we contact the East Anglian Division and tell them we've solved the Troxley case for them?" Brian laughed.

"You may jest, but if we don't get shot of this case, we may well end up out there."

"You mean a trip into the countryside? Great!"

"You *are* joking, aren't you?" Mike sighed and looked down the list of missing persons, then clicked on several items marked 'Found — West London'. A row of faces scanned in from photographs appeared on the screen. The 'found' items were posted when human remains were discovered during a house clearance. A list of possible names had been entered under each face, indicating that the remains of several of these people had been found at the same address as the photographs. After clicking on a number of such entries, Mike became depressed and started thinking of his parents, his wife and his daughter. He closed down the computer and switched it off.

Brian had finished reading the front page of the *Wisbech Echo* and had moved on to the inner pages. "Ninety-five thousand pounds. How much is that in euros, sir?"

"Ninety-five thousand euros," Mike replied, realising that for the second time that day Brian was taunting him with a relic from the turn of the century.

"So that means, if I saved up, it would take me..." He scribbled a sum on a scrap of paper. "It would take me, at forty euros a week, forty-five years to buy a house."

"People earned more than forty euros a week in those days. And anyway, they got a loan and paid it back at so much a month."

"Did you ever pay for a house?"

"Once, a long time ago." Mike glanced across at the newspaper. "When that was printed there were more people than houses. If it was like that today, *I* wouldn't be living in Ruislip and *you* definitely wouldn't be living in South Kensington. Well, not Queen's Gate anyway." He turned his attention to his desk and resorted to tidying, or at least rearranging, the contents of the drawers.

"'Bring this coupon to one of our restaurants. We will cut the cost of your evening meal by ten pounds. Christ, sir! How much...?'"

"Ten euros."

"Ten euros! And that's what they knocked *off*! That's nearly two days' pay. I'd starve to death!"

"People did, Brian, but not for the want of money."

"Says here, sir, that a man was convicted for hitting another car driver with a baseball bat. Says when the other motorist overtook him he became annoyed and chased after him. At the next set of traffic lights he got out of his car and hit him." Brian turned the page. "Huh! Man beats up his wife. She needed ten stitches." He went quiet and moved on to the next headline: 'Parents Start Campaign After Death Of Daughter'. He looked up at Mike, then back down at the page. Without further comment, he closed and folded the paper.

Brian sat in silence, looking out of the window. Suddenly, a small bottle of pills landed on his desk. He picked it up and read the label. "'Chitosan'. What's that?"

"Well," said Mike, "as you are so interested in relics of the late nineteen hundreds, I thought you might be interested in those."

Brian, smiled, unscrewed the cap of the bottle and shook two pills into the palm of his hand. "How many do I take then?"

"None, if you've got any sense."

"They're illegal then?"

"No. They're fat-busters. People took them if they were overweight."

"No-one gets overweight on what they eat at Ivan's."

"Exactly. So even though they're not illegal, being in possession of them is suspicious in itself."

"People used to eat so much that they got fat? And then had to take pills to lose the weight?" Brian looked puzzled. "So why didn't they just stop eating?"

"Compulsion. If you have food readily available all the time, you just keep eating it. Out of boredom, natural desire —or just for the hell of it."

"Amazing!" said Brian, putting the two pills back into the bottle.

"In those days, food was sold in shops and advertised on television. It was difficult to avoid it."

Brian took a closer look at the bottle. "But the label on this bottle is new."

"Those were taken from someone crossing the river a few weeks ago. Which means that somewhere in London there is a black marketeer, or a corrupt official, with a diet problem."

"Shouldn't be hard to spot them now." Brian tossed the bottle back to Mike.

Mike returned the bottle to his desk drawer. "Not hard to spot if we can permanently cut off their supply."

*

At four thirty Langford called Mike into his office. Langford's office was sparsely furnished and dark. There was a thin layer of dust on all the surfaces except the top of the mahogany desk, behind which the Deputy himself was sitting. Although most people in the building had grown used to the idea of cleaning their own offices, the concept seemed to be alien to Langford. Papers and folders, piled up on a long, narrow table set against the wall, awaited the attention of a filing clerk who, like the cleaner, did not exist.

"Take a seat, Mike." Langford waved his trembling hand at two faded leather executive chairs.

Mike selected the cleanest of the two and sat down carefully so as not to disturb the dust.

Langford slid himself down in his chair, which he then swivelled round so that he could gaze, skywards, out of the window. He stretched the few strands of thinning grey hair back over his scalp. "Anything interesting this week?"

"Not really," replied Mike, in a voice that was barely audible. He looked around the room, wondering if the crookedly hung landscapes were originals. As they were not faded, he assumed they were. "Oh, except for the dead American, of course."

Langford swung round and sat upright; his chair groaned and creaked as it slowly re-adjusted itself. "Yes. Found out what he was doing here? Economic migrant, was he?"

"Too early to say." Mike, conscious of the time, wanted to avoid lengthy explanations that would delay his journey home. However, he felt it was best, in view of the implications of what they had already discovered, not to hold too much back. Langford's label of 'economic migrant' seemed designed to provoke a reaction. He could see no other reason to trot out party propaganda about the USA. "It could end up being a party matter."

Langford's eyebrows rose, but his hooded eyes remained half shut. "And why do think that?"

Mike described the newspaper and the passport.

"But if he's dead, there's no problem." Langford stared into space, fixing his line of sight at a point just above Mike's head. Then, as if suddenly struck by an idea, he looked him straight in the eye. "It was suicide, I take it? There wasn't anyone else involved, was there?"

"As I said, it's a bit too early to say one way or the other. We'll know more next week when Hutch has had a good look. I just thought you might want to let security at the UKGA know."

"Yes, I see what you mean. Still, I think it can wait." He shuffled some papers around on his desk — a sign that he regarded the meeting as finished. "Nothing else?"

"Only about Tyler."

"Tyler?"

"Yes. Tyler." Mike watched the shuffling of papers become more agitated and decided that now was not best the time to broach the subject. "Well, actually that can wait until next week."

Langford made a half-hearted attempt to stand up and see Mike out. "Have a good weekend, Mike."

By now Mike was on his feet and had the door open. "Thanks,

sir. You too."

*

Back in the office, Mike found Brian clearing his desk.

"The Chief happy then?" asked Brian, throwing his rucksack over his shoulder.

"That'll be the day." Mike picked up his briefcase and followed Brian into the corridor.

By now the building was silent and their footsteps echoed as they descended the stairs. The guards at the main entrance looked relaxed and wished them a good weekend. To Mike's annoyance, they called Brian by his first name.

They stood together on the westbound platform of St James's Park underground station. The District and Circle lines were the only ones in the centre of London still operating. All the deeper tunnels were now permanently flooded and, for all anyone knew, they had collapsed.

"Busy tonight," said Brian. To him it *was* busy, whereas to Mike London seemed like a ghost town. "Well, the big event never happened. Just trying to keep us on our toes, I suppose."

"Probably," muttered Mike, as the train arrived.

Brian saw someone he recognised. He waved, but still sat down next to Mike and interrogated him about his plans for the weekend. Getting little response, he talked of his own plans.

Mike now realised that Brian had not been joking about the day out with the fire brigade.

By the time it reached Knightsbridge the carriage was half full, which was about as busy as it ever got. At South Kensington Brian stood up. "Have a good weekend then, sir. All the best to Linda."

"Thanks. You too, Brian, and be careful."

It was at Turnham Green that Mike first noticed something different: a small crowd in the street. He had only the briefest glimpse but, at the next stop, there was another crowd near the Ivan's Restaurant. At Acton Town he had to change trains and the Harrow-bound train was already waiting. Crossing the platform and getting into the carriage, he was conscious of a commotion in the ticket area, above. He felt some obligation to see if help was required, but the doors closed and the train pulled away before he could get off it again.

At each station along the route there was the hum of voices and glimpses of crowds. No-one got on, and by the time the train reached Rayners Lane he was the only passenger in the carriage.

A hundred metres from the station entrance a crowd had formed in front of the Rayners Lane Ivan's Restaurant. Mike began to push through the group of people but, as he did so, a woman turned to face him. She was pale and seemed to be in shock. "He's gone. Ivan's gone," she said.

Mike backed out of the crowd and set off for home on foot. Two peninsulas of settlement extended out into the wilderness that had once been the western suburbs. Mike lived at the very extremity of north-west London, in a settlement bounded by Harrow-on-the-Hill to the east and Field End Road to the west. The strip of settled land followed the old Piccadilly line from Acton Town. At some points its width was no greater than the railway line itself, but nearer the stations it ballooned out, and in places was up to three kilometres wide. East Harrow had been lost thirty years before, just after the great epidemics. Only a few farms remained. Efforts to keep South Ruislip viable had been in vain; it had been lost twenty-three years ago. There was now nothing but wilderness beyond Field End School, which had been reclaimed for use as a medical unit, district-council offices and an education centre.

Allchurch had laid claim to a four-bedroomed detached house in Malvern Avenue. His wife, Linda, complained at first that they were being too ambitious in taking on such a large place. However, as the population stabilised and most of the basic services in the district were restored, she became less concerned.

"Have you heard? Ivan's gone," Linda said, as Mike walked through the door.

"Yes. There's a crowd at the restaurant — well, all the restaurants actually."

"What will happen now? Do you think there'll be a war?"

"No, of course not. Nothing will happen," Mike said, gently stroking his wife's face, then putting his arms around her. "Why should there be a war?" He kissed her neck. "There'll just be an election and someone else will take charge."

Mike wondered why so many people regarded war as the solution to, or at least a logical outcome of, every major problem. Just because there was some political manoeuvring in a country on the other side of Europe, nations that a few years ago could not even feed and clothe themselves properly were expected to take up arms. Perhaps this was a hangover from the old twentieth-century way of thinking, a state of mind that should have changed — not least because, during the last fifty years, the major wars had been fought against starvation, disease and Nature itself.

*

On leaving South Kensington station, Brian called in at a book shop. He picked out an old hardback, filled in a loan card and left. The book shop was the main reason Brian took the train to work rather than cycled. Walking back towards the station, he descended the steps to the underground walkway leading to the Science Museum. Half way down the tunnel, a musician heard his footsteps and began to strum a folk song on a twelve-string guitar. People either avoided the walkway because the echoing music amplified the loneliness and emptiness of the city, or they deliberately took the route because the voice of the singer was a pleasant alternative to the silence of the street above. Brian was one of the latter group.

"Thanks," the singer said when Brian dropped three euros into an open guitar case.

"Have a good weekend, Jim," Brian replied, without making eye contact with the man.

Brian gave no thought to the fact that it had taken three hours to earn the money he had just given away. To his generation, money was meaningless. The economy had collapsed before he was born. Now everything was free: food, accommodation, clothes, travel were all, when available, there for the taking. If his clothes became worn or torn, they would be repaired or replaced at the laundry. If he wanted to travel somewhere, he just got on a bus or a train, though he had to bear in mind that the underground trains only ran between six in the morning and seven thirty in the evening. Entertainment was also free, when there was any. Any electronic consumer goods that had survived in storage were — with the exception of cookers, refrigerators and washing machines — available to anyone who could give a good reason why they wanted them. Brian assumed that money only existed as a comfort blanket for the older generation: something to hold on to. The value of the euro related to nothing within the government-controlled economy. It was exchanged for an hour's labour. But everyone was obliged, by law, to contribute forty hours labour a week. The coins themselves were a mixture of pounds, francs, Deutschmarks and, occasionally, newly minted euros.

Brian could imagine Mike saving his coins, waiting for the day when they would have some purchasing power again. He knew that Mike was irritated when large sums of money, sometimes up to two hundred euros, changed hands as wagers were settled over lunch. Anyone who couldn't pay wrote out an IOU. Mike became particularly annoyed when Brian, on getting back to the office, screwed up the IOU and threw it in the bin.

"That's paper money you're throwing away!" Mike would exclaim, with horror.

"You're right." Brian would pick up the paper and smooth it out. "I'll keep it and buy myself a sports car."

Exhibition Road seemed busier than usual when Brian emerged from the walkway. People were already crossing the road to the large Ivan's Restaurant in Prince's Garden. He took a left turn off Exhibition Road and within a few minutes had reached Queen's Gate. Although the houses were semi-derelict, the road itself was free of any shrubs. Half way down the row of well-weathered facades, the brown, rusting railings gave way to a short section of shining black metalwork. Window boxes crammed with lavender and carnations decorated a gleaming white house with a deep-red door and brightly painted window frames. The sound of music and voices from radios and televisions drifted out of the open doors and windows.

As Brian climbed the steps he called up to the round-faced soldier who, his hands behind his head, was resting his feet on a first-floor windowsill and soaking up the early evening sun. "Fancy a ride out with the fire brigade on Sunday, Trevor?"

"Sounds interesting," came the lazy reply.

"Starting out at six thirty."

"Pass."

"Counts as community service."

"So does Stef's floorboards, and I don't have to start doing that till ten."

The sun gave the walls in the hallway a red hue. The deep-blue carpet was covered with white footprints and flecks of sawdust. On the right, in a reception room, there was a neat pile of wood, resting on two trestles, and a collection of paint tins, brushes and jars set out on a dust sheet. Through the door, on the left, a television was delivering the evening news to an empty living room.

"Brian, have you heard the news?" A tall, late middle-aged woman emerged from the kitchen. She hugged Brian briefly, then led him by the arm into the living room. "Ivan has gone, resigned, just like that," she said in a matter-of-fact way, standing in front of the television with her arms folded.

The news reader was explaining that details were still sketchy and that no official comment was expected until Sunday at the earliest.

"Huh! And what is television if it isn't official comment?" Stef, or 'Aunty Stef' as she was called, was owner of the house — and Brian's landlady. She had been allocated the house on the understanding that she would provide much-needed accommodation for at least ten single men or women. That was eight years ago and this condition no longer applied. The amount of reclaimed property now in use as barracks, hostels and flats was more than sufficient. Young, single people, posted to the London Regiment or, like Brian, without a family home, had no trouble finding a room. However, it suited Stef to have 'her boys' (as she called them) around the place. She had lost her husband just before taking on the house, but still had three sons. The youngest was serving in the army in Herefordshire, another was an electronics engineer in Manchester and the eldest was managing a textile company in Yorkshire. She often claimed it was ironic that young men like Trevor, from rural areas, were posted to London, while her son was sent out into the countryside. 'Her boys' became her surrogate sons, and Stef became their surrogate mother — in Trevor's case, the only mother he had ever known.

One advantage of having sons strategically placed in key industries was that Stef was well supplied with fabrics, paints, building materials and even a working television and radio. 'Her boys', who were required to contribute the standard minimum of thirty-two hours' community service each month, provided the labour that maintained the house and the street. Community service had been introduced after the great epidemics had decimated the number of able-bodied people available to maintain essential services. Initially that had included clearing vegetation from streets and railway embankments, repairing water mains and, in certain circumstances, removing the dead for cremation. A generation on, people had begun to improvise around the central theme. Community service now encompassed a wide range of activities, including evening classes and home study. Some activities, such as the removal of wild animals from the suburbs, could be classed as leisure pursuits. The whole concept needed to be rethought, or (some said) abandoned altogether, but the government saw the scheme as a means of maintaining social cohesion. It was therefore likely to continue.

The main problem about community service was getting a responsible person to sign for it. As Stef served on Kensington District Council, this was no problem for Brian or Trevor. Tomorrow Trevor would be laying floorboards and Brian would be painting the house next door, which Stef hoped would eventually serve as lodgings for families visiting the city. In return, 'her boys' would have their hair cut, their laundry collected and sent off, their beds made, and generally be fussed over and pampered.

"Tea! I forgot the tea!" Stef dragged herself away from the television, disappeared into the kitchen and re-emerged with a cup of tea.

Brian thanked her and went upstairs. His room was hot and stuffy. Placing the cup on the bedside table, he lifted the sash window and manoeuvred his armchair into the sun. Then, like Trevor, he placed his feet on the sill and started to read his book.

At eight o'clock there was a call from downstairs — Stef was collecting everyone to go out to dinner. Trevor banged on Brian's door and told him to hurry up. When all 'her boys' were out in the street, Aunty Stef pulled the front door to and they set off for the Ivan's in Prince's Gardens.

Brian attempted to continue reading his book at dinner, but Stef, Trevor and the others were determined to stop him.

"Always reading. Your head will explode!" Stef laughed.

Trevor reached across the table and grabbed the book. "Let's see what it is this time then!" He read a few sentences and threw the book back to Brian. "That's gross! How can you eat and read that at the same time?"

Brian picked up the book. Trevor rested his head on the table so that he could read the author's name on the spine. "Patricia Cornwall. Who's she then?"

"A writer from the last century."

Stef turned to Trevor and smiled. "Classical literature."

Brian gave up trying to read when a group of girls seated nearby accepted Trevor's invitation to join them for the rest of the dinner.

Saturday 17th August 2041

At nine o'clock on Saturday morning Mike began his community service. He sat with three other district councillors at one end of the makeshift courtroom in Field End School. Nine people were brought before them. Four were ordered to do extra community service. One, whose crime was evasion of additional community service handed out at a previous hearing, was given a short custodial sentence on a penal farm. The rest were given conditional discharges. Linda was also in the school building, giving morning and afternoon classes in basic hygiene.

By three in the afternoon Mike and his family were back home, relaxing in their garden.

*

Brian, having been told repeatedly throughout the day that the ladder he was using did not look safe, that he was leaning too far out of the window, and not to drink tea with paint on his hands, was finally informed, at five o'clock, that he had done enough.

Aunty Stef and her boys went for dinner early. Afterwards, with the group of girls, they all walked to Hyde Park. Trevor and Brian carried a crate of beer between them. In five boats they rowed slowly along the edge of the Serpentine, alighting at a café which was still undergoing restoration. The sun disappeared behind the dense forest of Kensington Gardens and the trees that had enveloped the Serpentine Gallery and the Albert Memorial. They drank the beer and talked, rowing back to the bridge on West Carriage Drive when the light began to fail. In the darkness, as they sat on the bridge, bets were placed on how many shooting stars would appear in the next thirty minutes. But the heat of the evening and the alcohol had dulled their senses, so the wager was confused: no-one could work out who had won and they took it in turns to drop the coins off the bridge. Except for the faint splashes echoing under the bridge, and the sound of the water lapping against the crumbling, overgrown paved path around the lake, the park was silent.

Aunty Stef switched on a torch to light the way back to Queen's Gate. She told them they should have more respect for money. The group split, some of the boys following the girls down Exhibition Road. Brian stayed with Stef and Trevor. He had managed to convince Trevor that a day out with the fire brigade would be more exciting than house repairs.

Stef shone the torch across the facades of the tall houses around the Albert Hall. "Wouldn't they be something? Take you lot more than a week of Saturdays to get those into shape." Then her mood changed. "You ought to be with the girls, Brian."

Brian laughed. "Early start in the morning. Six-o-clock!"

"It's about time you stopped all this laughing and joking, and took life a little less seriously."

"That doesn't make sense."

"You know what I mean."

But he did not. Back in his room, he sat up in bed trying to read his book. The room swam and his eyes felt heavy. Downstairs Stef was locking up, the house fell silent and Brian drifted off to sleep.

Sunday 18th August 2041

Early on Sunday morning Mike slung his .22-calibre hunting rifle over his shoulder, stuffed his pockets with shells and set off with five others in the direction of South Ruislip. The hunting trip would count towards his community service and meant that he would have the following weekend to himself.

Mike disliked South Ruislip station; it brought back particularly bad memories. Now derelict, completely overgrown and charred by a series of fires, the area around the station was barely recognisable. Twigs cracked underfoot as the group walked in single file under the willow and horse chestnut trees. Fifteen years ago a four-hundred-strong community still clung on here, but it was under pressure from all sides. There was the constant advance of vegetation: ground elder, willows, towering leylandii, whitethorn and brambles. Then it was cut off from the rest of London by the collapse of Western Avenue and the failure of the Central line.

On the corner of Great Central Avenue and Primrose Gardens, just opposite the station, there had once been an Ivan's Restaurant. It was here, one Saturday twenty-five years ago, that the shooting took place. The guard was nervous. The remoteness of the posting was quite frightening enough for a boy of seventeen who had only been in the army for three months. The atmosphere of siege, the stories of raids on isolated restaurants, and the ever-encroaching vegetation all served to put the young guard on edge. He left the safety catch of his machine gun off. Meanwhile, a small girl had collected a bottle of water from Ivan's and was carrying it, carefully, in both hands, along Great Central Avenue. She dropped the bottle. The soldier turned and fired, cutting her body in two.

Apart from sanctioned executions, the shooting of a member of the public by a soldier had to be investigated by the civilian police. Mike and Padreep Kumar had arrived on the scene together.

Both were new recruits to the police. Kumar would eventually become commander of the West London Division, with responsibility for security at Heathrow. The South Ruislip incident was to have an impact on both the men and create a lasting bond between them.

The girl lay there like a broken doll. The legs and lower torso were in a pool of blood and water that had formed in the gutter. The upper torso, surrounded by broken glass, was wedged against a garden wall. Blood had sprayed across the pavement in the direction the girl had been walking. Mike turned the upper torso over. She was wearing a protective mask over her nose and mouth. She had a squint; her glasses, lying amongst the remains of the bottle, had been repaired with tape. There was no identification, not even an S-Card. The girl's tongue protruded slightly, as though it was swollen and too big for her mouth.

"Retarded." Kumar gulped and then coughed. "No S-Card. Her parents were probably frightened someone would take it from her." He turned and looked down the street. "Wearing a mask. So whoever sent her out has probably got something contagious. Too ill to go out themselves. Sent her out for water. And bang!"

Mike had then realised what Kumar already knew: somewhere, in one of the houses which were drowning in the rising sea of foliage at the end of the road, someone was waiting for the girl — and for the water she had been carrying. Over the years he had been asked to investigate many acts of violence: shopkeepers beaten to death by mobs, strikers shot by soldiers, and looters gunned down by vigilantes. But the death of the girl — or at least the slow, lonely, unseen death of the person who had sent her out to fetch the water — had stayed with him. It played with his imagination. It caused his darkest fear (one shared by many others who had seen London's population shrink by over two-thirds) to bubble up from his subconscious. It was the fear of being the last person left alive, hungry, diseased and dying of thirst, in an empty house choked by Nature itself. The fear he had suppressed for so long had found the visual stimulation it needed to acquire a voice.

Mike and Kumar had made some effort to find the girl's house. There was no shortage of people who had seen her walking backwards and forwards, collecting water from Ivan's, then disappearing into the undergrowth at the end of the road.

The soldier had returned to barracks before anyone could interview him. Mike had been due to see him the following day, but that morning the soldier was found hanging by his belt from the end of a bunk bed. That was Mike's lowest point. That was the day he finally admitted to himself that the world he had once known was gone for ever. He was freed from the shackles of the vain hope that, one day, everything would return to normal. Now everything could be measured from a new base.

A week after the shooting, the nightmares began: an ever-changing cast, a mixture of guilt, anxiety and panic acted out at first nightly, then weekly, then monthly. Even now, they made the odd unwelcome visit during the early hours. Sometimes it was the girl, sitting opposite him on the train. Sometimes it was his first wife or his mother. Sometimes the girl clutched the bottle of water. Sometimes she held his dead daughter. The doors would open and the girl would get out, walk across the platform, out of the gate and disappear down the path that led into the woods. As the doors of the train closed, the undergrowth swallowed up the carriage. He called out, but the girl had gone. He was awake, sweating, with Linda trying to soothe him.

All these years later, he was still browsing the London Police Network to search for the girl's face in the database of missing persons, or for requests to identify remains.

This was not the route Mike would have chosen, past the spot where the girl had died; along the path she would have taken through the undergrowth; through the now-abandoned houses, one of which she would have returned to, had she lived. He merely followed the person in front who, carrying four long wooden poles, had been charged with leading the hunt.

On the other side of the abandoned dual carriageway, the trees thinned and the track gave onto a large area of grassland. Everyone in the hunting party had their number. Mike was 'right two', which meant that when they saw the small herd of deer he was to aim at the second animal from the right. The person in front, 'left one', slid the wooden poles and his rifle from his shoulder, then took aim at the deer on the far left of the herd. In a whisper the leader counted down from five. On zero they all fired. Two of the animals fell; two others staggered. Everyone took a second shot at the two animals still standing.

They tied the hooves of the four deer and hung them on the poles. Supporting the poles between them, the group retraced their steps in single file along the path. It was the person behind Mike, a retired accountant, who started to reminisce, talking about foreign travel, cars, television and London's Theatreland. The rest of the group joined in, all contributing their observations and experiences. It was these tales of the past, a strange and alien land to which he could not relate, that had made Mike's son give up these hunting trips. Presumably that was why the sons of the other members no longer joined them.

Mike thought of how his parents had spent their Sundays: finishing off a light lunch in a pavement café, at the end of a weekend break in Paris, then heading home on Eurostar; sharing out the sections of the Sunday newspaper; planning their new kitchen, their holiday, and a retirement which should have been long and happy but ended up short and brutal. Perhaps they had had plans for their son. It was safe to assume, however, that these plans had not involved carrying a slaughtered deer through the streets of Ruislip.

The four animals were deposited at the Ivan's in Malvern Avenue. Here they would be butchered and then used during the week, with any surplus going to the restaurant in Rayners Lane. "What did you shoot this one with? A machine gun?" The restaurant manager looked down at the animal that had taken most of the second volley. He signed the community service forms which each member of the hunting party had presented to him, although Mike himself, as a district councillor, would be one of the people checking the forms at the end of the month.

The hunters drank beer, reminisced and lamented some more, then dispersed and headed home.

*

In Earls Court, at six thirty a.m., three hours before Mike had set off on the hunting trip, two other people were having their community service paperwork put in order. In this case, it was not quite so simple. Sam, the ice-cream van driver, had no authority to sign forms, so dockets already signed by his boss were being attached to forms for Brian and the young soldier, Trevor.

Brian and Trevor wandered bleary-eyed around the fire station. The large doors to the street were open, and cool morning air was funnelling between the two enormous, immaculately polished fire engines. A large, hand-drawn poster on one of the walls depicted two engines surrounded by caricatures of Sam and the other members of the fire crew. In big letters across the top it asked 'Thinking of Having a Fire this Weekend?', adding underneath 'Then Call Us First — the Earl's Court Fire Brigade — 999'.

The two new recruits climbed the stairs and entered a large office, next to the one where Sam was still completing the paperwork. A thickset young man was staring at a map of London. He held a large steel ruler against the map while listening to a radio being tuned in to various army frequencies.

"Sam!" shouted the man by the map. "You'd better come in here."

Sam handed the completed forms to Brian and Trevor, then walked over to the map. "That fire up north, is it?"

"Yep. We have a situation, as they say. I place it in Beech Hill Park." The man at the map placed one end of the ruler on a patch of green and swivelled the other end downwards. "Wind direction south, fifteen miles an hour."

"Are you sure that's where it is?"

"Triangulated from Centre Point and a patrol on the M1–M25 intersection. Both report a lot of white and a little blue smoke. Could be Trent Park, to the east. Even so, it doesn't make much difference. It's still going to hit houses."

Sam turned to the radio operator. "Any radio traffic from the fire service?"

The operator shook his head. "Probably haven't been called yet. The local residents may not realise there's a problem and the army doesn't seem particularly worried so far."

"Michael!" Sam shouted down the stairs. "What's New Barnet like?"

"The pits."

"Apart from that."

Michael came up the stairs. "No, seriously, it's the pits." He walked over to the map and pointed to the residential area just below the park. "These houses here, less than thirty per cent occupied, gardens overgrown and roofs missing." He traced the roads with his finger. "Grass, brambles and bushes down the edges of all of these. This one totally overgrown. Oh, and at two points along here the park goes half way across the road from the north and meets the gardens creeping over the road from the south."

"When were you there last?"

"May. I did send their district councillors one of our letters."

"Straight into the bin, I suppose."

"Wouldn't be surprised."

"Well, lads!" Sam turned to Brian and Trevor. "Some action for you!" He walked back to the office and hit the alarm. The building was filled with a deafening ringing.

The fire crew ran to the pole and, one by one, descended to the ground floor. Brian followed and, releasing his grip too early, hit the ground hard. His stomach rose and pushed the air out of his lungs. Trevor, observing Brian's plight, hung on to the pole too tightly and was left suspended half way up. Sam grabbed Trevor's foot and, giving it a sharp tug, pulled him to the ground.

"We'll just take one engine!" Sam shouted. "I'll give you a call if we get desperate." The fireman who had been climbing into the cab of the second engine jumped down again, nodded and gave a thumbs-up sign.

"It's not as if they will be left with nothing to do," said Sam as the fire engine roared out into the street and made a violent left turn. "After all this dry weather London's like a tinderbox." He pressed the accelerator to the floor, throwing Brian and Trevor back in their seats. "And we're the only fire crews who will go across the river."

It took just fifteen minutes to reach King's Cross station. From there they followed the roads along the railway line to New Barnet. In 1860 the population of Barnet had been just under three thousand; now it was just over two thousand. The pleasant northern suburb of London it had become in the interim, was no more. The parks and golf courses, which had made the area popular with middle-class commuters, were now dense woodland. Most of the remaining population occupied the houses around New Barnet station.

Barnet had the appearance of a sleepy English village, but Michael's description of it as 'the pits' was the view of a fireman rather than someone seeking a peaceful place to retire. In some streets on the outer edges only two or three houses were occupied. Roads had been reduced to narrow, winding footpaths. Even in the central areas the occupancy rate was only thirty per cent at best. The remaining houses had overgrown gardens that the summer sun had turned into a thick carpet of dried vegetation. Some of the houses had exposed roof timbers, empty window frames and floorboards, all of which had first rotted and then dried like paper. The picture was completed by a ramshackle collection of derelict garden sheds and broken wooden fences.

"They might as well all live in petrol-soaked tents," Sam remarked, as the fire engine rode over the hummocks of dried grass and brambles covering a road that was supposed to separate the overgrown park from the first row of houses.

Barnet had survived attacks from rioters, looters and disease. It was now about to be consumed by a fire that was tearing southwards through Beech Hill Park. The fire, advancing in a pincer movement, threatened to enter Barnet itself. Flames flickered amongst the clouds of smoke emerging from the woods. Suddenly, a ball of fire detached itself from a tangle of fallen trees and rolled lazily across the road in front of the fire engine. The tall, dry grass and bushes that had overwhelmed what had once been a lush lawn bounded by neatly clipped privet hedges, swallowed the flame, then spat it skywards, together with a billowing white cloud of smoke and fragments of carbonated leaves.

"Water?" Sam shouted.

"Beech Hill Lake if we can still get to it, otherwise Pym's Brook at the end of this road," replied Michael, without needing to refer to the map he had been studying *en route*.

The heat struck Brian's face. Until this moment, he really had thought this would be no more than a ride in a fire engine. He did not like the suburbs, preferring the security of the city centre to the wilderness that was laying siege to the edge of the capital. Now, as flames surrounded the fire engine, he became increasingly anxious.

A group of muntjak ran out of the woods. Terrified by the fire engine, they turned and ran along the road. "Look! Bambi!" shouted one of the firemen. Everyone laughed, except Brian.

Sam sensed Brian's apprehension. He stopped being the chirpy ice-cream van driver and took on the role of a military commander — the part he would play for the rest of the day. "Brian!" he shouted, without giving any indication that he had registered Brian's concern. "All these houses on the left need evacuating. Get hold of someone in authority and make sure everyone gets out. Move everyone right back to New Barnet station."

"Yes." Brian nodded.

"No possessions. No hanging about to watch. Right back to the station."

Sam looked over his shoulder. "Trevor, we will need some earth-moving equipment — a bulldozer, digger, whatever you can get that will rip the dried grass off the next road across. Then, if the fire hasn't already got that far, you can try clearing a firebreak in the gardens at the back of this row of houses."

"What about this row?" Trevor asked.

"No chance! These are going. The best we can hope for is the next one across."

The fire engine came to a stop at the point were the second pincer of fire was advancing towards them through the trees. A line of men and women, passing buckets of water along a chain, were dousing the road. Sam put on his yellow fireman's helmet. "Remember," he said to everyone, but looking at Brian as he spoke, "no heroics! No-one goes rushing into a burning house. If people want to stay put, that's tough. We are here to put out a fire." He pulled his coat over his burn-scarred arms. "Be careful," he added finally. "I won't have time to watch you *and* the fire."

Sam climbed out of the cab and walked over to the person at the head of the chain. "OK. You can stop that now. Save your energy."

A middle-aged man, sweat streaming down his blackened face, signalled to the rest of the chain to stop. "That was quick. We only phoned you fifteen minutes ago."

"One hour and fifteen minutes too late, by the look of this."

"We only just realised that it might jump the road."

"Well, it will." Sam took Brian by the arm. "This is Brian. He is going to help you evacuate everyone to the station. Get two of your people who know these streets to help him." He then took hold of Trevor's arm. "This is Trevor. He is going to need a bulldozer to build some firebreaks."

Brian and Trevor were assigned their helpers and set about their tasks. Michael supervised the setting up of the pump and the rolling out of hose. Within fifteen minutes one jet of water was blasting into the blazing undergrowth and another was dousing the houses.

After thirty minutes Sam climbed back into the cab of the fire engine and picked up the radio handset. "Earl's Court fire brigade calling Centre Point. Come in."

There was a delay, then the speaker crackled into life. "Centre Point. Go ahead, Earl's Court fire brigade."

"We are in Barnet, where that smoke you have been monitoring is coming from. We understand that the residents here placed a call to the fire service. No units have arrived. Can you progress?"

"Sam, is that you?" Ross's distorted voice came on the line. "Why aren't you boys in church today?"

"Come on, Ross. No time for chitchat. We have a problem here."

"Yes, I can see some black smoke."

"Other end of the street. Only one unit here. Our second is in reserve."

"Very wise on a day like today. We're chasing up the other

units and will advise."

At the end of the road, Trevor was standing behind the driver in the cab of a tractor fitted with a small digger bucket. Sam ran towards the tractor, waving his arms. It stopped briefly to let Trevor off, then continued scraping its way down the backstreet.

"Is that the best they could come up with?" Sam was exasperated.

"Sorry. It's from an old builder's yard. They're trying to get another one started."

"Shit and *shit*." Sam turned to walk away.

"Sir?"

Sam stopped and turned. "Sam, not 'sir'. Sam."

"Er, Sam." Trevor struggled to call this person, who had suddenly acquired such an air of authority, by his first name. "I don't know if this will help, but there's a team of army engineers based down the road at St. Pancreas. They've got some big earth-moving stuff loaded onto railway trucks." He waited for a reaction, but none came. He began to feel embarrassed. "I'm not sure I should have told you that."

"Why the hell not? Jesus! We're all on the same side, aren't we?" He turned to walk away again. "Come with me."

With Trevor standing beside him, Sam leant inside the cab of the fire engine and picked up the radio again. "Ross!" he shouted. "Sam here again."

"Go ahead, Sam"

"You've got some engineers and equipment at St. Pancreas."

"Er, yes. I think so. Why?"

"Can you get a bulldozer and a team of engineers up to New Barnet to cut us some firebreaks?"

"Sam, last week you were running the fire brigade. This week you're giving the army orders. Man, by Christmas you'll be doing Ivan's job."

"Ross, we have little time left. Yes or no?"

"Yes, sir!" Ross replied. "Oh, by the way, chased up the fire service. Get back to me if they're not there in fifteen minutes and we will send you some of ours."

"Thanks, Ross. You're a pal."

Sam turned back to Trevor. "Take this mobile phone. Just press 'M', then '1', and you'll get through to me. Go down to the station. When the engineers arrive, bring them up here and set them to work. If they're not there in thirty minutes, give me a call."

Brian had shepherded all the families out of the first two rows of houses. He led them through their back gardens, as the fire had now cut off the road in front. The sight of the first houses bursting into flames had made Brian's task easier. Apart from one couple, who had insisted on searching for a photograph album, he met very little resistance. The district councillor led the group of residents towards the station, while Brian returned to the fire engine to find out if the next row of houses needed evacuating.

Just as Brian reached Sam, another fire engine arrived. The driver got out and strode across to them. "OK, sonny." He smiled. "*We'll* take over now."

Brian expected Sam to fly into a rage, but he didn't. "Sure. No problem," he replied calmly. "Just tell me where you want to get your water from, and which houses you want me to douse first." The fireman seemed confused. He looked up and down the road, then across at the houses, before turning back to face Sam. He was about to speak but, before he got the chance, Sam cupped both hands around his mouth and shouted. "Michael! Over here a minute!"

Michael arrived. Looking the fireman up and down, he smiled at Sam and raised one eyebrow. "Michael," said Sam, ignoring the fireman, "show this crew where to get their water, then take them down to the end of the street and get them to douse the second row of houses and gardens."

Sam smiled as Michael led the fireman away, then turned to Brian and winked. In a matter of minutes he had not only taken command of the second fire crew, but had also delegated that command to his assistant.

The evacuation was to continue. With the wind still keen, Sam was not confident that two fire crews alone could arrest the fire. He confided to Brian that, in the absence of the engineers, there was no reason why the fire should not keep going until it reached the railway line. There was even the possibility that the two fires would meet to create a firestorm, within which the fire crews would be trapped. "Twenty euros say we lose this one, Brian," he said with a grin.

"You're on," said Brian, only half-believing he would collect. Rejoining the group of local councillors, he began the evacuation of the next two rows of houses. This time the troop of refugees was larger. Unlike Sam, who despite his reservations remained outwardly calm, Brian was hit by another bout of angst. The role he had taken on, like the fire itself, was growing to epic proportions. The authority he had assumed far exceeded that of

Mike Allchurch's assistant.

Trevor had a similar crisis of confidence. The train loaded with earth-moving equipment arrived at the station, and the seventeen engineers accompanying it immediately placed themselves under his command. Slowly and patiently, trying to forget he was only a private and had only been in the army for six months, Trevor explained the task to the drivers of the two bulldozers.

A councillor took the S-Card numbers of the fire crews and filled out a dispensation form, allowing food to be consumed outside a restaurant. Thirty minutes later, egg-and-ham rolls and a bottle of beer were issued to each man. The councillor explained that there was a fault on the terminal in the restaurant and most of the crew's S-Card numbers only showed 'basic' food entitlements. The councillor had, however, persuaded the manager to produce 'basic plus' meals.

By four thirty in the afternoon, thanks to some brutal garden clearance on Trevor's part, the fire had been stopped, with the loss of only one and a half rows of houses. The smouldering remains of five houses were demolished and the rubble hosed down.

The evacuees returned from the station. Those whose houses had been destroyed were picking through the rubble. As Brian walked past one group, on his way back to the fire engine, a woman ran up to him. She took hold of his hand and pressed an ornament into it. "Thank you," she said. He tried to refuse the object, but the woman turned and walked away.

At five thirty Sam's crew left the regular fire service to continue the damping down. Brian's eyes and throat were burning. He examined the ornament — a porcelain figure of a woman in a long blue dress, the base slightly blackened by smoke. Trevor was hoarse from shouting over the noise of the machinery. He looked at the figure. "Valuable?" he croaked.

"To somebody, once, perhaps," Brian replied, turning it over in his hands a few times before dropping it into his pocket.

Brian stood in the shower at the fire station for thirty minutes. As the adrenaline drained from his body, his legs began to ache. The burns from the sparks started to sting. Once he was out of the shower, he transferred the porcelain figure from his fireman's jacket into his rucksack.

Brian and Trevor collected their bicycles and pushed them towards the main doors. They shouted their thank-yous to Sam, who, when he realised they were leaving, ran across to stop them.

"Look, when my girl turns up, we're all going for dinner. You've got to come with us." They leant their bicycles against the wall again. Sam hesitated for a moment, then said, "You are a handy pair to have around. Any chance you could come along again?" Brian could see that, although Sam was addressing both of them, his main interest was in Trevor. This was confirmed when Trevor explained he was on duty most weekends.

"That's a pity," Sam said, adding, as if it was only of passing interest, "Who's your commanding officer?"

*

In Ruislip, the Ivan's Restaurant in Malvern Avenue fell silent when, at the beginning of the seven o'clock news, the image of Ivan Vlachos appeared on the television screen. "Hello friends," his tired voice said. "As you have probably already heard, I am to retire. We have known each other for many years. There was a time, not long ago, when a person would have counted themselves lucky to live to the age of sixty-three. Today it is different. Everything is different. When we first knew each other, times were so bad a person could not retire; they had to work until the end. Today that is no longer the case. Over twenty years ago, I told you I would cover the Ukraine, and the rest of Europe, with wheat — that there would be enough to feed us all. Today the fields are full and you all have enough to eat. All I now ask, in return, is that I should be allowed to live out the last of my years in peace, on my farm. My friends, goodbye and thank you."

Mike's son smiled as the two teenagers on the next table laughed and pretended to push their fingers down their throats. A waiter leant across their table and whispered to them. "Would like me to ask the guard to come in and see you?" The teenagers' faces flushed and they fell silent. Mike's son looked down at the table.

"Well, he deserves a rest. He certainly got us out of a mess," Linda said, still staring at the television. The newsreader explained that Vlachos's post of leader of the Ukraine Green Party would be taken over by his deputy, Lex Simitovich, who would also hold the post of leader of the European Green Alliance until the elections at the end of the month.

"I'm not sure everyone sees it that way." Mike realised that this was neither the time, nor the place, to contradict the widely held belief that Europe would be a wasteland if it were not for Ivan Vlachos. At the beginning of the century, Ivan's folksy speeches, delivered in a heavy Russian accent, would have been dismissed as politically naive, indicative of a politician who was neither sophisticated nor media-aware. All the older people seated in the restaurant that evening could remember the day they first heard of this over-friendly, ever-joking Russian; the day it was announced Britain would be taken under the wing of a Europe dominated by the Ukraine and ruled over by the Green Alliance; the day the shortages stopped and people started to believe that European civilisation might just survive. Although Mike liked to think that he was never taken in by the 'big friendly Green giant', tonight even he felt slightly apprehensive about life without Ivan.

As they walked home, Linda pressed him about his comment. "Well," said Mike, "there are some who believe that our friend Ivan stood back and watched us suffer; that he didn't step in until he was sure the Socialist government had been smashed and the Green Party were in place."

"That's not true."

"I didn't say it was. It's just the way some people see it. Ivan is, or was, a politician. Politics is all about power. Ivan did a trade with Britain: we got food and he got power."

Linda linked arms with him. "Of all people, you should know that isn't true."

*

The girl peered down the neck of Sam's shirt, then rolled up his sleeves and inspected his arms. "No new holes. Couldn't have been a very big fire." The rest of the crew laughed and started to recount their versions of the day's events.

"How do you get away with it?" Brian asked.

"Nothing to it. Just get in the fire engine and go."

"No. I mean the fire engine, taking charge, telling the army what to do."

Sam swallowed a mouthful of beer. "The fire engine was easy. One day they sent me to Earl's Court to pick up a fire engine and break it up for spares. When I got to the fire station, there were two engines, and the place had been unoccupied for years. So I thought, this looks interesting, and put in an application to live in the flat above it. I didn't tell them about the second engine, and did it up myself. Then I volunteered to do a few weekends' community service with the regular fire brigade, learned the stuff, met up with the lads here and away we went."

"But what about the real fire service?"

The crew fell about laughing. "The real fire service? You mean that bunch of prats that turned up late and didn't know where the water was?" Sam joined in the laughter.

"So why not join the real fire service and change it?"

"Because they won't change." Sam paused to choose his words. "Brian, we are surrounded by people who have either screwed up big time, or who stood back and let other people screw up. People like your boss. They are so used to things getting screwed up that all they can do is stand around waiting for the next disaster. They've got failure bred into them. If it was left to the real fire service, in three months we would be walking backwards into the Thames with flames all around us. We can't change people like that. They're dead brains, terrified to do anything — and just as scared to let us have a try."

"They let you have a go today."

"That's because we didn't leave them any choice. They were shit scared. As far as they were concerned, they'd already failed. When they get to that stage they are only too pleased to get shot of the responsibility. Two years ago I had a boss like that. If you had come to us then, you wouldn't have got a moped, let alone an ice-cream van." Sam smiled, and wiped the remains of a bread roll around his soup dish. "The guy we've got now — totally different, younger guy, sees the broader picture. Last week the army phones up, wants fifty trucks because the railway, up north somewhere, has broken. Next day, fifty trucks, drivers, fuel, the lot — all ready to go. Two years ago I couldn't even get the boss to sign the community dockets. Now I get dockets *and* diesel. He even disappeared a fire engine off the books for us."

Brian sat thinking. He was about to ask another question when Sam leant forward. "Look, Brian. We've got a blank sheet of paper. There isn't any past, no rules they can make us conform to. *They* screwed it all up. Now *we* can do what we want. As long as it makes sense, and you think it will work, just do it. What will your boss say? 'Oh, that won't work.' Of course he will, because, as far he knows, nothing has ever worked. If you can see where you want to go, just go for it."

The girl slid one arm around Sam's waist, put her face close to his, then pressed a finger against his lips. "Shsh now."

"Yes," said Michael, mimicking Sam. "Just go for it. That's if your girlfriend lets you, of course."

The group collapsed into laughter again, but stopped when

Ivan Vlachos started his speech. When it was over, Sam was the first to speak. "Shame. Good bloke."

Michael lowered his voice to a whisper. "Did he fall, or was he pushed?"

"All I know is that I wouldn't give up a job like that without a fight," replied Sam.

"Ten euros says Simitovich gets the European leader's job," said Brian.

"That reminds me, I owe you for the bet this afternoon." Sam reached into his pocket, but Brian told him to forget it.

"Simitovich won't be there long," said the girl. "Fairchild will beat him hands down at the election."

The mention of Fairchild's name stopped Brian in his tracks. Later that night, lying in bed staring at the porcelain figure on the bedside table, he was still considering the implications of what the girl had said.

2

Friday 20th April 2001

The morning after the attack at Whiteside's farm Sergeant Bryant thought his career in the police force was over. By Friday of the same week, however, he was well enough to walk across to the window of his seventh-floor hospital ward. He watched the streams of cars trickling out of Cambridge along the country lanes. True, he tired quickly, but the dizziness was going. Things were definitely looking up.

Two thousand five hundred kilometres away, in the Ukraine, Ivan Vlachos's week had not gone so well. He was now standing on the balcony of his sixth-floor flat. The keen westerly breeze was warm and felt just as humid as it had been two hours earlier, when he was sweating in his office. Vlachos had left work early. His head dropped, and he gazed at the knot in his tie. It still looked wrong. He pulled the tie undone and started again. This would have been the third attempt — but he stopped. Looking up, he stared, as he had on so many other evenings, at the power station three kilometres downstream and on the opposite bank of the Dniester. Before this week, in the few daylight hours when he was not actually working there, the sight of it had filled him with pride. Today he felt detached from the building and betrayed by his colleagues.

"Tanya, I can't get this tie right."

"What do you want a tie for?" The voice came from inside the flat. A slim young woman with short brown hair stepped through the sliding glass door, flicked Vlachos's hands away from his neck, and hurriedly tied a new knot. "These Greens don't wear ties. Why don't you just go in jeans and tee-shirt?" She straightened the knot, then ran her hands over his shirt to flatten the creases. "Look, you're sweating already."

"They're expecting an engineer."

"Well, they're getting an engineer."

"One that works in industry. A company man."

"Perhaps not for much longer..." She stopped herself, fully aware of the implications of what her husband was doing, and the effect it might have on their way of life. Still, it had to be his decision. What was the point of the hi-fi, the holidays and the new car if he was going to spend the rest of his life brooding?

"Do you think I'm doing the right thing?" he asked. As if on cue, their ten-month-old daughter woke and her cries echoed through the flat.

"That's for you to decide. Whatever you decide, I'll support you." She stepped back into the room.

Vlachos took one last look across the river. They had betrayed his trust and now he would betray theirs. Yes, he did worry he might lose his job and, with it, the money to pay for the car and this flat. But he did not really believe it would come to that. Next year he would still be here. — In the event, this was not to be.

As the train pulled into Lvov station, Vlachos removed his tie, carefully folded it, and put it in his jacket pocket. Even though the sun was now low in the sky, the city was holding on to its heat. Sweat ran down the side of his face. He removed the jacket and rolled up his shirtsleeves. As promised, outside the station in Ploshcha Vokzal'na, the red Volkswagen was waiting.

The driver looked over his shoulder, then swerved out into the traffic. "Have you brought any overheads?"

"Yes." Vlachos patted his briefcase.

"Only I see you have no portable computer." The car came to a halt, sandwiched between a tram and a parked lorry. "It doesn't matter. We have a PC with PowerPoint." The tram wheels screeched deafeningly along the rails.

"Actually, I haven't brought a computer presentation," Vlachos shouted. "Just overhead transparencies. I didn't think you..."

The driver laughed. "Ivan, we are not against all technology. You know we have a website?"

"Yes."

"Well then."

The lecture theatre, in the economics department of the Ivan Franho State University, was large. It was also more oppressive than the ones at Kiev University, where Vlachos had studied engineering. Perhaps it only seemed that way because he was now surrounded by strangers. After all, he was used to public speaking. Until now, however, his audiences had been made up of people he knew and who were of a like mind.

The personal computer that had been set up on the lectern left little space for papers. A young woman was talking to the driver. She looked over at Vlachos, then left the theatre. She returned pushing an overhead projector mounted on a trolley. Vlachos felt embarrassed, out of place and slightly disoriented. He ran his fingers down the edges of the lectern. Looking up at the sea of faces, he searched for someone he might recognise, or even someone who bore the slightest resemblance to one of his managers or colleagues. There was no-one.

The girl stepped forward, leaned across the lectern, and spoke into the microphone. The introduction was brief: "Good evening, everybody. Please welcome Ivan Vlachos. He is an engineer with the Ukrainian Nuclear Industry Inspectorate." His lecture had already been discussed in some detail by members of the fledgling Ukraine Green Movement. As far as Vlachos was concerned, this made starting the talk that much harder.

"Good evening. I am Ivan Vlachos." He could hear himself repeating the girl's words. "I am an engineer with the Nuclear Industry Inspectorate." Pausing momentarily to take a breath, he scanned, once more, the faces in front of him. These were not his colleagues; these were not his managers or university tutors. These were strangers, and the next sentence would be his first step into another world. "Any engineering system, or organisation, designed or created by man can be regarded as an extension of man the living organism. Society itself can be regarded as a single living organism. Agriculture is its mouth, food processing is its digestion, and the sewage system its lower gut and bowel. Healthcare, with its hospitals and pharmaceutical companies, is to society as a whole what the immune system is to the human body. In fact, you could say that, apart from being conscious of its own existence, society is a complete macro- or meta-man."

Vlachos wasn't expecting a round of applause. Then again, he *was* expecting *some* reaction — some positive-sounding noise. Had he stated the obvious? Perhaps he had misjudged the audience. He picked up the glass of water, observing his hand tremble, and took a sip.

"As man has created large-scale industrial plants — for example, chemical works and nuclear power plants — we should consider the extent to which these processes have a model of man, the biological entity, built into them. We should also consider the implications of this subconscious modelling, particularly in the field of risk analysis."

He thought he saw someone nod, but there was still a barrier between him and them. It was as though he was still speaking to a group of engineers at the plant, as though these people here were watching him remotely, on some sort of screen, with no obligation to react.

It was then that Ivan began to change, to adapt his style to the audience. In future years, dissenters would claim that Vlachos was just a front for the Green Party; that the simplistic gloss he put on complex scientific issues, the constant references to his own family, the empathising, and relating his own plight to that of the people, were all carefully scripted. Some thought that Vlachos was just a puppet and that the waspish, German-born Peter Aul pulled the strings. Then there were those who thought it was Vlachos who had hijacked the Green Party, using it to further his own political career, just as he used Ukraine's grain surplus to force Green parties into government across Europe.

"Man is pre-programmed to die." Vlachos was suddenly more confident. His hands no longer gripped the sides of the lectern but made sweeping gestures. "Macro-organisms also have a predefined life span. In the autumn, the individual wasp remains outside the nest and dies of cold. In so doing, it avoids becoming a burden on the resources the queen will consume the following year." He moved out from behind the lectern so that his whole body was visible to the audience. "I stay out late sometimes. Get rat-arsed, come home and bang on the door at two in the morning. The wife shouts 'You stay out there till you sober up.' But these guys do it big time, and every night." The audience started to warm to him, and he relaxed slightly. "Our body will die when it reaches a certain age. Sometimes our own behaviour leads to its destruction. So we should consider whether social structures and industrial processes have a mechanism — either implied or subconsciously designed into them — which, when activated, will end their lives."

In America they were to call him 'the Green Joseph Stalin'. He would be accused of deporting the strong and fit from the countries he annexed, and putting them to work in Ukrainian labour camps; of supporting an unsustainable Green economy with an army of slaves. These accusations were toned down when shipments of grain were negotiated. Then American television viewers were introduced to 'Uncle Ivan'. It would be suggested that he was politically naive; that he played poker with all the cards face upwards; and, again, that he was no more than a front man for a government that was engaged in a bizarre type of political brinkmanship. "We do not want a war with anybody," he would say. "Our nuclear weapons are in the dustbin and all our soldiers are gathering the harvest. We can't fight you today. If you really want a war, you will have to fight yourselves." But what country had the resources to wage war, or an army fit enough to fight? And who would be foolish enough to attack the land that was producing a significant proportion of the world's grain?

Now some of the audience were taking notes. Others were just listening intently and wondering why this engineer from the nuclear power industry was being so candid. What role did this person, who had such unconventional ideas, play in a safety executive? — an executive that was widely perceived as being no more than a rubber stamp for the programme itself.

"Man can model most events, can replay them as memories or envisage them as future actions. He can imagine many conditions his body is likely to find itself in. He cannot, however, model death. Complete failure of the body is, for logical reasons, unimaginable. As a child, one may have a strong fear of death, and make an effort to model the experience. As we age, the risks that we felt might lead to our death present themselves — in most cases, without our suffering any ill effect. So we stop even attempting to model our own death. Consciously, we now consider ourselves immortal, despite the presence of a time bomb that will eventually trigger our own destruction.

"As man designs and builds complex processes and systems, and programs into them a total-destruct mechanism, he also builds in subsystems which, as time goes by, provide the illusion of immortality.

"In a nuclear power plant there is a somewhat feeble attempt to model man's consciousness within the physical power plant itself. Networks of alarms and sensors, linked to a central computer, provide the basis for what could possibly be regarded as consciousness. But this still falls short of what man regards as awareness, and the plant cannot possibly envisage its own destruction."

Vlachos's role within the safety inspectorate was already coming under review. These unconventional ideas were part of his post-graduate thesis. His tutor at college had tried to persuade him to stay at university and work on a doctorate. Vlachos, however, wanted practical experience and was worried about becoming overqualified. As a compromise, he persuaded the management of the safety inspectorate to let him work on a thesis. Then the university refused to accept the finished work, claiming it was too unconventional, and the inspectorate's management refused him permission to publish, claiming that the thesis represented a security risk. Seeing himself as both deceived and betrayed, Ivan decided to ignore his manager's ruling. Tanya had told him not to be bitter, not to travel to Lvov with the intention of taking revenge on his manager and tutor. She told him that people would detect the spite in his voice — and that would devalue his work.

Vlachos braced himself, tensed his muscles, and launched into the technical section of his talk, reading out the next heading: "'How Man Tricks Himself into Believing a Nuclear Power Plant is Safe.'" He paused and looked around. He saw the audience lean forward in their seats, suddenly becoming more attentive. "A shut-off valve has a failure rate of once in two hundred years. The backup valve also has a failure rate of once in two hundred years. The chances of both the main and the backup valves failing at the same time is the product of the two possibilities: once in forty thousand years. The coolant pump has a failure rate of once in a hundred years; with its backup, once in ten thousand years. The chances of both pumps and both shut-off valves failing at the same time is once in four hundred million years.

"But backup systems should not be given the same failure ratings as primary systems, because they are inevitably considered as being less crucial than primary systems. So they receive less attention during maintenance. Secondary systems also stand idle for long periods. Valves may stick and pumps may suffer uneven corrosion of their moving parts. More important to this thesis is the fact that backup systems always operate in a different environment from the primary system — i.e. one in which a similar device has already failed.

"When valves and pumps are considered as part of a complete system, the failure of a shut-off valve changes the environment in which the second valve, and the two pumps, are operating. The likelihood of a pump continuing to work is reduced when the shut-off valve fails. It is no longer working in the environment the designer envisaged when specifying the chances of failure. We now have the beginnings of a failure cascade that could possibly end with the total destruction of the power station. In the event, it does not. But now the operator has seen a rare failure occur — one which, despite being potentially dangerous, resolved itself.

"The illusion of invincibility, or immortality, has been created. With each incident — because the coincidental failure of a second device, then a third, is highly unlikely, in theory — the operators feel that the plant is becoming safer. In reality, the plant is becoming more dangerous. However, as each incident or failure is resolved, the operators perceive the likelihood of total destruction as increasingly remote.

"Has a self-destruct mechanism been designed into the nuclear power plant? Well, we have now seen that the plant contains a mechanism that mirrors our own illusion of immortality. We can conclude that this mechanism is present in order to mask a feature that the engineer, subconsciously, embedded into the design itself — the *ability* to self-destruct."

If that had been all there was to Vlachos's thesis, then perhaps, after a short discussion and some questions, he would have returned home having got the whole thing off his chest. But there was more. He switched on the overhead projector. The light temporarily blinded him and he fumbled in his briefcase for the folder of acetates. For each overhead, he explained the computer simulations he had run. He described the historic data used and the worrying conclusions he had reached. He claimed that the nuclear power plant, the one he was working in, would suffer a minor failure in the first year, a major failure within the following three years, and a catastrophic failure within fifteen years.

The analysis could not be faulted. During the question-and-answer session, Vlachos explained in greater detail the assumptions and factors which underpinned the formulae that drove the computer simulation.

In the event, Vlachos did not have to wait fifteen years. In the spring of the following year, a spike in the electricity supply in Ukraine's newest nuclear power plant burnt out the solenoid on a primary shut-off valve. The jolt of electricity also destroyed the insulation on the windings of the primary pump motor. The primary valve refused to open; the secondary valve had jammed shut. A second water supply was turned on. At this point, the armature windings of the primary pump burnt out. The secondary pump started. The operators breathed a sigh of relief, remarking how amazing it was that so many unrelated failures had occurred at the same time. Twenty-five minutes later — and unnoticed for fifteen minutes — the main bearing on the secondary pump shattered. The control system assumed that the primary pump had been restarted. The water supply to the reactor was lost. A meltdown began.

A hundred and fifty thousand people — including Vlachos, his wife and his daughter — were forced, at three o'clock in the morning, to leave their homes for ever. It was to be the Green Party's press officer who led the news reporters and camera crews to Vlachos. It was to be Vlachos who became a spokesman for the displaced residents, and an unofficial expert on the reactor itself. When the government fell, he became at first *a* spokesman, and then *the* spokesman, for the Green Party. At the beginning of the election campaign, he became the leader of the party. When the Green Party won, he became prime minister.

His first task as prime minister was to explain to the people why the World Trade Organisation had allowed countries around the world to boycott Ukraine's exports. He explained the US's retaliation to his decision to scrap the nuclear programme. He justified Ukraine's ban on the import of GM crops and foods. And during the global crop failures he became 'Uncle Ivan' — only too happy to take care of the family of anyone who wanted to travel to the Ukraine and help feed the world. When the epidemics came, he was the one who shared people's grief. "This month, here in the Ukraine, three thousand two hundred and one people have died of influenza. Too often we hear these large numbers. Sometimes we wonder who the 'one' was. This month it was my daughter." Some people said that Vlachos was just a cynical politician, one who used his own daughter's death to score political points. Others, who found the loss of some, or all, of their family too great to articulate, or who were frightened to advertise to their peers a possible weakness or flaw in their own genetic make-up, could now express their grief by proxy — by publicly mourning the death of Lena Vlachos.

Vlachos returned the notes and the overheads to his briefcase. The girl moved to unplug the projector. "That was a very interesting talk. Thank you." She was about to push the projector towards the door, but hesitated. "Would you mind if we posted your thesis on our website?"

"No. That's fine," he replied, without considering the implications.

"Do you have the text on a disk?"

Vlachos reached into his briefcase and took out a disk. The girl pushed it into the drive of the computer on the lectern and copied the contents onto the hard disk. "Thanks," she said, returning the disk without further comment.

'The Vlachos Thesis', as it became known, was read widely by members of Green movements and nuclear protest groups around the world. In a cell in London's Brixton prison, a copy of the web pages lay on a small writing table. On each page, scribbled in pencil, someone had made notes.

For digestion read food chain. Immune system read National Health Service. Poison read BSE, failure cascade, animal feed,

CJD. Total destruction — 5 to 35 million victims, euthanasia, social collapse. False alarm. Relief, complacency — the illusion of immortality. Genetically Modified crops. For digestion read food chain, failure cascade...

Next to the notes was a series of flow diagrams for chains of events that ended in catastrophe. These were the rough notes that David Fairchild used to turn 'the Vlachos Thesis' into one of the Green movement's most important documents. Perhaps the thesis was flawed. Perhaps its analysis did not bear close examination. Perhaps it was, as some scientists claimed, witchcraft for the new dark ages. But the decades ahead would bring death, suffering and the destruction of a whole way of life. In the absence of religion, without the comfort and distraction of materialism — and faced with the failure of conventional science — Vlachos's, and Fairchild's, thesis fulfilled the basic need for an explanation.

Monday 19th August 2041

Brian was first in the office. Despite an extra cup of coffee at breakfast, he still felt tired. Pains in his legs, arms and neck, which had eased during the walk to the station, returned after he had been sitting down for a while. Taking the newspaper from the Troxley file, he read the front page again. Brian sat for a moment, deep in thought, but when he heard Mike's footsteps in the corridor outside, he returned the newspaper to the file and closed the filing cabinet.

"Hello. Here early. Good weekend, was it?" Mike sat down heavily, leaned forward and switched on his computer.

"Not bad."

"Get your ride in a fire engine?"

"Yes."

"Big fire up at Barnet, wasn't there?"

"So I heard. Was the hunting good?" Brian wanted to move the subject away from fire fighting.

"Not bad. Four deer."

"If you like that sort of thing."

"Oh yes, of course, you're a veggie." Mike tapped a few keys, then stared at the screen. "Well, back to law reform then."

"What about Troxley?"

"Oh, yes!" Mike turned to face Brian, as though he had been taken by surprise. "I was thinking about that on the way in. I don't think we'll need to worry about it anymore. Not with Ivan going and Fairchild lined up for the top job. The party will bury that case somewhere quiet. Langford will have the file up to Park Lane in no time."

"Maybe."

"No 'maybe' about it."

"Five euros?"

At first, Mike ignored the challenge, then had a change of heart. "OK. You're on."

Brian looked out of the window. Wisps of white cloud were dissolving into a pale-blue sky. "We've still got the forensics to sort out."

"Yes. Might as well do that now. Come on."

Brian followed Mike out of the office "Do any of these laws and regulations you're amending deal with fire control?"

Mike smiled. "Er, no. Well, not many anyway. Why?"

"Just wondering."

Placing his index finger on a mark on Brian's neck, Mike asked, "Is that a burn? You really ought to tell your girlfriend not to smoke until after sex."

Brian smiled. It seemed that, for a Monday morning, Mike was in a particularly good mood. Perhaps it was the thought of getting shot of the Troxley case. After all, it was not often that a case got pushed upstairs to the party. Most came the other way. "I was just wondering if regulations could be drawn up which forced district councils to stop residential areas turning into firetraps."

"Sounds like a good idea. I draft a regulation saying let's make sure all the dried grass and bushes are cut down. Then someone draws up a law to go with it. Someone forgets to cut the grass in Rayners Lane and I get two months on a penal farm. Sounds good so far."

*

Brian pushed open the door to Amanda Pearce's laboratory. In an office just inside, the briefcase, mobile phone, gun and passport were laid out on a desk. Amanda ushered them into the office and handed Brian a sheet of A4-sized paper.

"Well, the person who pushed the redial button on your phone certainly had a good look inside this briefcase. They picked up the passport and handled the gun."

"Curiosity?" suggested Mike.

Amanda frowned and tilted her head slightly. "Perhaps, but they left several prints on the handle of the case. Is it possible she moved the case from one room to another?"

"Could have," replied Brian. "What about Troxley? Did you find his ...?"

"Of course she did," Mike interrupted. "It was his case and his passport."

Embarrassed, Amanda looked down at the floor. "Well," she said to Brian, "his prints were on the case but not on the passport. There was a set of prints on the passport — but they were not Troxley's."

Brian considered this for a moment, then asked, "And the gun?"

"Oh yes. He left a lovely clear fingerprint on the trigger."

"Well thanks, Amanda. I'll have my phone back." He turned to Mike. "What do we do with the rest of it?"

Mike did not reply. He dragged the briefcase to the edge of the desk, placed the passport and the gun inside it, closed the lid and carried it out of the office.

Amanda held the laboratory door open. "Seeing Hutch next, are you?"

Brian smiled. Amanda drew air between her teeth. "And on a Monday as well. Just try not to upset him."

*

"What do you think this is, laddie?" Dr. Hutchinson waved a long bone in front of Brian's face. Mike could see that both men were already sparring with each other. The best thing he could do was move back from the table, on which Troxley's body was laid out, perch himself on a stool and watch from a safe distance.

"A bone."

"Right. Good. Yes, it's a bone. A femur." He jabbed Brian's chest with it. "Notice anything about it?"

Brian took the bone and rolled it around between his fingers. "Er, very small scratches. Possibly made with a knife and fork," he murmured. "Oh no!" he exclaimed suddenly. "You've started to eat Troxley!"

Hutch grabbed the bone and banged one end of it on the table, then he waved it in front of Brian's face again. "Contrary to the rumours which some people have been putting about" — he leaned forward and stared into Brian's eyes — "free meat is not one of the perks of this job." He turned and looked at Mike, to see if there was any reaction. Mike avoided eye contact. "The owner of this bone," Hutch continued, "has probably never missed a meal between the time he was born and the age of twenty-seven. Now how old would you say this chappie was, eh?"

Brian raised his hand to his mouth, then looked down at the body. "Fifty?"

"Over sixty. This man has led a charmed life: plenty to eat, no disease, no stress. That's why he only looks fifty, laddie. What does that mean?"

"It means he hasn't been living around here."

"Good. That's right." He pointed the bone towards Mike. "Cut off Mike's leg and what do you think you'll find?"

"He goes around in circles?"

Hutch flinched. He wanted to laugh but chose to ignore the remark and continued with his performance. "On *his* bones you'll find marks where growth slowed during the famine. But this character here" — he prodded Troxley's remaining leg with the bone — "seems to have been somewhere else when all that happened."

"We know that," Mike said. "We found a US passport on him."

Hutch and Brian looked at each other. "Have you spoken to Amanda Pearce?" Hutch asked, in a near-whisper.

"Yes," replied Brian, still looking Hutch straight in the eye.

"Good. Good. Next then." Hutch held up Troxley's right hand. "Our friend here is right-handed." Brian was about to speak, but Hutch continued. "Before you ask me how I know, no great feats of forensic analysis were needed to spot nicotine all over his right hand." He walked around the table and picked up the left hand. "But, he somehow managed to shoot himself with his left hand."

Letting go of the hand, Hutch walked to the end of the table and ran his fingers across the top of Troxley's head. "Glass fragments in the hair."

"Er, that was me," said Brian. "I broke a window."

"To get into the room?"

"No. I was letting some air in."

Hutch slid his hands under Troxley and gave a violent tug. "Where are you learning police procedures, laddie? Cowboy books?" The body rose up, turned over and landed face down, with both arms and the remaining leg draped over the edge of the table. "Here, here, here and here." He pointed to discoloration of the flesh between the shoulder blades, on the upper part of the buttocks and on the remaining calf muscle.

"Hypostasis," said Brian.

Hutch looked surprised. "What?"

"Hypostasis. It's where the blood settled after he died."

"I know that." Hutch looked up at Brian as he leaned over the body.

"So after he shot himself, he had a lie-down, then decided he would be more comfortable in a chair." Brian smiled.

"Probably thought it would get rid of the stomach-ache."

"How do you know his stomach was aching?"

"Everyone gets stomach-ache after swallowing cyanide."

"He had a really crap day, didn't he?"

Hutch looked up and smiled. Then he mimicked an airline pilot: "I hope you enjoy your stay here in London and we look forward to welcoming..."

Mike gave a short cough in order to get Hutch's attention. "So what's your opinion then?"

Hutch turned to face Mike "Well, judging from the contents of the stomach, someone took our friend here out to dinner, then gave him a glass of vodka and lemon laced with cyanide. They placed him on the floor, or possibly in the back of a van," — he glanced at Brian — "which didn't, as it turns out, have fragments of glass in it. They then put him in an armchair and blew his brains out. The gun left a powder burn on the hand and, when it arrived here, a finger was still wrapped around the trigger."

"So murder dressed up to look like suicide," Mike suggested.

Hutch did not rush to agree with this verdict. Instead he turned, looked down at the body, and bit his lip. "Someone was sufficiently on the ball to realise that they had to wrap the finger around the trigger before rigor mortis set in in the fingers. They must have seen he was right-handed when he drank the poison, but still they chose the wrong hand — and overlooked the hypostasis."

"A murder, dressed up as a suicide, dressed up as a murder then?" Brian suggested.

Mike thought that Hutch would lose his temper. However, he did not. He looked up and waved his finger slowly in front of Brian's face. Picking up the report he had prepared, Hutch folded it twice, then ran his fingers along the crease. He pushed it down hard into Mike's top pocket. "There you go, Mike. All yours, and the best of luck."

"What about the body?"

"The incinerator."

"But don't we have to inform the American Embassy?"

"We'll send them the ashes. They can send him home by air mail and cash in the return half of his ticket. They'll probably be glad of the money."

"Thanks, Hutch," Mike said

Brian was already walking towards the door. "Yes, thanks, Dr. Scarpetta," he called out, without turning round. As the door closed behind them, Mike and Brian heard Hutch give a short laugh.

"Ticket!" Mike exclaimed as they were about to climb the stairs. "There wasn't any ticket!"

"Perhaps the girl took it and cashed it in."

"Without the passport? Oh, what the hell! We've done our bit. It's someone else's problem now."

Mike took the Troxley file out of the filing cabinet. The two reports were added to it and the whole lot went into the briefcase. Mike then put the case next to the computer on his desk. Moving the mouse around, and clicking the button a few times, brought up the dialog box for gaining access to the internal network. "I take it you are serious about those fire regulations?"

Brian was taken by surprise. "Well, yes."

"Good, because I'm volunteering you to work on amendments to environmental laws and regulations. When you're contacted just explain what you want to add. If Park Lane and the ministry are happy you'll get a password." He entered Brian's name, hit return and then closed the connection.

"Thanks."

"You won't be thanking me in a couple of months' time. Switching off the computer, he grabbed the briefcase. "Now to get shot of Mr. Troxley. See you later."

*

Hearing the knock on the half-open door, Langford looked up. "Come in, Mike," he murmured. He also seemed to be in a particularly good mood and less stressed than he had been on the previous Friday. Nevertheless, his hand still trembled as he pointed to one of the chairs in front of his desk and invited Mike to sit down.

Mike assumed that Langford's spirits had been lifted by the thought of off-loading the Troxley case onto the UKGA's security division. "It's all here," Mike said, laying the case on the desk.

"Yes. You've obviously heard about Ivan?"

"Of course," Mike replied slowly, already fearing the worst.

"Well, I've spoken to Park Lane and they feel..." Langford looked up to the ceiling as he struggled to find the right words. "At a time like this, and given that there could possibly be... And really a newspaper with Fairchild's name in it is hardly conclusive..."

"And the fact that Troxley, the man with the hole in the head, was also mentioned in the article?"

"Well, quite. Anyway, the party feel that if they were to take on the case it could be misinterpreted. Seen as a cover-up. An independent body should carry out the investigation, they feel."

Mike could not decide which was more annoying — having the case bounced back or that Langford enjoyed doing it. "Which independent body is that?"

"Us." Langford scratched the side of his face. "There's no need to be facetious." He drummed his fingers on the briefcase, making it clear he no longer wanted it on his desk.

Mike slid the case off the desk and put it on the floor next to his chair. "If I'm going to work on this, I'll need some assistance."

"You've already got Tyler."

"I'd rather have someone else. Someone a bit more mature."

"Less flippant?" Langford put both hands behind his head and leant back in his chair. "Most young people, today, are like young Brian. They haven't lived through the things we have. But he's keen and intelligent."

"A clowning boy scout." Mike thought he would try another tack. "Anyway, he's tied up on some law-amendment work."

"You know as well as I do that law amendment is just a fill-in job." Standing up, Langford rolled up his sleeves. "Another hot one. Fancy coming over the road for a spot of lunch?"

Mike picked up the briefcase and made one last attempt. "I really think I could handle this one better on my own."

"Give it a week. After all, you'll be visiting that farm in Norfolk. Do you really want to go out there on your own?"

"I don't really want to go there at all, actually." He had given little thought to how the investigation would proceed, because he had hoped that his involvement would end with this meeting.

"Well then, perhaps you can delegate that to young Brian."

*

Brian gave up waiting for Mike and decided to go for lunch on his own. After collecting his food, he saw Mike and Langford sitting in the far corner of the restaurant, next to a window that looked out on Queen Anne's Gate. Dr. Hutchinson was sitting on his own at a table in the centre of the room. Brian almost failed to recognise him without his white coat. "This taken?" he asked, holding his tray a few inches above Hutch's table.

Hutch's expression did not change. He merely shook his head slowly, without appearing to acknowledge Brian's presence.

"Hot again." Brian dug his thumbs into the bread roll and tore it in two.

"It is." Hutch took a knife and cut an apple in half.

"What do you know about GM crop technology?"

"Nothing. You need to speak to a biologist or a botanist."

"So if you found a seed, or a leaf, in the hair of a body, you wouldn't be able to tell what sort of plant it came from?"

Hutch did not answer at once. He slowly chewed both halves of the apple down to the core before speaking. "It's so noisy in here, you can hardly hear yourself think. Why don't you call into my office when you've finished your lunch?" He stood up abruptly and walked out of the restaurant.

*

Brian found Hutch sitting behind his desk in a small office at the back of the main forensic laboratory. Still without his white coat, he was thumbing through the loose-leaf pages of a large ring file. As Brian entered the room, Hutch closed the file and replaced it on a shelf behind him. Turning back to face Brian, he removed his glasses, let them fall on a blotter, put both elbows on the desk and rested his chin on his hands. "So, young man, you want to know about GM technology."

Brian, without waiting to be asked, pulled up a chair and sat down.

"Genetically modified crops." Hutch almost spelt out each word. "Is your enquiry in any way connected with Mr. Troxley?"

"Yes."

"I thought it might be. So what do you want to know?"

"Everything really."

"Everything? Where do we start?" Hutch sat back in the chair and retrieved his glasses from the blotter. "Well, we have been modifying crops ever since we started farming. When we first grew wheat, most of the grain fell out of the ears before it could be harvested, but the grain which was collected, and re-sown, was from plants which held on to their seeds. After a few harvests, all the wheat was related to the plants that held on to their grain the longest. So by doing nothing, other than grow it as a crop, we have modified wheat."

"But that's not really a modification of the actual plant."

"No. It's not even hybridisation. Just enhanced natural selection. But over the years we became more sophisticated in our approach, and farmers cross-pollinated plants that had desirable properties. A hybrid of a wheat might have a large ear but a short stem, so the plant would not collapse in a storm or under the increased weight of the ear itself. It would also produce more wheat for a given amount of straw."

Hutch waited until Brian nodded to confirm he was keeping up, then continued. "GM crops are, or to be more precise were, plants which were constructed from other plants or animals. 'Frankenstein foods' they were called. You've seen the film 'Frankenstein', have you, laddie?" he asked, with a smile.

"Read the book."

Hutch stopped smiling and tried to adopt a more serious tone. "Well, rather than take limbs, scientists took genes from another plant, or sometimes even from a fish or insect, and added these to the genetic code of the wheat, maize or whatever."

Brian, noticing that Hutch was being less aggressive, relaxed and hung one arm over the back of his chair. "What was the point of that?"

"The intention was to use the new gene to make the plant resistant to herbicides and, in some cases, even make it kill insects which were trying to feed on the plant. So that's GM crops." Hutch watched Brian, waiting for him to stand up, or at least ask another question. He did neither, so Hutch continued. "But what you really want to know is why it all went so horribly wrong?"

"Er, yes."

"Heard of Genesis Natural Products Inc.?"

"I've heard the name."

"Well, forty years ago they were the fourth- or fifth-biggest biotechnology company in the world. They had developed a herbicide-resistant family of crops with large seed heads and the minimum of stem. They patented a range of plants — maize, corn, barley and Soya — all with the same properties. It was, so it is said, the most expensive biotechnology research-and-development project ever undertaken. The company used most of the money it had earned from agricultural antibiotics, and it also raised a massive amount on the US and European money markets. By the way, I assume a keen party member like you understands the evil nature of capitalism?"

Brian smiled. "Institutionalised greed, a non-violent means of waging war on other countries, a..."

"Yes, OK. Anyway, the reason Genesis were able to raise so much money was their claim that the new seeds lasted for only one growing season. If you planted a seed from one of their plants, it just wouldn't grow. That meant the farmer had to go back to Genesis each year to buy more seed.

Well, and here it becomes a little hazy, just as Genesis brought the products to the market a university announced it had developed a hybrid with the same properties — but the university's hybrid could be replanted the following year. It was also rumoured that the modification which Genesis had hoped would prevent the second generation of seed from germinating, didn't work."

"And that was a problem?"

"A problem for Genesis, whose shareholders were getting nervous. If farmers used the hybrids there would be no way Genesis could recoup its investment." Hutch drew a deep breath. "However, as if by magic, Genesis announced they had cracked the problem and rushed the product onto the market ahead of the hybrids. At the launch, they announced that a limited amount of seed would be offered free of charge to farmers around the world. The rest you might know."

"A record harvest world-wide was followed, a year later, by a fifty per cent shortfall."

"Followed by a halving of the previous year's crop in each of the four years that followed."

"And that was Genesis's fault?"

"Well," — Hutch gave a short laugh — "it became fairly obvious what they had done. Not only were their own seeds failing to germinate, but so were everybody else's." He swivelled his chair around and pulled from the shelf a thin book that he placed on the desk in front of Brian. The cover read: 'Final-Year Project — Melissa Hutchinson'.

Brian slowly opened the journal. "Melissa Hutchinson?"

"My sister," said Hutch casually. He leaned over the desk and, using a pencil, flicked through the yellowing pages, containing maps and charts, until he reached one near the back. "She died of cholera a year after graduating." He pointed to a series of pictures.

76

"This column here, pictures of fields of wheat, oilseed rape, Soya, barley and so on. And the next column, pictures of the same crops in the following year. And the third, the next year."

Brian inspected the pictures carefully. "A bit threadbare."

"Each year the crops got thinner and yields went down."

"What caused that?"

"A gene. Genesis called it 'poppy 7b'."

"From a poppy plant?"

Hutch shook his head. "Maybe that's how it got its name. But there's nothing in here about it."

Brian turned the pages of the book. "So your sister carried out these experiments?"

"No. They wouldn't let an undergraduate loose on the poppy 7b gene. What you've got there is only her interpretation of test results from government laboratories. She had to put on some sort of space suit just to go onto the site."

A schematic representation of the poppy gene filled half of one of the pages. Brian scrutinised it. "A clever piece of technology, was it?"

"Oh yes, very clever. The plant had large flowers with masses of pollen. Everyone was surprised when they realised how sophisticated it was — and that Genesis had produced it so fast. It was just the way it was used that wasn't so clever."

"Because the second generation plants didn't grow?"

"The poppy gene was a so-called terminator. All the big biotechnology companies said they would never use such a gene. They claimed there was too much resistance from farmers. Cynics claimed that the only reason the companies didn't use it was because they couldn't get it to work."

"So why did the farmers use Genesis's products?"

"Greed. The crops had twice the yields of conventional crops. For a twenty per cent increase in yield it wasn't worth selling your soul to a chemical company — but two hundred percent? With returns like that, who cares about buying new seed each year? Added to that, tens of thousands of farmers were given free samples as part of a marketing promotion."

Brian shrugged. "So what was the problem?"

"The problem was that the poppy-gene crops started to neutralise the other crops on the farms where it was used. Wind and insects carried the pollen into surrounding fields. The problem was made worse by the increased size of the plant's flowers."

Hutch used the pencil to open the book at a page that had a copy of a Genesis brochure attached to it.

Brian read the title out loud: "'A Complete Agricultural System for the Farmer looking for High Yields and Flexibility.' Cute."

"Yes. Some conspiracy theorists even suggested that the company had actually designed their product to attack conventional crops."

"So why didn't the farmers kill the stuff? Use some sort of chemical on it?"

"Because" — Hutch sat back in his chair — "Genesis's crops were not only herbicide-resistant, they were resistant to other companies' herbicides — which increased speculation about a conspiracy. Genesis had their own herbicide, but they never got the chance to use it. When farmers found out what the company had done, they were pretty annoyed. Well, actually, that's an understatement. Soon there was a blanket ban on Genesis's products, and embargoes right, left and centre from governments around the world. Within months the company was bankrupt."

"Why not rotate the crops?"

"Where would the farmers get the seed from? The gene had contaminated all the seed they kept back. And each year the contamination got worse."

"Checkmate."

"Yes. It certainly was a poser. A farmer could only save his farm by leaving it barren. Not many farmers could afford to do that. Even if they could, if the farm next door had been abandoned, leaving the land untreated, the problem came back. The rest you probably know."

"Complete economic collapse, famine and epidemics."

"Well, on its own it wasn't disastrous, although people may have gone hungry and some may have died. However, it was just the first failure in what Fairchild and Vlachos were calling a 'failure cascade'. And the end of the world as we knew it." He smiled at Brian. "Or the beginning of the world as you know it."

"So you believe in the failure-cascade theory?"

Hutch turned his hand palm upwards and shrugged.

Brian thumbed through the rest of the book. On the second page was a picture of a group of students sitting on a low brick wall in front of a large greenhouse.

Hutch reached over, closed the book and returned it to the shelf. "One collects these things. Should really throw it out, I suppose. Have you got any family?"

Brian had noticed that Hutch's tone had softened during their conversation; but he was still surprised by the question.

"No. Well, my mother is still alive, but she's remarried and lives in Birmingham." He now saw that Hutch was struggling to cope with the loneliness and sense of loss that haunted so many of the older generation. Embarrassed, Brian changed the subject.

"If Genesis wasn't the largest GM company, why didn't the others put pressure on the government to ban the product before it even went on the market?"

"No-one realised what the product was capable of — until the second year."

"So the poppy-gene modification came out of the blue?"

"Out of the blue." Hutch put the pencil into a cracked mug with no handle. He stood up and started to put on the coat that had been draped over the back of his chair. Brian saw this as a signal that the conversation was over.

"But weren't there tests?"

Hutch had been waiting for this question. The previous Friday, as soon as Brian and Mike had left her room, Amanda had brought the newspaper down to his lab. If he hadn't seen the newspaper, Troxley's death would have remained just what, at first glance, it appeared to be: suicide. Pulling his coat tight across his shoulders, he sat down again, and whispered. "Brian, this is the bit that you listen to very carefully."

Brian ran his fingers over his lips, then laid both hands on the table in front of him. Hutch was waiting for the sarcastic comment or flippant remark that would give him the perfect excuse to dismiss the question and return to work. But Brian remained silent.

Hutch sniffed and rubbed his nose vigorously. "There are two versions of this story: the one you probably know off by heart, and the one that the chief executive of Genesis told at his trial. Which do you want first?"

Brian looked down at the corner of the desk. "The party line?"

"OK. The tests were a cynical marketing ploy to get farmers to use GM crops. Just as suppliers of tractors and combine harvesters lent a farmer a machine for a few weeks, hoping he would find it indispensable, so the seed suppliers hoped the farmer would get hooked on GM crops." He saw from Brian's blank expression that this version needed expanding. "Fairchild," he continued, "said that the tests were not scientific, as no data had been collected from the sites in the years immediately before the tests. And precious little data was collected from the surrounding area."

"And the devil's advocate?"

"I assume the devil you are talking about is the chairman and chief executive of Genesis Natural Products Inc.?" Hutch smiled. "Yes, he claimed that the trials were valid and that the poppy-gene modified crops, along with all their other GM crops, were extensively tested. There was even a government-backed committee to oversee the trials. Apparently, all the tests proved that the crops were safe: there was no cross-contamination. Unfortunately, as he later came to realise, some of the trials were flawed and others were disrupted by so-called 'eco-terrorists'."

"People actually believed that?"

"Obviously the judge didn't, because the Genesis bosses were locked up and the key thrown away." Hutch stared at Brian for a moment before continuing. "You obviously haven't grasped the implications of all this."

"No. Sorry. What do you mean?"

But Hutch did not explain what he meant. Once again he leaned across the table and spoke in a whisper. "Look, Brian, I know you aren't going to spend your whole life acting like a clown. The right case will come along, something you can get your teeth into, you'll get your act together and start behaving like a real policeman. But, believe me, this is not that case."

"I was only asking about GM technology."

"No, Brian. You're asking about a group of people who wrecked a GM trial. One of them is about to become the most powerful politician in the western world. Another is lying out there on a slab, dead. This case is a mixture of politics and murder. That's unhealthy at the best of times. It's especially dangerous when the politicians can make up laws as they go along."

Brian looked away. "It will probably go over to Park Lane anyway."

"You know it *won't* now. Not after the resignation. And if it does end up on your desk, just pin a few reports together and file it away as unsolved. Whatever you do, don't go digging around."

"Sure thing. Thanks for the chat, Hutch." Brian stood up to leave.

"There's one other thing, Brian."

"Yes?"

"As you haven't taken a blind bit of notice of what I've just said — watch your back."

*

Mike lay back in his chair, pushing against the legs of the desk with his feet so that the chair swivelled from side to side in a quarter circle. He did not speak when Brian entered the room, but continued staring up at the ceiling.

Sitting down, Brian attempted to work out what he had missed in Hutch's explanation. Then he noticed the stack of five euro coins in the middle of his desk. As Brian picked up the coins, one by one, Mike spoke. "The hotel, first thing tomorrow morning. We interview the man and the girl again — and have a proper look around."

3

Tuesday 20th August 2041

In retrospect, it was obvious that everything that had happened in the Adelphi Hotel in the past ten years had happened during the last two weeks. On closer inspection, the paint on the sign outside was fresh. The room where the body had been found was the only habitable one in the hotel. All the others contained rotting furniture, covered in a thick layer of dust and upholstered in fabric that disintegrated when touched. Brian had noticed the absence of electricity on his first visit. He thought Mike had asked to use the mobile because he knew the hotel's telephones were not working. Now he realised that his boss had only done so to avoid touching the grime-covered handset in the room. And in retrospect both the man and the girl should have been taken back to the Home Office for further questioning.

From the window on the first-floor landing Brian noticed the disturbed earth in the garden below. A spade lay on the paving stones, next to a raised flowerbed. "Someone's been doing a spot of gardening then," he said.

"Christ!" Mike exclaimed. "They came back for them!"

Until this point Brian had assumed that Mike at least understood the situation and was merely turning a blind eye in order to avoid excessive paperwork. Had he realised how wide of the mark his boss was, he would have been more assertive when voicing suspicions of the girl's involvement. But, after all, Mike was the boss; he was in charge of the investigation; he had the reports and was there when Hutch explained the forensic evidence.

"Two euros says it's not the girl."

"You're on," said Mike, without hesitation, as he returned to the room where the body had been found. The telephone was dead. Dropping the handset back into the cradle, he was about to turn on the table lamp when he remembered there was no flex. It dawned on Mike that the room was no more than a stage set. Enter, stage left, the old man — just as the questioning of the girl was about to reveal that the hotel was a sham. Is that how it worked? Just as he asked about the telephone calls, in came the old man trotting out his lines: 'I don't want any trouble.'

Had he cared a bit more, made an effort, the girl might still be alive. But in truth Mike did not care; still did not really care. His view of the Troxley case had not changed. It was trouble, and all he wanted to do was get shot of it as soon as possible — without making any waves. Go through the motions and act out his role, just as the old man and the girl had acted out theirs. Hand in the report and get a polite round of applause from Langford and a pat on the back from the party. Down would come the curtain. Solved or not — it did not really matter. 'Solved' would mean a trial and possible embarrassment for the party. Langford would have to confirm it of course, but Mike felt that either 'unsolved' or 'remains open' would suit most people.

All that stood in the way of a successful conclusion to this case was Brian. The flowerbed downstairs was not the only place where his assistant was digging furiously. Now that he had chanced upon some dark deed perpetrated by his elders, there would be no stopping him. Like other young men with no God or religion, Brian was prey to conspiracy theories. Langford should have removed him from the case. The fact that he had not was a problem, but not an insurmountable one. Brian must be led to the largest information source possible, where he would quickly become distracted and eventually drown in a sea of irrelevant rumours and half-truths. After all, there were other equally dark misdemeanours: the corruption of minor party officials, and the framing — even murder — of opposition politicians.

"Yes!" came the shout from down in the courtyard. Feeling in his pocket for two euros, Mike made his way down the stairs.

Standing naked from the waist up, Brian wiped the sweat from his brow. "There you go! She shot him in the head."

The body had been buried, fully clothed, under half a metre of earth. The face was a mass of blood. "Someone's shot him in the back of the head," Mike said.

Brian picked up his shirt, put it on and rolled up the sleeves. "Meaning?"

"Meaning she probably didn't do it."

"I can't see why not."

"Because we've got the gun, remember." Mike bent forward to take a closer look at the old man's body. "The same people who killed Troxley came back to stop this one talking."

"It wasn't the only gun in London," Brian mumbled. "And why didn't they kill the girl as well?"

"They've probably abducted her, or she made herself scarce before they got here." Mike shrugged. "Anyway, we've got things to do. I'm going to arrange a visit to Harry the Print. You cover the old man up again, then find out what *The Guardian* has got on the Whiteside Farm attack."

"No autopsy?"

"What, on him? What's the point? He was shot and that's it."

After shovelling the dirt back over the body, Brian threw the spade on top of the mound of earth. "If you don't mind, I'll call back to the office before going to *The Guardian*. One of us ought to put together a photofit of the girl."

*

Amanda sat at the keyboard of her personal computer while Brian recited a description of the girl in the hotel. Slowly, a face took shape on the screen. "That's about it," he said, realising (having met two girls over the weekend) that the photograph was no more than a composite of them and the suspect.

*

The power a police officer, even one as junior as himself, could wield never failed to impress Brian. Everyone, from petty crooks to high-ranking party officials, was only too pleased to assist with an investigation. Brian was under no illusions, however. It was not his charm or strength of character that encouraged the public to open their hearts to him. Most people only tolerated policemen — even ones as confrontational as Mike — because obstructing them would lead to a visit from another, less friendly branch of the security services. So when Gerald Petrie turned down a simple request for access to *The Guardian* newspaper archives, Brian was more than a little surprised.

"You can't just come in here demanding to see our archives," snarled Gerald.

"*Asked*. I asked to see some back issues." Brian stared at the twenty-eight-year-old assistant editor, wondering what he had done to upset him. Maybe Brian was beneath him in the party hierarchy. Unlikely, he thought. "I could get a warrant," he said.

"Yes. I suppose you could." Gerald hesitated for a moment, then opened the metal gate beside the reception desk. "I suppose you'd better come and have a look then. But we're short-staffed. If you can't find the information, that's just tough."

Gerald led Brian up the stairs to the main editorial office. Despite his slight build, the newspaper man took the stairs two at a time and was waiting for Brian on the second-floor landing. He pushed open the door to the newsroom when Brian caught up. "When people see *The Guardian*, they think there's not much work involved in producing it. What they don't realise is the sheer amount of news we put together every day, compared with the small amount which is actually selected for printing."

In the newsroom, three journalists were sitting behind terminals. None of them looked up when Brian and Gerald walked past. "Is this all the staff who work on the paper?" Brian asked.

"No. There's a couple of reporters on assignments, there's the Brussels correspondent, and ten regional correspondents around the country. Oh, and the senior editor upstairs." Gerald held open the door to the research department and lowered his voice to a whisper. "We get pretty much a free hand with what is put on the web, but the senior editor decides what goes into the printed issue — eyes and ears of the party."

"What did you expect?" said Gerald, noting Brian's surprise on finding that the research department contained only three PCs on Formica-topped tables. "There's no paper here and no printers. All the archives are on-line. If you want printed issues, you need to go to the British Library."

"I need access to some stories from April 2001."

"That far back! Well, they should be archived — *The Guardian* was on the web before 2001." Gerald switched on a PC. "Take a look out of the window for a minute while I log you in."

Brian looked down into a deserted Farringdon Road. He could hear the sound of keys being tapped behind him.

"You can go ahead now. The archives are all web-based but are password-protected. I take it you know how to use a browser and a search engine?"

"No problem." Brian sat down in front of the computer. Entering the 'W' of 'Whiteside' opened a small window containing a list of suggested words gleaned from enquiries made by previous users. Brian immediately stopped typing and looked up at Gerald.

"I'll leave you to it then." Gerald smiled as he left the room.

Brian thought for a moment, then backspaced over the 'W' and entered 'GM crops'. The first headings, from 10 of 38,747 articles, appeared. Brian confined the search to the years 1999, 2000 and 2002; the number of articles reduced to 11,920. Adding

'Genesis' reduced the count further to 1,840. After clicking on the first heading and retrieving a pad and pencil from his rucksack, Brian began to take notes.

An hour later, Brian wandered out of the archive and asked one of the journalists for directions to the nearest Ivan's Restaurant. The Farringdon Road Ivan's was next to the underground station. It was quiet, with only a few diners. Brian assumed they were either office workers or media professionals.

During the meal, he noticed Gerald and another *Guardian* journalist entering the restaurant. They did not join him but sat at a table near the back of the room. Conscious of being talked about, Brian looked in their direction on several occasions. Each time, Gerald was staring back at him.

Forty minutes after Brian returned to the archive, Gerald reappeared. Walking slowly around the room, he eventually pulled up a chair and sat down next to Brian. "Difficult, isn't it?"

"A bit tedious," Brian replied, still looking at the screen and taking notes.

"This anything to do with that body in the hotel then? A politician, wasn't it?"

"No, this is just something I'm doing for my evening classes."

Gerald scoffed. "That's what it would have said on the warrant: 'Permission to search the archives — justification: homework.'" He paused for a moment, then added, "You should have said, 'What body?'"

Brian realised he was dealing with someone significantly sharper than his boss. He turned to Gerald. "So how do you know about the body in the hotel?"

"An anonymous tip-off."

"Man or woman?"

"I don't know. One of the journalists took the call."

"A known source?"

Gerald held up his hands. "Now, hold on a minute! This is starting to sound like an interrogation."

Brian shrugged and continued taking notes from the screen.

Gerald smiled. "That's a hard way of going about it. Still, I suppose you've got no choice really. After all, if you type in what you're really looking for, I'll be able to read it when you've gone."

Brian tapped his pencil on the table.

Gerald took the pencil and pulled the notepad towards him. He tore out one of the pages and wrote two words on it. Folding the page, he said, "A trade: this username and password, valid for a month, in exchange for the name of the politician in the hotel room."

"What makes you think it was a politician?"

"That's what the caller said."

"Well, they were wrong." Brian looked down at the piece of paper in Gerald's hand. He thought for a moment, then typed 'Troxley' and hit the return key. A list of headings scrolled onto the screen. Brian clicked on the one that read 'Missing Activist Thought To Have Returned To The US'.

"You're kidding," said Gerald, moving closer to read the story.

"About what?" Brian asked, as he took the piece of paper. Gerald did not answer. Instead, he scrolled down the page, reading the text at breakneck speed before returning to the list of headings and clicking on the next story. Another young man with no God or religion had fallen prey to a conspiracy theory.

*

In Bermondsey, East London, an armoured car was parked between two derelict warehouses. The driver was watching the door of a small factory unit on the opposite side of the street.

While Brian had been having lunch in Farringdon Road, Mike, wedged between two soldiers, was being driven across Southwark Bridge in the back of an armoured car. He saw little of the East End as the driver picked his way through the rubble-strewn streets. Now he peered out of the small window in the side of the vehicle at the seemingly deserted factory. "Are you sure he's in there?" Mike asked the driver.

"So I'm reliably informed." The driver started the engine and edged the car out into the street, turned right and slowly drove past the factory door.

"Alone?"

"So they say." The driver slammed the car into reverse and pressed down on the accelerator. After they had travelled backwards for twenty metres, he pulled at the steering wheel. The car swerved and came to rest with only three metres between its rear doors and the large sliding metal doors of the factory.

The two soldiers jumped out and swung a ram towards the small hinged panel in one of the larger sliding doors, but before the ram could make contact the door swung open.

The small boy looked impassively at the two soldiers. "Yes," he said, in a squeaky voice.

Mike stepped forward. "We're here to see Harry."

The boy turned and shouted, "Dad! Some people here to see you."

Mike pushed past the boy. In the centre of the large workshop, leaning on a table set between two full-colour printing presses, was a short, balding man with a toothbrush moustache. He wore a full-length white coat, the front of which was covered in multicoloured smears of printing ink. There were bicycle clips around the bottom of his trouser legs, and print splashes on his boots.

The man tipped his head forward as Mike walked towards him. He peered over the horned-rimmed women's glasses perched on the end his nose and reached across the desk to pick up the phone. Mike pulled a revolver from his pocket and pointed it at Harry's head.

Taking his hand from the phone, Harry threw his head back and laughed. "'Well, Mr. Allchurch,' they'll say, 'we're going to bring back paper money next year. You'd better ask Harry to come and see us. After all, he's the only printer left who can produce banknotes.' And what will you say, Mr. Allchurch?" Harry stepped forward and looked Mike straight in the eye. "'Well, actually, sir, I shot him in the head last week.'" Harry laughed again as Mike put the gun back in his pocket.

"I need some help."

"That's bloody obvious! You come in here, terrorising my kid, then start waving a gun about. Trouble is, I'm a printer, not a bloody psychiatrist."

Mike laid the briefcase on the table and flicked the catches. As he lifted the lid, Harry reached down to the floor and picked up a lunchbox.

Staring at the S-Card Mike had placed on the table, Harry bit into a sandwich. "Only a German would think of using the National Lottery system to check food-ration cards. You see, they don't understand irony, Mr. Allchurch."

"You printed this, didn't you?"

"You're joking, Mr. Allchurch. That's a hanging offence. Why would I risk that?"

"For money. Isn't that why you forge things?"

"I don't forge things."

Mike laughed. "A legit printing business, eh? Is that why you're tucked away in an East London backstreet? Get much passing trade?"

"Doing a nice line in 'So Long, Ivan' cards this side of the river."

"I didn't think you were that keen on the anarchists."

Harry groaned. "True. They haven't done the East End any favours."

Mike picked up the card and waved it under Harry's nose. "So if it wasn't you, who did print this?"

Harry took the S-Card and examined it under a desk light. "No-one. It's the genuine article."

"It can't be." Mike snatched it back, took out his own card and compared the two.

"I wouldn't get those mixed up if I were you. That card is a 'high seven'."

"What's a 'high seven'?"

"I don't know exactly, but that's one." Harry took another bite from his sandwich as he eased himself up onto a metal chair. He studied Mike as he chewed. Swallowing hard, Harry took hold of the S-Card again. "They say if you are going to forge one of these, and I hasten to say I'm not, avoid numbers above forty-five."

"I'm sure I've seen numbers above forty-five." Mike tried to recall his wife's, children's, and then Brian's numbers.

"You hand that card over in a restaurant and you'll be dragged out of the place before you can finish your veggie-burger."

"Who by?"

"The consensus is, it's you lot. But if *you're* asking *me*, then obviously it's not."

Mike took the card and dropped it into the briefcase. Before he could close the lid, Harry had reached in and grabbed the passport. Mike tried to snatch it back, but Harry half-turned and held it at arm's length. "Aha! Let's have a look then!" he said, as he slowly turned the pages.

"I know that's a forgery," said Mike dismissively.

"If it is, there's a better printer around than me. And they've got access to some fifty-year-old paper."

"What?"

Picking up a magnifying glass, Harry pushed his glasses up onto his forehead and examined one of the pages of the passport. "There is something strange about the print, but it's probably the real thing — just age, I suppose." He flicked over a few pages. "Expiry date's been tampered with and the photo isn't genuine." He thought for a moment, then snapped his fingers. "Berlin. There was a guy in Germany. Gunter something. He used to doctor passports. Could be his handiwork."

"Not you?"

"Please, Mr. Allchurch." He opened the lunchbox again and took out another sandwich. "Fancy one of these? They're bacon. Have you noticed how much bacon there is around at the moment?"

"No thanks."

"Ah yes, you're a vegetarian."

"I'm not actually."

"I thought you were. Oh no, of course. That's your sidekick. Brian."

"Tyler."

"Now, I thought he seemed like a decent bloke. Can't see him breaking down doors and waving guns at people." He studied Mike for a while, then added, "Of course, he's got a sense of humour."

"It doesn't do him much good."

Harry put his hand on Mike's shoulder. "I dunno. When half of London has disappeared, there's no electricity or gas, and the streets look like the set of 'The Day of the Triffids', it would be a shame if we lost our sense of humour as well."

Mike took back the passport, and then grabbed Harry's glasses. "Let's slow down the flow of dodgy paperwork for a few weeks, shall we?"

Harry tried to snatch the glasses back, but Mike had already put them into the briefcase and closed the lid. "You're a mean sod, Mr. Allchurch."

*

Mike stood on the platform of St James's Park underground station, waiting for the westbound train. Now he felt bad about taking Harry's glasses. Brian, who had seen him put the glasses in his desk drawer, did not help by pointing out that the lenses seemed fairly unusual. It was partly because of Brian that Mike had taken the glasses, having been provoked by the unfavourable comparison between him and his assistant.

A poster on the wall of the station depicted a queue of people standing in a restaurant. One of the figures had been blanked out. The caption read, 'Is there someone you haven't seen recently? — Look out for your neighbours.' Mike stared at the poster.

"Time goes by." Mike turned, and found Padreep Kumar standing beside him. "Now *you* look like a man with a problem."

He smiled.

"You've heard?"

"I've heard gossip, rumours."

When the train arrived, Padreep was first on. He walked to the end of the carriage — the empty part, Mike realised, where their conversation could not be overheard. The doors closed and the train pulled out of the station.

When Padreep felt the noise level had risen sufficiently to render their voices inaudible to the other passengers, he turned to Mike. "So the body has ended up on your patch then?"

"What do you mean?"

"Well, when was the American killed?"

"Last week, sometime on Thursday night. How do you know about all this anyway?"

"Like I said, gossip and rumours." Padreep shrugged, sighed and then went silent as the train pulled in to the next station. Mike thought he had lost interest, but as the doors closed again he continued. "Funny thing happened on my patch last Thursday night. About two in the morning, the duty officer at Heathrow police station gets a call from the manager of the Penta Hotel. Apparently, one of the guests, who had arrived that afternoon, went out to dinner and didn't come back. The man's suitcase was still in the room and he hadn't checked out. In fact, he had told the receptionist he was only going out for a quick bite to eat. The duty officer told the hotel manager someone would call around in the morning."

"Not so strange. The guy was probably an illegal."

"Mike, he was an American. And there was more."

The train stopped again, and one of the new passengers took a seat opposite Mike and Padreep. The conversation turned to wives and families, and the current state of Southall and Ruislip. At Earl's Court, two young men with close-cropped hair and wearing workman's boots got on the train. They too slumped in the seats opposite. When he was younger, Padreep would have been filled with terror at the sight of two men like these. When the food shortages started, bands of thugs of every ethnic background roamed the streets of London. They stopped cars, broke into shops, and beat up pedestrians. Every group had their favourite targets and their own hierarchy of prejudices. The Jews were hoarding money, the Asians were hoarding food, the Blacks were spreading disease, the Chinese were kidnapping children, and the Whites were trying to enslave everyone else.

But the epidemics ended the distinction between Blacks, Asians, Chinese, Jews and Whites. They eroded the dividing lines between the young and the old and between men and women. Soon there were only the living and the dead, the sick and the well. The two young men were exhausted. They worked in the London Transport repair depot at the old Olympia exhibition centre.

One of the engineers was reading a brochure entitled 'Railway Workers' Exchange Scheme — Deutsches Bahn.' Perhaps their manager had identified the first signs of withdrawal. It was not uncommon for workers without families to block out a drab, lonely existence by throwing themselves into their work. One of the aims of the exchange scheme was to prevent withdrawal; another was to provide a constant cross-fertilisation of ideas. Judging by the objections being voiced, including not being able to speak German and losing time on the current job, their manager would have an uphill struggle getting the two men to take a break.

The train lurched violently and Padreep banged his head against the window. "It's still there," said one of the engineers, "two hundred metres from Barons Court."

"I'll tell the track-maintenance manager about it tomorrow," the second engineer replied, wiping the sweat from his face with his sleeve. "God, I'm thirsty today!"

Both Mike and Padreep reached into their bags and took out a bottle of water. "Thanks," said the engineer with the brochure, "but we're off at the next stop."

The carriage emptied. Mike turned to Padreep. "So you think this American is the same one I've been lumbered with. He could just be an illegal." He then thought over what Padreep had already told him. "What about the suitcase? Was there an ID in it?"

"Now that's where it gets really strange. The next day we visit the hotel and the manager denies the man is missing. In fact, he denies he ever existed. Says it's the result of confusion between the receptionist and the reservations department."

"And you don't believe it."

"Until I heard about your case, I didn't give it a lot of thought. Now I'm wondering..."

"Wondering if the American was picked up and killed, and the killers returned the next morning to collect the suitcase and keep the manager quiet." Mike rubbed the side of his face. He was tired and would have preferred an evening off the Troxley case. "Is there any chance you can get hold of a list of all the Americans who flew into Heathrow on that Thursday?"

"That's a good idea. It shouldn't be too much of a problem. I could get a list to you tomorrow morning."

"Thanks." Closing his eyes, Mike rested his chin on his chest.

"Do you get the idea that your case is fitting together rather like a simple jigsaw?"

"Yep. We're being led through it by our noses."

"Big trouble."

"Only if we get it wrong." Mike opened his eyes again and looked at Padreep. "Only if my over-enthusiastic assistant goes off-message. Looks under the wrong stone."

"Brian? He wouldn't do that. He's a party man. Knows which side his bread is buttered on."

"Let's hope so."

4

Wednesday 21st August 2041

At eight fifteen, the list of American arrivals appeared in Mike's e-mail in-box. He scrolled down the list. "Oh well, end of that lead." He looked at his watch. "Let's get over to King's Cross."

"What do you mean?" Brian looked over Mike's shoulder.

"See for yourself. No Troxley."

"Perhaps he arrived the day before."

"No. Padreep said the American arrived on Thursday. Or at least that's what the hotel manager said before he changed his story."

"Wait a minute." Brian jabbed his finger at the screen. "I've seen that name before." He copied the name from the screen onto Mike's notepad, tore off the page and returned to his own desk. Mike watched with interest as Brian took a small piece of paper from his pocket, unfolded it, then typed the two words on it into his computer. *The Guardian*'s archives appeared on the screen. Brian entered the name from Pradeep's list. "There! I knew I'd seen the name before!" Brian read from the newspaper article: "'Clifford Passmore, Head of Security at Genesis Natural Products Inc., today complained about the lack of police protection for GM crop trial sites in the UK.'"

Brian turned to Mike. "Now he's back."

"Some sort of reunion," Mike said, with more than a hint of sarcasm in his voice.

Brian was studying the newspaper story. "No. It's far more interesting than that." He reached across the desk and picked up the telephone, lazily tapped out a number, and waited for an answer. "Hello. Immigration? Brian Tyler here. Is it possible to search your computer records back to the year two thousand?"

Mike felt a sinking feeling in the pit of his stomach. "Brian, we've got a train to catch."

"Plenty of time yet. We'll still get there before lunchtime."

Within fifteen minutes, Brian had received an e-mail listing all the dates on which Clifford Passmore had flown into or out of Britain. The list included a 'no show' for a flight from London Stansted airport on the evening of the 16th of April 2001, the flight he caught the following week, and — forty years later — his return last Thursday.

Mike and Brian only just caught the nine-fifteen Peterborough train from King's Cross station. What should have been a straightforward rail journey had become a logistical nightmare that had taken a secretary a whole day, and Mike an afternoon, to organise.

The rail network was one piece of Britain's infrastructure that remained in relatively good shape. It was deemed important enough to warrant its own ministry and employed more people than agriculture. Freight scheduling and timetable planning attracted the best mathematics graduates, and the country's top civil, electrical and mechanical engineers were employed on a project to re-establish electrification of the network.

The motorway and road networks were subject to a policy of managed decline: routes which were once dual carriageways had been downgraded to ordinary roads. Trunk routes had now been reduced to single-lane roads with passing places. The Ministry of Transport ignored b-roads and country lanes altogether, and their maintenance was left to the whim of district and local councils. The Ministry of Railways, on the other hand, were given all the penal workers and community labour they required. Moreover, all workers over sixty-five and still fit enough to work were given light duties in railway stations and goods yards. Semi-retired railway enthusiasts were only too happy to take over the running of small branch lines. Those people who had been hoping for a leisured retirement were less pleased.

Despite the railways' first call on the county's resources, there were still problems. Two major derailments had isolated most of East Anglia from the rest of the network for over a week. In normal circumstances, Mike and Brian would have travelled to Downham via Cambridge and Ely. Now they either had to delay their journey until Friday, or travel to Peterborough and complete their journey by car. As he intended to travel to Brussels on Friday, Mike decided on the latter alternative.

Most trains were classified as freight and had one or two passenger carriages tacked on the end. There were few, if any, dedicated commuter trains. Their train had just been loaded when Mike and Brian arrived on platform eight; the diesel locomotive was about to drag it out of King's Cross station.

As the train passed through Barnet, Brian noticed the semicircular bite the fire had taken out of the housing estate. He felt increasingly uneasy: each station they passed was more derelict than the previous one, and houses gave way to vast expanses of impenetrable undergrowth. To distract himself, he took out the Troxley file and thumbed through the pages he had added the previous day.

Mike had a lot of catching up to do. It was difficult enough to get authorisation just to enter an agricultural district, let alone carry out an investigation in one. But getting permission to arrive there by road had turned into a Kafkaesque nightmare. Eventually the local police in Downham were persuaded to provide a car and driver to collect Mike and Brian from Peterborough station, and obtain the necessary clearance from the East Anglian Regiment.

"So what's your theory then?" Mike asked.

"Too early to say," replied Brian, without looking up.

"Long-running feud between Troxley and Passmore?"

"No."

"Troxley finds out that Passmore is visiting Britain and decides to hunt him down. Passmore kills him and then escapes? Blackmail perhaps?"

"Impossible."

"Why?"

"Because Passmore and Troxley probably are, or were, the same person."

"You mean Troxley used Passmore's identity to get into the country?"

"No. I mean it looks as though Troxley was Passmore. There is no record of Troxley ever passing through UK Immigration — on his way from, or back to, the US. Immigration have a record of Passmore returning to America a week after the Whiteside Farm attack."

"Probably got fired. Anyway, that doesn't make sense. Passmore was head of security at Genesis. What was he doing wrecking their trials?"

"What indeed?" Brian toyed with the idea of telling Mike about his conversation with Dr. Hutchinson, but thought better of it. He was not sure his boss would appreciate the addition of an extra level of complexity to a case he was already having trouble getting to grips with. He replaced the file in his rucksack, took out a book and started to read — while trying to ignore the fact that the last station the train passed had barely been visible amongst the trees.

"Know much about this farmer Whiteside?" Mike asked.

"Only that he was twenty years old when the Greens attacked his father's farm. Made a big fuss when the television cameras arrived. Judging by his performance then, I don't think we'll get much from him now." Brian retrieved the file and handed it to Mike. "There are some newspaper cuttings in there."

"Probably a wasted journey then."

"There might be a few other things worth checking," although, at the moment, Brian could not think of any.

*

Matt Spencer, a tall, unshaven youth with a shock of black hair hanging down over one eye, was leaning against the front wing of a green Rover 90 P5. He held a card with 'Allchurch' and 'Tyler' scrawled on it. Paying little attention to the small group of passengers leaving the station, he continued his conversation with the elderly railway worker even after Mike and Brian had identified themselves. Eventually, standing up straight, he said goodbye to the old man and held out his hand to Mike. "I'm Matt. And you are?"

"Mr. Allchurch I said, if..."

"And I'm Brian," Brian interrupted.

"So, Brian, you're taking your holiday in Downham this year." Matt laughed.

"Hardly," he replied apprehensively.

"Don't believe all you've been told about the countryside — it's far worse than that."

The car groaned and whined across the station forecourt.

"This is ancient." Brian shouted above the noise of the engine.

"Some of it's nearly eighty years old," Matt replied, "but most of it I've made up myself. The last thing you want to drive out here is something complicated that you can't patch up with a few bits of tin."

At the first road junction they encountered after leaving the town, a soldier flagged down the car. "Papers," he said, leaning forward to get a better look at Mike, who was sulking in the back of the car. Matt handed his own and his passengers' ID cards to the soldier. Stepping back from the car, the soldier read the names on the cards into his radio. After a short delay, the radio crackled briefly and the soldier handed the papers back through the car window. "Picked the wrong time to go home."

"You mean the convoy?" Matt put the car back in gear.

"Yer. Take care, Matt," the soldier shouted, as they drove away.

"This is going to be a long journey, lads," Matt said, working his way up through the gears.

"Only thirty-five miles. Shouldn't take more than an half an hour," said Brian.

Matt laughed. "You reckon?"

"Two euros says less than an hour."

"You're on." Matt and Brian shook hands on the bet.

After twenty minutes, Brian noticed a flashing blue light in the distance. "What's that?"

"Your two euros going down the toilet."

As the blue light got closer, Matt pulled the car onto the overgrown left-hand side of the road. An army Land Rover threw up a cloud of dust as it rattled past. As the dust had settled, the first of a series of large lorries thundered towards them. Each lorry buffeted the car and shook the ground as it passed. Getting out of the car, Matt walked around to the passenger side to open the doors for Mike and Brian. "We'll wait through there," he said, pointing to an opening in the bushes.

The three walked up the incline leading from the road into a small housing estate. A sign told them they had got as far as Thorney. Another sign, more recent, stated that the settlement was no longer viable. 'Anyone removing property from this area will be severely punished' — to which someone had added, 'Executed, if you're lucky.'

The remains of a chalet bungalow, one of a group arranged haphazardly amongst the tall brown grass and rambling bushes, were just visible behind a row of trees. "Housing estate," said Matt, waving his hand in the direction of the other houses, as he led the way towards a large rectangular opening in the front of the bungalow. "Empty for years."

"Everyone died?" Brian asked.

"No, it was cleared." The grass stopped two metres short of the house, and the ground was covered with an uneven scattering of paving stones.

Stepping carefully over the remains of a patio door that had fallen out of its rotten frame, Mike entered front room of the house. The floor was strewn with broken glass and lumps of plaster. Brian stood surveying the surrounding buildings and the procession of lorries moving along the road. Matt kicked the rusted remains of a barbecue to one side. "Most of the people who lived here had jobs in Peterborough or London. Without their cars they were stuffed. Those who didn't die or move out themselves were cleared out by the army twenty-five years ago."

"Tough for them," mused Brian.

"The army aren't the best removal men in the world." Matt bent down and picked up the remains of a portable CD player. "Most people were rehoused in the towns. Some stayed in the country but, if they did, they were expected to work here and not many fancied that."

"Is that why there was a soldier at the road junction, to stop people moving back?"

"No, that was to make sure you haven't come to steal food."

"You're kidding?"

"No. All road traffic in and out of East Anglia is checked by the army. When the food ran out, people were coming out of the towns at night and stealing from all the farms. The police couldn't stop it, so the farmers set up vigilante groups. That got messy, so the army stepped in. And they are still here." The casing crumbled away from the outside of the player. Matt carefully slid a plastic disc out of the mechanism. He blew away the shiny flakes covering it and then held it up to the light. "My dad says there used to be dead bodies tied to stakes by the side of the road, with a sign saying 'Thieves Keep Out'. He skimmed the disc across the top of the grass and took one more look at the mangled remains of the CD player. "Well, I reckon the people who lived here must have died. No-one could live without one of these." He smiled and threw what was left of it onto the barbecue.

Inside the house, Mike was shuffling around in the hallway, pulling open cupboards and picking items off the floor at random. Brian observed that he was being far more thorough than he had been in the hotel. The floor of the front room was covered in a mixture of pink dust, which had once been the ceiling, and fragments of fabric which, over the years, had absorbed enough dirt to support a crop of bright-green moss and grass. Mike's attention was next drawn to the mantelpiece. Two porcelain figurines stood either side of a clock and a row of photograph frames. The photographs themselves, where they had not simply disintegrated, were barely more than bleached pieces of paper.

Brian was about to step forward to pick up one of the figurines but, before he could do so, Mike swept his hand along the mantelpiece and sent its contents crashing into the fireplace. He offered no explanation for this action, which Brian saw as nothing more than petty vandalism. Mike left the room without speaking. His anger was born of frustration. The more he looked around this house, the more he thought about the house in Ruislip — the house the girl with the water never got back to.

At the back of the house, the noise of the passing lorries was little more than a muffled drone. Rising from the tangle of hawthorn and blackberries were three fruit trees. A misshapen plum tree had lost most of its branches, which had broken under the weight of fruit during years when frost or wind had not destroyed the blossom. The greengage tree had grown tall, and all of *its* fruit was well out of reach. The other tree, however, was weighed down with large green apples. Matt returned to the car to fetch two hessian sacks and helped Brian fill them with the fruit. Mike watched them as first they picked all the apples they could reach from the ground; then Matt sat on Brian's shoulders to retrieve enough to fill the second sack.

The convoy had passed by now. The two sacks were put on the back seat of the car. Mike was annoyed. Not only would the apples make the remainder of his journey uncomfortable, but he rather fancied eating one of them. The young party 'Boy Scouts' sitting in the front, however, would take exception to such an anti-social act.

As the car moved off, Mike listened to their banter. Its structure and content differed little from the mindless chatter in the ice-cream van the previous week. Was it the party, the education system or this new way of life that produced uniformly flippant and irreverent and apolitical youths? They were so uniform that when any two were put together you would think they had known each other all their lives.

Why was there no resentment? Brian was a policeman and it was the police who controlled Matt's life. At any moment they could come knocking on Matt's door and tell him to hand over his car and do some useful work.

But Matt *was* being useful. He, like Sam in London, had made himself indispensable to the police and the army. He knew East Anglia like the back of his hand. He was familiar with all the routes to the coast and was accepted by people living in Black Fen — where even the army were reluctant to go. "Well, let's see if we can get to Downham before the next convoy," Matt said, revving the car's engine.

"What happened to the railway?" Brian asked, as he looked at his watch. "And I owe you two euros, don't I?"

"They think someone sabotaged the lines. There were two derailments in as many days: one near Cambridge and the other outside Peterborough."

"Why would anyone do that?" Mike chipped in from the back of the car.

"Some people are getting a bit tired of all the extra food we are producing disappearing into the cities without us getting anything in return." Matt looked over his shoulder and the car drifted into some potholes. He pulled at the steering wheel; the car bounced back onto the relatively smooth centre of the road. "Farmers just making a point, I suppose."

Matt took a sack of coins out of the glove compartment. "Whatever you do, don't call them euros in Downham. The farmers hate the word. Call them pounds. If you've got any foreign coins, swap them for pound coins out of this sack."

"It's really that bad?" Brian took the sack, dropped the two euros he owed Matt into it, and then exchanged all of his francs, guilders and Deutschmarks for pounds before passing it over his shoulder to Mike.

"Bad, Brian?" said Matt. "There's some places around here I wouldn't drive without a spare can of petrol."

"In case you run out?" Brian asked.

"No. In case I break down. I'd just get the petrol, pour it over me and set myself on fire. It's not as bad as what they do to young men they find out there on their own." Matt laughed.

The landscape was opening up all around them. Bushes and grass gave way to rows of sugar beet and maize, and large fields of wheat and barley. Brian had seen pictures of agricultural land on television and in the party magazine, but he found the scale of it, stretching to the horizon on every side, impressive.

Three kilometres from Downham, on the outskirts of a small village called Nordelph, the car coasted to a standstill by the side of the road. Matt pressed the horn, and people from the nearby fields converged on the car. The farm workers stood in a circle as he read names from a list, handed out cardboard boxes and collected money.

Realising he was witnessing the black market in action, Brian walked away from the car and surveyed the countryside, pretending not to notice the excited chattering behind him. Mike appeared beside him and smiled. "Well, Brian, going to arrest them?" At that moment, two soldiers jumped down from a lorry parked in the field and strode purposefully towards the car. As the voices of the farm workers were not silenced by the arrival of the soldiers, Mike and Brian returned to the car to find out what was happening. The two soldiers laughed and joked with Matt as they tried on leather gloves.

Matt did not comment directly on the impromptu car-boot sale but, seeing that Brian was uneasy about the incident, he said, "Don't worry, Brian. This isn't just the countryside — it's a different country."

Once through the abandoned village, the car swerved off the road and slid between two tall metal gates, which stood open at the head of a long gravel drive. Matt brought the car to rest between an army Land Rover and an open lorry parked in front of a large red-brick manor house. The three-storey building had white-painted window frames on the first two floors and lead-cased dormer windows in a stone-tiled roof. A soldier stood guard in front of an open doorway at the top of a wide set of stone steps. All around the edge of the semicircular gravel car park were tangles of bicycles, either leaning against trees or lying on the grass.

"Well, this is it," Matt said.

Brian stared up at the building, which was almost as well maintained as Stef's house. "We're staying here?"

"No." Matt opened the car boot. "You're staying at the Swan Hotel. But this is where I was told to bring you." He looked at the two rucksacks. "Do you want me to run your stuff up to the hotel?"

Mike had got out of the car and was rubbing the tops of his legs to get the circulation going again. He leaned into the boot and grabbed his rucksack. "No thanks," he snapped, then walked briskly towards the door of the house.

Matt took a cardboard box out of the boot of the car. "Bundle of laughs, your mate." He had intended to accompany Brian to the house but changed his mind. "Look, save me going in, can you take this? Tell them if it's wrong I'll change it." He handed over the box. "Thanks. See you later." He said without waiting for an answer.

Brian, slightly confused by Matt's sudden change of heart, took the box. "Yes. Thanks for everything."

*

The polished floor of the oak-panelled reception area was made up of a mosaic of diamond-shaped tiles. There were no ornaments or pictures, except for a party poster showing rolling fields of ripened wheat. A central wooden staircase with elaborately carved railings divided before it reached the first floor. The clatter of keyboards and the sound of voices came from a room to Brian's left. Just inside the main door, a soldier sat behind a reception desk. He asked why Mike and Brian were visiting Nordelph Manor, but paid little attention to their explanation. Laying out their ID cards side by side, he checked the numbers against a list pinned to a clipboard, then picked up the phone.

Mike frowned as Brian handed over the box and relayed the message. The soldier was speaking on the telephone as he took the box and slid it under the desk. He had only just replaced the receiver when the large oak door behind him creaked open. A second soldier appeared and, holding the door ajar, asked Mike and Brian to step into the room.

Expecting something at least as grand as the reception area, Brian was disappointed to find himself in an office whose walls, far from being oak-panelled, were painted a pale green. Instead of paintings and sculptures there were maps and charts. Even the large polished table in the centre of the room was covered only with computers, printers and piles of papers.

An army officer, who had been sitting on one the dining chairs, stood up when Mike and Brian entered. "Hutley. East Anglian Regiment," he said, holding out his hand. "Here to sort out this Whiteside business, are you?" Hutley was a youth of medium height, with a bulbous nose and dull grey eyes. The fact that he was red-haired and seemed to be bottling up a tremendous amount of anger left Mike feeling ill at ease.

Mike shook Hutley's hand. "Yes, that's right. I'm Mike Allchurch. Metropolitan Police..."

"Metropolitan!" exclaimed Hutley. "That's no good to me..."

The second soldier leaned forward and whispered in Hutley's ear. Hutley looked down at the floor for a moment, then glanced up at Mike and Brian. "Sorry. Bit of a mix-up," he said. "We were expecting the local police — and it doesn't look like they're coming." Hutley walked to the door and shouted to the soldier at the reception desk. "Get hold of the surgery! Tell them I'll be picking up a doctor and taking them out to Whiteside Farm in about ten minutes!"

Hutley slammed the door, returned to his desk and picked up his hat. "If you want to visit Whiteside Farm you can tag along with us, I suppose."

"Well, actually, we also need to speak to the person who owns the farm. They do live here, don't they?" Mike asked.

"Miss Parks is unavailable at the moment," Hutley barked, as he snatched a bunch of keys from the desk. "And I'm going to the farm, so if you want to come you'd better follow me." He strode out of the room without looking back.

The Land Rover roared down the drive and out into the road. This time, Brian rode in the back. All the same, Mike could not help feeling, given Hutley's agitated state and reckless driving, that, yet again, he had drawn the short straw. It took just thirty minutes to get into Downham, pick up the doctor and then return to Nordelph. Instead of returning to the manor, the driver turned into West Farm Way and after three hundred metres steered onto the track that led to Whiteside Farm.

When the track was smooth enough to allow him to speak, the doctor remarked that he was less than happy at being pushed around by the army. "You know the rules!" Hutley shouted over his shoulder. "The shooting of a civilian requires a police investigation — and as I can't get the police to get off their fat arses you'll have to do."

"But I thought that was only..." Brian stopped speaking when he saw the doctor shaking his head and putting his finger to his lips. The Land Rover encountered a particularly rough section of road and Brian was thrown onto the floor. By now he was beginning to feel sick.

Hutley turned to Mike. "So what's your interest in Whiteside Farm?"

"We've come to ask Gerald Whiteside questions."

"About what?"

"The crop attack."

"That old chestnut! The number of people we get up here about that..." The Land Rover's wheels fell into a set of ruts and Hutley had to tighten his grip on the steering wheel. "Well, you've had a wasted journey."

"Why's that?"

"Because the old man topped himself this morning."

Whiteside Farm was located on the northern bank of the Bedford Drain — a hundred-foot-wide man-made channel which drained water from the Fens. The farmhouse itself faced onto a lane that ran parallel with the waterway. It was along this badly rutted lane that the Land Rover was travelling.

At the rear of the house a large concrete yard was enclosed on one side by a long wooden machinery shed and on the other side by two cottages and a corn dryer. In the centre of this yard, the Land Rover came to a halt. A flock of sparrows flew up and circled around before returning to the corn spill they had been feeding on. Hutley marched towards the farmhouse, while everyone else was attempting to regain their balance. Brian took a few steps, then vomited onto the ground.

"You OK?" Mike asked, concerned that Brian might have contracted food poisoning.

Leaning forward, Brian raised one hand. He was about to speak but was sick again. Eventually he stood up straight, his face bright red. "Sorry about that. Can't ride in the back of a car."

Then Mike remembered. Travel sickness was common among the younger generation. As small children, most of them had never ridden in cars, and so suffered motion sickness later in life. He now realised why Brian was always so eager to ride in the front seat of the vehicles they travelled in.

By the time Mike and Brian reached the house, Hutley had already forced the door. "There, plain as the nose on your face," he said to the doctor. "Suicide. Just sign the paper and we'll clear up this mess."

"OK, OK, calm down." The doctor drew back the curtains to let some light into the kitchen. Gerald Whiteside's body was sitting in an armchair next to the fireplace. The top of the farmer's head was missing, and there was a large red mark on the ceiling.

"Calm down?!" Hutley snapped, as he picked a shotgun up off the floor and laid it on the table. "We want to move another family in here next week. Don't forget, we're half way through the harvest."

"I'm sure Morris will keep everything ticking over for the next fortnight. And anyway, I think Miss Parks decides who moves into her farms."

Hutley was going to respond, but thought better of it, deciding instead to pace nervously to and fro across the large kitchen.

"Do stop doing that. You keep blocking the light," the doctor murmured as he leaned over the body.

"I'm going to see if I can find Morris." Hutley stormed out of the room, brushing past Mike and Brian, who were standing in the doorway.

"The man's scared out of his wits," the doctor said, as Brian approached the body.

"Was scared, you mean."

"Oh no, not Gerald here. Hutley. Fear, that's what all the

shouting is about. He's caught between a commander who wants to keep the peace and a woman who is as tough as old iron — and creates merry hell."

"Mrs. Parks?" said Brian, crouching down beside the body.

"Miss Parks. Her family owned all the land around Downham." The doctor sighed. "She still runs the place. I don't think anyone has plucked up the courage to tell her it all belongs to the government now. Hutley is supposed to be in charge of the soldiers guarding the farms — and the penal workers." The doctor took a form from his bag and started to fill it in. "Therein lies the conflict, and Hutley usually comes off worst." He paused for a moment and looked down at the body. "Of course, it doesn't help that he's as thick as shit. The police don't have to attend suicides. Everyone knows that. That's why they didn't turn up."

"Mind if we take a look?" asked Brian.

The doctor scribbled his signature on the bottom of the form. "Be my guest."

Mike was already working his way through a pile of papers stacked on the Welsh dresser.

Brian examined both of the farmer's hands, turning them over to look at the palms and then the backs. He took a wooden box containing two glass jars and a scalpel from his rucksack. After running the blade of the scalpel under the farmer's fingernails, he carefully placed all the dirt in one of the jars. "So, Whiteside was depressed then?"

"Well no, not really." The doctor watched Brian's work with interest. "Miserable, but not depressed."

"No family?"

"No, but he was very close to Miss Parks. You see, when her father was killed she was left without any family, so Gerald here more or less adopted her. She came out here to see him every day, and he spent a lot of time up at the house. Lucky it was Morris and not her who found the body."

Taking the second jar and the scalpel, Brian collected fragments of paint from the frame around the back door. "I thought you said she was tough."

"Not this morning. Apparently she's in bed crying her eyes out." He snapped his bag shut and returned his pen to his jacket pocket. "I'll leave you to it then," he said as he left the kitchen.

"See a pattern?" Mike asked, without turning away from the papers.

"Well, it looks a bit like my mother and father holding a small dog."

"What?" Mike spun round to find Brian staring up at the bloodstain on the ceiling. "What the hell are you talking about?"

"Sorry. I thought you were giving me a Rorschach inkblot test." Brian undid the top button of the farmer's shirt and pulled the collar away from the neck. Then he undid the cuff and rolled up the sleeve.

"Bruising?" Mike said, crouching down and examining the exposed arm.

"Fair amount, especially around the neck." Brian walked over to the back door. "Probably surprised outside, dragged indoors, strangled and then shot in the mouth to make it look like suicide — and hide some of the evidence."

They both walked out into the sunlight and crossed the lane to the steep bank that rose up in front of the farmhouse. From the top of the bank they could see a straight channel of water stretching to the horizon in each direction. "Suppose this is what stops East Anglia from becoming part of the North Sea." Mike smiled. "So who is going to ask Hutley where he was first thing this morning?"

Brian was not listening. His attention had been caught by a row of wooden boxes surrounded by swarms of insects on the opposite bank. "What do you think those are?"

"Mosquitoes."

"Why would anyone keep mosquitoes in hives?"

"I don't know. Anyway, do you think it was him?"

"Who?"

"Hutley. Do you think he killed Whiteside?"

"Very keen to get it officially classified as suicide." Brian looked back at the house, then surveyed the countryside beyond. "But it took at least two men to do it."

"In case you didn't notice, he's got access to hundreds of men."

"So you think the army did it?"

"Who else? Look at all the checks they made on the way here."

"Yes, it is hard to see how anyone else could get into this place. But if the army killed Whiteside, it changes the angle on the Troxley killing."

Mike climbed back down the bank. "To tell you the truth, I'd rather not think about it. To think we're stuck here for two days. If we'd known about this earlier, we needn't have come at all."

"Could get Matt to run us back to Peterborough this

afternoon."

"No, we can't." Mike became agitated. "Apparently it would have to be cleared with the army. That would take two days. So we can't travel out of here until tomorrow."

"There's still the local police to see." Brian stumbled down into the lane. "We might make some progress with the Troxley case."

"Oh yes? A forty-year-old assault and battery? We can't even solve a murder that happened five hours ago."

Hutley was waiting at the entrance to the farm, glancing from side to side, and occasionally turning on his heels to look behind him. "Have you seen Morris?"

"Who?" asked Mike.

"Morris. Morris Haswell," Hutley said, raising his voice as if it was obvious who he was talking about. "The farm worker."

There was an ear-splitting bang and Hutley threw himself to the ground. A few of the sparrows that had been feeding on the grain spill in the centre of the yard took to the air — but the majority stayed. Those still moving fluttered around amongst the dust and feathers, trying to fly. From one of the barns a stooped figure, dressed in overalls and carrying a shotgun, walked over to where the birds lay. Following him was a cat, which grabbed an injured bird and ran into the garden of one of the cottages.

As he used the heel of his boot to squash the life out of the remaining injured birds, Morris looked across to where Hutley was sprawled on the ground. "Drop something?" he called out.

"You bastard!" shouted Hutley. "What the hell do you think you're doing?"

"Killing sparrows," he said, adding sarcastically, "As we're not supposed to use poison, they have to be shot. Nasty job, but someone has to do it." He swung the gun upwards and pointed it at Hutley, who was now back on his feet. "Dust shot. Sometimes you can kill sixty at a time."

Hutley retrieved his cap and brushed it against his sleeve. "Well, playtime's over. I'll give you a lift back to the manor and we can get this lot sorted out."

"I've got my bike, thanks." Morris walked away, only to be pursued by Hutley.

Mike and Brian followed at a distance. "Was he killed with dust shot?" Mike whispered.

"No," Brian replied.

"Still, worth keeping in mind."

Brian shook his head in disbelief and quickened his pace in order to reach Hutley before he climbed into the Land Rover. "Mind if we have a lift into Downham?"

"We're going back to the manor," snapped Hutley, directing his anger with Morris at Brian. "The best thing you can do is walk back to the road and flag down a passing lorry. At this time of day, most of them are taking people back to town for their lunch break."

Although unhappy about being abandoned in the middle of nowhere, Brian was relieved not to be in the back of the Land Rover, which was now bouncing along the track in front of him.

"He could have taken you as far as the road," said Morris as he cycled past, weaving around some of the larger ruts.

"I was thinking the same thing myself," Mike muttered under his breath.

A lorry approached only moments after they had reached West Farm Way. Brian held out his arm as if he were flagging down a bus on Park Lane. The driver did not ask them where they wanted to go. Two passengers sitting in the back of the lorry lowered the tailgate and pulled Mike and Brian on board. Before they could take their places on the wooden benches that ran down each side of the open vehicle, the tailgate was slammed shut and the driver resumed his journey into town.

Sitting opposite Mike was a middle-aged man in oil-stained overalls. His feet were resting on a large toolbox. Lying on the floor next to the toolbox was a grime-encrusted piece of metal from a tractor. "Not from round 'ere dressed like that," the man said.

"Up from London," replied Mike.

"Ministry of Agriculture?"

"Police."

The man smiled. "Ah, it was your lot sent me up here."

Mike glanced at the other passengers and wondered if they too were serving time on a penal farm. The absence of a guard should have put him at ease, but it did the opposite. "How long have you been here?" he asked, feeling it was better to keep the conversation going.

"Ten years."

"Well, you should be home soon then." Mike wondered what sort of crime the man had committed to warrant such a long sentence.

"Oh no!" The man laughed. "I was only sent here for a year. I just decided to stay."

"Stay?" Brian joined in. "You're here from choice?"

"Why not?" the mechanic asked.

Brian shrugged. "It's a lot different from London."

"I wouldn't go back. It's like a ghost town down there. At least here there's plenty happening. Well, in the summer at least." He leaned forward and retrieved the toolbox, which had bounced across the floor of the lorry. "Anyway, I met my wife here. She's a local girl."

"She must be really special." Brian said.

The mechanic looked across the fields. "No, I wouldn't go back," he murmured.

Brian began to feel unwell again. An old woman sitting opposite leaned forward. "Concentrate on something in the distance and don't look back at the road." He took her advice, but it didn't help much.

Downham was a small market town. During the famine and epidemics it had shrunk to a quarter of its original population and split into two small hamlets. The northern settlement was grouped around the railway station and flour mill. Opposite the station were the grain silos, dryers, several factories (including a machinery-repair yard), and a large supermarket which had been converted into an Ivan's Restaurant. The Swan Hotel, police station, army control centre and the local Green Party offices were half a kilometre away in South Downham. In between lay a number of empty shops and houses that were gradually being reclaimed as the population of the town grew.

Today, as the lorry carrying Mike and Brian entered North Downham, the town was a hive of activity. Lorries, some carrying grain from the fields and others returning empty from Peterborough, queued along the road. Those coming in from the fields either deposited their loads in the corn dryers or, after the civilian driver had been replaced by a soldier, were redirected to Peterborough. Behind the lorries, tankers waiting to be filled with flour were parked up on the verges.

The mechanic climbed out of the lorry as soon as it stopped. Brian passed the toolbox down to him. "This railway breakdown is causing real problems!" the mechanic shouted above the noise. He threw the broken piece of machinery over his shoulder and staggered towards the repair yard.

The rest of the passengers moved briskly towards the restaurant. Mike and Brian followed them. Inside, the activity was as frantic as it was outside. A constant flow of people moved between the serving counters. The floor was pockmarked with the holes left when the supermarket's refrigerators and shelves had been removed. In one corner of the entrance hall a large notice board displayed a pictorial history of the building — complete with samples of packaging and magazine advertisements. Mike studied the notice board but walked away before Brian could pass comment.

Lunch was over quickly and the two were back outside in less than thirty minutes, standing in the blazing August sun and the swirling dust. "Bit like eating on a production line," Brian said, putting two water bottles into his rucksack. "I thought life in the countryside was supposed to be relaxed and tranquil."

*

Downham police occupied the building that had once housed the local council. The door closed behind them, shutting out the noise of the town. A policeman, working at a desk at the back of the room, stared at the two visitors for a while, then stood up and walked over to the counter. "Can I help?" PC Peter Pardoe asked, trying to sound as polite as possible, just in case Mike and Brian were part of the group of party officials and civil servants overseeing the emergency transport of grain and flour.

Peter was a lanky, awkward-looking young man. His eyes were bloodshot from staring at the computer terminal. Born in Downham, he had only lived away from the town for three of his twenty-five years, while he studied accountancy in Birmingham. On his return, it had been impossible to find work as an accountant. Instead, he had joined the police service.

Mike made the introductions and explained the events of the morning — omitting his theory that Whiteside had been murdered.

"So they dragged the doctor out there. What a waste of time!" Peter yawned and rubbed his eyes. "You'll be heading back then?"

"We were wondering if you had any records relating to the Whiteside Farm attack?" Mike asked.

"You mean the attack on Sergeant Bryant?" Peter said enthusiastically. "Yes. We've got a whole file on the case."

"What about Bryant himself, and the other policeman? Are they still alive?" Brian opened up his rucksack and took out a notebook and pencil.

"Both dead," replied Peter, without hesitation.

Brian was surprised by the speed of his reply. "Is there a file on the case?"

Peter walked out of the room and returned, in a matter of seconds, carrying a well-worn box file that he pushed across the counter.

"You've been asked for this file before," Brian suggested.

Peter laughed. "About once a month. Students, amateur historians, all sorts. Most of the stuff in there was written up for the trial."

Brian picked up three sheets of discoloured paper, held together with a rusting staple. 'Transcript of radio transmission Bryant, Parnell and Control — 16th April PM.' He turned the pages carefully. "How long after the event were these written up?"

Taking the papers, Peter turned to the last page and pointed to the date. "A week. I think most of it was done in a rush when the press got hold of the story. Sergeant Bryant's version came a lot later."

Brian started thumbing through the rest of the papers.

"It's not there," said Peter. "No-one has ever seen it — or his notebook."

Brian raised his head and gave Peter a quizzical look. Peter shrugged and looked down at the box.

Mike leaned across the counter. "What about the relatives of Bryant and Parnell? Are any of them still alive?"

Peter left the room again and returned with an older policeman. The old man puffed and wheezed as if merely trying to recall Bryant and Parnell was draining the energy from his body. "Bryant?" The old man rubbed his chin and stared into space. "No, I can't think of anyone left alive." He studied Brian as if seeking inspiration. "Ah, Parnell," he said, as if the recollection had taken him by surprise. "His wife remarried. Her name's Rolt now. Lives in Wisbech and works in that vegetable-packing place."

"Brown's?" suggested Peter.

"That's it. Brown's. She's a supervisor." The old man turned to Peter. "OK?"

"Yes. Thanks."

The old policeman looked at the two visitors, then, shaking his head, he shuffled out of the room.

Working his way through the transcripts, Brian made the occasional entry in his notebook. Peter obtained the telephone number of Brown's Food Packaging from his computer and gave Mike directions to the factory — drawing a crude map of Wisbech as he did so.

The bus was packed with farm workers returning to the fields after a late lunch. Four kilometres later it was almost empty. The windows and the door had been left open, but the air rushing through the bus was not cool enough to prevent Mike and Brian sweating profusely. At least the smell of stale sweat and dust was not so bad after most of the other passengers had got off.

Brown's Packaging was only a few hundred metres away from the railway station, the third stop the bus made in the town. The factory was big enough to render the policeman's map unnecessary.

Brown's had started life as a supplier of tinned foods. When the food shortages became acute and supermarkets closed, the canning industry was thrown into crisis. Like other high-volume packaging manufacturers, can-makers disappeared. There were attempts to keep the industry alive and to continue to use tin cans as a means of distributing food. However, when the epidemics started, a shortage of skilled workers made it difficult to keep complex can-manufacturing plants running.

The last gasp came shortly after the government decided to consolidate all food-can manufacture in Leicestershire. All the surviving workers were relocated, some forcibly, and plants around the country were cannibalised to build ten production lines at Braunston, near Leicester. The first problem was an outbreak of tuberculosis at the chemical works that manufactured the lacquer to coat the inside of the tins. Then tin-plate supplies were disrupted when a cholera outbreak closed the main European tin-plate mill in Italy. Even when production did get under way again, transporting what was essentially fresh air took up too much capacity on the railways and had to be diverted onto the disintegrating road system.

The complete breakdown of the motorway system and the concentration of food consumption in Ivan's restaurants, combined with an outbreak of dysentery amongst tool setters in the Braunston works, sealed the fate of the tin can. What looked like a perfectly straightforward piece of engineering proved too complex for a society no longer geared to mass production or the consumerism that supported it. When the problems of the can-manufacturing industry were explained to him, a minister at the Department of Trade and Industry declared that it was apparently simpler to make a car than a modern tin can.

The Braunston works was scaled down and concentrated on making stainless-steel drums with resealable lids. The European Ministry of Food had produced a specification for such drums, as well as for large resealable glass jars and two-litre bottles. Containers made to these specifications were being unloaded from the lorries parked in the 'goods inwards' area of Brown's. Mike and Brian dodged between the convoy of vehicles as they made their way to the main office.

A guard, sharing a joke with a young secretary, was leaning across the counter in the reception. As the main door opened, the soldier snapped to attention — although he relaxed slightly when he saw it was Mike and Brian rather than his sergeant. Stepping forward, he asked to see their IDs. The girl phoned through to the factory and asked for Sharon Rolt. There was a short conversation, then the girl said, "She'll be with you in a moment." She pushed the visitors' book towards Mike and turned her attention back to the guard.

While Mike was filling in the book, Brian studied a glass cabinet containing samples of Brown's packaged products, past and present. The miniature exhibition made great play of the environmental advantages of present-day packaging over that of forty years ago. "Brushing up on your history?" Mike said, crouching down beside Brian, who was looking at the row of tins of vegetables on the bottom shelf.

"They sold those in supermarkets like the one we were in today?" Brian asked.

"Yes," replied Mike, not knowing whether Brian really was as naive as he appeared. A lot of the time, Brian's pretence of ignorance was an effective means of ridiculing consumerism — and having a dig at the older generation. In this case, however, Mike was prepared to give him the benefit of the doubt. Brian had already revealed some rather surprising gaps in his knowledge of the late twentieth century. And, after all, he had never seen inside a functioning supermarket or encountered tinned food. It was also unlikely he would have come across them in the sort of books he read.

"So if I lived in one of the villages outside Downham, I would have to carry those home with me. A bit heavy, aren't they?"

"Car."

"Oh yes."

"So you bought food in a tiny tin like that," he said, standing up. "And when you'd eaten it you'd take it all the way back."

"No. You threw it away." Mike pointed to the small card explaining the benefits of the present-day stainless-steel drum and the glass jar.

"'...even dog food.'" Brian read out in a surprised voice. "Was that during the famine? People started eating dogs?"

"No. They used to buy tinned meat for their dogs and cats."

"To fatten them up before they killed them?"

"No." Mike became slightly irritated. "You must have seen films where people kept dogs and cats as pets." He tried to recall one, but couldn't. "You remember that farm worker we saw today? He had a dog and a cat."

"I thought they were for hunting animals." Brian sank down onto one of the chairs that had been set out in a row with their backs to the window. "Did you have a dog?"

"Yes." Mike sat down beside Brian and rested his head in his hands. "A red setter. We called her Tammy."

"You didn't eat it?"

"No!" snapped Mike.

"What happened to it?"

"It disappeared."

Brian looked over his shoulder at the queue of lorries making their way very slowly across the car park. "Probably someone else ate it."

Mike wondered if Brian knew how hurtful he was being. He glared at him, but Brian took no notice. Mike decided that it would be a waste of time trying to explain the concept of pets to Brian. What would be the point? Brian was the product of an education system heavily influenced by Green Party propaganda. He had been exposed to ideas formed long after Green thinkers — no longer needing the support of animal-rights campaigners — had radically reassessed man's relationship with the animal world. What was it Vlachos had said? 'Societies which treat animals like humans encourage the confused thinking that leads a society to treat people like animals.'

Mike could not imagine Brian showing affection to another person, let alone to an animal. Had Brian just been having a go at him? After all, he was a vegetarian and Mike was not. Brian took the party line that raising animals for meat was wrong because it wasted resources and, in the long term, was not sustainable. The countryside, with its abundance of wild animals, must present him with a confusing image.

For a moment, as the door opened and closed, the background hum of the factory turned into a deafening clattering of glass jars and steel drums. A woman wearing a white coat, cotton hat and ear defenders walked over to where Mike and Brian were sitting.

"Hello. I'm Sharon Rolt," she said, sitting down beside them. "Hot today, isn't it?" Sharon took off the ear defenders and, pulling a handkerchief from the sleeve of her coat, mopped the sweat from her brow.

Ten years ago, Sharon — who was sixty-six years old — would have been forced to continue working, but now she worked from choice. Some older workers still felt obliged to work, but Sharon only did it because she needed the company. The management had cut her hours and promoted her to supervisor, so she no longer had to do any manual work. It was just that there was nothing for someone with no surviving children or grandchildren, no outside interests and a husband who was still working, to retire to.

"We'd like to ask you some questions about your former husband," Mike said.

Sharon did not respond straight away. She was still savouring the comfort of the chair. "Oh, Dick," she said eventually, rubbing her legs.

"Yes. We were wondering if he ever talked to you about the Whiteside Farm attack."

Sharon laughed. "Did he talk about it?! He never stopped. Whiteside Farm... Huh."

Brian took out his notebook. Sharon, on the off chance that she was going to be asked to read something, took off her glasses and wiped the lenses on her handkerchief. "On the night of the attack, did he say why they were waiting in West Farm Way?" Brian asked.

"Well, you know, over the years Dick changed his story quite a lot. Every time there was something on the television or in the newspapers about it he would come up with some new theory." She looked at Brian and smiled. "A bit of a storyteller, Dick was." She paused to draw breath. "What he said at first was that he thought it was strange they had waited so long. Usually they only waited there at closing time or if they thought someone from Downham had carried out a robbery in one of the villages." She paused again, taking another breath. "He thought that Ian — that's Sergeant Bryant — had been tipped off that the field would be attacked."

"Did he give any other reason why he thought that?"

"Yes. Something about the way they were told about the attack."

Brian looked at the notes he had taken in the police station.

The transcript of the radio message had also caught his eye: "'Are you still in place?'"

Sharon thought for a moment. "Yes, that's it. As though they expected them to be waiting there."

Brian turned a page in his notebook. "He asked the controller if the person who reported the attack was still on the scene. Why did he do that?"

Mike sighed, stood up and walked back towards the glass cabinet containing the packaging. Sharon ignored him and sat thinking about Brian's question. "He said, later, that Ian wondered why they didn't see the person who reported the attack go past them while they were waiting in the lane." She shrugged her shoulders. "Dick thought it might have been reported by someone on the Littleport road."

Brian closed the notebook. He saw Mike making a point of looking at his wristwatch, but continued with the questioning. "Did he think there was anything else odd about that night?"

"Only that he thought they were ambushed."

"What do you mean?" Brian saw, out of the corner of his eye, Mike pointing at his watch.

"He thought the attackers could have got back to the van without hitting Ian."

Brian opened the notebook again and scribbled a couple of sentences before snapping it shut and getting to his feet. "Well, thanks very much, Sharon."

"I don't know how much help that's been. It was a long time ago," she said.

"It certainly was," Mike muttered under his breath.

Brian shook hands with Sharon and followed Mike out of the building. "What does it matter who did what, where and to whom some forty years ago?" Mike persisted. "What really matters is who killed Troxley last week."

"It could provide a motive," Brian said.

Mike stopped walking and lowered his voice. "It could also turn up something about Fairchild we'd rather not know about."

Brian took no notice and continued walking towards the railway- station bus stop.

The packed bus arrived in North Downham just as most of the farm workers were going home and the day shifts were leaving the flourmill and machinery-repair yard. Army vehicles fought their way along the main street between large groups of cyclists and pedestrians. "Do we eat now or later?" Brian asked.

Mike threw his rucksack over his shoulder and pushed his way into the crowd. "Later. Let's find out what the Swan Hotel is like."

Two workers with large yellow patches on the backs of their overalls came out of he entrance to the flour mill and made their way towards the restaurant. "Penal workers, without a guard," whispered Brian. "Why don't they run away?"

"How, and where to?"

"Good point."

Most of the crowd had dispersed into the side streets before Mike and Brian reached South Downham, even so the pavement outside the Swan Hotel was still busy. The door to what had once been a public bar closed behind them and, at last, there was silence. "I think I've seen more people today than I see in London in a month."

"At least," said Mike, approaching the bar and banging his hand down on the bell.

A fair-haired youth appeared. "Hello. Can I help?" He was already reaching under the bar for the register.

"We've two rooms booked for tonight," said Mike.

"You're from London." The young man placed the register on the bar and laid two room keys on top of it. "If you could sign in, please. You'll find the rooms at the top of the stairs." He began to move back towards the door.

"Before you go," Mike said, "are there telephones in the rooms?"

"Yes," the youth replied, continuing his retreat.

"Working ones?"

"Yes. If there's any problem you'll find me in the lounge bar."

As Mike and Brian entered their names and their S-card numbers in the register, they could hear a group of men engaged in conversation in the other bar. Every so often the voices would be raised in what sounded like a cheer.

Brian looked at the list of guests who had booked in. There was one other person, a low-ranking army officer, staying at the hotel. He also noticed there had been a steady stream of visitors since the previous weekend. Brian showed the list to Mike. "Bit busier than the Adelphi." He laughed.

But Mike was not amused. He snatched one of the keys off the bar and climbed the stairs. While the room itself was basic, with plain emulsion-covered walls and bare floorboards, the furniture was elaborate. The wooden bed had carved legs and a headboard. The polished writing table and chair were finished with inlaid wood. The air was dry and the lace curtains billowed into the room as a warm breeze blew in through the French windows, which opened on to a balcony with a view over the street.

Brian dropped his rucksack onto the bed in his room, walked over to the window and stepped out onto the balcony. Below him, people were still making their way along the street. The occasional lorry, tractor or army Land Rover drove past. In the distance he could see the Wisbech road snaking between the fields and disappearing somewhere just beyond Nordelph Manor. He jumped up and down. Mike, who was also standing on the balcony outside his room, winced. "Seems safe enough," said Brian. He grabbed a chair from inside the room, sat down and put his feet up on the balcony rail. "What's the plan for this evening then?"

Mike looked out across the town. "Well, I want to get through to Linda. She wasn't feeling too good last night."

"What's the problem?" Brian put his hands behind his head and tilted the chair back.

"Nothing too serious. Just a touch of toothache." Mike turned to go back into the room. "I'll make the call, then freshen up. See you downstairs in fifteen minutes."

Having taken off his shirt, Brian spent five minutes sunning himself before going back into his room. Unpacking his rucksack, he took out his pyjamas and laid them on the bed, then put his small washbag and a bottle of water on the shelf over the basin. He hung his jacket, which had spent most of the day strapped across the top of the rucksack, on the coat hanger in the wardrobe. The cold tap gurgled for a few seconds after it was turned on, and there was a hiss of air before rust-coloured water swirled into the basin. Brian put the plug in the drain and watched the basin fill up. He cupped his hands to splash water on his face, then thought better of it. Taking his flannel out of the washbag, he soaked it in the cool water, then wiped it over his face and under his arms.

Mike spent twenty minutes trying to get through to his wife on the telephone. He obtained a variety of recorded messages: everything from the abrupt 'There is a fault' to the more specific 'The line is busy — please try later.' It was unlikely that the messages bore any relation to the real problem. When Mike arrived in the lounge bar, Brian was already sitting at one of the tables, his notes spread in front of him. In the corner of the room, two soldiers were deep in conversation.

*

"So what's the verdict then?" Mike asked as he sat down.

"Well, reading through the transcript and from what Parnell's wife was saying, there was definitely something strange about the attack at Whiteside Farm. It's amazing really that she remembers so much about it."

Not that amazing, thought Mike. He still remembered precise details of conversations with his first wife. He hung on to the memories and found, as time went by, that he could remember more rather than less. "But does it really matter that much?"

"It could provide a motive for killing Troxley. And if we find the motive, we're a step nearer to finding the killer."

"After this morning, I think we know who the killers are," said Mike, lowering his voice and tilting his head towards the soldiers.

"No, I don't think so."

"Of course it is. Who else could it be, out here?"

"OK, it's likely, but we can't rule out other possibilities."

"Meaning?"

"Meaning we shouldn't put all our money on one horse just because it is ahead at the first turn." Brian waited for Mike to respond. He didn't, so Brian decided to provoke a reaction. "It's not a good policy to rely on just one line of investigation and dismiss all the others."

"So you're an expert on police investigations now." Mike smiled and leaned forward. "In case you hadn't noticed, there are only two of us. That rather limits the lines of investigation we can follow up, doesn't it?"

"To two."

"OK, have it your own way. What do you suggest we do next?"

"Well, I was thinking of having a look at the field where the attack took place..."

At that moment, one of the soldiers stood up and walked across to the bar. He pressed the bell and the youth appeared at the door.

"With you in a second," the young man said, then disappeared again. The men who had been in the lounge bar filed into the room and the youth re-appeared behind the bar. Some of the men, and the youth, placed bottles on the bar. The soldier put down two glasses. The glasses were filled, and the soldier returned to his companion.

"I've a feeling they're not drinking water," Mike said.

Before Brian could respond, the youth brought two glasses to their table. "Local brew," one of the men at the bar called out, as these glasses too were filled.

Another man left the bar and approached their table. Brian recognised him as Morris Haswell, the labourer from Whiteside Farm. "Parsnip. Careful how you drink it — it's stronger than anything you'll get in London."

Mike took a sip. He was used to rosehip wine, which most of the Ivan's served up in the winter to fight off colds. This was a lot stronger and, on an empty stomach, seemed to have an immediate effect. Mike felt his face flush and his head begin to swim. Brian took a sip. Having often drunk quite heavily at the weekends, the wine had little effect on *him*. On occasion he had drunk far stronger brews in the privacy of Aunty Stef's cellar.

Pulling one of the chairs out from under Mike and Brian's table, Morris sat down. He stared at the two policemen for a while, then drank his glass of wine in one gulp. "So you found out who did it?" he asked, but did not give Mike or Brian time to answer. "I tell you who did it. It was those Green fascists from London. They came up here and killed him, and now you're here to cover up the mess."

Although Mike took Morris's rant in his stride, Brian was shocked and glanced uneasily around the room. The barman laughed, and one of the soldiers was shaking his head slowly. Nothing he saw put Brian at his ease. He felt he ought to say something, before Mike got into an argument with Morris.

"It looks like suicide. Apparently a lot of farmers take their own lives," said Mike calmly.

"It's the only way out of this prison."

"Prison? What are you talking about?" Mike scoffed.

Morris nodded his head in the direction of the two soldiers. "Just take a look around. You lot tell us how to run our farms, how to use the land. We have to grow crops without proper chemicals and fertiliser, and you send soldiers to stand at our backs and make sure we meet your targets — and don't keep too much food for ourselves." Morris's face was weather-beaten and scarred with a mass of broken veins. He moved it closer to Mike's and whispered, "What did we ever do to deserve having our homes turned into prisons, and for life, eh?"

Mike looked down his nose at Morris. "How far back do you want me to go?" He guessed that the farmer's rant was a general all-encompassing gripe and probably not as serious as it sounded.

He therefore decided to provoke Morris. "Let's see. You spent years pocketing huge subsidies from the taxpayer *and* charged over the odds for food. Then you poisoned people by turning cows into cannibals. After that, you got really greedy and in the process contaminated your own seed stocks. And, as if that wasn't enough, you bred a family of superbugs strong enough to wipe out over half the population of Britain. Now don't get me wrong, but somehow I can't see how you can be trusted with anything more complicated..."

"Now, you listen to me!" roared Morris. "It was the government who told us to turn our land over to grass for meat and poultry production when all the crops failed! We told them we couldn't expand livestock farms without more antibiotics. Did they listen? No! And by the time they realised, it was too late and nothing could stop the disease. And another thing," — he lifted his hand to stop Mike interrupting — "another thing, we weren't the ones who were pushing GM crops. That was your government as well."

"It wasn't the Green government."

"But it's the Green government who have turned the countryside into a prison camp. The only difference between the penal workers and us is that the penal worker's sentence ends and he can go home. We have to stay and watch our hard work disappear in railway wagons. That devious shit Ivan steals the lot. He was the one who made our money worthless. It's not the first time in history the fascists have devalued another country's money so that they could bleed Europe white. The Germans have done it twice, and the second time they lumbered us with their worthless euros. And Ivan has got camps as well. He's not satisfied with taking our food. He takes all our young people too." Morris lowered his voice, but still spoke loudly enough for everyone in the room to hear. "People are taken out to those camps and they never come back."

Mike stared at Morris, who was waiting for his last statement to sink in. Resting his elbows on the table and scratching the side of his face, Mike said, "Yes. I spent two years in one."

Morris realised his trump card was now worthless. He stood up, nodding his head, and — waving his empty glass in front of Mike's face — he backed away from the table. "Well, there you are then!" He turned towards the bar. "You know what I'm talking about then."

The group of men at the bar laughed, and pretended to calm

Morris down. The soldiers peered out of the window.

"Come on. Let's get something to eat," Mike said.

Brian gathered up his notes and left the room, careful to avoid eye contact with anyone standing at the bar.

Once outside, Mike turned to Brian. "I want you to get that man's details: name, S-Card number, address — the lot."

"You're not going to arrest him?"

"No. But if the party ever debates the re-introduction of democracy, I want to make sure that man is the first speaker."

Brian smiled and tried to remember the last time his boss had made a remark that could have been mistaken for a joke. "Two euros says it's apple pie."

"Pounds, Brian. Do you want to get us shot?"

It seemed that getting away from London had helped Mike relax. During dinner he even seemed receptive to some of Brian's ideas on the Whiteside Farm attack. However, this new-found enthusiasm did not extend to accompanying Brian on a cycle trip to the scene of the crime.

"Now? It's six kilometres. It'll be dark soon!" Mike exclaimed as they left the Ivan's.

"Not for a few hours yet."

"Why not get the driver to go back that way tomorrow?" Mike pushed his hands into his pockets and looked down at his feet. "You go. You know what I think about it." He looked up the road towards the hotel. "I really want to talk to Linda."

"Didn't you get through?"

Mike shook his head. "No."

"Try e-mail," Brian suggested. "And don't worry about the field. I'll go alone."

*

The booking clerk at Downham railway station wrote Brian's S-card number in the bicycle-loan book. Brian tried to recall the route the lorry had taken from the farm, and was attempting — unsuccessfully — to turn the police transcripts and stories from *The Guardian*'s website into a mental map. At the junction of the Wisbech road and West Farm Way he stopped. He knew this was close to where Bryant and Parnell had parked their police car. However, there was no point riding down the lane if he did not have a clear idea where the actual field was. Although the sun was still quite high in the sky, it was already acquiring a red tint.

Perhaps Mike was right and this was a pointless exercise.

It was then that Brian realised he was close to Nordelph Manor. Remounting the bike, he continued along the Wisbech road.

The guard at the front door waved Brian past after no more than a casual glance at his police ID card. Inside, the house was silent and the reception desk unattended. There was a faint rustling noise coming from the main office, and Brian assumed that Hutley was still at his desk. The door was ajar. Pushing it open, Brian stepped into the room. The early evening sun poured through the tall windows.

The noise was not Hutley. Beside the desk stood a woman. Her dark-brown hair was cut in a simple pudding-basin style. She was wearing a short black dress with small white polka dots, which revealed her shoulders, a substantial amount of cleavage, and her long pale legs. On the floor, draped around the heavy working boots she was wearing, lay a heavy tweed skirt. A pale-yellow blouse was hanging over the back of the chair behind the desk. On the desk lay the cardboard box Brian had handed to the soldier earlier that day.

"Yes!" the woman snapped.

Brian raised his hand to shield his eyes from the sun. "I'm Brian Tyler. I'm with the police in London."

"There's no need to salute!" The woman snapped again.

Brian stepped forward into a shadow and lowered his hand. He was aware that he was staring at the woman, but he was unable to prevent himself — or think what to say next. He smiled at her.

"Something strike you as amusing, Mr. Tyler?"

The rebuke provided the jolt Brian needed to gather his thoughts. "I want to take a look at the land around Whiteside Farm and wondered if you could give me some directions," he said, sounding more aggressive than he had intended.

"OK." The woman's tone was marginally softer. She bent down and took hold of the hem of her dress, then looked up at Brian. "If you would excuse me for a moment."

"Yes," said Brian, still staring at her.

"I think what I'm trying to say, Mr. Tyler, is that I want you to turn and face the other way while I change my clothes." Her voice had hardened again and she spat the sentence out, one word at a time.

Brian mumbled an apology and turned around. He could hear the rustling of cloth behind him. "So why do you want to look at

Whiteside Farm?" The voice was strained and muffled as the woman pulled the dress over her head.

"I want to take a look at the field where the policeman was attacked."

There was a short laugh. "Don't tell me you've caught someone after all these years?"

"Well, actually..."

"What?" The voice was muffled again.

"Nothing. I'm just interested in the case."

"OK. Done."

Brian turned around. The woman was now dressed in the yellow blouse and the tweed skirt. The black dress lay screwed up in a heap in the cardboard box.

Snatching open a desk drawer, the woman pulled out a wad of maps. She threw one after another down on the desk. The last map she unfolded, and carefully smoothed it out with both hands. "This is very old, but if you are looking for the Genesis trial site it is the best one," she said, pointing to a field marked on the map.

Brian stepped forward and glanced down at the map. The woman's finger was trembling. He looked up and found he was standing closer to her than he had realised. A band of freckles ran across the top of her cheeks and the bridge of her nose. Her eyes, watery and red-rimmed, were a bluish grey, with small yellow flecks. She had obviously been crying before Brian entered the room. He maintained eye contact with her for just a moment too long. Suddenly, she looked away, hurriedly gathered up the map, folded it, and pushed it into his hand. "Take it with you. It's self-explanatory."

Brian backed away. "Thanks," he said. "I'll bring it back later."

"No hurry."

When he reached the door, Brian turned and looked back. The woman had already seated herself at the desk. "I'm sorry to hear about your loss," Brian said. The woman did not reply. Her face was hidden in the shadows and he could not gauge her reaction.

Brian rode to the far end of West Farm Way before he opened out the map. He realised immediately that he had overshot the track that led to the field. He also saw what the woman meant about the map being self-explanatory. The trial site was marked in red, as were a series of concentric circles, with their centre in the midpoint of the field itself. — a feature which looked curiously familiar.

Standing in the field, at the spot where (according to Parnell's account) the attack had taken place, Brian scanned the horizon, or at least the parts of the horizon which were not hidden by trees. He looked for evidence of the squares that were spaced around the circumference of the concentric circles on the map. Although the inner circle was only two hundred metres in diameter, there was no sign of any objects. On the eastern side of the field, a line of trees hid the Wisbech-to-Littleport road. Cycling along the road confirmed the suspicion that Parnell had confided to his wife. The field was not visible to passing motorists — or, for that matter, cyclists. So if the call had not been made from here (and Parnell had seen no-one on the West Farm Way), it had probably come from the field itself.

Leaving the bicycle at the side of the road, Brian walked to the trees. Amongst the young willows were the remnants of older trees, trees more than forty years old. One of the squares marked on the inner circle was on the bank of a small stream. Brian had no difficulty locating the stream and quickly found the spot were the feature was supposed to be. He searched the area and discovered the badly rusted remains of a metal cabinet. The louvered door of the box came off its hinges when Brian pulled at it. Inside, there was a tangle of metal, glass and wires.

The light was failing and the long shadows the trees cast across the fields were fading. Brian realised it would be dark by the time he got back to Downham. Some traffic — indeed, *any* evidence of human activity — would have made him feel happier during his journey back along West Farm Way. The light mist forming above the ditches and spreading across the road brought to mind some of the ghost stories he had read.

It had been his intention to return the map, but on reaching Nordelph Manor Brian found the gates shut and locked. This should have been no more than a minor inconvenience. After all, he could return the map later, or even post it from London. But as he continued his journey, the feeling of being locked out in this wasteland played with something in his subconscious. He found he was experiencing, and could not control, a feeling of total alienation. No longer able to appreciate the space and beauty of the East Anglian landscape, or to savour the warm evening air, he pedalled furiously. All he wanted was to get back to the hotel and lock himself in his room, or sit down and talk to Mike. He imagined that the road in front of him was the walkway between South Kensington station and the museums; imagined he could hear the echo of the guitar and the voice singing 'Tambourine man'. He sang the words out loud, and the panic subsided.

*

The public bar of the Swan Hotel was empty, but as Brian approached the stairs he heard voices coming from the end of the hallway. On the off chance that Mike was still up, he pushed open the door to the lounge bar. A group of men standing in front of a dartboard turned towards Brian, and stared at him, in silence. He was just about to close the door again when someone called out his name and walked over to him. It was then he recognised Matt Spencer, the driver.

"Sorry, Matt. I didn't realise it was you. I'm looking for my boss," Brian explained.

Matt laughed. "Now that's a man who could seriously ruin someone's evening."

The young bartender was pouring a round of drinks. He turned towards Brian. "It's OK, you can come in. Morris has gone home."

Everyone else burst into laughter, and someone called out "Get orf of moi land", which caused even more merriment. It was clear that either Matt or the bartender, or perhaps both of them, had provided the rest of the group with enough information about Brian to render introductions unnecessary. They had also heard a description of Mike that earned Brian their sympathy.

The darts players were a mix of farmers, mill workers and engineers. The two soldiers who had been drinking in the public bar earlier were also playing. "Play darts?" Matt asked.

Looking at the pile of money on the table next to the dartboard, Brian worked out that each player had contributed two euros. He added two coins of his own, then joined Matt's team — which Matt came to regret as the night wore on. Perhaps if Brian hadn't joined them the group of men would have dispersed earlier, but stories of London, and Brian's curiosity about the countryside, kept the conversation going until the early hours. It also meant that everyone drank far more then they should have done.

Brian's casual mention of the visit to Nordelph Manor was greeted with the sound of air being sucked through teeth.

"So you've met the ice maiden, have you?" Matt said.

"Funny, his voice doesn't sound any higher," one of the soldiers chipped in. There was another burst of laughter and the darts match broke down in confusion. Drinks were finished and everyone except Brian, Matt and the bartender, who remained in the hallway, made their way noisily out into the street.

Brian steadied himself against the banisters at the bottom of the stairs, then turned and sat down heavily on the second step. "Thanks for letting me join the game. I enjoyed that," he said.

"No problem," Matt replied, leaning against the wall. "Now if you want some real fun, you need to be here on Saturday night."

"We would be carrying him back to London," the bartender said, as he returned to the lounge to clear away the glasses and bottles.

"So that was Miss Parks, was it?" asked Brian.

"No, that's Eddy." Matt laughed.

"No, no." Brian tried to stop himself laughing. "I mean that was Miss Parks I met at the manor."

Matt levered himself away from the wall and sat down on the stairs next to Brian. "Hildee Parks."

"Hildee?"

"Short for Hildegard."

Brian laughed.

"Oh, and not as funny as Hildegard," said Matt, joining in.

"She could certainly have done with a laugh this evening. I suppose losing Whiteside was a bit of a blow."

"Probably, but she's not been happy for a long time." Matt gazed down at his feet, and brushed the hair back from his face with his hand. "Do you know, I go into Peterborough once a week. And for the last six weeks, I've been bringing her back a dress. She writes down exactly what she wants. Sometimes she even draws a little sketch. Every week she sends it back. No explanation, just sends it back." He got to his feet. "I know her measurements better than I know my girlfriend's." He glanced at his watch. "Talking of which, time to go. I'll pick you and your boss up by the station at eight." He leaned over and looked into Brian's face. "Think you'll make it?"

Brian stood up. "No problem," he replied, missing his step and crashing into the banister.

Thursday 22nd August 2041

Following a restless night, Mike woke as the first vehicles started moving through Downham. Had he managed to get through to Linda by phone rather than having to exchange e-mails, perhaps he would have slept better. After washing and dressing, he stepped out onto the balcony. The town hummed with activity and the roar of lorries setting off in convoy for Peterborough. Footsteps and chattering voices in the street below reminded him of London before the epidemics.

Mike peered over the balcony. "Are you awake yet?" he called out. Brian stepped from of his room carrying a cut-throat razor, he had a strip of shaving cream down one side of his face. Mike envied Brian's ability to shave without the inconvenience of finding scarce razor blades or a working electric razor.

"Yep. Ready to go," Brian replied, dragging the razor across his face one last time.

"You look like death. Did all that noise keep you awake?"

"What noise?"

"Some party the local yobbos were holding downstairs."

Brian looked down at his watch. "We'd better get a move on. We're being picked up at eight outside the station."

"How do you know that?" Mike asked, but Brian had already walked back into his room.

*

"Bit of a problem I'm afraid," said Matt, as he drew up in front of the station. "I've got to take a piece of medical equipment and an engineer to Peterborough station, but it isn't ready yet."

"Can't you come back for it?" Mike asked icily.

"No. It's urgent. You can get some breakfast while you wait."

"We've already had breakfast!" Mike snapped.

"Where is this equipment?" Brian asked, in an effort to defuse the situation.

"Just across the road, Brian."

Mike registered the familiarity between Matt and Brian. He also noticed that both of them were excessively dark around the eyes. It did not take him long to work out why the noise of the previous night's party had not disrupted Brian's sleep.

Brian turned to Mike. "Why don't we go over there and take a look? It might be interesting."

Mike looked at his watch. "Well, why not?" He sighed as he followed Brian across the road to the line of factory units.

"Couple of people want to have a look around while I wait for the machine," Matt called out as he led Mike and Brian into a large workshop. Medical instruments in various states of repair were laid out on desks. A grey-haired man with a neatly trimmed beard and wearing glasses with heavy frames stood up behind one of the desks. "Yes, you're very welcome. I'm sorry we are holding you up but the parts only came this morning." He started to lead them out of the room, but stopped suddenly and extended his hand to Mike. "Oh, I'm terribly sorry. I'm Andrew Cameron."

"Mike Allchurch." Mike shook hands with Andrew, but noticed that Brian had crossed to the other side of the office and was inspecting a cardiac monitor attached to a personal computer. The machine produced a series of simulated traces. "And that's my assistant, Brian Tyler," Mike said.

"Hello, Brian," Andrew called out, as he led Mike out of the room.

"Now, this is the piece of equipment that is holding you up," Andrew whispered. It's the slide assembly for a tunnelling electron microscope. It's supposed to be in the Central Middlesex Hospital by the end of today." An engineer was carefully screwing a set of stainless-steel guide rails to a complex piece of cast metal. The screws were so small that he needed a large magnifying lens to see them.

Mike and Andrew returned to the main workshop. "Well, that's about all there is to see really," said Andrew, sitting down behind his desk.

Sitting down on a chair in front of the desk, Mike noticed that Brian was still working his way along the line of instruments, studying each one carefully.

"Matt said you're from London," said Andrew.

"Oh, yes." Mike turned his attention back to Andrew. "Ruislip. Do you know it?"

"Yes. I used to work in Hayes for a company which made microscopes."

"How did you end up out here?"

"We never did like living so near London. My wife preferred the countryside. When the troubles started, we thought it was a good time to get out. The instrument maker who owned this place had just died so I took it on."

Perhaps it was because he was so tired that Mike asked the question nobody asks a stranger: "And your wife has settled in?" He realised his mistake, but it was already too late.

"She's dead," replied Andrew in a matter-of-fact way. He looked over his shoulder at the street outside. "She would have loved all this. Equality, community spirit, no cars, no pollution or waste, organic food, and no money worries." He stared at Mike for a moment, drumming his fingers on the desk. "That's the trouble with utopias — there's always a shortage of tickets."

*

Brian failed to find what he was looking for in the workshop where Andrew and Mike were chatting. A carpeted corridor led from the reception area to the stores at the back of the building. In a small office, off this corridor, two youths were hunched over a computer keyboard. The screen was white, except for a small black square through which lines of numbers scrolled each time a key was struck. As Brian stepped into the room, the second youth reached across and hit a key on the top left of the keyboard. The screen changed instantly, to display a spreadsheet. Although the youths did not acknowledge Brian's presence, one of them suddenly began reading numbers from a drawing on the desk, while the second youth entered the numbers on the spreadsheet.

The next room contained racks of small boxes and several large pieces of machinery. A white-coated technician sitting at a workbench was fitting lenses into the frames of a pair of glasses.

On his return to the main workshop, Brian looked in on the two youths. The computer screen had reverted to its former state, and this time they failed to notice Brian standing behind them.

*

"You've got enough to keep you busy here," said Brian, as he sat down next to Mike.

"It's not as frantic as it used to be," Andrew said. "Organisation is a bit better than it was."

"And you do some computer programming?"

"No. My stepson and his friend use the computer to track down and order the components we need. E-mail, newsgroups and the web — that sort of thing."

"Glasses?"

Andrew tilted his head back and laughed. "When we started getting this place off the ground again, we put up a website explaining we specialised in optical engineering. Anyway, someone in Northampton found an abandoned optician's and was looking around for anyone who might be able to use the stock and equipment. They thought 'optics' was close enough and it arrived here unannounced." Andrew smiled at Brian. "So if you ever need a pair of glasses, we're your people."

Brian looked at Mike. "As it happens, we know someone who just lost a pair."

Mike glared back but said nothing.

A technician carried a wooden box into the room. "Ready for the off," he said.

*

"Mind if we stop off at the manor?" Brian asked, as the car approached Nordelph. "I've got to return something I borrowed."

For reasons that Mike did not understand, Matt drew air between his teeth and the technician laughed. "Why not?" said Matt. "Might as well pick up the dress while you're at it."

Brian met Morris on the steps of the manor house. The two men gave each other a sideways glance as they passed. The reception desk was manned again, but as the soldier (who looked the worse for wear) recognised Brian he merely waved him through. The door to the estate office was closed, so Brian knocked on it gently and listened carefully.

"Enter!" shouted the voice on the other side of the door.

Hildee Parks was alone in the room, sitting behind her large desk, which faced the door. "Ah! Mr. Tyler. How are you today?" She stood up and walked round the desk.

Brian took a few steps into the room and held out the map. "I brought this back. Thanks."

Hildee took the map with her left hand and extended her right. "I must apologise for yesterday. I'm Miss Parks, Mr. Tyler."

"Brian," he corrected her.

Hildee took no notice. She threw the map on the desk. "Did you find everything you were looking for, Mr. Tyler?"

"No, not everything."

"Oh well. Perhaps another time. You are welcome to borrow the map if you ever need it again."

"Well, actually, I'm on the way back to London."

"Matt taking you?" Hildee asked, without softening her voice.

"Yes."

"How was the Swan?"

"Er, adequate." Brian wondered if Hildee had taken the same course on interrogation techniques as he had.

"Yes, a good description. I hear you had a bit of a run-in with Mr Haswell yesterday evening."

"A bit. Nothing serious."

"He may go over the top, but in the main he is only saying what a lot of other farmers think. Still, I am sorry if we have all made you feel slightly less then welcome."

Brian was considering asking Hildee what her definition of 'slightly' was, but he didn't get the chance. She grabbed the cardboard box from the desk and held it out in front of her. "Please give this to Matt Spencer. Tell him it is not suitable. And sorry for the inconvenience."

Once again, Brian made eye contact. Unlike the previous day, her eyes were not bloodshot. Perhaps it was the flecks in her eyes that again held his attention for just that second too long. He saw her take a breath but he interrupted as she began to speak. "I thought it suited you, Hildee."

She looked away. Brian could see she was confused, perhaps thrown by the use of her first name. However, it did not take long for her to regain her composure. She looked at him — not at his face, but at his jacket, with its leather patches and the crude repairs Stef had made to the pockets and sleeves. "You are an expert on clothes, are you, Mr. Tyler?"

As Brian turned and walked out of the room, he could hear Hildee's footsteps behind him. When he reached the door, her footsteps stopped. He assumed that Hildee was following him in order to give him the box, but he was too angry to turn around. He did, however, glance back as he passed the reception desk. Hildee was standing in the doorway. Her right hand was holding the top button of her blouse; her left was gripping the doorframe.

It was only after he was in the car, and Matt had asked him where the dress was, that Brian realised Hildee had not been holding the box when he last saw her. Looking up at the window, he noted that she had returned to her desk and to the documents she had been reading when he entered the room. As the car turned out of the front gate, Brian looked back at the house. He could see Hildee standing at the window, watching the car leave.

They were only a few metres past the West Farm Way junction when Morris Haswell flagged them down.

"Oh no!" exclaimed Mike. "It's that bloody idiot again. Can't we just drive straight on?"

Brian was still on edge after his meeting with Hildee "We'd better hear him out," he said. As the car came to a halt, he grabbed the door handle and leapt out. "What's up?" he asked Morris.

"You come with me. I want to show you something," Morris said, walking back down the road in the direction of West Farm

Way. After looking at Mike and shrugging his shoulders, Brian followed Morris.

Getting out of the car, Mike ran to catch up with Brian. "You've just seen Miss Parks?" he asked.

When Brian admitted he had, Morris sniffed. "Well, that's all right then."

Brian was not at all sure what was 'all right'. When the three men reached the junction, Morris pointed in the direction of Whiteside Farm. "See that bank by the drain where you were standing after you looked at the body? Well, yesterday morning I saw two men go over that bank and get into a boat."

"Where were you?" asked Mike.

"In the barn."

"So you got a good look at them?"

"Yes. One was short and fat and the other one was tall with a moustache."

Mike buried his face in his hands for a few seconds, then turned to Morris. "So why didn't you tell us this yesterday?"

"Told you now, haven't I?" With that, Morris mounted his bicycle and set off back towards the manor.

Mike looked down at the ground. "I wonder if I can find a decent-sized stone before that daft bugger gets out of range!"

This was the second time that Morris had brought out the previously hidden humorous side of Mike's personality. Brian wondered whether Mike had a soft spot for the old man.

During the journey back to Peterborough, Brian said little, other than asking Matt how long it would take to get from Downham to Peterborough on the river, and where in Peterborough you could hire a boat.

"Thinking about a sailing holiday?" Matt laughed.

When they reached the railway station, the technician grabbed the box from the boot of the car and ran to catch the London train. Brian and Mike stayed in the car. "Oh no!" said Matt. "You want me to take you to the marina."

"Yes please," said Brian.

"Highly irregular. I'm not supposed to deviate from the route."

Mike leaned forward, over the back of Brian's seat. "How far is it?" he asked, looking at his watch.

Matt thought for a moment. "Three kilometres."

Mike sighed. "Well let's do it then, and put Brian's mind at rest."

Only five of the thirty boats in the marina were still floating. Several, pulled clear of the water altogether, had been cannibalised for parts.

A round-faced man was repainting the hull of a boat. "My wife looks after all the paperwork," he said. "She's in the booking office."

The booking office was a partitioned corner of the boat-repair shed. The 'wife' looked young enough to be the round-faced man's daughter.

"That's right," said the woman. "Two men. One was tall with a moustache and the other was short and stocky."

"Did they have an accent?" Brian asked.

"Not really. They could have been from London. They sounded a bit like you."

"Did you get their S-Card numbers?"

"No. They said they were from the ministry."

"What ministry?" asked Brian.

"Waterways, or something like that." She started rummaging around amongst the papers on her desk. "Here it is," she said, handing a sheet of paper to Brian.

"'Home Office — Inland Waterways Security Division" Brian read from the top of the page. "There's a number here. Did you ring to check that these people were genuine?"

"Yes," said the woman indignantly. "I mean, they didn't have S-Card numbers, did they?"

"And someone answered?"

"Yes. They said it was OK."

"When you made the call, did you get put through to someone else, or did the person who answered confirm the men's identity?"

"No. She didn't put me through to anyone else."

"She?"

"Yes. It was a woman."

Becoming increasingly agitated, Mike glanced at his watch.

"Can I take this? Brian asked, as he examined the sheet of paper.

"No!" the woman snapped. "I mean, how do I know who you are?"

Brian realised that in the light of their questions it would be difficult to convince the woman he was a genuine policeman — even if he gave her the telephone number of the Home Office.

Taking the sheet of paper, he laid it face down in the desktop scanner which stood next to the PC. "Scan it into your computer so that you've got a copy." The woman clicked one of the icons on the screen and the scanner whirred briefly. The scan complete, Brian took the original, folded it, and slipped it into his pocket.

*

"I owe you," Brian said to Matt when they reached the station.

"No problem." Matt walked with Brian towards the train. "Just tell me one thing. Did she really keep the dress?"

"Yes."

"I don't believe it. I bet you forgot to ask her for it."

"OK. When you see her wearing it, you owe me five euros."

Matt laughed. "*Pounds*. Five *pounds*. You aren't back in London yet."

"Come on! For goodness sake, get a move on!" Mike shouted.

The train was about to leave as Mike and Brian jumped on. The late night and early morning were catching up with Brian, and he drifted into a light sleep as soon as he sat down. Mike moaned about having to miss lunch.

Brian woke as the train was leaving Stevenage. He swallowed a mouthful of bottled water, took a book from his rucksack and started to read.

"Let's have a look at your S-Card," Mike said.

Brian reached into his pocket. "Why? Do you think it's a forgery?"

"No. I'm just interested." He studied the card, then handed it back. "Have you ever seen an S-Card with a seventh number higher than forty five?"

Brian thought before answering. "I'm sure I have."

"I thought I had too, but according to Harry the Print the seventh number is special. He thought it was used to trace people."

"What about Troxley's card?"

"That's why he mentioned it. The seventh number on Troxley's card was high."

"A good way to track him down, especially if you didn't know when and where he was arriving."

Mike gazed out of the window. "It makes me think we are up against someone with a lot of clout."

"Like who?"

"The army," Mike murmured.

"More likely someone very small."

"What do you mean?" Mike scoffed.

"Well, if *we* wanted to find someone, what would *we* do?"

"Alert all the constables on the beat, the local police, councillors, Ivan's managers..."

"And the army would give a description to guards at railway stations and Ivan's. More likely it's someone with limited resources — or with a day job. Or even someone who shouldn't be in the country at all."

"Not the army then?" Mike said, obviously not taking Brian seriously.

"Probably not."

"Just because some yokel flags us down and tells us some cock-and-bull story about a boat."

"Which turned out to be true."

"Which could have been set up. Remember the Adelphi Hotel." Mike jabbed his finger on the table. "And while you were with Miss Parks, we saw Haswell come out of the manor house. Hutley had probably told him what to say."

"Haswell had already told us that someone killed Whiteside."

"No he hadn't."

"He did. Last night he said it was Green fascists who came up from London."

"That was a drunken rant. And he didn't tell us about the boat."

"Because he thought we were involved. Remember what he said about us being there to clean up the mess. The *last* thing he was going to do was tell us he was a witness. All that happened this morning was that someone told Haswell we were genuine."

If Mike was honest with himself, he couldn't remember the conversation, but the argument was beginning to sound compelling. "But Haswell's performance was probably just the warm-up act."

"You credit him with that much intelligence?"

"No, but Hutley or Miss Parks could have put him up to it."

"Hutley?" Brian laughed. "I'm not sure he has any more nous than Haswell." He gazed out of the window at the dense undergrowth and began to wish they had eaten before leaving Peterborough. "Anyway," he said, turning back to Mike, "I think Hildee Parks told Morris to spill the beans. She seemed pretty upset about Whiteside."

Mike stared at Brian without speaking.

"She had been crying yesterday when I saw her," Brian said, still looking out of the window.

"'Hildee?'" Mike said. "'Hildee?' I thought you didn't see her yesterday."

"I called in yesterday evening before I went out to the farm. She'd been crying," Brian repeated.

Recalling the state he had found Brian in that morning — and his obvious lack of sleep — Mike had been wondering if Brian had spent the whole evening in the bar. Perhaps Brian's socialising had been more extensive than he first thought. A broad grin spread across Mike's face. "Is there something you're not telling me?"

"No!" Brian retorted.

"What's she like then?"

"Let's see. Arrogant, sarcastic, humourless and mean-spirited." Brian resisted the temptation to suggest that Hildee and Mike would make an ideal couple.

"A woman like that could turn the tears on and off like a tap."

Brian remembered seeing Hildee's finger tremble as she identified Whiteside Farm on the map. There *were* tears, but they were tears of rage. He felt the desire to defend her but realised this would only fuel Mike's sarcasm, so he changed the subject. "What will you ask Fairchild when you see him?"

"If I get to see him."

"Well, whoever you see in Brussels."

"Oh, I'll probably start by asking him where he was the night Troxley was shot. Then I'll take his shoes away to see if there is any chicken shit from Whiteside Farm on them..." Mike noticed that Brian was ignoring him. "What will you be doing?" he asked.

Brian was reluctant to answer after Mike's previous outburst, but thought he might be able to turn the conversation back to the subject he wished to broach. "I was going to track down the phone number on that Inland Waterways authorisation, then see if I can find the person who issued Troxley's S-Card." He took a breath. "Is there any chance you could find out if Fairchild can remember someone making a call on a mobile phone during the Whiteside attack?"

"And you think, even if he could remember, that he would tell me?"

"Just a thought."

"Only just."

Brian was becoming annoyed with Mike. He knew really that he should take a walk down the train and cool off, but was reluctant to admit defeat. "There was a soldier staying at the Swan," he said, with a hint of aggression in his voice.

"Yes. We saw his name in the register. So?"

"He was only a low-ranking officer."

Mike shrugged. "Probably something to do with all those lorries."

"I don't think so. I don't think an officer from the transport division would be staying in a hotel. Not with all the barracks in the area. I think he was from army intelligence."

"Don't tell me," Mike sneered. " He was there spying on us."

Brian wondered whether to continue. In the end he decided that, even if Mike wasn't receptive, the opportunity to talk through his theories would clarify his own thoughts. "What if the army started an investigation at the same time we did? Even if it was only a casual inquiry involving plugging Troxley's name into a few databases? It wouldn't take them long to come up with the Troxley, Fairchild and Whiteside Farm connection."

Mike became visibly more attentive.

"Then," Brian continued, "just a few days later, and while the same policemen who are investigating Troxley's death were visiting Downham, Gerald Whiteside, a potential witness, is murdered. Now if you were in army intelligence, wouldn't you be asking yourself a few questions?"

"You mean the army think it's us?"

"What happens if they pick up on this S-Card trick?"

Mike shrugged again.

"All right then. Who has overall control of S-Card administration?"

"We do. The police."

"Who would have issued Troxley's S-Card number?"

"Immigration."

"Which is?"

"Part of the Home Office. Look..."

"Us again!" snapped Brian, reaching into his pocket and taking out the letter of authorisation the boatyard manger had been given. "Take a look at the signature on the bottom of that." He thrust the sheet of paper at Mike.

"That's the Home Secretary!" Mike exclaimed in horror.

"Us again." Brian snatched the sheet of paper back and returned it to his pocket. "Even Hutley could put all of that together in his sleep. If the army think that we are meddling in politics, they are going to start to wonder which way all the farmers will jump. Brian realised he had provided Mike with the ultimate wake-up call.

Mike went pale, ran his hand over his mouth and sank back in his seat. "We're really in the shit."

"And we're not alone. I think the person behind this has managed to get the army suspecting us and us suspecting the army — which probably gives them a completely free hand." Brian laid his notebook on the table and began to write. "Whatever you say, I think we need to look back a long way to find the answer to this. It's got something to do with Genesis and Whiteside Farm." He tore a page out and gave it to Mike. "If you can get the answers to these questions from Fairchild, we may get to the bottom of it."

Mike was in a daze. Until a few moments ago he had been able to dismiss Brian's contribution to this inquiry as a muddled collection of conspiracy theories. This was no longer possible. He read the list of questions, then looked up. Brian had buried his face in a battered hardback book. Mike tilted his head to read the title on the book's faded spine: 'All the President's Men', by Carl Bernstein and Bob Woodward.

*

"Take it easy, and keep your head down tomorrow," Mike warned Brian as they walked through the main entrance of the Home Office.

"No problem, sir," Brian replied. They went their separate ways at the second level. Mike needed to prepare a few things for his trip to Brussels, and Brian wanted some information from the data centre.

The room housing the Home Office mainframe and server farm still bore the scars from the time when a series of windows had been crudely cut into the partitioning walls. Most of the strip lights had gone and the computer centre now relied, for most of the day, on natural light. Moreover, the working hours of data-centre staff had been brought into line with those of the rest of the department, which, in the main, operated during daylight hours.

The IT manager was a tall over-friendly young man. If the S-Card system *could* be used to track down people, he would probably say so. But there was a chance that he had made the requisite modifications himself. In that case, the enquiry would be passed on to whoever ordered the changes. Did Brian really want to tweak the tail of the person who delivered Troxley to his killers

— and who could find out where he ate at night?

"We've found a stolen S-Card terminal," sighed Brian. "It's probably just some idiot who doesn't realise you need access to a phone line to make it work, but I'd rather check it out. Have you got a manual that gives a basic overview of the S-Card system?"

"Sure." The IT manager walked across the open-plan office and picked up a 30mm-thick spiral-bound manual. It had a blue cover, criss-crossed with tape, and was entitled 'S-Card Network Overview'. "This covers most of it. A bit heavy going in places. The connection details for the terminal are in the appendix."

"Thanks."

"Er, when do I get it back, Brian?"

"Tomorrow."

The IT manager laughed. "Not going to get much sleep tonight then."

*

'The S-Card system is based on national lottery terminals and X25 telephone connections. The terminals have been modified to accept one set of seven numbers instead of five sets of six (see appendix A). The supporting communications software is basically unchanged. Added as a backend system is a network of Windows NT servers which support an object-oriented database of users. Users in this case are all persons living within England, Scotland and Wales who have been issued with S-Card numbers.

Within the database each person is considered as an object with a list of attributes, such as their entitlement to food, their health etc. (see Appendix B). Another database contains Ivan's Restaurants, Health Centres, Hospitals and Crematoriums (see Appendix C). Attributes from objects within this database are exchanged with the user-database.

The backend software consists of Active Server Pages, dynamic HTML, Visual C++ routines and a number of conventional Microsoft Access databases within a client-server architecture. The development environment used is Microsoft Visual Studio Version 6.

By the time his train had reached South Kensington, Brian had thumbed through the manual several times. "Computer books," the man in the book shop said with astonishment. "*Now* you'll see some dust." He led Brian to the back of the shop. "You may have to go up the road to the college. All we have got are these," he said, pointing down at two shelves of thick, faded paperbacks. Just as the assistant had said, they were all covered in a layer of dust.

"That's the one, 'Client-Server Architecture'," Brian said, crouching down to pick up the book.

"Oh yes, brilliant it is! Just don't tell me how it ends. I'm only half way through it myself." The assistant laughed and returned to the counter.

*

By the time Trevor knocked on the door to say that everyone else was going to dinner, Brian had already got an elementary grasp of the S-Card system. He took the book with him to the restaurant. This time it was Stef who took it away from him and pretended to read it. She put on her glasses and folded back the first page. "'Networking for Dummies.' That sounds a good idea — computer programmers never seem to get out much." Even Brian, despite the fact that the joke was aimed at him, managed to laugh.

*

It was almost dark when Brian stopped reading. The manual, books, and the elementary computer experience gained at technical college, had provided him with a general understanding of how the S-Card system worked. For the purposes of the Troxley investigation, he had reached a sufficient level of understanding two hours ago. Since then, he had just carried on reading as a displacement activity. What Brian should have been doing was thinking about the investigation as a whole. So far, all the evidence fitted the hypothesis that Troxley was silenced because he had information that would embarrass Fairchild. On the surface, it looked like a cover-up by the party. But this was like a forged painting. It appears to be an original — until you use a magnifying glass. Only a closer examination reveals that some of the brush strokes are wrong.

*

Mike was not sure how long the two men had been following him. They seemed to have appeared from nowhere as he left the Ivan's Restaurant at Turnham Green. One man was tall and thin, the other was stocky. They fitted the description given by both the farm labourer and the woman in the boatyard. Perhaps the tall one had a moustache. Mike did not turn around to check. The last time he had looked, one of the men was unbuttoning his overcoat. Instead, he concentrated on losing them before he reached the underground station. He ducked into a side street, quickened his pace and disappeared down a narrow alley on his right. The alley led to a second side street, which connected with the main road. It would force the pair to split up; perhaps only one of them was armed.

But a mound of brick rubble blocked the alley. Mike, realising there was no time to double back, began to climb the pile of masonry. He slipped and almost fell. By the time he regained his balance, both men had entered the alley. The tall one did have a moustache. Both men had pistols in their hands.

*

On his return to the office, Mike had taken Troxley's S-Card from the briefcase found in the hotel room. Already he was toying with the idea of trying it; just to see if Harry the Print and Brian were right about the high seventh number. It would be the easiest way to flush out the army — if they were the ones behind the killings. He almost changed his mind about using the card. After all, it had been used on Troxley and was probably invalid by now. In the event, Mike decided nothing would be lost by a little experimentation.

The Ivan's chosen was a few hundred metres from Turnham Green underground station. At five-thirty in the evening it was busy. Mike thought he would be able to lose himself amongst the other diners and, at the same time, watch the street outside through the large windows of the restaurant. The operator reacted with surprise after entering the card into the machine. He grabbed the face mask which had been hanging around his neck and pulled it over his mouth. He said nothing as he hurriedly pushed a red badge across the counter and made it clear that he wanted Mike to pass through to the segregated section of the restaurant.

Far from being lost in the crowd, Mike was almost on his own in the part of the restaurant reserved for diners with potentially contagious diseases. After collecting his food from the unmanned serving counter, he sat as far away as possible from the pale young man wheezing in the corner of the room who was encouraging his equally pale son to eat.

That was how it worked; how they found Troxley. Troxley's number flashed up on a computer screen somewhere and the guard was alerted. Mike had been right about everything except the guard. He had bolted his food, and periodically glanced at the guard to see if he was using his radio. Preoccupied with the soldier, Mike failed to notice a car stopping a few metres down the road from the restaurant. He did not see the two men who got out and positioned themselves in an alleyway on the opposite side of the street. He did not notice the taller of the two men watching the restaurant through a pair of binoculars.

*

Now, as Mike tried to walk backwards up the pile of brick rubble, it was the taller of the two men who raised his pistol first. While in the restaurant, Mike was still convinced it was the army who had tracked down Troxley and who were about to arrest him too. Now he gave little thought to the prospect that Brian was probably right all along — he was just waiting for the shot. When it came, he felt nothing. There was a sound no louder than a door closing. At first, he thought the gunman had missed. Then the tall man staggered and fell forwards. The stocky man grabbed his own pistol and turned. As he did, there was another shot and he too fell to the ground.

A young man dressed in jeans and a tee-shirt walked slowly down the alley. "Down on the ground! Face down! Now!" he shouted, pointing a pistol at Mike's head.

Mike lay face down on the ground. Footsteps got closer and one of the wounded gunmen groaned. There were two shots and the groaning stopped. Mike felt the cold barrel of the gun on the back of his neck. "Papers," the man in the tee-shirt whispered, in an accent Mike could not place. Reaching into his pocket, and grazing his hand on the paving as he did so, Mike retrieved his ID. "Slowly," the man hissed.

After a few seconds, Mike's ID card dropped onto the ground, beside his head. Again the gun was pressed into the back of his neck "Count to fifty, then get up," the man said. Mike counted, and listened to the gunman's footsteps fading into the distance.

*

"You look terrible," Linda said, when Mike walked through the door.

"Bit of an accident on the way home."

144

"Anyone hurt?"

Mike was going explain what had happened, but decided against it. "A man collapsed in the street at Turnham Green. I spent an hour getting someone to take him to hospital."

"Have you eaten?"

"Yes," Mike replied, but omitted to say that his dinner was spread across the alley and between the bodies of two gunmen. It was then that he noticed that Linda also looked pale. "Still hurts, does it?" He gently stroked the side of her face.

"Don't," she said, wincing. "I'm going to have it looked at tomorrow. I think it must have an abscess under it."

Mike put his arms around her "I'll stay. I'll tell Langford I can't go."

"No. There's nothing you can do. I'll be right as rain by the time you get back." Linda kissed him and smiled. "You go and enjoy your holiday."

Mike laughed. "Some holiday."

5

Friday 23rd August 2041

The train crawled slowly through the Kent countryside, through the overgrown orchards and decaying towns. At one point, Mike caught a glimpse of the bridge that formed part of the unused high-speed rail link from London to the Channel Tunnel. Every year there were promises, or rumours of promises, that work would recommence on the link, but there was still a labour shortage, and the manpower needed to bring the new line into service was fully occupied maintaining existing track. Once through the tunnel, the train picked up speed. Outside was the wildness that was northern France: a dense young forest that extended from the coast to Paris. The only roads that connected Calais to the capital and Lille ran alongside the railway line. These roads were for use by railway workers and the army. Every two or three kilometres the train passed an armoured car or a lorry filled with soldiers.

Mike watched the other railway line. It did not waver by a millimetre. Once, such precision engineering was taken for granted. Now, like air travel, it was a marvel: a minor miracle performed by twenty-five per cent of all the railway engineers in France and Belgium.

*

Deputy Commissioner Stephen Langford stood in the doorway of Brian's office. "You're going to be all right today while Mike's away?"

"Yes. He's left me with one or two things to follow up." Brian picked up the copy of the authorisation the Home Office — Inland Waterways Security Division had provided for the boatyard owners. "I hope you don't mind, but I've asked Johnny Coates to check this out." He handed the sheet of paper to Langford. "It's something we picked up in Peterborough. There's no such thing as the Inland Waterways Security Division at the Home Office. I thought if Johnny could track down the address where that phone was installed we might be able to catch someone red-handed."

"Very good." Langford turned to walk away, then realised he had not answered Brian's question. "Oh yes. That's fine, by the way. Using Coates, I mean."

Pressing the 'alt' and tab keys on his computer, Brian recalled the browser software he had hidden just before Langford entered the office. The phone rang. It was Johnny. Brian closed down the web browser completely. "Well, what did you find out?"

"Well, Brian, er sir, it's right next door. Well, Lewisham Street anyway. British Telecom thought I was mad. Apparently the order was placed by us."

"That figures. Where are you now?"

"I'm at the Storey's Garden end of the road. When I walked past the address there was someone in there, working in an office on the second floor."

"Wait there. I'll be along in a few seconds. Don't do anything until I get there."

*

Johnny heard Brian approach. "No-one's gone in or out," he said, without taking his eyes off the street.

"Got a gun?" Brian asked, quickly realising that Johnny had and that that was the only reason he was wearing a jacket on a blazing hot August day.

"Yes, but I've never fired it. Is this person dangerous?"

"Well, she hasn't killed anyone this week."

"And last week?"

"Two that we know of."

Reaching into his pocket, Johnny took out a .38 calibre revolver and checked that it was loaded. "Well, I'm ready if you are."

The door to the house was unlocked. None of the blackened brass plates on the wall outside said anything about Waterways Security. Brian went in first, edging his way along the first-floor landing while Johnny stood half way up the stairs, pointing his gun at the office door. There was no answer when Brian knocked, but the door flew open when he kicked it. Stepping backwards, Brian pointed his revolver into the room and waited for Johnny to come up the stairs.

The room was empty. Brian and Johnny searched the adjoining rooms. Eventually Johnny discovered the fire escape. He climbed out of the window and descended the metal spiral staircase. Brian ran back down to the front door and out into the street. They met up at the intersection of Old Queen Street and Storey's Garden. "Anything?" Brian asked.

Johnny shook his head. "Not a sign."

Brian pulled the photofit picture out of his pocket. "This her?"

Johnny studied the picture. "Could be. I only saw her side view. I didn't want to stare in case I gave myself away." He shuffled his feet. "She must have noticed me anyway. Sorry about that."

"Well, that's the way it goes. You can't expect to run a proper surveillance operation with just one person."

They returned to the house. "Combined fax, voice and modem," Johnny said, crouching down next to a junction box fixed to the skirting board.

"Still warm," Brian said, putting his hand against the kettle standing on a tray on top of a filing cabinet. He ran his finger across the tray. "Been eating food — obviously didn't want to be seen at the local Ivan's." Pulling on his gloves, he reached across the desk to the small fax machine. "Let's try 'last number redial'."

"I wouldn't bother if I were you." Johnny pointed to the wire that ran up the wall. It had been cut in two places, and a section a metre long had been removed.

"Why the hell do that?"

"You answered that one yourself," Johnny replied.

"What good does that do them? British Telecom can give us a list of all the calls to this number."

"It buys them time." Johnny looked at his watch. "It will take Telecom at least three hours to get back to me. As it's Friday, they may not have an answer until Monday — especially as they've done me one favour already today."

"See your point." Brian crossed the room to a large drawing board. Clamped onto it was a complicated mechanism consisting of a set of links. Moving the larger arm of the mechanism caused the smaller one to mimic its motion in miniature.

"What's that then?" Johnny asked.

"Some sort of copying machine." From under the larger arm Brian extracted a piece of paper, marked out in squares, and held it up to the light. "This gets more puzzling every day." He placed the piece of paper on the desk. "Right! Let's leave this lot for Amanda to sort out. What I need you to do is get that list of calls from Telecom and find out who owns this place — and who it was rented to."

"Yes, sir," Johnny said.

It was only when Johnny snapped to attention that Brian realised he had acquired an air of authority.

"It's still 'Brian'. I haven't been promoted yet." Brian smiled.

"And the way this is going you won't be calling me 'sir' this side of Christmas."

*

"Is Mike Allchurch there?"

Brian recognised Dr Tim Hutchinson's voice. "No, he's in Brussels today."

"Very funny, laddie. Now put him on."

"Seriously, Hutch, he took the Eurostar this morning."

There was a moment's silence at the other end of the line. Brian raised his shoulder to keep the receiver against his ear while he returned to his web browsing. "Well, you had better come down here yourself then," Hutch said eventually. "And look in Mike's drawer — if his gun is there, bring it with you." Brian sighed deeply and put down the phone. When he pulled Mike's drawer open, a bottle of water rolled to the front. He found the bottle of fat-busting pills, Harry the Print's glasses, a notebook and, right at the back, a revolver. Taking his handkerchief, Brian carefully wrapped it around the gun and put it in his pocket. Seeing Harry's glasses in the drawer reminded him what a callous bastard Mike could be at times.

*

"Voilà!" Hutch pulled the covers off two bodies. Standing between the two trolleys, he held his arms up and let the sheets fall to the floor. "That's French, by the way." Walking slowly towards Brian, the doctor waved his hands over the corpses. "One minute a mild-mannered middle-aged civil servant — the next a crazed assassin. They were right, you know. If you want to cut the murder rate, just lock up all the 'ordinary blokes next door who keep themselves to themselves'.

"What are you talking about?" Brian gazed at the two naked cadavers.

"Your boss, Mike Allchurch. And these — his handiwork." Hutch stepped back again. "Take a look for yourself. One shot in the back, the other in the chest. Both finished off with a bullet in the head."

Brian laughed. "You're joking! Are you saying that Mike did this?"

"That's what the guys who brought them in said. Your boss

149

called in last night and asked for a meat wagon and this is what the driver found. Did you bring the gun?"

Brian took the revolver out of his pocket. Hutch noticed the handkerchief. "Being careful, I see. The investigation's getting a bit fraught," he muttered under his breath. Holding the gun to his nose, he shook his head, then peered down the barrel. "Huh, there's dust in there. Well, I guess it wasn't him after all."

"Anything come in with them?"

Hutch pointed to two plastic bags on the lab bench. Each bag contained a pistol and a mobile phone. One of the bags contained an S-Card. "This card was the only ID there was," he said, handing the bag to Brian. "Neither of the guns had been fired recently."

Through the bag, Brian could see that the card was Troxley's. "The idiot!" he said.

Picking up the two sheets, Hutch started to cover the bodies. "Worked it out then? Good! So what do I do with these?"

Brian reached down, squeezed the leg of one of the bodies and smacked his lips, then waited for Hutch to explode with rage.

"Very funny, laddie!" Hutch snapped.

Brian, puzzled that he had got off so lightly, wandered out of the room.

*

Why were only half the sites attacked? Brian was tempted to type the question, word for word, into the search engine on *The Guardian*'s website. Why Downham? Why not Saffron Walden or Newmarket? The location of all the GM test sites had been published the previous year. Saffron Walden, in Essex, was next to the M11 motorway, and the Newmarket site was 300 metres from a junction on the A11. The Downham site, however, was over two kilometres from the A10 — itself not a major road. At first, Brian had thought it might be the type of crops. Maybe the oilseed rape was being singled out. But at Royston, in Hertfordshire, a field of wheat had been attacked.

Now something else was troubling Brian — something Hutch had said. What was there to 'work out' about the bodies? Mike had tried Troxley's S-Card. The two gunmen had tracked him down. Then the two gunmen... No, he *hadn't* worked it out. If Mike hadn't killed the two gunmen, who had? Who were the gunmen anyway?

Something at the Adelphi Hotel had been wrong. Perhaps it

was the passport. Then there was Downham and the letter at the boatyard. What was puzzling Brian most, however, was Hildee Parks — something she said or did. He thought back to his two meetings with her. Without Mike, would he be allowed to go over the whole picture again with a magnifying glass? Were the two gunmen Mike stumbled across acting alone, or were there others? Was it only 'high seven' numbers that could be tracked using the S-Card system, or could his own card be traced?

Then he remembered the map. It was the first thought that had entered Brian's head when he woke that morning. Hildee Parks had walked over to her desk and taken out a map that was forty years out of date. Why was it there? Why hadn't it been filed away somewhere? She had been using it herself. She either knew or suspected why Gerald Whiteside had been killed. The excitement of solving the puzzle, however, gave way to apprehension once Brian realised what he had to do.

Brian telephoned Hutch's lab. "You won't need those mobile phones. Mind if I borrow them?" Hutch refused at first, claiming that they were needed for fingerprints, and only relented when Brian pointed out that any prints on them were likely to be either Mike's or the victims'.

Hildee Parks and her map. Brian thought about it again. Each time he did so, it was harder to put it out of his mind. How would he get to her in the middle of the military-controlled rural zone? The first meal he ate would flag him up on the S-Card system. How could he drop out of sight for a weekend?

*

A large map of England hung on the wall of the Army Liaison office. All the army-controlled zones, including the rural ones, were marked in red. The East Anglian zone stretched from Cambridge to the coast. At the coast itself, however, there was a demilitarised corridor two miles wide. "Why the gap?" Brian asked the liaison officer.

The officer shrugged. "Army doesn't like fish?"

"No, seriously, does the zone really stop short?"

"Yep, and, strangely enough, it is down to fish. Boats come in from Belgium, Holland and France. The European navy control fishing. If a soldier gets into a fight with a French fisherman — not that he would, mind you — then we would end up with a diplomatic incident on our hands." The officer smiled. "An even worse one if the navy and our army start slugging it out in the streets of King's Lynn." He studied Brian for a moment, watching him trace his finger along the railway line from Cambridge to King's Lynn, then down the coast of East Anglia. "Why do you ask?"

Brian stepped away from the map as though he had been caught doing something wrong. "Oh, a friend of mine lives on the coast. They've asked me up there for the weekend."

"Bandit country." The officer noticed the worried look on Brian's face. "It's OK. Just tell the guards on the train that you're passing through."

One problem solved, but that did not overcome the difficulty posed by the S-Card system. Brian would be treading on the tails of people who had unconventional access to data he generated each time he ate. He could take a bicycle, which would mean he didn't have to borrow one in Downham and give his number to the stationmaster — but he could not skip a weekend of meals. He too needed access to the S-Card system. Brian then remembered what he had seen on the computer screen in Andrew Cameron's factory. It was certainly not a computer game, and the two youths had been anxious not to be observed. Brian regretted having been so keen to return the S-Card system manual that morning. He recalled seeing the youths studying a black window containing groups of numbers: eight or ten lines, more than four groups in each line, separated by dots. He was as sure as he could be that the numbers were network addresses and that the youths were hacking into something.

Next, the travel plan. He would be travelling, as far as the guards on the train were concerned, to the coast. If he arrived as everyone was returning from work, he could slip off the train at Downham station without being noticed. Brian checked the hotels in the coastal towns to find a likely place for a holiday-maker to stay.

Now it was time to obtain some background information about Hildee Parks, to make sure that when he appeared on her doorstep she would not call the army and have him arrested. Brian thought back to his last encounter with her — perhaps being arrested by the army would be preferable. *The Guardian*'s website revealed several articles about the Parks family: typically vocal farmers bemoaning the destruction of the countryside by a government with an urban agenda. Then he found the Parks's farm bed-and-breakfast website. Brian printed off the front page and the booking form. Then he read the article about Hildee Parks's father a second time.

It was settled. He would go. But in truth Brian had decided two days ago that he would return to Downham. This unofficial investigation was merely a way of justifying the trip.

*

David Fairchild surveyed the Brussels skyline from the window of his office in the Rue de Rivoli administrative building. The city, like London, and most others in Europe, had retreated into the centre and left the rest to decay. Once, the botanical gardens below had been a retreat for office workers escaping the noise and fumes of the cars that thundered around the six-lane inner ring road. Now the wilderness they had become was a constant reminder that what Nature had done to the suburbs and the residential sectors it could do to the rest of the city.

"Why Troxley?" Fairchild murmured. "Of all the things they could have picked on..." He returned to his seat behind the large glass-topped desk. Facing him, a file resting on his knee, was Alan Mitchell, head of security for the UKGA. In addition to dealing with overall security for the party, Mitchell acted as Fairchild's right-hand man. Having joined the Green Alliance a month after Fairchild had been released from prison, he knew full well what 'all the things they could have picked on' were.

Why choose Troxley and the Whiteside Farm incident? Why not call Fairchild to account for his treatment of the Church? For the way the party reacted when the Church of England's access to food supplies threatened to undermine the party's hold over the population of Britain? Using their large and efficient publicity machine, the party made sure the media received detailed accounts of every food-poisoning case which could be traced back to a Church-run shop or soup kitchen. It was the right thing to do, of course. The Church was using food to boost its congregations. But it was politically naive, and the power base it had built up could have been hijacked by the Socialists or one of the other parties. Then what? Chaos again.

There was the penal system and the way it was used to bolster the ranks of farm and factory workers decimated by successive epidemics of influenza and cholera. And yes, the crackdowns on petty theft and evasion of social responsibilities were driven by the need for more labour. But what was the alternative? At least everyone got enough to eat, eventually.

If someone wanted to attack Fairchild, why not dig out the piece of paper which gave members of the armed forces immunity from prosecution during their struggle to contain the anarchists in East London? Or the document which waived the right to free association and travel within rural zones? His signature was on both of them.

He never actually signed anything associated with euthanasia. However, a tidal wave of ageing baby-boomers from the previous century was swamping hospitals already overburdened with malnourished flu victims. The party had prioritised health care in favour of people of working age. Doctors, obliged to reduce suffering, participated in assisted suicide for aged cancer victims. The more resources were stretched, the more widespread and formal assisted suicide became. With an eye to the immunities being offered to the armed forces, doctors too sought protection from future retribution. No one regulation or statute saw euthanasia pass into law. The legal framework supporting it was still confused. Nevertheless, despite the fact that fingers could be pointed at any one of a hundred people with varying amounts of blood on their hands, it was Fairchild everyone held responsible.

Fairchild slammed his hand down on the desk "It's got to be Simitovich. He's the one with most to gain. Ivan's out of the way. With me gone he would be home."

"Home in a nest full of shit," Mitchell said, without looking up from the file. "If he destroys you over Troxley, he destroys the party. Simitovich is too strongly associated with the party to survive that."

"But Troxley is a double-edged sword. If Troxley and I conspired, then I'm a villain. If Troxley hoodwinked me, then I'm a fool. The only way I can prove I'm innocent is to prove I'm an idiot." Fairchild tilted his chair backwards and stared at the ceiling. "Perhaps he's going to make me an offer: resign, and the investigation ends. Perhaps that's what he said to Ivan."

"We would have heard if that was the case."

Fairchild let the chair rock forward and rested his elbows on the desk. "OK. So who are we ruling out and who are we ruling in? Simitovich out. The Americans?"

"Out."

"But Troxley was American. Has lived in America for the past forty years. Well, until a week ago."

"The Americans have got too much to lose. We are on the verge of signing a trade agreement covering technology and oil.

Ivan was negotiating a huge contract for grain. You've heard the way Simitovich talks about the Americans. No. I think they are only interested in maintaining the status quo."

"Well, that just leaves the conspiracy theories. Farmers, the police, the army..."

"Farmers? Not a happy bunch but too much to lose. The police?" Mitchell looked up and smiled. "Well, that's me really. Do we rule that out?" Fairchild laughed. "That just leaves the army — and they have got more to lose than anybody."

"Well then?"

"Another conspiracy. Simitovich and someone else."

"Who?"

Mitchell shrugged. "This is just thinking aloud really. Simitovich has been talking a lot about liberalisation and democracy recently."

It was 'liberalisation' that worried Fairchild. Once the party's stranglehold on the press was relaxed, it would only be a matter of time before an ambitious journalist began reassessing Fairchild's reputation. Liberalisation would go hand in hand with increasing prosperity — and a new chattering class would start passing judgement on his leadership. He had taken many difficult decisions, some of which had caused a great deal of suffering. Judged from the comfort of a society where starvation, violence and disease were no longer the norm, he might well be viewed as a latter-day Eichmann or Pol Pot.

"But *we've* been talking about liberalisation — and so has Ivan."

"In a way, we've got Ivan to blame for this situation," Mitchell said.

Fairchild gave Mitchell a quizzical look. "How do you work that one out?"

"Well, he started talking about democracy a year or so ago..." Fairchild was about to interrupt, but Mitchell raised his hand. "And, he started to implement the constitutional reforms that would make it possible."

"Well, that made sense. Anyone who has seen what happened to Russia when it liberalised forty years ago realises you have to do that. There have to be some controls."

Mitchell smiled. "Even if only to make sure we are the only party that can be voted into government."

"You know that isn't true. Having a constitution that encompasses environmental issues wouldn't stop elected representatives forming social-democrat or conservative groups."

"But it does limit their flexibility. If all economic policies have to be drawn up with sustainability as a primary consideration, then elected representatives have little room for manoeuvre. Most of the opposition policies would be identical to ours. What Ivan is saying is, 'yes, you can vote for anyone you like, but they must do exactly what we say.'"

"That's far too simplistic."

"It may sound that way, but if you were hoping that democracy was going to change everything, you would be a disappointed person. And if you were a person who had a vested interest in change, you might throw your weight behind someone who was willing to introduce democracy without a lot of constitutional reform."

"Such as Simitovich."

Mitchell nodded. "Yes. Such as Simitovich."

"So who do you suspect?"

"Well, if I am right the list is a long one: budding industrialists, black marketeers hoping to become legitimate retailers, farmers, you name it."

"I still think the farmers aren't that unhappy with their lot."

"Maybe, but we'll probably never find out. Whoever is pushing will disappear as soon as the investigation is over."

"How long will it take?"

"The end of this week."

"This week?" Fairchild said with surprise.

"Simitovich is in London for a series of interviews and television appearances. My guess is that the investigation will be made public so that he can make the most of it during the television broadcast on Saturday."

Fairchild sat back and ran his fingers through his hair. "This week. So what are we doing about it? What about this policeman? All...?"

"Allchurch." Mitchell looked down and read from his notes. "Mr. Mike Allchurch. Commander of the Central London Division of the Metropolitan Police." He looked up again. "Well, what we are not going to do is let him interview you. That would suggest you are implicated in the killing of Troxley. I can't force him to close the investigation, because that would suggest a cover-up." He stood up and walked over to the window. "We have to be careful with this one — someone is leaking information to the press."

"Do we know who?"

"Could be anyone. Probably someone spreading rumours in the Ivan's in Farringdon Lane, where *The Guardian*'s editorial staff eat, but we haven't managed to track them down yet. The UK press we can control; the American press we can't. So far, only *The Guardian* has picked it up. We have told the editor to make a big show of digging around — just to keep the informant happy. If we try to put a lid on the story they will start talking to US publications."

"Why haven't they done that already?"

"My guess is that they would like you to resign rather than have to push you. Going public before the police report is finished would be messy. Leaking the story to *The Guardian* is just an easy way of applying a bit of pressure."

"But what about Allchurch?"

Mitchell gazed down at the street below, then looked at his watch. "Aul's man should be taking him out of the loop."

"You're having him *killed*, *here*, in *Brussels*?"

*

Mike walked down the Rue de Jardine towards Rogier. He had given up weaving his way along the pavement. Every few metres it was cordoned off, forcing pedestrians to walk in the road. Mitchell's claim that Fairchild was tied up for the rest of the day was less than convincing. The booking for the hotel had obviously been made before Mike arrived at the office. They were just buying time.

There were more barricades at Rogier. The square looked as though it was being cleared after an explosion. Groups of workers, watched over by a guard who was leaning on the railings at the top of the steps leading down to the métro, shovelled broken glass and masonry onto the back of a lorry. There was also a guard outside the rear entrance to the Palace Hotel. This entrance could only be reached through a small gap in the barricades that had been erected along the edge of the square. The tall glass-clad building in front of Mike was not accessible at all. Signs hung on steel mesh told passers-by to beware of falling debris. The warnings were academic: the panes of glass which fell from the upper stories of the deserted eleven-floor hotel would often glide across the width of the square before smashing on the ground.

This was not where Mike wanted to be. With Linda ill, he should have been returning to London. The decision to book him into the Astoria seemed to be some sort of put-down. Most visitors from outside Belgium were accommodated in the Palace Hotel. The Astoria was used, in the main, for low-ranking party officials and bureaucrats from other parts of the country. Unlike the Palace, the Astoria had no computerised registration system. Mike had to write his S-Card number in the register, then wait while the receptionist checked the entry. It would be Friday, when the register was taken over to the Palace and all the entries were logged in the computer there, before Mike would show up on the system. He did not realise that this was precisely the reason Mitchell had chosen that particular hotel.

Mike climbed the stairs to the second floor. His room tapered towards a narrow window that looked out onto the crumbling brickwork and grime-covered windows of the neighbouring building. Paint flaked from the walls, one of which was curved, further reducing the already limited floor space next to the single bed. Mike was reluctant to close the door and propped it open with his travel bag. Intending to open the window, he had only taken three steps into the room when the travel bag was flung onto the bed and the door slammed shut. Turning, he immediately recognised the shoes, jeans and gait of the person who had dispatched the two gunmen in London. The gun, with silencer attached, also looked familiar — and for the second time in two days it was pointing at his head.

Even though he knew that his own gun was still in his desk drawer in England, Mike nevertheless plunged his hand into his jacket pocket. "Easy now, Mr. Allchurch," the gunman hissed. "Unlike in London, the discovery of a dead body in a Brussels hotel room generates very little interest."

*

Mitchell turned to face Fairchild. "No chance. Good help is hard to find these days." He walked back across the room and sat down. "He's not so much being taken out of the loop as being sent round a bigger one."

"What are you talking about?"

"Well, you see," — Mitchell crossed his legs, then clasped his hands together and rested them on his knee — "Peter Aul has a plan."

Fairchild groaned, and tilted his head back. "As if things weren't bad enough."

"No. Hear this out. Aul is lying low in Germany at the moment. He was there visiting his son when Vlachos resigned. If he hadn't been in Germany, who knows? Uncle Ivan would probably still be in power."

"The plan," said Fairchild impatiently.

"At the moment, Vlachos hasn't got anyone to investigate the allegations which forced his resignation. Now, Allchurch seems to be an Ivan fan. He spent a couple of years in the Ukraine when the volunteer work camps were set up. We could send him to the Ukraine to be briefed by Ivan — he might even be able to dig around a bit. I suspect that the person who dished the dirt on Ivan is also dishing the dirt on you. If Allchurch can come up with something before the weekend, we might be able to piss on Simitovich's firework."

"Slim chance." Fairchild thought for a moment. "If this policeman is such a fan of Ivan and, supposedly, a friend of ours, why don't we leave him in place to continue the investigation?"

"It seems there may be a problem with doing that. Aul's man stumbled across Allchurch when he was trailing the hit men who killed the farmer — and, for all we know, Troxley as well. It seems that our friendly policeman would have been the next victim if Aul's man hadn't terminated them."

Fairchild sighed. "'Terminated.' Now I remember why I don't like Aul's plans. If this man Allchurch goes to the Ukraine, will the investigation in England come to an end?"

"That's what we thought. The only other person on the case is Allchurch's assistant." Mitchell thumbed through his notes. "Tyler. According to Aul's man and my contact at the Home Office, Tyler is a bit of a clown. Young man, likes a drink. Didn't seem to be taking the investigation seriously." Mitchell smiled. "Apparently he collected Troxley's body in an ice-cream van."

For the first time that day, Fairchild laughed. "So we are fairly confident his report is not going to do us any damage."

"Well, that's what we thought."

"You seem to be referring to Mr. Tyler in the past tense. Don't tell me Aul's man has 'terminated' him as well."

Mitchell pushed a piece of paper across the desk. "Read that. It's a list of the questions that Tyler wanted Allchurch to ask you."

"'One: On the night of the attack, did Troxley make any calls using his mobile phone while he was actually in the field? Two: Did the minibus enter West Farm Way from the Littleport direction? If so, did Troxley choose this route? Three: Did Troxley choose..."' Fairchild read the rest of the questions to himself, then dropped the list onto the desk. "Damn! The report might be dull but the appendix is going to make interesting reading."

"We may have to deal with Mr. Tyler when the time comes."

Fairchild glared at Mitchell. "The 'we', I assume, is 'you' — not one of Aul's people." He waited until Mitchell shook his head, then picked up the list, folded it, and handed it back across the desk. "Anyway, what if Allchurch doesn't want to go?"

*

"And what if I don't want to go?" Mike picked up the Kiev guidebook and the ticket the gunman had thrown onto Mike's travel bag.

"There's a piece of paper inside, telling you how to find Ivan's house." The gunman had ignored Mike's protests. Putting his gun in his pocket, he pulled a chair from under a small writing desk and sat down. "When you arrive in Kiev you are to say that you are going to question Ivan Vlachos about an attempt to impede an investigation into the affairs of David Fairchild. Then passport control will call security, security will call someone at the party, and in thirty minutes you will be on your way to see Ivan Vlachos. When you get there, tell him Peter Aul sent you."

"I still haven't said I'll go."

"Mr. Allchurch, my job is to persuade you to go to see Ivan in Kiev and to make sure you don't cause us problems in England." Aul's man slipped his hand into his pocket. "How I do that has been left entirely to me."

"How will you explain *your* presence in Kiev?"

Aul's man smiled "I will not be accompanying you. I will be staying in Belgium, for reasons connected with my health."

"So there's nothing to stop me going to Kiev and then flying straight back to London?"

"As far as I'm concerned, nothing at all." He shrugged. "But your boss may ask who you met in Kiev if you didn't go there to interview Ivan."

Mike sighed. "OK. When's the flight then?"

*

The interior of the carriage glowed orange as the early evening sun flooded through the windows of the small diesel train gliding lazily across the flat Fenland landscape. People seated around Brian were in high spirits. With another week of work behind them, most were planning their weekends. He had seen the two guards get on at Cambridge. Train guards carried revolvers instead of the rifles or machine guns used by the soldiers guarding the railway stations. They were also more jovial than other soldiers. Brian could hear their light-hearted banter in the next carriage. Once again, he ran through his story and tried to recall the bus and railway timetables he had memorised earlier that day.

The original plan had involved a weekend break in Hunstanton, but this was shelved when Brian could find no evidence of habitable hotels. There was only one boarding house on the East Anglian coast, in the small town of Cromer, which still advertised rooms on the World Wide Web.

Plans based on a fiction seldom bear up well under scrutiny. Brian was to find his imaginary itinerary no exception. The sliding door in front of him was rammed open and the two guards marched into the carriage.

"IDs pl-ease." The first guard, cap pulled down over his eyes, was imitating a drill sergeant. Most of the passengers took little notice of him; some did not even bother looking up as they held out their identification cards for inspection. He worked his way down one side of the carriage, checking cards, mumbling 'yes' or 'OK', and sometimes exchanging a few words with the regular passengers. Brian took out his ID and offered it to the second guard.

Stepping back, the soldier steadied himself against the seat opposite.

"Police. Here on official business?"

"No, just a weekend break," Brian replied, reaching out to retrieve his card. Realising that this was a mistake, he withdrew his hand.

The soldier was a regular in the East Anglian Regiment. His face was thin and tanned. He had a sharp nose, on which was balanced a pair of reading glasses. He studied the photograph on the ID card at length, then looked over his glasses at Brian. There was no doubt that the photograph on the card was of Brian. The guard merely wanted to make eye contact and assert his authority over someone who, possibly, outranked him. Once he had bolstered his ego sufficiently, the card would be handed back and the game would be over. Brian had been guilty of doing exactly the same thing on numerous occasions. But the card was not handed

161

back.

"And where are you going?" The guard's voice trailed away.

"Cromer."

"Changing at Ely for the Norwich train?"

There was no point in lying. The guards themselves would be getting off the train at Ely. "No, I'm travelling to King's Lynn — getting a bus to Hunstanton, then another to Cromer."

"A strange route."

"I wanted to travel along the coast."

"Is that your bicycle on the other side of the door?"

"Yes."

"Don't they have bicycles in Cromer?"

"I don't know. I haven't been there before."

The soldier unbuttoned the top pocket of his tunic and took out a small notebook and a pencil. "Where are you staying?"

"Cromer."

"So you said. The name of the hotel, please."

"Fairview."

The soldier wrote down the name of the hotel and then copied down some details from Brian's ID card.

The first soldier had finished checking the passengers on the other side of the carriage and those seated behind Brian. Now he was waiting, filling in the time by talking to a middle-aged couple. Like others who had decided to stay in the army, he had managed to get a posting near home. Most of the passengers he knew by sight, and some by name.

Brian's soldier was less convivial. "You realise that it is an offence to be in a rural zone without permission?" he asked, making the question sound like the preamble to an arrest.

Refusing to be rattled, Brian replied calmly. "I'm just passing through."

"Have a pleasant journey." The soldier thrust the ID card at Brian and, replacing the notebook in his pocket, rejoined his colleague.

The two soldiers, and many of the passengers, got off when the train stopped at Ely. Brian watched the jovial guard run across the platform to join a group of soldiers who were laughing and engaging in mild horseplay. The soldier who had interrogated Brian did not join the others. As the train pulled out of the station, Brian watched him take the notebook from his pocket and walk towards the ticket hall.

*

A man wheeling a bicycle off a train was a memorable event. When he failed to show up at King's Lynn, the army would soon track down someone who remembered him getting off here at Downham. So when the train came to a halt, Brian did not stand up straight away. It was not only the army he was worried about. Someone might contact London and ask why a policeman from the Met. was wandering around East Anglia. He looked at his watch. Was the office empty now? If it was, he would be able to explain away his trip in person first thing on Monday morning. Were his assumptions about Hildee Parks as wide of the mark as his belief that travelling into East Anglia by train was simple?

As far as Brian could tell, no-one noticed him pushing the bicycle out of the station. Once in the street, he rode off, as confidently as possible, in the direction of Nordelph. It struck him that travelling here by train, rather than by car, had altered his perception of Downham. Then he remembered something Mike had said, about how the car distorted everything. So this was what he meant. For the first time Brian appreciated how much Mike's perception of the world must have changed when private motoring ended — but still he failed to understand how a car provided anyone with freedom.

A face appeared briefly at one of the windows when Brian hammered on the door of Nordelph Manor. After a considerable delay, the door slowly swung open.

Outwardly at least, Hildee did not seem surprised. "The policeman, Mr. ...?"

"Brian Tyler."

"Yes. Mr. Tyler. You need the map again?" Hildee stepped back and pushed the door wide open. She was dressed in a tee shirt and shorts. Her right hand was in her pocket and stayed there, even when Brian stepped forward to shake hands.

Brian did not notice Hildee become tense when he reached into the pocket of his jacket — or relax again when he retrieved a piece of paper. "I noticed that you do bed and breakfast, and I thought it would be a nice place to spend the weekend."

Taking the piece of paper in her left hand, Hildee flicked it open. She read the page printed from the manor's website. "Very droll, Mr. Tyler." She stared at Brian for a moment, then sighed. "You had better come in."

The door slammed behind Brian as he walked towards the

office. "Not in there," Hildee called out. "In the study." She held open a door on the other side of the entrance hall.

The study was the same size as the office. It contained two sofas and three matching chairs, set in a semicircle around a large fireplace. In front of both the windows stood polished mahogany tables, on which collections of framed photographs and china ornaments had been arranged. Brian hung his rucksack on a dining chair that stood beside the first table. Seeing Hildee frown, he lifted the rucksack off the chair and put it on the floor. "If it's going to be a lot of trouble, I can go back into town and stay at the Swan. It's just that the last time I was here you said..."

"Yes, I did. If you ever come back, you can stay here, I said." She took a breath — something that Brian remembered his schoolteacher used to do before delivering a lecture. "You know how, when you meet someone while you are away from home, you sometimes say, 'If ever you are in London, look me up.'"

"Well, no....," Brian started to reply.

"Well, what would happen if they all took you up on it? You would have a house full of people. I was only being polite. Perhaps you have a problem with such concepts. I imagine..." Then she noticed how dejected Brian looked. Lost for words, she stared at him as he picked up his rucksack and walked away. "Are you here in some official capacity?" she asked, just as he reached the door.

"No," Brian said, without turning around.

"Here without permission?"

"Yes." He looked over his shoulder at her.

"What did you tell the army?"

"Said I was just passing through, on my way to Cromer."

She gave a short laugh. "Who the hell would be going to Cromer?" Then, shrugging her shoulders, she pointed to one of the chairs. "Sit down, you silly man. It will take a few minutes to get a room ready." Brian had just enough time to leap to one side as Hildee strode out of the room and slammed the door behind her.

The room fell silent, apart from the sound of Hildee's footsteps as she marched up the stairs, followed by the creaking of floorboards overhead. Brian wandered around the room, studying the photographs: pictures of babies in their mothers' arms, family groups and men working in the fields. There was a picture of Gerald Whiteside, the farmer whose body he had examined earlier that week. Whiteside was supporting a young girl who was learning to ride a bicycle. Brian sank down onto the chair and looked out of the window. He felt weary as he stared across the gardens and the fields that lay beyond. He now regretted this excursion, and recalled the advice both Mike and Hutch had given him about keeping his head down. What had possessed him to embark on such a madcap scheme as this?

Doors slammed and more footsteps echoed in the rooms overhead. Brian waited for the stairs to creak again, but they didn't. He picked up one of the photographs: a man and woman on a beach. The man was wearing a suit and the woman wore a wedding dress.

"So that is your game — stealing the silver!" Brian stood up with a start. Hildee was standing in the doorway at the back of the study. She wiped her brow and walked over to a bureau in the corner of the room. Opening the top drawer, she put her hand in her pocket and took out a revolver. Brian felt a cold sensation at the back of his neck and in his arms. He sat down slowly. Hildee dropped the gun into the drawer and turned to face Brian again. "My parents' wedding photograph."

"What?" asked Brian.

"In your hand."

Brian realised that he was still holding the photograph. "They're on a beach." He put it back on the table.

"Malibu. They were married on the beach at Malibu."

"Long way to go to get married." Brian looked at the photographs again to see if there was another wedding photograph. "Are *you* married?"

"Are you offering?"

Brian glanced up. Hildee blushed slightly and giggled, holding her hand up to her mouth. Then she blurted out, "Have you eaten yet? Answer the second question first."

Brian smiled at her. "Marx Brothers."

"'Night at the Opera.'"

"'Duck Soup' actually." Brian stood up. "And no, I haven't eaten yet."

Hildee reached into the top of the bureau. From where Brian was standing, he could not see what she was picking up, but whatever it was it was too small to be a revolver. "Is there a Mrs. Tyler?" she asked, walking across the room towards him.

"Yes, there is," Brian replied.

"Oh." Hildee raised one eyebrow, then looked out of the window. Her face was tanned but smooth. The dark skin below her eyes revealed a sadness that until now had been disguised as anger, annoyance or tears.

"My mother," Brian added.

"That is not what I meant," she said, leaning forward and grabbing the sleeve of Brian's jacket. "So is she the one who has been patching up your clothes?"

Brian glanced down at the repairs Aunty Stef had made to his sleeves — just long enough for Hildee to make her move. He looked up as the knife descended.

*

Mike had not flown in an airliner since he was seventeen years old. It had been a business-class flight, paid for by his father, to the Munich beer festival. He had also flown to Spain, Sweden and the west coast of America, but he always used to feel out of place amongst the businessmen hunched over their laptop computers. Three years on, his degree behind him, he would have been part of all that. It never happened. Now, looking around the small passenger cabin of the ageing Ukraine Air A310 Airbus, he realised it never would.

As on all other forms of European transport, the only thing that went first class was freight. Passengers were second-class baggage. Unless it was urgent, everyone travelled by train. No-one, for any reason whatsoever, was allowed to fly between London, Brussels and Paris, which were all served by Eurostar. Most of the fleets of the major airlines were in mothballs. Aircraft were only brought into service to replace those that were beyond repair. New planes were turboprops, built to designs dating back to the previous century.

When Mike was seventeen, Germany was a patchwork of small fields and managed forests. Today Mike saw below him a landscape that looked much the same as East Anglia, or any other agricultural region: small towns and villages were surrounded by a few fields, beyond which lay a wilderness stretching to the horizon. Railway lines cut through the dense forest, linking those small towns with what had once been major cities. Here and there, still visible amongst the trees, were isolated — and deserted — stretches of autobahn.

There were only ten people on the flight. The Green Party had succeeded in stigmatising air travel to such an extent that most of the passengers were too embarrassed to talk to each other. They either read or looked out of the window. Mike opened the guidebook and read the instructions again.

*

Just as Aul's man had said, in thirty minutes Mike was clear of the airport and travelling by shuttle bus into the centre of Kiev. The instructions had told him to catch the Irpen train and get off two stops after the town itself — 'easy to spot because of the large number of guards'. Here his passport and ID were scrutinised. A number of phone calls were made before he was allowed to leave the station and take the bus to Ivan Vlachos's house.

The soldier on the gate disappeared into a guard hut and picked up a telephone. He held Mike's ID card out in front of him and read the details to the person at the other end of the phone. At the far end of the drive, two people emerged from the front door of the large single-storey, ranch-style farmhouse. One person remained by the door, while the other walked slowly to the gate. A heavily built man in shirtsleeves took the ID card from the soldier, studied it, glanced at Mike and then indicated that the soldier should open the gate. The man in shirtsleeves did not speak as he led Mike down the drive. It was the second man who spoke. "What business have you with Mr. Vlachos?"

The acceptability of Mike's answer would depend on whether Ivan was a prisoner and these people were warders, or whether this was the ex-leader's home and they were his bodyguards. Mike tried to work it out. In the end, he played safe. "I am here as part of an investigation concerning David Fairchild."

Mike had met Ivan Vlachos before — on 18th September 2010. Of course, Ivan would not remember him. That day he had met hundreds of people. He shook them by the hand before addressing them during his tour of agricultural work camps. Tanya Vlachos was as beautiful as ever. She was the first person to step forward and shake Mike's hand as he was shown into the large living room. Vlachos himself was seated on a sofa, his feet resting on a low table covered with newspapers and magazines. The corners of some of the pages lifted as the cool evening breeze entered the room through two sets of French windows. "So, someone else looking for answers to something I know nothing about," Vlachos said, getting to his feet and walking over to the window.

Mike looked around the room. Still unsure of the role of the man in shirtsleeves, he followed Ivan to the window, where he was gathering up one of the billowing curtains. Stepping out onto the veranda, Mike leaned on the wooden railings and waited for Ivan to follow. "Peter Aul asked me to come here to see you," Mike said.

Vlachos's face broke into a smile. He rested his hand on Mike's shoulder and led him back into the room. "This man has been sent by Peter." The shirt sleeved man, and everyone else in the room, relaxed visibly. "How is he? More to the point, where is he?"

Mike began to tell the story of his encounter with Aul's man in Belgium. Ivan was bombarding him with questions, but Tanya interrupted. "Before you get carried away, has Mr. Allchurch eaten?" Ivan repeated his wife's question and Mike explained that he had had a late lunch at Brussels airport. "Then I will go and get a room ready for you," Tanya said. "I'm sure you must be very tired." Until then, Mike had not considered where he would be spending the night.

"Yes, it must have been a long day," Ivan said. "We will talk about these things in the morning." He stood up and beckoned to the shirt sleeved bodyguard to follow him. The two men left the room.

Mike realised they had gone off to discuss what to do with their prize catch, rather than to give him the chance of some rest. He began to make his own plans for the next day. Sit and listen to Ivan's theory about Troxley and protestations of Fairchild's innocence? Stay long enough to make Aul happy — just in case his man was waiting back in Brussels? Why not fly back to Heathrow? Who was going to stop him?

The room was plain. The furniture looked Scandinavian. No elaborate ornaments. No ostentatious displays. A row of photographs, in silver frames, had been fixed with screws to the brickwork of the wide chimney breast: Ivan and Tanya surrounded by relatives at their wedding; Ivan graduating; Tanya graduating; then, in a much smaller frame, a photograph of Lena.

This was the Lena Mike had seen thirty years ago, gripping her mother's hand, looking down at the ground as the crowds flocked around her father. Then she died, and became an icon representing everyone's loss. By the time his own daughter had fallen victim to cholera, Mike had thought he was all cried out. Like a lot of people, however, he found a few more tears when Lena died. Sometimes, in his more cynical moods, he blamed Ivan's publicity machine for whipping up the hysteria and generating this collective grief, but it went deeper than that. He remembered a man who, looking twenty years older than his forty-five years, was watching over the bodies of his wife and two children. Mike had helped him load those blanket-clad bodies onto the back of the disposal lorry. The man had stood as if in a trance, staring down the road until the lorry was out of sight. Then, his eyes red and his face drained of colour, he had turned to Mike and said, "It's a shame about Lena, isn't it?"

"Are you all right?" Tanya asked. "Can I get you a drink of water?"

Mike had not noticed her come back into the room. "Yes, that would be nice. It's been a long day."

"Your room is ready. It's probably best you get to sleep before my husband comes back. He will have you up all night. Talk, talk, talk." She smiled.

Tanya got Mike the glass of water and showed him to his room. The room was furnished in the same style as the living room. The carpets, the bed, the cupboards and the chair all looked new. It was obvious that, until his resignation, Ivan and Tanya had spent little time here.

"Is it possible to contact my wife in England?" Mike asked.

Tanya frowned. "We had the house swept and it is OK, but the telephone — we cannot tell." She saw that Mike was disappointed. "We have encrypted e-mail. Is there any way your wife could read it?"

Mike wondered if it was safe to send an encrypted e-mail to Brian or Kumar and ask them to pass it on. But did he really want them to know he was in the Ukraine? "No, it doesn't matter," he said.

Sleep did not come easily. Mike was thinking about Lena again. *He* still had a family. True, it had been patched together from bits and pieces of other people's, but he had not been left on his own. He remembered Ivan's broadcast. He thought of the girl carrying the water. He thought of the girl's mother, abandoned and dying alone. He did not want Brian or Kumar to know he was here — because he had changed his mind about the investigation.

*

The blade of Hildee's knife penetrated the sleeve of the jacket at a point where she was holding the cloth clear of Brian's arm. In one movement she pulled the knife towards her, tearing the sleeve down to the cuff.

"Come on then. Dinnertime." Hildee tossed the knife onto the table and walked to the door without turning around.

Brian looked down at the knife and then at his sleeve. Slowly he followed Hildee out of the room, through the hall and back out into the gardens. His doubts about his visit had returned. Picking up his bicycle, he stood beside it for a while. Hildee locked the front door, then collected her own bicycle from under the trees and set off down the drive.

If there was to be another conversation with Hildee, Brian felt it really ought to start with some sort of explanation on her part. He attempted to examine his sleeve and estimate the amount of work needed to repair the only jacket he owned. In the event, there was no conversation, as Brian had difficulty keeping up with Hildee, and even when he drew level with her he was too out of breath to speak.

On entering Downham, Hildee rode past the restaurant and up the hill into the southern half of the town. She stopped in front of a row of shops, leaned her bicycle against the wall and disappeared into the laundry. Brian stood for a moment, trying to get his breath back.

"Glad I caught you. I thought I'd be too late," Hildee said to one of the women behind the counter.

"Hello, Miss Parks. Just about to close up, dear."

"I'm afraid we have had a bit of an accident. My friend here tore his sleeve on a fence." Hildee turned to Brian. "Take your jacket off, Mr. Tyler."

Brian stared at her in amazement.

"Off! Take your jacket off, Mr. Tyler."

Brian slipped his jacket off. Hildee grabbed it and put it on the counter.

The woman gave the jacket a cursory examination. "Ruined," she muttered. "Can't repair this one, dear." She picked up a pair of scissors and cut the label away from the collar, then emptied the contents of each pocket onto the counter. The woman turned, threw the jacket unceremoniously into a large cardboard box in the corner of the room and disappeared behind a bank of racks at the back of the shop. She emerged carrying two new jackets. "Which?" she said, holding them up.

Brian looked confused.

"Choose then," Hildee said.

Brian stood riveted to the spot. Eventually, Hildee reached forward and took one of the jackets.

170

"That's better, dear." The woman laughed. "Mine wasn't wrapped very well when I got him." She looked Brian up and down as she ran the jacket under a sewing machine to attach the label, with Brian's name and number on it, to the collar. "Mind you, mine wasn't that special when I got him unwrapped either." The second woman burst out laughing and pushed a book across the counter towards Brian. "Name, date and S-card number," she said, dropping Brian's possessions into the pockets of the new jacket.

Brian hesitated before entering his details in the book. This explained Hildee's performance with the knife. Now, whatever else he did, there would be one record of his visit that he could not hide. A record which Hildee herself would have access to. She must have planned this while she was getting his room ready. Perhaps he had underestimated her. Brian wondered what else she had in store for him.

"Now, that's a lot better," Hildee said as they rode back to the restaurant.

"It's a waste. There was nothing wrong with my old jacket."

Hildee shrieked. "You were a walking fashion disaster! *You* may not mind walking around looking like a heap of rags, but *I'm* not going to sit and eat with someone who gets small change left on their plate because they look as though they are down on their luck." She watched Brian examining his new jacket. "Why didn't you choose?"

"Never had to choose anything before." He continued to examine the garment after he had placed his bicycle in the rack outside the restaurant. "Quite good quality cloth, isn't it?"

"Welcome to the countryside, Mr. Tyler."

*

At one time or other, every pair of eyes in the restaurant was turned in Brian's direction. Hildee was either unaware of the attention they were attracting or she was distracted by the stream of people who visited their table to talk to her. Hildee spent most of the meal discussing manning levels, deployment of penal labour, grain storage and the transport backlog caused by the derailment earlier in the week. "You had better tell me what you have got planned for tomorrow, Mr. Tyler," she suggested. Before Brian could answer, someone else had interrupted.

Towards the end of the meal, Matt Spencer, the driver,

slumped across the end of the table. "Brian! Back so soon?" He turned to Hildee. "Anything you need running back into town?"

"Not at the moment, Matt."

Matt glanced at Brian, then addressed Hildee again. "Don't leave it too late. May have to leave early on Monday."

"I'll let you know."

"Coming to the film tonight? It's a good one — 'Star Wars'."

"Maybe," Hildee replied.

Matt pushed himself up from the table. "Well, see you there perhaps."

*

Half way through the film Brian forgot himself and slid his arm around the back of Hildee's seat, as he might have done with any other girl he had taken to the cinema. Either Hildee was too engrossed in the film or she pretended not to notice.

"Escapist rubbish," Brian said as they rode back to Nordelph.

"People liked it." Hildee reduced her speed so that Brian could catch up. "I liked it and you seemed to enjoy it. I think people like to escape for a while."

"Matt seemed edgy this evening. Was that because of me?"

"Why should you make him edgy?"

"Jealous..."

"Jealous!" Hildee laughed. "Oh, you mean because you are with..." She laughed again. "No, I hardly think so." She pedalled harder, forcing Brian to do the same. "Matt likes to act the big man. Likes people to believe he is more important than he is. So he tells people he chooses the film himself. Really he has to take what they give him in Peterborough. Last week it was 'Mad Max' — not a popular choice."

"Can't he get pirate copies?"

"From where?"

"From the same place he gets the clothes."

"Those clothes come from a party warehouse."

"Stolen?"

"No. You really understand nothing about the countryside, do you? The party know that the farmers are restless. That they resent having to work all hours only to see all their produce disappear into the cities. They are told what to grow and how to farm. And they have the army standing over them all the time. You must know. You spoke to Mr. Haswell."

"Well, listened to him actually."

"Anyway, the party tries to keep everyone happy by handing out goodies. Matt pretends he knows a man — but that is just Matt."

"So his story about euros not being accepted here...?"

"Matt and his friend collect foreign coins. They probably have one of the largest coin collections in East Anglia."

"And people being shot and tied to telephone poles?"

Hildee did not reply. She slowed down and let Brian draw level again. "So what films do you get in London?"

"There's a choice, mostly. Clint Eastwood, Bruce Willis. I saw 'Fatal Attraction' a few weeks back."

"And you called 'Star Wars' rubbish! You really know how to give your girlfriend a decent night out!"

"There isn't... There's a small cinema in Kensington that shows special-interest films. Ealing comedies."

"And Marx Brothers?"

"Yes. They ran through the whole series. Most of the people from work went to see them. My boss does a good imitation of Groucho Marx."

"Not something I imagine a policeman doing."

"Oh, it's entirely unintentional."

Hildee started giggling. Eventually she was laughing so much that she had to stop and get off her bicycle. "Sorry! I'll be all right in a minute," she said, turning away from Brian. "I just had this image of you as Harpo, running around behind your boss honking a car horn."

Arriving back at the manor house, Brian went straight to the office. Hildee followed him into the room and watched him switch on the computers and examine the wiring behind them. "This computer here, I'd like you to report it as faulty tomorrow morning. Ask that optics engineer who works near the station to come and fix it."

"Andrew Cameron, his..."

"Yes, his son is a computer whizz kid. If you could ask for him specifically."

"We could have done that tonight. He was in the cinema."

"No, we'll do it after breakfast."

Hildee felt strange, being ordered around in what she regarded as her own home. She was also surprised how quickly Brian had transformed himself from a carefree lad into an officious party operative. She should have been angry, but instead felt herself warming to him. The feeling troubled her. "I am going to bed now, Mr. Tyler. Your room is ready. It is upstairs on the left. The light will be on and the door is open. Goodnight."

Hildee had left by the time Brian looked up "Yes. Goodnight," he said, to an empty room.

Outside, the countryside had fallen silent. The combine harvesters had stopped working and lorries no longer whined and rattled along the roads. The walls of Nordelph Manor were thin and Hildee could hear Brian unpacking his rucksack. She tried to guess what each sound represented. The metallic clunk on the shelf above the basin — a razor. A dull thud on the bedside cupboard — a document perhaps. The sound of him taking off his clothes, the buckle of his belt hitting the metal bedstead. 'Untidy,' she thought. Then, like a whisper, the sound of the sheets being pulled back and the creaking of the bed. The light had not been switched off. He must be reading, but there was no sound of pages being turned. A book perhaps. After thirty minutes Hildee heard a gentle thump on the bedside cupboard, and the click of the light switch. Definitely a book.

Hildee woke in the early hours and lay still, wondering what had disturbed her. There was a groan from the next room, mumbled words, then a voice crying out. 'Stop! Wait!' it shouted. The sound of the bed creaking, as a body writhed on it. Hildee recalled the stories she had heard about London, and wondered what images haunted Brian. The house fell quiet again and she slept once more.

6

Saturday 24th August 2041

"Why not start from the beginning? Why did you resign?" Mike was walking back to the house with Ivan and one of the bodyguards. Tanya and the second bodyguard had walked on ahead. Over breakfast, the conversation had been confined to the weather, the grain harvest and Vlachos's move to the countryside. Now, away from the soldiers, farm labourers and office workers, amongst whom the bodyguard suspected there was at least one of Simitovich's men, Ivan felt free to talk.

"One day a police report landed on my desk." Ivan shrugged and seemed to be speaking to the world in general. "It said that someone had been tampering with archived data from a disused nuclear power plant." He spoke slowly, as though he was disclosing the information reluctantly. Then he drew a deep breath. "It was alleged that someone had destroyed access records for the computer that controlled the plant where I worked forty years ago. Then it said that when they looked at what was left of the access data, it appeared that, forty years ago, I had been logging into the computer that controlled the plant. It strongly suggested that I had a hand in causing the accident that destroyed the plant."

"Had you?"

"What?!" Ivan shouted.

"I mean, had you been accessing the computer?"

"I had to finish a report, but I no longer had access from within the plant. They hadn't removed my password. So what could I do? I carried on accessing the computer, of course."

"Let me guess. The data that was destroyed related to all the accesses leading up to the day of the accident which, by some chance, remained intact."

"Yes, that's about it." Ivan stopped walking and surveyed the surrounding countryside. "If it had been made public, it would have been disastrous — not just for me, but for the party as well. I had to resign. That's all there was to it."

"You must have been quite annoyed."

"Quite annoyed!" Ivan shouted at Mike. "Quite annoyed!" His face turned red. Tanya looked around and began to walk back to where they were standing. As she approached, Ivan held up one hand. "Sorry. Sorry. I'm just taking time adjusting to the English art of understatement."

Ivan continued walking until he reached a seat next to the path. "So, tell me what they are saying about David," Ivan said, when Mike and Tanya had caught up with him. Mike described the discovery of Troxley's body and the killing of Gerald Whiteside. "People being killed. It sounds like someone's getting desperate," Ivan said. "But still it's the same trick. Now Fairchild has to decide whether to tough it out and risk wrecking the party."

"There's a thought that Simitovich is behind it. I suppose because he has most to gain," Mike suggested.

"What would he gain by wrecking the party?"

"He's assuming that Fairchild will back down, just as you did."

"But it's still dangerous. Even if he doesn't publish all these stories about me and David, they will be there for others to pick up."

"Perhaps he will use the allegations. When he gets into power, he will announce that the party has been corrupted. Simitovich will put himself forward as a reformer." Mike sat thinking for a moment. "But then, *you* started talking about reforms before he did."

"Ah! Now I think you are getting closer to the real reason for all of this." Looking at his watch, Ivan got to his feet. "Come on, Mr. Allchurch. Mike. It is Mike, isn't it?"

"Yes."

"We can't spend all morning talking politics. We've got to get you on the move."

Mike suspected that the informal tone of the conversation meant he might not like where he was 'on the move' to.

*

Brian washed and dressed. Before he went downstairs, he transferred Harry the Print's glasses from his rucksack to his jacket pocket. Brian was well aware that he shouted out in his sleep. Stef rarely mentioned it, but Trevor was always teasing him about it: 'Thought the house was on fire' or 'Grisly murder in the house on Queen's Gate again last night.'

"I hope I didn't disturb you," Brian said.

Hildee was sitting in the study, sipping water from a glass and reading. "Not at all."

"If you want to move me to another room, I wouldn't mind."

"Don't worry about it," she said, acknowledging that Brian

had indeed woken her. "Shall we get some breakfast and then put this master plan of yours into action?"

*

The Downham Ivan's Restaurant was filled with people in the halfway house between work and play. What passed for community service in the countryside bore even less resemblance to work than it did in the city. Fishing, regarded by many as a sport, often involved no more than taking a boat trip along the river. For this reason, everyone was in good humour. Once again, Hildee was more relaxed with Brian than he was with her, especially as people on the next table were openly speculating about where Brian had spent the night.

*

"Sorry to trouble you, Andrew." Hildee wandered around Andrew Cameron's office, occasionally stopping to inspect the electronic instruments set up on the benches. "It's just that one of my computers has stopped working. I wondered..."

Andrew Cameron did not look up from the microscope he was working on. "Tony!" he shouted. A small screw fell from the pair of tweezers he was holding and bounced across the desk. "Damn! Tony, get in here!"

"All right! Coming!" The voice grew louder as Tony walked down the corridor.

"Tony will sort it out for you. It'll keep him out of my hair for a little while." Andrew stood up and rubbed his eyes.

A stocky youth with a tired expression entered the room. "Hello, Miss Parks."

"Miss Parks has a problem with one of her computers," Andrew said.

Tony's face came alive. "Hardware or software?"

Hildee turned to Brian.

"Oh, software," Brian said. "I think one of the low-level internet access routines needs modifying, or possibly it's been corrupted."

Tony frowned. "Are you sure? That shouldn't happen. Do you think it's a virus?"

Brian shrugged. "Could be."

By now, a second youth was standing in the doorway.

"Mind if Adam comes to help?" Tony asked.

"The more the merrier." Brian smiled.

"We'll take a PC and our development software up there on the bus," Tony said, as both the youths left the room.

Brian took the glasses case out of his pocket. "I realise you're busy, but would it be possible to put these lenses into new frames?" He watched while Andrew prised open the case and carefully took out the pair of women's glasses. "Only, when I was here before, I noticed that you had lots of frames."

"Yes, you were here with that policeman. I thought I recognised you." He glanced at Hildee. "And you've found a problem with Miss Parks's computer." He gave Brian a quizzical look. "Don't leave the boys alone in the room with it. Internet and development software is a touchy subject around here."

"Oh, no problem," Brian said innocently. "I'll keep a close eye on them."

Andrew inspected the glasses. "Nothing wrong with these."

"They belong to a printer I know but don't really suit him."

"Him? Yes, that would be a problem. We've got some 'Silhouette' frames which look rather nice."

"Some what?" Brian asked.

"'Silhouette.' They were designer frames, very expensive."

"Designer?" But Brian decided not to pursue the issue. "How much will they cost?"

"Let's see. When they were made they cost four hundred pounds. With inflation, and bearing in mind the demand we get for them..." Andrew furrowed his brow, and Hildee could tell that he enjoyed teasing Brian as much as she did. "Let's call it a round zero."

"Free?"

"Why not? You can owe me. Sort it out next time you're back up here. He is allowed back, is he, Miss Parks?" Andrew smiled when he saw Hildee blush. "Seriously, when do you need them?"

"Well, I'm catching a train back to London tomorrow morning."

"Tomorrow morning?"

"Is that a problem?"

Andrew laughed. "Not for me, but..."

"I'll pick them up tonight before dinner," Hildee interrupted. She then turned to Brian. "Come on, Mr. Tyler. We must leave Mr. Cameron to get on. We have to get back to Nordelph before the bus gets there."

At first Brian thought it strange that Hildee seemed in such a hurry to get him out of Andrew Cameron's office. Then he recalled the long conversation Mike had been dragged into, and he assumed that Hildee wanted to get away before the same happened to him.

The bus had just left Nordelph Manor when Hildee and Brian arrived. Tony and Adam were carrying a large box, with handles fitted to each side, down the drive. They unpacked the box in the office, carefully taking out the system unit, monitor and keyboard, and assembling them on the desk next to Hildee's computer.

Leaning on the wall by the window, Hildee watched the two youths wire up and switch on both computers. Once all the icons had appeared on the screens, Tony turned to her. "Exactly what is the problem?"

Shrugging her shoulders, Hildee turned to Brian. He had just entered the office, carrying a brown folder and two mobile phones. Putting the folder and the phones on the desk, Brian picked up two chairs and placed them either side of the one Tony was sitting on, so that both he and Adam could sit down.

"First things first. Tell me why you've been breaking into the S-Card database."

Hildee felt faint. Tony looked at her, seeking an explanation, but she turned away, sank down into an easy chair and rested her forehead against the palm of her hand. How could he do this to her? What would Andrew say when his son was put in prison? Her mind raced. Was the death sentence for sabotaging the S-Card network still in force? What would people in the village think of her? Why did he have to involve her in all this?

*

"So the answer is in America," said Ivan, concluding his long and detailed analysis of the events of the past month. The shirt sleeved bodyguard, reclining on the sofa in the living room of the Vlachos's house, nodded in agreement. "That's where Troxley came from. Find out why he came back — and who invited him — and you'll know who is pushing Simitovich."

Mike stared across the low coffee table at Ivan and the bodyguard. "So you expect me to go over to America and track down someone who knows Troxley. And who might know why he returned to England." He frowned. "In a week. You realise America is a big place."

Ivan laid a sheet of paper on the table. "Martha Snyder. CIA in

Langley, just outside Washington."

"The CIA. Why should they help us?" asked Mike.

"Because we had a grain deal, and a technology deal, and an oil-exploration agreement. And when they listen to Simitovich, all they hear is a lot of talk about how 'democracy' and 'liberalisation' will make Europe strong enough to stand on its own two feet."

"That's just electioneering for domestic consumption. They don't really believe it."

"The Americans have had their fingers burnt by Russians before. They are not going to risk losing the grain deal, especially as their harvest may not be too good this year."

Mike still looked concerned. For the first time, the bodyguard spoke. "Look, it's straightforward. I can take you through all the problems you might run into in the US. Martha will be able to fill you in on anything I miss. We've already e-mailed her. She has arranged your flight and will meet you at the airport."

Mike laughed. "Sounds easy."

Ivan leaned forward, clapped his hands together, then glanced at his watch. "One, two, two and a half. Yes, there's time for lunch before you go back to the airport." He strode towards the French windows and called out. "Tanya, we are going to lunch."

*

The restaurant was stifling. Mike realised after only two mouthfuls that this was not a good day to eat goulash soup. Sweat trickled down the side of his face. Tanya sat next to him, and Ivan opposite. The bodyguards had surveyed the restaurant. Everyone around Mike was relaxed. It was clear that the identities of Simitovich's spies were common knowledge and that, at the moment, there were none in the room.

"You said that your version of liberalisation was different from Simitovich's."

Ivan looked at Mike, and swallowed the mouthful of bread roll he was chewing.

"Is there still that waxworks in London, Mr. Allchurch," Tanya said, before her husband could speak. "I went there once, when I was a child."

"Madame Tussaud's. Yes, but there are only a few exhibits. Unfortunately, none from this century," Mike replied.

Ivan waved his spoon in front of Mike's face. "The difference is," he said, ignoring Tanya's attempt to guide the conversation into a less controversial area, "the liberalisation that Simitovich is proposing will be introduced without the implementation of a suitable constitution."

"But England has never had a written constitution anyway, so where's the problem?"

"The problem is," — Ivan took another mouthful of soup — "the problem is, Mike, that without a Green constitution democracy will drag us backwards into the same mess we were in at the turn of the century."

"A Green constitution, which only the Green party can work with. That's hardly democracy."

"Did you get a chance to look around when you were in Brussels?" Tanya asked.

Mike turned to her. "No. I was only there for a few hours. I've been there before though."

"That's rubbish!" Ivan said. "Any party can work with a Green constitution. In fact, a democratic party has certain duties and responsibilities which make up the core of the Green constitution."

"What about freedom of speech, freedom of the press, freedom of movement?"

"Freedom to be poisoned by any corporation the government thinks will turn a quick buck and create a few jobs before the next election? Is that the sort of freedom people want?"

"I think we have to educate people, then leave the choice to them..."

"When we were in Brussels last year, we saw that model village with buildings from all the capitals of Europe. Did you know that it is maintained by schoolchildren?" Tanya said, but by now Ivan and Mike were too engrossed in their argument to listen to her.

"Where in your precious constitution, written or otherwise, does it say anything about education?" Ivan shouted. "Or are you going to rely on the goodwill of big business? Look where that got Russia at the turn of the century! It liberalised and the capitalists raped and robbed them blind. Look at what happened in England with BSE! The government didn't educate people to understand that if suddenly you can afford to eat beef every day of the week, instead of just on Sunday, the quality may not be the same. Where does it say that people should be told if the animals they eat have been fed on their own shit? And where is your precious freedom of speech when scientists are too scared to express any opinion that differs from the one the government and the producers are spinning?" Ivan put his elbow on the table and rubbed the side of his face with his hand. "Look at the research into BSE! Some scientist thought that the prions entered the human body through the lungs and eyes — not just the gut; that victims, some of them vegetarians, contracted CJD by breathing in dust from dried animal feed and pet food — or from the clothes of husbands who worked in abattoirs. But scientists were put under pressure to withdraw this information, told they would lose funding, or their jobs. Discussion ceased. Pages were removed from university websites. Just because people might start asking why the government converted all the infected cows into powder and stored them in leaking warehouses across England. Then, when it suited the government," Ivan held up his hands, "suddenly all the dissident scientists were right — again without free debate. Who was educating the people then? The same thing happened here in the Ukraine with the nuclear power industry."

Mike blew on a spoonful of soup. "So basically what you are saying is that people are just too ignorant to be trusted with democracy."

"No, no. Mike, you have to understand that the sort of constitutions we had at the turn of the century were there to protect labour against the oppression of the capitalist — not to shield the consumer from the ravages of global corporations. In a consumer society there's no education, only advertising. Back then, the food producers were only interested in making money. They didn't lobby governments for more spending on education, only for fewer restrictions on pesticides and the use of GM crops. They didn't listen when scientists explained that squeezing millions of pigs, all of them full of antibiotics, into factory farms would cause a pandemic. A government that relies on the food producers to teach the public what a healthy diet is ends up with everyone eating their own shit and paying for the privilege."

"How is your soup, Mr. Allchurch?" Tanya asked.

Mike returned the spoonful he had been about to put in his mouth to the bowl. "It's a little bit hot for me, actually."

"My husband feels very passionately about these things." She sighed wearily. Then suddenly her voice became sharper. "But what you should remember is that we are no more than parasites on the surface of Mother Earth. Most of the time, she doesn't even notice us. Sometimes we irritate her and she scratches a little. Sometimes we irritate her a lot and then" — Tanya flicked her hand — "she sweeps us away. Yes, we can play our little games. We can grant each other freedoms and speak of democracy. All I know is that the last time we annoyed Mother Earth she took away my only child." For a moment, there was look of sadness in her eyes. She picked up a glass of water. After taking a sip, she said softly, "Mother Earth is the limit of our freedom. Her decision to take Lena was not based on a vote lost in some irrelevant parliament. It was a demonstration of her power over all of us."

Ivan fell silent and concentrated on his lunch. The only sound in the restaurant was the clatter of spoons on the stainless-steel bowls.

*

"Troxley was important to someone," Ivan said, as Mike's train approached the station. "It isn't Simitovich — the man's not that clever. Just being used probably. It could be a group of farmers; it could be one of the old banks or corporations. They're still around, waiting for the return of the 'good old days'." He shook Mike's hand and then, in typical Ivan style, slapped him on the arm. "Good luck, Mike!" he said.

As the train pulled away, Tanya waved, then took hold of Ivan's arm. Mike watched her lead her husband away. She was more than the homely woman Ivan joked about in his broadcasts. He remembered Ivan describing the loss of his daughter, how everyone shared Ivan's grief that day. Tanya was carrying her grief alone.

*

"Just tell me why," Brian said softly.

"It's only a game," Tony stuttered. "Just a game. That's all."

"Show me."

Reaching over the desk, Adam took the modem lead out of the back of Hildee's computer and plugged it into a socket on the back of his PC.

After moving the mouse across the desk, Tony clicked the button a couple of times. The screen went blank, except for a dialog box asking the user to log in. Nervously, Tony tapped on the keyboard. The letters 'ARGON5' appeared in the box momentarily, before the screen cleared to display a 3D graphical representation of an Ivan's Restaurant. One by one, blue and green figures appeared at the tables and in the queue by the counter.

"Switch to self-view," Adam whispered.

Tony hit a key and the rear view of what looked like a robot appeared at the front of the screen. Tony turned to Brian. "It's better with a joystick."

Adam leaned forward. "Try Peterborough. There might be someone there."

Tony clicked the mouse again. A menu containing a list of towns in alphabetical order appeared in the top right-hand corner of the screen. He clicked on 'Peterborough'. The Ivan's cleared and then began to fill with new figures. This time, one of the figures was dressed as a gangster.

"There he is!" exclaimed Adam.

Tony hit two of the keys on the keyboard. Gunfire raked the restaurant. Blood spurted from the blue and green figures as they were cut down in a hail of bullets. The gangster got up. Using two of the figures as cover, he headed for the pillar in the centre of the room. The robot that Tony was controlling could not redirect his fire in time to catch the gangster. There was a delay, then the gangster re-appeared, guns blazing, from behind the pillar.

"Oops, trouble," said Adam.

"Damn!" Tony called out. "Can't do it without a joystick." He sighed.

Brian pressed his hands together and held them to his mouth. "That's OK. I've seen enough."

Tony and Adam looked worried again. Both the youths, and Hildee, were staring at Brian.

"So, what you are doing is lifting all the recorded visits to restaurants and using them to create these..." Brian frowned and pointed at the screen.

"Actavars," Adam suggested.

"Actavars," Brian repeated, turning to Tony. "And you add a virtual version of yourself?"

"Yes. So that we can be seen by other players on the network."

"There are other players then?"

"Yes, all the time." Tony relaxed and tilted his chair back, not questioning why Brian had asked the obvious.

"For that you need read-and-write access to the central database on the S-Card server." Brian opened his folder and took out a hand-drawn block diagram of the S-Card network. "According to this, no-one has direct read-and-write access to the S-Card database. A few secure and trusted servers have *read*

access, but only two *secure and trusted* servers have *write* access."
Brian paused, pretending to study the diagram and waiting for
either Tony or Adam to contradict him. The youths remained
silent. "So unless you have got into the old lottery computer or the
server in the Ministry of Health, I can't see how you're doing it."

"There is another server," said Adam, with an obvious sense
of pride.

"Well, I haven't found it."

"It's there." Tony leaned forward again. "The S-Card server
trusts itself. If a software routine is placed on the S-Card server, the
database will accept read-and-write instructions from it."

"So this game talks directly to an application on the S-Card
server itself?"

Tony took the mouse and restarted the game. "Yes. When you
start, it generates a dummy S-Card number."

"What if the number already exists?"

"The first number is always 255 or FF in hex. The remaining
numbers are generated by translating the time of day into six
numbers — that way you don't get the same number as another
player. The FF tells this program that the number belongs to
another player. That's why it generates a custom Actavar instead of
a blue or green figure. The dummy number lasts as long as you're
logged in. When you log out, it's deleted."

Hildee wanted to tell the boys to stop talking. It was obvious
to her that they were being tricked into filling in gaps in Brian's
knowledge. All of this would be used as evidence against them.

"But surely you can't just drop a piece of software onto the S-
Card server?"

Tony nodded. "There's a whole development environment on
the server."

Brian looked puzzled.

"Compilers, programming languages, debugging tools," Adam
explained. "And there's a facility for remote debugging so that
programmers can work on software from other locations."

"Why?"

Adam shrugged. "Probably been there since the software was
written. The password is common knowledge and it gives us a back
door into the server."

"How did you find this out?"

"From Ivan World News." Tony clicked on the top corner of
the screen and the game shrank to an icon. Then he clicked on
another icon and a newsreader appeared. He selected 'refresh' and

that produced a list of documents. There was a name next to each entry.

"All these people are involved in developing this game?" Brian asked.

"Yes," said Tony.

'Bloody fools,' thought Hildee, as she watched Brian studying the list.

"Go back to your game again," Brian said.

Tony clicked on the game icon and the restaurant was displayed once more. Slowly the blue and green Actavars populated the tables. Sometimes one of the figures would stand up and walk out of the room, eventually being replaced by another, which entered carrying a tray.

"Where is this?" Brian asked.

"Peterborough," Tony replied, pointing to the top of the screen, where the name of the restaurant was displayed.

Brian looked puzzled. "I can't believe there are that many people eating at this time of day," he said, glancing down at his watch.

"There aren't." Tony pointed to the time of day displayed next to the restaurant name. "This data is taken from the last meal break — breakfast. If you play in the evening it is taken from dinner; in the afternoon it uses the lunch data. The program takes an hour of data. The software gives each person twenty minutes to eat their food. That's why some of them are leaving."

"So if you went to the restaurant in Downham, you could find me and Miss Parks eating breakfast."

Tony clicked the mouse a few times. The restaurant cleared and then began to fill with new characters.

Hildee stood up and strode towards the door. Hearing Brian refer to her as 'Miss Parks' was the final straw. Almost as soon as he arrived, he had called her by first name. Now, having got what he wanted, he was distancing himself from her.

"Before you go," Brian called out, "have you got any paperwork relating to Whiteside Farm?"

Hildee turned and walked towards the library. She held the door open for Brian, slamming it hard once he was in the room. Grabbing three box files from one of the shelves, she dropped them, one at a time, onto the reading desk. "'Accounts', 'Trials' and 'Crop Experiments'. If you are really interested." She turned and snatched open the door. "I shall be upstairs tidying your room." She glared at Brian, then marched through the office and out into the entrance hall.

Brian returned to the computers. He could hear Hildee's footsteps pounding up the stairs.

"You'll need to take your shirt off now." Tony laughed. "It'll get a lot warmer in here."

"What do you mean?" Brian asked.

"Well the ice maiden has gone," Tony said.

Adam chuckled. "Are you *really* staying here — with *her*?"

Ignoring the question, Brian sat down and stared at the screen.

"There's Morris!" exclaimed Adam. "Kill Morris!"

Tony held down two of the keys on the keyboard. The restaurant was raked with fire. Two of the figures fragmented, their body parts falling into pools of blood. "Sorry about that, Mr. Tyler."

"What's the problem?"

"Well, you've been caught in the crossfire." Tony smiled.

Brian pointed to the screen. "Dare I ask what that yellow thing is?"

Tony placed the cursor on the body and clicked the mouse button. A box of data appeared on the screen. "Egg. You had a 'basic' meal and that included egg."

Brian stared at the screen in silence.

"It has hospital wards as well," said Tony excitedly, as he clicked the location menu.

Brian held up his hand. "No, no. I'll use my imagination, thanks." He took a sheet of paper, drew a box on it and divided the box into small rectangles. "How long would it take you to put together a piece of software which read all the details of my visit to that restaurant out of the database? Then allowed me to change the location, using the location list, before writing the whole record back to the S-Card database?"

Tony turned to Adam. "All the routines are there. Each visit is just a data object. All it needs is a dialog box." Both youths thought for a moment.

Adam leaned back in his chair so that he could see Brian. "About an hour."

*

Hildee was sitting on the chair in Brian's room. She had grabbed the rucksack with the intention of searching it for clues to what else he might have in store for her. She sat trembling with rage, unable to do anything. Then, standing up, she upended the rucksack over the bed. The book landed on the pillow but the porcelain figure rolled onto the floor and broke. Hildee scooped up the remains of the figure and examined them. Slightly fire-damaged but inexpensive, she thought. Perhaps it was of some sentimental value.

Hildee dropped the pieces of the ornament back into the rucksack, then grabbed the book off the bed. 'Summer', by Albert Camus. Not the sort of book a Clint Eastwood fan would be carrying around. She sank down on the bed and flicked through the pages. Stopping at a description of the seashore, she read a few paragraphs. She felt strange, slightly disoriented. She could hear Brian's voice reading the words; could visualise sitting with him in some small café, looking out to sea. The feeling was discomfiting. She closed the book gently and returned it to the rucksack.

Brian's sheets had been screwed into a knot and hung over the end of the bed. Hildee pulled at the under sheet to straighten it out. She was about to smooth the creases in the top sheet when, to her own surprise, she scooped it up and held it to her face. Closing her eyes and taking a deep breath, Hildee could smell Brian's body. She could hear his voice again. She felt both aroused and vaguely disgusted by her own behaviour.

After remaking the bed, Hildee took a second look at the book. Contradictions, or just the romantic and sentimental side of someone who was also devious and ruthless? Or a hidden weakness? After all, both the book and the figure had been secreted away. Then again, they might have been stolen during a house search. Perhaps this was not the book she heard him reading the previous night. Either way, she would not be distracted from implementing her original plan.

*

Brian left the youths working on the program and returned to the library. He thumbed through the papers in the 'Whiteside Farm Accounts' box. There was no mention of crop trials, and the records ended abruptly half way through 2003. At first sight, the second box, 'Whiteside Farm Trials', looked more promising. However, the large bundle of punched papers held together with a metal clip turned out to contain nothing more than reports on equipment loaned from suppliers and on chemicals and fertilisers supplied free by manufacturers.

188

The third box, 'Whiteside Farm Crop Experiments', also contained a bundle of papers. The first page bore the title 'Genesis Natural Products GM Oilseed Rape Trial'. The next page was an index. However, there was a line of rust across the retaining clip where it had been straightened and then bent again. Brian realised that a large number of pages had been removed from the bundle some years ago.

Hildee came into the room, dragged a chair over to the desk and sat next to Brian. "Are Tony and Adam in serious trouble?"

Brian turned to the page where the trial results should have been. They were missing. "Hacking into the S-Card network is a serious offence."

"So what will happen to them?"

Brian referred to the index again: 'Data from other trials — page 85.' He thumbed through the papers. Page 85 was missing. He sighed and stared across the room. "Let's see. They could be sent to London. A quick trial. It's a capital offence, so there won't be an appeal."

Hildee tried to swallow, but her throat was suddenly dry. She lifted her hand to her neck.

"If they put real names to that list of other players, the sentence might be commuted to life." Brian looked up at the gap on the shelf left by the three box files. "Then the search would start for the other hackers." There it was, another box file: 'Whiteside Farm/Genesis.'

Brian turned to Hildee, who by now was visibly pale. "Of course, once it became common knowledge that Tony and Adam had been arrested, the other hackers would disappear off the face of the earth. Create themselves travel permits. Go abroad somewhere. The S-Card network would start behaving in strange and mysterious ways. The food supply and health system would break down and the only people who really knew how to fix it would be hiding somewhere in America."

"So nothing is going to happen to them?"

"No. If something was going to happen to them, it would have happened by now."

Hildee watched Brian take the box file from the shelf. "Oh, sorry. I forgot about that file. It has been years since I looked at that one." She waited for Brian to respond, but he merely stared blankly at her. "You mean people know about Tony and Adam?" she said.

"The term is 'tacit approval' — more experience gained than

harm done," Brian mumbled as he opened the box.

"But the police must have their own computer programmers?"

"Yep. A whole department, in fact." Brian turned his attention to the box file. It contained the same newspaper he had found in Troxley's briefcase, together with a bundle of papers punched in the corner and held together with a legal tag.

"But you do not trust them, do you?" Hildee asked. "You do not trust your own programmers."

On top of the bundle of papers in the box was the map Hildee had lent Brian earlier that week. He picked it up and threw it down on the desk. "To tell you the truth, Hildee, I don't know what to believe — or who to trust."

Hildee leaned forward and was about to touch Brian on the arm when there was a knock on the door. The door was already open. An embarrassed Adam stood watching them. "Sorry to trouble you, Mr. Tyler, but your software is ready."

*

Tony clicked on an icon and what looked like a spreadsheet appeared on the screen. He entered Brian's S-Card number in one of the boxes. "We got your number from the restaurant after we shot Morris."

Hildee looked puzzled. "Morris?"

"In the game, Miss," said Tony. Hildee nodded slowly, hoping that if she appeared to understand Tony would keep his explanation brief. "Now there are your records: breakfast at Downham, dinner at Downham and lunch at London, Queen Anne's Gate. All the data: what you ate, the time, the lot."

Brian examined the list. "How do I change the last two records?"

"Simple." Tony moved the cursor to the location entry in the last record and clicked twice. The alphabetical list of restaurants appeared. "Now you can scroll down the list, but it's easier to start typing the name in. Where do you want to go?"

"Cromer."

"Cromer?" cried Hildee.

"Cromer," Brian repeated softly.

Tony entered 'Cromer' and the record changed. "Is Miss Parks going with you?"

Brian laughed. "No."

"Wise move," said Adam.

"What do you mean by that?" snapped Hildee.

"Oh, just that a lot of other records would have to change as well, Miss." Adam smiled and gave Tony a sideways glance.

Tony clicked on the game icon, ran the cursor across the restaurant, and clicked on each of the characters in order to display windows of data. "See? You've gone." He changed the location to Cromer and repeated the process. "There you are! Breakfast in Cromer." Tony returned to the editing program and moved the dinner Brian had eaten the previous evening to Cromer. "There's no way of testing that, of course"

"Why do you keep rolling the data over? Why not just use one dinner session?" Brian asked.

Tony returned the game to Ivan's in Downham. "In case someone starts checking database accesses. If one session was accessed over and over again, for months on end, it would stick out like a sore thumb." He ran the cursor over the diners, clicking on each one. Brian thought he saw something and leaned forward to take a closer look at the screen. "There he is," Tony murmured.

"Fire!" both youths shouted. "Die, Morris!" The figure's stomach exploded in a cloud of red before falling to the floor.

"That was awful," Hildee said indignantly.

"Let me have a go." Brian reached over and took hold of the mouse.

Hildee looked at Brian in disbelief. "Really! How childish!"

Brian moved the cursor onto one of the diners in the corner of the restaurant and clicked the mouse button. "Not there."

"We can't tell where people sit. They're just sent to tables at random," Tony said.

"Silly. Of course not." Watched by Hildee, Brian checked each diner in turn. Then he found what he was looking for: 'Captain Ian Taylor. MI/SI Hereford Regiment.' But he had seen a second soldier when Tony had been clicking on diners. Brian continued the search. 'Captain James Nunn. MI/SI Hereford Regiment.'

"That is wrong," Hildee said. "There was only one soldier at breakfast."

Brian knew Hildee was right, and that meant that the second Military and Signals Intelligence officer in the restaurant that morning had been in plain clothes. He stood up. "Probably came in later." He saw that Tony was about to correct him and turned to face Hildee. "Talking of eating, shall we all go and get some lunch?"

191

Hildee looked at her watch. "It is about that time."

"Is that it now?" Tony asked.

"I need that editing software on a disk, then I'd like you to look at something else for me, but we can do that after lunch."

Tony looked at Adam, then back at Brian. "If you don't mind, we'd rather get on with it."

Brian flicked through the pages of the folder then placed a sheet of paper, with Troxley's S-Card number written on it, in front of Tony.

"High seven!" said Tony and Adam in unison.

"Does the Ivan's Killer game produce these 'high seven' numbers?" Brian asked.

Adam scoffed. "No way!"

"Why not?"

He shrugged. "It's a special code used to track down people who have got contagious diseases."

Brian pulled up a chair and sat down. He moved the cursor to another character and clicked the mouse button. By chance, the data that came up was Hildee's. Brian pointed to the window. "This item here: 'Health'. Next to it, 'Normal'. Now, if someone is ill, this field changes. So why change the number?"

Adam shrugged again. "I don't know. It's just what people say: 'Don't touch high sevens.' We used to use random numbers up to 254 for the second to sixth numbers. Then someone said it was dangerous and we gave them an upper limit of 50. Perhaps someone used one and the restaurant was raided."

"If a restaurant was raided, how would anyone in the games network be able to link it to what they were doing? After all, they are never in the restaurant in real time."

Tony frowned, bit his lip and looked up at the ceiling. "Good point, but does it matter how the 'high seven' was discovered?"

"I don't think anyone did discover it," Brian said. "Go back to your Ivan's Killer bulletin board." Tony recalled the newsreader and the list of entries that had scrolled down the screen. "Now search for the first entry which mentions 'high sevens'. Tony typed in the words 'high' and 'seven', as well as the number '7'. The list of entries contracted. Tony selected the first entry.

ALERT, ALERT Number usage warning
Be aware that using a number which has a seventh entry greater than 49 will alert the security services.
A number of restaurants and hospitals have been raided —

arrests made.
Be careful out there.
Trailblazer

Adam read the message, then turned to Tony. "He's right. How would he know? And who did they arrest?"

"Who is Trailblazer?" asked Brian.

Tony shrugged. "Don't recognise the name." He cleared the message from the screen and looked at the list again. Once more, Hildee began to feel uneasy. "trailblazer@rebafing.com," Tony said, turning to Adam. "Ever heard of them?" Adam shook his head.

Brian picked up his notebook and scribbled down the e-mail address. "Right now, what you need to do is look for all the entries posted by this 'Trailblazer' person."

Tony created a new search. This time the list was reduced to just two entries. The second entry was the alert that they had already read. The first had been posted twelve months earlier.

Help needed.
Hi, fellow gamers
I'm working on a variant of the Ivan's Killer game and would appreciate any help accessing the database and copies of any driver routines.
Please be discreet as I am using the company's PC.
trailblazer@rebafing.com

Brian sighed. "And someone would be daft enough to believe that?"

Tony clicked the mouse button and brought up Trailblazer's details. "He's really 'e.monk@rebafing.com'." Clearing the screen and opening a web browser, he entered 'www.rebafing.com'. The home page of Rebafing Technology Ventures appeared. Tony clicked on a button labelled 'contacts', which produced a second page. "There he is: Edwin Monk — Junior Programmer."

"See your point," Brian said.

Adam took the mouse from Tony and clicked on the browser's 'back' button. Rebafing's home page reappeared. "Boston, Massachusetts. How would he know that restaurants were being raided?"

Brian thought for a moment. "He didn't. He had used the seventh number for his own version of the program. Then he found that your random number generator was interfering with it."

Adam shook his head. "So why not use another number in the first position? They could have changed their software to use another number in the first position — say 254 instead of 255."

"Or any number in the first position above 49 and below 255," Tony chipped in.

"Too late," Brian said. The youths looked puzzled. "My guess is that the cards had already been issued. Trailblazer found that his program didn't work when they tested it in Europe. But by then the person they wanted to catch had already been given one of the cards. The victim would get suspicious if they were asked to give it back."

"So, what now?" Tony asked.

Brian picked up one of the mobile phones. "A bit of real hacking for you. Get into rebafing.com and find a piece of software that links the 'high seven' S-Card number with this mobile phone. But, whatever you do, don't run it and don't switch the phone on until we get back." He turned to Hildee. "Lunch then, Miss Parks?"

"Yes, lunch." Hildee paused and looked at Brian thoughtfully. "Mr. Tyler," she whispered under her breath.

*

"This must be great for kids," Brian said, looking around at the open fields.

They were half way between Nordelph and Downham. Hildee was too far ahead to hear exactly what Brian had said. She slowed down. "What did you say?"

"It must be great to be born in the country."

Hildee shrugged and looked around. "If it is what you are used to, you do not take much notice. Have you always lived in the city?"

"Yes, most of my life. But my father was born in a small village in Nottinghamshire. After he died, my mother took me to stay with some relations there."

"Is your..."

Brian interrupted Hildee before she could finish the question. "I just think you're lucky not having to worry about bringing up children in the city," he said.

Hildee stood up and pressed down on the pedals of her bicycle. Brian did not catch up with her again until she stopped outside the restaurant in Downham.

Lunch was over quickly, but Hildee got into a long conversation with Andrew Cameron when she took Brian to collect the glasses. Both she and Andrew wanted to transfer some of the penal workers from the farm to the workshop the following week. The stumbling block was Hutley, who claimed there were not enough soldiers to guard a split working party.

It was another hour and a half before they got back to Nordelph "We are virtually unscathed, I hope," Brian said, as they walked into the office.

Tony looked up from the computer. "Oh yes, Mr. Tyler," he replied, looking at Hildee.

Brian suspected that Hildee had not been so lucky. This was confirmed by Adam. "Enjoy the salad, Miss Parks?" he asked.

Tony held up a floppy disk. "All on there, tested and ready to install."

Brian was sure that it had been tested thoroughly. The temptation to use the software to the full would have proved too much for the youths. In the last hour, Tony and Adam had probably found out more about him than Hildee had learned during a whole day of subtle probing. In fact, even he could not have imagined the extent to which his life had been investigated.

Tony and Adam now knew that Brian spent most of his spare time with a soldier called Trevor. He lived in a house with a woman called Stephanie — who was too old to be his wife and was probably his landlady. They concluded that he was single, never visited his parents and was probably a volunteer fireman. All this data had been gleaned using search software that created a cross-linked database of diners in Brian's local restaurant. Adam joked that if Brian tried to arrest them, they would tell Miss Parks he was unattached, and she would lock him in his room.

Brian, as far as the youths could tell, was an 'OK sort of person'. They had been impressed by the way Trailblazer had been detected. In normal circumstances, they would have been reluctant to hack into the server of a fellow hacker. In their eyes, however, Trailblazer was already a lesser person for being so careless.

"Still working on Trailblazer. We've got his source code. Just going through it now."

"He won't know you took it, will he?" Brian asked.

"No chance! We put a piece of software on another server.

That dragged in Trailblazer's code, then deleted itself. We did that with another server before we collected it ourselves."

"You don't use Euro Telekom On-line then?"

Tony scoffed. "No way!"

When the collapse had come, in the early part of the century, all the economic models supporting the major on-line services failed. Most of the internet reverted to a collection of government-controlled networks. Across the world, the larger on-line services and the telephone companies were taken over by the state. In Europe, the party had bundled all the telephone and service providers together as 'Euro Telekom'. Hackers avoided transferring data across the heavily monitored Euro Telekom network. They preferred their own servers, linked with dedicated ISDN connections. If data like Ivan's Killer News was transferred across Euro Telekom Net, it was heavily encrypted — much to the consternation of the party's security section.

*

Brian picked up the map of the trial site. Hildee had followed him into the library. "I am sorry," she said, sitting down beside him. "After you borrowed the map, I took another look at my uncle's notes."

"That's what all of these are." Brian took the bundle of papers out of the box file and dropped it onto the desk.

"Yes. He spent a long time in here. He became obsessed with it."

Brian went back to the office to collect his notebook. When he returned, he closed the door behind him. "Your uncle was killed, wasn't he?"

"Yes," Hildee said softly.

"How did it happen?"

"Some men came from Peterborough to steal food from the fields. My uncle ran into a group of them and was shot."

"He was in charge of the manor?"

"He took over when my parents died. Until then, he had been working in London, at one of the universities. He studied microbiology. That is probably why all this interested him."

"How old were you when your parents died?"

"Really, Mr. Tyler, so many questions."

Brian realised that Hildee was going to be evasive. He feigned a frown, flicked open his notebook and with a pencil scored two lines under the notes he had taken when Tony was searching the internet. "You're twenty-six now, so your parents died when?"

Hildee was surprised by the sudden change in Brian's tone. "Oh, four. No. Six."

"Sorry, you were six when?" Brian asked, pretending to be confused.

"I was six when my parents died."

"Both parents?"

"They died within weeks of each other."

Brian scribbled down some more notes. "Then your uncle came to take over Nordelph?"

"Yes, but..."

"And when he was killed you were?"

"Fourteen."

"Fourteen? You took over the running of all this when you were fourteen?"

"Gerald Whiteside."

"Gerald Whiteside what?"

"I was trying to tell you. Gerald Whiteside took over most of the day-to-day running of the manor when my uncle died. I took over from him when he got old, when it got too much for him."

"Grew up fast." Brian took a deep breath. "So your uncle was killed fifteen years ago." He flicked over the page of his notebook. "But the army closed off East Anglia over twenty years ago. How did these raiders get here? By boat?"

"I do not..."

"Did they catch them?"

"Yes, I think so. I really don't remember."

"You never thought it was raiders who killed your uncle?" Brian did not give Hildee time to answer. "You thought he was killed because of something he saw in here." Brian pulled the box towards him. "How many hours did you spend going through this lot? Wondering why the police were lying in wait that night? How the passer-by saw the raiders when the field is hidden from the Littleport road? Then when Whiteside was killed, you took the map out and started wondering all over again. What happened then? Did you get scared? You don't seem the sort of person who scares that easily." Brian stopped. Hildee looked as though she was on the verge of losing her temper. He wanted to give her time to calm down before resuming his attack.

Hildee had been holding her breath. She swallowed hard, then breathed out slowly. She had only returned the map to the file that morning. "No. I was not scared. Not for..." She looked down at her hands, which were trembling.

Brian waited until Hildee looked up again before he spoke. Once again, the small yellow flecks close to the dark ring around the edge of her blue-grey irises held his attention, as they had earlier in the week. This time, however, it did not seem to worry her. "Bit of a Pandora's box, isn't it?" Brian said softly.

Leaning forward, Hildee took the papers out of the box. She was close enough to Brian for both of them to feel the warmth of each other's faces. Hildee quickly sat back in her chair. Brian suddenly lost all enthusiasm for the interrogation.

Brian spread the map across the desk. "I found some sort of box in the trees by the Littleport road. It seems to tie in with the little squares marked on these circles."

"It does. I must say, I never realised there were any left." Hildee was searching through the papers.

"They had bees in them? Like the ones by the river opposite Whiteside Farm?"

Hildee looked puzzled, then realised what Brian was talking about. "No. The boxes behind the farm are hives for wasps and lacewings. We use predatory insects instead of insecticide. Father was one of the pioneers of the technique in Europe. My uncle refined it. It is quite widely used now. No, what you found was one of the monitors used for the trial. They were placed on a series of concentric circles. The diameter of the inner circle was twenty metres greater than the length of the field itself. The outer one was five hundred metres in diameter. The cabinets were divided in two: the bottom half was a conventional beehive and the top contained a particle collector. The idea was to monitor both the amount of pollen that drifted from the trial site in the wind and the amount collected by bees." Hildee took the pencil out of Brian's hand and pointed to the edge of the map. "One or two monitoring stations were even set up a kilometre from the field."

"Quite an undertaking."

Hildee found what she was looking for. "The map only tells half the story," she said, folding the pages back so that the one headed 'Data from Other Trial Sites' was uppermost. She ran a pencil down the list of sites. "See, only half the sites are marked as having monitoring equipment, and someone has written something by each one.'

Brian thumbed back through the pages of his notebook, until he found the notes he had taken when searching *The Guardian*'s website: "All destroyed in the two weeks before the Whiteside Farm attack."

"Yes, but the rest of the trial sites were left untouched." Hildee pointed to the list again. "See, 'Trial Complete and Reported'."

Brian picked up the papers and leafed through them. These were the key sections that had been removed from the other file. "But if the Whiteside Farm trials were destroyed, why are there still all these pages of data?"

Hildee took the papers from Brian. "Those relate to the year before the trial. It is called 'base data'. The monitoring stations were put in place to assess how much pollen would be collected in normal circumstances." Turning to the next page, she pointed to a paragraph of text. "See, here it says that pollen from the field of oilseed rape was detected in both the cabinets and the monitoring units up to 200 metres from the field. 'It is proposed that further units are added to the trial during the GM phase and that these units are placed one kilometre from the field.'"

"So even though the trials were destroyed, there was evidence that pollen could travel at least 200 metres from the field. Was this ever published?"

"No. The whole trial was considered invalid. The only data used, what data there was, came from the unmonitored sites."

Replacing the papers in the box, Brian picked up the newspaper and reread the report of the attack. He was following in the footsteps of someone who had already investigated the Whiteside Farm attack — and he was coming to the same conclusions. Turning the page of the newspaper, he reread the stories of the man attacking his wife, the campaign for the dead child and the road-rage incident. Then, realising Hildee was studying him intently, he closed the newspaper. "I don't understand these people at all. Do you?"

Hildee shrugged. "Never had time to think about it."

"What was your uncle like?"

"Oh, great! Happy-go-lucky. Intelligent."

"Married?"

"Yes, he was," Hildee replied.

"Is his wife still alive?"

"No. She was not one of life's survivors. Perhaps if she'd stayed in London she'd have been all right, but she only lasted a year out here." Brian noticed a hint of bitterness in Hildee's voice. She had also developed a slight, almost imperceptible, accent.

"You didn't get on?"

"Ha! An understatement! I did not dress right. I did not walk right. I would never find a man if I spoke like a country girl." Hildee drew a breath. "She hated it here and took it out on me."

"So we can't talk to her. Any children?"

Hildee started to answer, hesitated, and then fell silent.

"When your aunt died, did your uncle remarry?"

Once again, Hildee started to answer, but thought better of it.

"It is rather important." Brian stared at her. "Hildee?"

"If you keep this to yourself. Please." Hildee waited until Brian nodded in agreement. "Well, after my aunt died, my uncle became friendly with a woman in Downham. Her name was Janet Spencer. She died two years after my uncle was killed."

"Any relation to Matt Spencer?"

"His mother."

"So, let's see. Matt is about nineteen?"

"Eighteen, and yes, he is my cousin."

"But probably no help to us with this." Brian closed the notebook and began returning the remaining papers to the box file.

"I would ask you to be discreet. You see, Matt does not know."

"I doubt that." Brian closed the file and replaced it, with the others, on the shelf. "But if he doesn't, he won't find out from me."

*

The gangster, the robot and three other characters were contributing to a bloodbath in a crowded Ivan's somewhere in Liverpool. Tony and Adam jumped up and terminated the game when they realised that Brian and Hildee were standing behind them. "All done, Mr. Tyler. Clever piece of software."

"All stolen from someone else," Adam added.

Brian took hold of a chair, turned it around and sat down with his chin resting on its back. "Why didn't you tell me you'd finished?"

Tony looked embarrassed. "We didn't want to disturb you."

Hildee turned away, but Brian had already seen her blush. "I will make us all a cup of tea," she said as she left the room.

"Well," Tony stammered as he picked up the mobile phone.

Now Brian was beginning to feel embarrassed. This was silly, he thought. It wasn't as if he and Hildee had suddenly become intimate. "Right!" he said loudly. "Show us what you've got and let's hope you haven't been spotted."

Tony snapped into action. Program source code scrolled down the screen, stopping now and then as either Tony or Adam explained how one of the functions worked.

"Not so much detail. Let's cut to the chase," Brian said. "Just tell me how it works."

Tony rubbed his hands together. "First you send an e-mail to 'tracker@rebafing.com' with the S-Card number of your target in the main body of the message. You also have to supply the names of the cities you want to track your target in, and how many days you want the search to run. The program takes the S-Card number out of the e-mail and uses the modified Ivan's Killer software to scan the database every fifteen minutes until it finds a match."

"And the mobile phones?" Brian asked.

Tony clicked on another file, and a new page of computer code appeared on the screen. "Hard-coded into the software are three phone numbers: two mobiles and a number in London. When the target has been located, a web page with the restaurant's location is created and posted to a site hosted by the Rebafing server. Then the program uses a TAPI-based routine to dial all three numbers. Each connection is terminated as soon as the call is answered."

"Seems a bit silly, hard-coding the numbers," Adam commented. "Can't see why they didn't send them as part of the e-mail message."

Brian ignored Adam's observation. He was too busy thinking about the London number. It belonged to the answerphone Johnny Coates had tracked down on Friday. Brian switched on the two mobile phones and keyed one of the numbers on the screen into the first phone. "Engaged. That's encouraging." He dialled the second number. The other mobile phone rang twice. Brian stared at it. "What happens now?"

Tony took the phone. "This button here. The one that says 'Web'." He pressed the button, glanced at the display, and handed the phone back to Brian.

Brian read out the displayed text: "'Toby Troxley — Turnham Green, London SW8.'" He switched the phone off and put it down on the desk. "That explains a lot. Thanks, lads."

Tony conferred with Adam, then turned back to Brian. "We were wondering if we could keep the mobile phones."

Brian laughed. "Using these would be like eating a jam sandwich in front of a wasps' nest."

Tony's face fell. "Good point," he said.

Hildee returned with the tea. Both Adam and Tony left theirs, and even Hildee seemed to have difficulty finishing hers. "Sorry, Miss Parks, can't drink mine. I think you forgot something," Tony said, as he and Adam packed the computer into its carrying case.

"Sorry, it is the best I can do — at the moment," Hildee replied, giving Tony a black look. Unfortunately, only Brian understood what she was trying to tell the youths. Because a policeman was present, the tea had been served without the usual milk and sugar.

After signing their Community Service forms, Hildee walked to the door with Tony and Adam.

Sitting alone in the office, Brian installed the editing software. After moving his lunch break to Cromer, he brought his notes up to date by adding a detailed description of the tracking system. He heard Hildee walk up the stairs. Gathering up his notes, and the two mobile phones, he crossed the entrance hall to the study. Now the collection of photographs on the table in front of the window made more sense. Parents, aunt and uncle, then just her uncle. In each picture a girl was growing older and taller — and as she aged, her smile became progressively more forced. Then Whiteside appeared in the pictures. He was teaching her to ride her bicycle, or sitting with her on a tractor. More recently, the old man was leaning over the desk she was working at. In these pictures her smile was genuine.

"Mr. Tyler." The voice came from the other side of the hall. Hildee had assumed that Brian was still in the office.

"Over here!" Brian called out.

Hildee seemed tense when she appeared in the doorway. Brian thought he was about to be chastised for being in the study. "I was wondering... I know it may seem rather tame after London," she said, her voice seeming to tremble as though she was nervous, "but I was thinking of going to the dance in town tonight." She waited for a response from Brian, but none came. "It starts just after dinner." She persisted. "There will be drink and usually Matt and a few of the other men..."

Brian suddenly realised how awkward Hildee was finding the relatively simple task of asking him out. "Lovely," he snapped, then seeing Hildee had taken his abruptness the wrong way, he added, "If you don't mind, of course."

Hildee sighed with relief. "No, of course not." She looked down at her feet. "Well, I will just get ready then."

While Hildee was upstairs, Brian returned to the library. He took down the box file labelled 'Whiteside Farm Accounts' and removed the papers from it. Then, after placing his own folder and notes in the box, he laid the original papers on top of them before returning the file to its place on the shelf.

*

Even in the shade of the trees the evening air felt warm. There was no breeze. If there had been, perhaps Brian would not have noticed movement in the bushes at the edge of the garden. Towards Wisbech the road was clear. At the West Farm Way junction, Brian stopped. The lane was also clear. He looked at his watch.

"Something wrong?" Hildee asked, turning her bicycle around and riding back to where Brian was standing.

Brian had expected her to carry on without him. Now he had to think of an excuse for hanging back. "All this cycling — this the third time today. Why don't we take the bus?"

"Make the most of it. When winter comes, you will be sick of waiting for the bus."

Brian was preoccupied and failed to notice Hildee betray herself. He pressed a button on his watch to reset the second-counter. "I thought I might time myself on this run."

"Really, for a policeman you are very childish." Hildee laughed as they set off towards Downham.

Brian looked down at his watch: twelve seconds. He glanced back over his shoulder. A cyclist had just rounded the corner in front of Nordelph Manor. They could not have covered the clear length of either West Farm Way or the Wisbech road in twelve seconds. The cyclist must have started out from near the manor house itself. Now Brian was sure he was being watched — luckily by someone who was not particularly clever.

*

The music was a mixture of rock and roll and pop. As they entered the dance hall, Brian realised that Hildee had not changed out of her jeans and tee-shirt. Most of the other girls were wearing summer dresses or blouses and skirts.

As Brian hung his jacket in the cloakroom, Hildee tapped him on the arm. "Won't be a moment," she said, swinging her bag over her shoulder and disappearing into the Ladies.

"That's the last you'll see of her." It was the repair mechanic.

"Mine went in there ten minutes ago and still hasn't come out." He laughed. "Some sort of conference."

Brian took a handkerchief out of his pocket, placed his police ID card on it and folded the handkerchief over three times before returning it to the pocket. "In that case, is there anywhere we can get a drink?"

The mechanic led Brian to the bar, where Matt Spencer and most of the other men from the Swan where drinking. Live music in London, when there was any, tended to be a mixture of blues and folk, mostly played on acoustic instruments. Equipped with electric guitars and microphones, the band here was working its way through their repertoire of Rolling Stones and Beatles songs.

"Seems I owe you five euros," Matt said.

"What for?" Brian shouted to make himself heard above the howl of feedback caused by the band's lead singer conferring with one of the guitarists.

Matt made a gesture in the direction of Hildee, who was standing on the other side of the room. She was wearing the black dress Brian had caught her trying on three days earlier. "How's she treating you?" Matt asked.

"Very well," Brian said, unable to take his eyes off Hildee.

The mechanic laughed. "Remember what I said about meeting the right girl and not being able to go back to London?" He slapped Brian on the back. "See if you can get a train tonight before it's too late."

Hildee was talking to a group of girls. One of the girls looked towards Brian and smiled. Hildee looked ill at ease, and even though she was much older than the other girls she seemed less confident. There was no sign of the aggressive stance she adopted when discussing farm management and manning levels with soldiers and factory managers. As the evening wore on, more people took to the dance floor. There were fewer girls standing in groups and fewer men at the bar. Hildee looked lost and glanced nervously around the room.

"Dance?" Brian asked. Hildee did not answer but merely followed him onto the dance floor. "Why didn't you come over to the bar?"

"You seemed to be having a good time." Hildee bent her knees and swung her arms gently in time with the music — movements that Brian thought hardly qualified as dance. "I didn't want to disturb you," she shouted above the music.

Back home in London, if Brian found himself with a girl who

danced like Hildee, he would look for an excuse to move on as quickly as possible. Sometimes Trevor would come to his rescue. Tonight, however, he felt differently. He didn't want to see her looking lost and alone again. "What sort of music do you like?" he said, trying to make conversation. Hildee pointed to her ear and shook her head. Again she glanced self-consciously around the room, then looked down at the floor.

The band was hammering out 'Brown-eyed Girl' Brian saw Matt look in his direction, nudge the mechanic, then walk across to the band. The guitarist crouched down at the front of the stage, exchanged a few words with Matt, and walked over to the lead singer. When the song finished, the singer and the drummer left the stage. The guitarist grabbed the microphone and, when the feedback had faded, said, "We are slowing things down a bit now."

Hildee shrugged and turned to walk away, but Brian reached out and grabbed her by both arms. She was taken by surprise as Brian's arms slipped around her. She looked down at the floor. Her hands moved nervously across his back, unable to settle in any one place for more then a few seconds. By contrast, Brian held her firmly, with one arm around her waist and his other hand on her shoulder. Across the room, she could see Matt, the mechanic and their girlfriends watching her. Wanting to hide, she moved closer to Brian. As she did so, her lips brushed against his neck. She smelled his skin and tasted the sweat. She smiled to herself. 'Nice enough to eat' one of the other girls had said when she saw Brian. Hildee pushed her lips against his neck again — not quite a kiss. Brian moved his hand across her shoulder and gently stroked the back of her neck, then kissed her on the forehead. Over her shoulder, he watched as the soldier disappeared into the cloakroom.

The sound of the guitar died away. "Time for home," Hildee said, running her hand down Brian's arm and interlocking her fingers with his. Brian looked towards the cloakroom.

The soldier had not returned. "One for the road," Brian said, leading Hildee towards the bar. The soldier reappeared and leaned against the wall on the opposite side of the dance hall. He was watching Brian finish his drink. Brian asked for a second beer. He downed it with such speed that both Matt and the mechanic gasped with surprise. He slipped his arm around Hildee's waist and gave her a squeeze. "OK, I'm ready," he said.

Outside in the cool air, Brian staggered and grabbed the railings to steady himself. He reached into his pocket for a handkerchief to wipe his brow. His police ID card fell on the pavement. He swayed, then stooped to pick it up. Hildee emerged from the dance hall just as Brian lurched upright again. She had changed out of her dress and back into her jeans and tee-shirt. "Are you all right?" she asked.

"Fine," Brian replied, his speech slurred.

"Hold on a minute, Brian!" Matt called out from the entrance of the hall, searching through his pockets as he walked over to him. "There you go: five pounds. Congratulations! It must be your magic charm." He slapped Brian on the back, then looked at Hildee and smiled.

Hildee got onto her bicycle and rode into the darkness. Brian grappled with his, only succeeding in mounting it at the third attempt.

By the time Brian reached the edge of Downham, all he could see of Hildee was a small red light in the distance. A kilometre from town, he slowed to a stop and the dynamo-driven lights on his own bicycle flickered and died. He watched Hildee disappear from view. Ten minutes passed, and still there were no lights on the road leading out of Downham. Whoever had followed them into town had decided not to follow them back. Perhaps, now that they had positively identified him, they would give up. Or, more likely, they too needed their sleep. Brian was beginning to get a feel for the strength and capabilities of the people who were trailing him. Probably only two people of limited experience — judging by the mess they had made of replacing his handkerchief and ID card after rifling through his jacket pockets.

*

Hildee was sitting on the stairs when Brian came into the entrance hall of Nordelph Manor. "At last! I thought you might be spending the night lying drunk in a ditch!" She stood up and walked towards him. Her hand struck him hard on the left cheek. She stepped back, half-expecting him to retaliate. Brian was about to speak, but Hildee did not give him the chance. "And do not ask me what that was for! You made some vulgar bet with Matt Spencer! It obviously involved me." She turned and strode towards the stairs. "You really are the most disgusting, drunken lout I have ever met!"

Brian's left ear was ringing and his face throbbed. He wanted to shout at her, but his throat was suddenly dry and he felt as if he was being strangled. "It was about your dress." He noticed Hildee falter. "Matt bet me you wouldn't..."

"Goodnight, Mr. Tyler." Hildee continued on her way up the stairs.

"Oh, what's the use?" Brian whispered to himself. He walked through the office to the library and retrieved his notes from the 'Whiteside Farm Accounts' box file. Above, the door to Hildee's room slammed.

*

Back in his own room, he was placing the file in his rucksack when he noticed the broken ornament. There were small fragments of porcelain on the floor. Obviously he had been right to hide his notes, but he was amazed how clumsy the search had been. Perhaps the soldiers had wanted to make their presence obvious. How had they broken in? Did they have a key? Had they been let in earlier? These questions ran through his mind as he undressed. He laid Camus's book and the broken figure on the bedside cupboard.

All Brian wanted to do was sleep. He looked at his watch. In nine hours he would be on his way home. It would be nice to sleep for seven of them, but he knew he would not be able to sleep while his face was stinging. He tried to read the book but could not concentrate. He picked up the broken figure, put the arm back on it, then put the pieces down again. This time tomorrow he would be home. Perhaps he would get back in time to go out with Trevor and Stef. He desperately wanted to see Stef. What on earth had possessed him to come out here in the first place? What had he achieved? Nothing that he could think of. All he had done was confirm what he already knew from speaking to Hutch — and from reading the S-Card computer manual. In fact, the main achievement of the weekend was the creation a computer program that removed any evidence of his visit.

Another nine hours and he would never see her again. Perhaps Tony and Adam were right. Perhaps she was mentally disturbed, unhinged by years of living on her own. No-one had ever taken him on such an emotional roller coaster ride. The pain was fading at last. No one had brought him so close to tears. Ten and a half hours and he would be in Cambridge. Two hours there, and then two hours on the train back to London. Back with Stef by tomorrow evening.

*

Hildee lay staring up at the ceiling. She had deposited her clothes in the corner of the room, on top of the black dress, which lay screwed up in a ball. She heard Brian's door close, the thud of the book being dropped onto the bedside cupboard, the clink of the remains of the ornament. Why had he got drunk? There were so many contradictions. The childish behaviour that had seemed so out of character. Timing himself on the ride into town, but not bothering to check how long it took to reach Downham. His tenderness when they were dancing, then his loutish behaviour a few minutes later. Which was the act? He did not seem to be drunk when he finally arrived back at the house.

Gradually Hildee's anger subsided enough for her to begin to rationalise the events of the evening. She too had glanced back and seen someone following them into town. Now she realised that Brian had been timing them, not himself. The drunken staggering had probably been an act, to persuade their tail that he was not worth pursuing, or to lull them into a false sense of security so that he could attack them on the journey home. Why did he not want to be followed? It had not bothered him before. He wanted to be alone. So that he could be in bed with her without worrying who was outside.

She heard the bed in the next room creak as Brian got into it. Hildee wondered if he had really thought he would be sleeping with her tonight. Had he bet Matt he would? If so what was all that about the dress? That too began to make sense. Twice Matt had asked pointedly whether she wanted anything taken back to Peterborough on Monday. That could only have meant the dress. What could she do about it now? Knock on his door and say sorry perhaps? She heard the clink of the broken ornament. Say sorry for that as well? Gerald Whiteside used to tell her never to take today's anger into tomorrow. He had seen her fly into a rage with a boyfriend on more than one occasion. If she had listened to him, she would not be living alone now. Tomorrow she would act on his advice. Tomorrow, however, Brian was likely to be very angry with her.

*

"The thing to remember is," Martha Snyder shouted over the noise of a taxiing aircraft as she held the car door open for Mike, "here we have to pay for everything." She slammed the door shut, then walked around to the driver's side. "You walk out of a restaurant without paying or sit down on a bus without buying a ticket and you give yourself away."

Apart from one or two buses and some yellow cabs, the freeway was deserted. Martha was forty years old. Most of her long brown hair was tied at the back of her head; a few strands blew across her face. The sleeves of her light-blue shirt rippled in the wind as the open-top sports car headed out of Dulles airport. She took an envelope out of the glove compartment. "There are two thousand dollars in there. You can sign for them later. You're booked into the Ritz-Carlton at Tyson's Corner under the name of Mike Andrews." She waited to see if Mike would ask why, but he didn't. "Mike Andrews is a member of a team negotiating the grain deal. I think that's it. Oh, don't worry about the bill for the hotel. We're paying that as well. That reminds me, I'll need your passport until tomorrow." Martha took a pair of glasses out of her shirt pocket. She had small, piggy eyes. Mike guessed that that was why she wore glasses with such large frames.

Swapping his passport for the envelope, Mike stuffed the two thousand dollars into his wallet without bothering to count them. After the fifteen-hour flight he should have felt tired, but his adrenaline had started pumping as soon as the plane had touched down in Washington. During the stopover in Brussels he had considered catching the train back to London. It was not just the thought of Aul's man lying in wait that had persuaded him to transfer to the American Airlines flight. He had promised Ivan, and he could not get Tanya out of his mind. It was also becoming clear that both he and Brian were being used. Whoever was using them would find Mike's visit to Ivan disturbing. There was a chance that he could have saved his neck by implicating Ivan in the Troxley murder. But by the time he had run through all the options — including the unpalatable ones — the Boeing 747 was in the air.

The in-flight meal was served on china plates, the drinks in real glasses. He had relaxed, slept and missed the in-flight movie. Now, having ignored the advice he had given Brian, he was committed to finding Troxley's real killer.

"This is Mr. *Andrews*," Martha said to the receptionist as Mike filled out the registration form. She put a slight emphasis on 'Andrews', in case he had forgotten. "We will settle the bill," she said, putting her identification card on the desk.

As Martha was CIA, the receptionist did not ask for identification and guessed that Mike was not really Mr. Andrews anyway. "Don't worry about filling in the address. Just sign," she said. Mike scribbled a barely legible signature. "That's great." The receptionist retrieved the form and put a key on the counter. "Second floor. The elevator is on the left. Have a nice day."

"Elevator," Mike muttered to himself.

"Air conditioning, pool, minibar and room service. No expense spared for our rich European cousins," Martha said, taking her car keys out of her pocket. "Ten a.m., as it's Sunday. Will that be OK?"

"Sorry?"

"Pick you up at ten tomorrow?"

"Oh, yes," said Mike, only now beginning to take in the plush surroundings: the polished wood panelling, the piano and the large vases of dried flowers. "Fine. See you then. Have a nice day," he said, as Martha jogged towards the main entrance.

*

In the early hours of the morning, Hildee woke with a start. The shouting was louder than it had been the night before. The same words — 'no' and 'wait' — but sounding more desperate. She heard the bed in the next room creak as Brian thrashed in his sleep. Eventually there was the click of the light switch and footsteps pacing the floor. The bed creaked again, then there was a moaning sound and, after a while, silence. "Sorry, Brian," Hildee whispered to herself before falling asleep.

Sunday 25th August 2041

Brian threw the tangle of sheets onto the floor and sat upright on the edge of the bed. He could hear the sound of birds singing outside the window and footsteps on the gravel drive below. Drawing back the curtains, he winced and screwed up his eyes. Below, Hildee Parks was tying two long, thin canvas bags to the small trolley attached to her bicycle. She glanced up briefly, then looked away again without seeming to acknowledge Brian's presence.

The tap squeaked. After Brian had turned it several times, cold brown water dribbled into the basin. He splashed two handfuls onto his face. He felt tired and dizzy, and had to steady himself against the basin while shaving.

Hildee was sitting on a wooden seat under the trees. She was wearing a white tee-shirt and a thin, crudely printed floral-patterned skirt. On seeing Brian, she stood up, walked back to the house and locked the front door.

"What are those?" Asked Brian pointing at the two canvas bags.

"Fishing rods. I thought we would spend the day down by the river," Hildee replied, pushing her bicycle along the drive. "I have packed some bottles of wine, water and, as you seem to like it so much, beer."

"But I'm leaving straight after breakfast," Brian said apologetically.

Hildee mounted the bicycle, pushing down hard on the pedals as the wheels ploughed through the deep gravel at the edge of the drive. "That's a shame," she said, without changing the tone of her voice.

Brian attempted to set off after her, but the accumulated gravel brought his bicycle to a standstill. He then wheeled it to the relatively bare track that other vehicles had created in the middle of the drive. Hildee was already on the main road. "You own all of this land!" Brian called out as he caught up with her.

Hildee applied her brakes and slowed down so that Brian could keep up. "You know better than that. No-one owns anything. I just manage this."

"What I meant was, your family..."

"Yes. My father, and his father, owned all of this."

"And they let you stay on here."

"By 'they' I assume you mean the party?"

"Yes," Brian gasped, still out of breath. He was going to ask whether the party or the army gave her any problems, but decided it was unlikely that anyone would risk incurring her wrath.

"A bit fragile this morning?" Hildee laughed, pedalling harder and increasing the pace. "My father was well connected with the party from the beginning. He backed them against the Socialists after the crops were contaminated. He argued against the switch to livestock."

"Why?"

"He said it would cause disease."

"He was right."

"In a way. He thought we would see something like BSE back again. When viruses from pigs in Holland and Germany started to infect humans, father was very vocal in his condemnation of the government."

"And backed the Greens."

"Yes, and that is why I am still here."

"So how did the farm survive?"

"If it had depended on my father, it wouldn't have. He was a real dreamer. Mother was the businesswoman. She had been running the bed and breakfast for years, and a farm shop that sold organic produce. Anything new that made money, she was on to it." Hildee gazed across the open fields. "Drew the line at building a golf course, though. Said she was not having vulgar little businessmen with their mobile phones traipsing past her window every weekend."

Brian thought for a moment. Hildee was smiling. But still he hesitated before speaking. "Do you think they will let your children stay here as well?"

Hildee giggled and pedalled harder, leaving Brian trailing behind.

*

"As much as you can spare," Hildee told the woman behind the serving counter. "This man has got a long day ahead of him."

The old woman smiled, took a sideways glance at the manager, then put an extra spoon of scrambled egg on both Hildee's and Brian's plate.

Brian ate his breakfast in silence. He felt unhappy about leaving, especially as Hildee's mood had improved.

Two tables away, Matt Spencer was slumped over his half-eaten breakfast. "Been here since last night, I should think," Hildee whispered. "Good job you aren't going anywhere today."

Hildee's refusal to accept the fact that Brian was leaving made him feel particularly uneasy. Perhaps she was going to make a scene. "Look, I'm sorry about having to go," he said nervously. "It's nothing to do with..." he struggled to find the right words.

Hildee swallowed a mouthful of egg. "Last night," she said, without looking up. "I'm sorry. I behaved terribly. I don't blame you for not wanting to stay. Really."

"I would like to stay," Brian lied, "but there's just too much to do."

"Fine, fine. Shall I move this breakfast to Cromer when I get home?"

Brian resisted the urge to look across the room at the soldier who had followed them into the restaurant. "That's OK. I'll do that tomorrow."

"Would she miss you if you didn't get back until tomorrow?"

"There isn't anyone."

"I meant your landlady."

"Oh. No. I've got a couple of things to sort out."

"A conspiracy to thwart and criminals to bang to rights." Hildee glanced up at the clock above the counter.

"You'd better hurry or you'll miss the train."

"Yes, you're right." Brian wondered whether he should lean forward and kiss Hildee on the cheek. He settled for standing up and extending his hand.

"Goodbye, and good luck," she said, shaking his hand. "Hope you find what you're looking for."

Brian was relieved that Hildee had not made a scene and surprised that she remained seated in the restaurant. Perhaps he had misread the signals she was giving off. As he pushed his bicycle onto the deserted platform of Downham station, the inspector's office door opened. A man wearing jeans and a tee-shirt staggered out onto the platform. "You were there last night," the stationmaster said, screwing up his eyes. "With Miss Parks. Are you going for a bike ride down the tracks?"

"No. I'm catching the next train."

"You've got a long wait. The next one is five thirty tomorrow morning."

"Tomorrow!" exclaimed Brian.

"No trains Sundays — track repairs. I'd have thought Miss Parks would have told you that."

Without replying, Brian pushed his bicycle back towards the station entrance. "Perhaps Matt Spencer will drive you to Peterborough," the stationmaster shouted after him.

In the station car park, Hildee was leaning against her bicycle. She grinned as Brian approached. "The river is only a ten-minute bike ride away."

Brian felt a mixture of annoyance and anger. Annoyed that he would not be able to keep to his schedule, and less than thrilled by the thought of spending another day with Hildee. "You knew damn well there weren't any trains," he said.

"Well, I thought, perhaps, as you are an important policeman, on such an important mission, that you had your own train." She giggled, betraying her excitement. "Of course, you could get Matt to drive you..." She snapped her fingers. "No, no. He is dead to the world for the rest of the day."

Brian got on his bicycle. "To the river then, I suppose," he muttered, setting off after Hildee. The road led west out of Downham, winding down a gentle incline through the deserted village of Denver. He caught up with Hildee as the road petered out and became no more than a track. They then pushed their bicycles past the giant sluice gates that controlled the flow of water draining from fens into the River Ouse.

The track ran along the southern bank of one of the straight channels that ran parallel with the road to Nordelph. This waterway passed through Whiteside Farm, and had provided Gerald Whiteside's killers with a means of escape.

Half a kilometre from the sluice, Hildee stopped and began treading down a patch of the long grass that covered the river bank. After a while she let Brian take over and unpacked the two fishing rods. Hildee spread two blankets on the ground and set up supports for the rods. The reel screamed as she cast the fly three-quarters of the way across the river.

Brian started to wave the second rod backwards and forwards, the fly circling around his head. Hildee took the rod from him. "Like this," she said, flicking the rod and sending the fly across the river. "I don't want to spend the next hour trying to get a hook out of your ear." She handed the rod back to Brian. "One day you will have to learn to do that properly." She sighed. For the second time in as many days Hildee had betrayed her innermost thoughts. And for second time neither she nor Brian noticed.

"So how many do you usually catch?" Brian asked.

"Fifteen to twenty," Hildee replied.

"And a novice? How many are they likely to catch?"

"Is that important?"

"Well, I need to know the form."

"Form?"

"To work out the odds of me catching more than you. I mean, if a novice usually catches, say, eight, then there's a fifteen..."

"Yes. I can probably work that out myself. If I had wanted to spend the day doing maths, I could have stayed at home juggling the manning levels."

Brian shrugged and stared across the river at the float, which was slowly drifting downstream. Hildee felt guilty for snapping at him. She waited for him to restart the conversation, but it became obvious that he was not going to. She saw him take a long hard look at his watch.

Brian felt uncomfortable. It seemed that Hildee had not

forgiven him for yesterday evening. Worse still, it looked as though he would be punished for it for the next six hours at least. He toyed with the idea of getting up and going for a walk.

"So what is your boss like then?" Hildee said eventually.

"A bit of an idiot actually," Brian replied, without looking at her.

"I never realised policemen regarded each other as idiots."

Brian found the remark amusing and smiled. "Yes, actually he does treat me as though I'm stupid."

Hildee smiled. "All the older generation think we are simple."

"Why do you think that is?"

"Because we are." Brian's float disappeared under the surface. He pulled at the rod and the reel screamed. Hildee reached forward, took hold of the rod and turned the handle on the side of the reel. "Like this," she said, pulling at the rod and reeling in the line. The trout writhed at the end of the line as it was pulled clear. Hildee held the rod upright and the fish landed with a thud between her and Brian. "Then you take out the hook, like this." The hook, weights and float swung back out over the river, leaving the trout motionless on the blanket.

"Now what?" Brian asked, looking down at the fish.

"Now you take it and put it in the keep net."

He picked up the fish and carried it down the bank. As he reached forward, the fish wriggled free and propelled itself over the net and into the water. "Blast!" Brian exclaimed.

Hildee laughed. "Time to reassess your form, Mr. Tyler?"

Brian picked up the rod and cast out across the river, the float falling short of where Hildee had previously cast it. He was about to reel it back.

"That will be OK," Hildee said, trying not to laugh at him again.

"Simple?" Brian asked, sitting down. Hildee looked at him quizzically. "You said we're simple."

"Oh yes. It's a simpler world." Now Hildee's float disappeared and she began pulling the fish across the river. "You see, consciousness is a memory of what is happening now. Your boss grew up in a complicated high-tech consumer society, where lots of things were happening all the time. They confused stimulation with awareness." She struggled to tire the thrashing fish, giving it more line, then reeling it back in again. "They thought they had reached some sort of advanced level of consciousness because they were over stimulated by endless streams of trivial nonsense." The fish swung clear of the water and landed on the bank. "Whereas we, Mr. Tyler, are not. All we have to worry about is survival — day-to-day survival." With a flick of her fingers, she pulled the hook out of the trout's mouth. "Getting enough to eat, not getting sick — the basics." She took the fish and threw it down the bank into the keep net. It writhed for a few moments and then was still. "So that makes me 'your favourite', does it?"

"Odds-on favourite," Brian said, not realising he was being teased. He watched as Hildee cast again. "That explains it, does it?"

"It explains a lot. It explains all those stories in that newspaper yesterday."

"Such as?"

"Well, about the woman who made all that fuss about her dead child."

"I can't see it."

"Well, that woman probably never gave a second thought to day-to-day survival. Certainly not at the level at which it concerns you and me. Survival was a collective experience. Society dealt with the life-and-death issues, such as food, drink and health — not very well, as it turned out. She was protected from all of that and filled her life with trivia instead. The only time she had to worry about survival was when her child became ill. The child, a product of her own genes, was flawed."

"And that explains why she started collecting money?"

"It was easier than admitting she was flawed. The survival of her genes was everything, even if it meant convincing the rest of society that her child was viable."

"I don't believe that," Brian said, turning away.

"What happens in London when a woman gives birth to a deformed baby?"

"How should I know?"

"You are a policeman — you know everything that happens," Hildee said sarcastically. Brian did not answer, but she persisted. "Well?"

Brian sighed. "I've never seen it, but they say that the doctor, or midwife, just doesn't start the breathing." He paused for a moment. "Or they leave it face down on a pillow." He turned and looked at Hildee again. "We are told that if we come across a stillbirth, it is not to be documented, and the body is sent for disposal without paperwork."

"And that is it. The woman can have another one and no-one

will ever know. She does not have to walk around advertising her own vulnerability. She does not end up with a constant reminder that her genes may have reached an evolutionary dead end."

"That's a very hard way of looking at the world."

"It is a very hard world I am looking at, Mr. Tyler." Another fish had taken the fly — a smaller one that could be reeled in without a fight. "The alternative, even if we could afford it, would be a lot worse."

Suddenly Brian's float disappeared. "What do you mean?" he asked, tugging at the rod and slowly reeling in the line.

"If we did try to support every mentally ill and deformed child that was born, what would happen to them if things took another turn for the worse?" Hildee could see that Brian was struggling with a large fish but she was still reeling in the one she herself had caught.

"We would have to deal with it when it happened," Brian said, his voice strained.

"You mean, like they did in the last century?"

"No. It wouldn't come to that."

"More sophisticated societies than this one have found some pretty gruesome ways of coming to terms with threats to their gene pool." Hildee landed her fish, then laid down her rod and helped Brian land his. "Well, that is a definite improvement on the last one," she said, taking the hook out of its mouth. "Shall we keep this one or do you want to throw it back?"

Brian smiled at her. "It's getting hot, isn't it?" He stood up, took off his shirt and threw it to the ground. After recasting the line, he sat down by the water's edge. "It still doesn't explain all their other neuroses, their obsession with cars — or the wife-beating."

Hildee dropped Brian's fish into the keep net. "Yes it does. All those things were ways of expressing their unconscious fears about their own survival. They had to demonstrate their own superiority. Their genes drove them to do it, even though it was irrelevant. Their cars had to be the best, their jobs had to be the most highly paid and their wives had to be the best-looking. Flaws in any one of a countless number of material possessions were interpreted as threats. Any threat was an excuse for a violent reaction."

Brian sat quietly for a while, looking down at his feet. He then looked up and surveyed the opposite bank. "Still, it's all behind us now."

"Or in front of us. That is what all this trouble is about. All this political in-fighting that you seem to have got caught up in."

"That's not the way I see it."

"We are producing more food than we need. That is obvious. We can see trainloads of it leaving here every day. Sometimes we cannot find enough work for locals, let alone for the prisoners you keep sending us. It will not be long before someone decides to start making things we do not need just to keep people busy. Before long, we will all get weekends and holidays to buy things we do not need." She paused for a moment, waiting for Brian to turn and face her, but he did not. "Then we will start filling our lives with trivia and meaningless images."

"You really think we'll go back to all that?"

"Oh yes! We are easily seduced. We will all forget where food comes from. What our health depends on. Then it will be back to the good old consumer society..." She stopped speaking. Her voice trailed away as she realised Brian was brooding. She waited for him to speak again or turn around, but still he did not.

Fifteen minutes passed. The silence was agonising. Hildee watched the beads of sweat forming on Brian's naked back. "What is your mother like?" she asked.

"I don't really know."

Hildee laughed. "You mean indescribably beautiful?"

"No. I haven't seen her since I was five."

"Oh, I thought she was..."

"Dead? No. She lives somewhere in Birmingham." Brian hoped a fish would bite and end the conversation. He waited, but the floats continued, undisturbed, on their lazy journey downstream. "She didn't cope very well with the death of my father. My elder sister looked after me for a couple of years and then I went into a children's home run by the party. I can't remember much about my mum — I think she was violent, sometimes." He sat in silence for a while, before asking, "How does that fit into your grand theory?"

Until now, nothing Brian had said or done had changed Hildee's view of him. He was an opportunity, someone to play around with and to poke fun at. He had been easy to keep at arm's length and she had felt little remorse after teasing him, or even after she had struck him yesterday evening. Now she could feel her fingers tingling. "I am really..." But she could not say the word. He was getting too close to her. She stood up to walk away, trying to collect her thoughts. The reel on her rod screamed. She sat down again and dragged the fish onto the bank.

218

"Sorry," she said eventually. Brian's shoulders rose and fell. Hildee watched the muscles tense and then relax. She reached out to touch his shoulder. Just before her fingers reached him, Brian turned. She was looking straight into his eyes. "You will burn in this sun," she said, knowing full well he would not. His skin, like her own, would tan before it burned.

Hildee picked up the trout and slid down the blanket until she was sitting next to Brian. "Hungry?" she asked.

"A bit."

"Want some fish?"

"You mean go back to town?"

Hildee lowered her voice. "No, silly, " she whispered. "One of these. Here. Now. You get a fire going and I will prepare it."

"Don't be silly, we're taking them back to the restaurant."

"Not this one." Hildee stood up and took a knife from the basket. With one stroke, she cut off the trout's head. She then turned the fish round in her hand and slit open its belly, emptying the contents into the grass. Crouching down, she opened up the fish and held it in front of Brian's face. "That make you feel really hungry?" Brian looked down at his feet and did not answer. Hildee ran her finger down the exposed inside of the trout. "Imagine how this would taste, cooked until it was pink, dripping with butter."

Brian looked up. Hildee was smiling. She dropped the fish and the knife into the grass at the edge of the blanket. Her lips were soft and tired — as they might have been after sex rather than before it. Until she kissed him, Brian had not realised how much he wanted her. Now the desire gripped every fibre of his body. She pushed him away violently, then hurriedly took off her tee-shirt. Before Brian could kiss her again, she pushed him down and was tugging at his belt. When he was naked, she removed her own pants, pulled him onto her and they made love.

Brian became aware of every skylark singing and every splash of the river against the bank. He felt the strength drain first from his arms and then from the rest of his body. Hildee smiled up at him and slowly rubbed the side of her face against the inside of his forearm. He could feel her left hand gently stroking his back, then her fingers gently massaging his ribs. He noticed too late that her other hand was fumbling in the grass at the edge of the blanket. Her arm rose rapidly in an arc. Still tired from lovemaking, and with Hildee's left arm holding him, Brian was unable to push himself clear in time.

"Do you need any help?" the waitress asked.

"I was just..." Mike did not have to say any more. He did not have to explain he was European. It was obvious from his clothes, and his accent merely confirmed the fact. It was twenty-five years or more since he had helped himself to food. Each day breakfast and, come to that, every other meal had been passed over the counter of an Ivan's. No choice, and no touching the food until it was on the table. Day after day, until he had stopped noticing. Now he stood paralysed, unable to make a choice, or even touch the serving spoons.

The waitress picked up a tray. "Continental or English?"

"English, please."

The waitress put a pile of scrambled eggs and several pieces of bacon on the plate, together with two rolls, some butter and a glass of orange juice.

"That's fine," Mike said, taking hold of the tray.

The waitress was reluctant to let it go. "Sure?"

"Yes, really. That's plenty," he replied. Despite missing dinner the previous evening, Mike was still not particularly hungry. The waitress released her grip and promised to bring some coffee to the table.

'President Promises US Will Be Self-Sufficient In Maize And Wheat In Four Years.' the headline on the *Washington Post* read. At the bottom of the page, there was a small story about New York: 'Marines and National Guard Hope to be in Control of the City by Christmas.' Mike was reminded of the British army fighting its way into the East End of London. In many respects, the US was lagging fifteen years behind Europe. Biting the bullet and at last trying to restore some semblance of order.

The other tables in the restaurant were sparsely populated with visitors from around the world. Mike wondered how many other hotels of this standard there were in Washington. This might be the only one. It was fourteen miles from the centre of the city. Away from the riots? Perhaps this was the equivalent of Park Lane Towers in London: a high-class hotel for visiting diplomats and party officials. Here, however, the hotel had been preserved in, or restored to, its former glory. Park Lane Towers was clean and well maintained, but had been stripped of its ostentatious decor. Mike gazed out of the window. When he and Martha had driven up to the tall white tower block, he had been struck by the apparent absence of armed guards. Now he could see, hidden amongst the trees, soldiers grouped around a pair of armoured cars.

*

"Have you been to the US before?" Martha asked, knowing full well he had. Despite what she had said the evening before, Sunday was just another day and she had started work at eight a.m. as usual. Letting Mike have a lie-in had given her plenty of time to run his passport number through the computer.

"Yes. A long time ago. New York and California." Mike watched the deserted houses and overgrown gardens slipping past.

Martha glanced up at the mirror, then braked. "New York, New York," she whispered under her breath. "Where in California?"

"Silicon Valley."

"That could be useful." Martha wound down the window and handed her pass and Mike's passport to one of the guards on the gate. The guard stepped back from the car then leaned forward to get a better look at Mike. He ran his finger down the clipboard he was carrying, then nodded to a second guard standing in the gatehouse. The barrier lifted slowly in a series of short jerks

Two high barbed-wire fences surrounded the CIA headquarters. Mike noticed that the fences, and the warning signs, were recent additions. "Have you ever been to Europe?"

"Fifteen years ago. Ukraine and Germany mostly." Martha omitted Britain, which she had visited on a forged Ukrainian passport when working as a field operative. For three months she had lived in East Anglia, pretending to be a postgraduate student spending her vacation doing volunteer agricultural work. During that time, Martha had developed a keen interest in the history of the Green movement. She had searched local newspapers for stories about crop attacks, had studied the field at Whiteside Farm and had come to the same conclusions about the attack as Brian Tyler. She returned to the US with a detailed knowledge of Europe's grain-producing capability. As a result, she had been promoted to 'analyst' in the European Section — of which she was now head, and which was under extreme pressure while the grain contract between Europe and the US was pending.

Because she had been able to extract information from the police station at Downham with ease and was not challenged even once by the authorities during her stay in England, Martha had

221

little respect for English policemen. This was reflected in her attitude to Mike. "Take a coffee?" she asked, as they arrived at her desk. Her office was a large glass-walled room containing a boardroom table surrounded by chairs and a row of filing cabinets. A PC had been set up at one end of the table and wires trailed across the room to a socket in the floor near her desk.

"Yes, that'll be fine," Mike replied.

In the next office a young man sat with his feet up on the desk. A keyboard was resting on his lap and a phone was wedged under his chin. "This place rattles a bit at the best of times," Martha said, putting the coffee on the desk. "But on a Sunday there's hardly anybody in." She sat down at the end of the table. "Well, Mike, are you just going to keep saying everything is 'fine' or are you going to tell me what Ivan sent you over here for?"

Mike sat down, shrugged and took a sip of the coffee. "I'm not sure what Ivan Vlachos wants. I'm here to find out what you know about Toby Troxley."

"So, do you know why Ivan resigned?"

Mike wondered if this was a trick question. Did Martha really not know? Was she pumping him for information, or just testing him? He sat in silence, looking around the room.

"OK. Ivan's been framed. Someone has been doctoring forty-year-old network-access data. We looked at the data ourselves — years ago. It looked innocent to us." Martha shrugged. "Well, it did until someone deleted half of it. The whole thing came like a bolt out of the blue. As it probably did to Ivan. It's my section's job to monitor all threats to European leaders, but there was no way we could have seen *that* coming."

"So what about Troxley?"

"Yes. Troxley. Now that's different. We always knew Fairchild was exposed and that Troxley had access to information that could embarrass him."

"How did you know?"

Martha thought for a moment. She did not want to admit that she had questioned Troxley, twice, since her return from Europe, The alternative was to jump in at the deep end, which she did. "Toby Troxley was the cover name for Clifford Passmore..."

"Yes, we know that." Mike took another sip of coffee.

"Clifford Passmore is, or was until a week ago, one of our agents."

"Passmore was CIA?" Mike put the coffee cup down slowly. He recalled Brian's list of questions and all the talk about conspiracies. But why was Martha being so candid and, more to the point, why was Ivan being so naive about the motives of the Americans?

Martha noticed the colour drain from Mike's face and wondered how to put him at ease. "Mind if I start right from the beginning?"

"I think you'd better."

"Fine. Damn! Now you've got *me* at it!" Martha laughed. Mike smiled, relaxed, and sat back in his chair. "Well, back in the days when America ruled the world, we realised that if global population growth continued to accelerate, certain basic resources were going to become strategic. The obvious one was water, but as far as the US was concerned, water was irrelevant. It could cause trouble in the oil-producing countries, but apart from that, we didn't give a damn. Anyway, we couldn't patent or license water."

Martha swivelled her chair round to face Mike. "But *food* now, that was different. With genetically modified crops, we could effectively *patent* food. So forget the internet and electronic commerce, forget oil, and forget nuclear weapons. We wanted to be first out of the trap in the GM race. It was the cold war all over again: we developed the weapons and you Brits were cut in on a small piece of the action."

"But I still don't see how Troxley, or Passmore, fitted in."

"I'm coming to that. You see, one of the main US players in GM technology was Genesis Natural Products. They were, so we thought, years ahead of anyone else in the world — even the British biotech companies. But then they screwed up. The product they had bet the farm on didn't work. People on Capitol Hill got worried, and then people here in the CIA got leaned on. We had GM technology in-house. It had been developed years before, when drugs were seen as a big threat, to neutralise poppy fields in South America and Asia. We never got permission to use it on any scale, so the technology just sat on the shelf.

"The CIA were told to hand it over to Genesis. We said no, but the guys on the hill leaned on us and we compromised. The deal was that we would hand over the technology if we could put someone into Genesis to oversee the deployment of what was called the poppy-gene project."

"Passmore," Mike murmured.

"Yep. Clifford Passmore was, officially, moved off our books and became a Genesis employee. First he was an M.R. director. Unofficially, he was still on our payroll."

"M.R.?"

"Media Relations. Then he took over security. No-one saw that it was a disaster waiting to happen. Passmore was now working for two bosses."

"Divided loyalties."

"Yes. Although, strangely enough, it was when the interests of the CIA and Genesis overlapped that the real damage occurred." Martha saw that Mike was puzzled. "Well, we — the CIA — weren't keen on our GM technology falling into the hands of other governments, so we didn't really want British companies getting their hands on it. Genesis knew the technology didn't work the way it was supposed to. So, successful trials in Britain weren't in either of our interests. Passmore saw trashing the tests as serving the best interests of both masters."

Martha paused again, putting both her hands together and placing them in front of her mouth as if praying. "There was another vested interest. I've never seen any documentation, but the British government was also very keen to get its biotech industry off the ground. In public, they played it cool over GM technology. Behind the scenes, however, they realised it was as strategic as nuclear technology had been twenty years before. And they knew that we in the US were reluctant to share it. The main problem for the government was the Greens. They were making a lot of noise about everything from the effect of rogue proteins on babies to the danger of cross-pollination by wind and insects. Even though, in most cases, crops wouldn't cross-pollinate, it was still a strong argument. 'Letting Frankenstein technology loose on the environment' was how the newspapers described it. So in public they played the concerned politicians, but behind the scenes we reckon they had someone in their security service undermining the Greens and distributing disinformation."

"And you think the British government had a hand in sabotaging the trial?"

Martha smiled. "Well, we *would* say that, wouldn't we? No, I just had the impression that Passmore got out of Britain a bit too easily. And don't forget that after the attack, the media saw the Green movement as just another bunch of violent thugs — rather than as a respected group of pragmatists. That put the government in a far better position." Standing up, she walked over to the glass wall and rapped on it with her knuckles. The young man in the next room looked up. Martha indicated that he should come into her room. She sat down again. "This is our Mr. Andrews," she said when the man appeared at the door. "He needs a change of clothes."

Martha then turned to Mike. "You say you know Silicon Valley. Where did you stay and where did you go?"

Mike had to think for a moment. "It was San José. Yes, I stayed in San José and visited a company in Mountain View. Then I spent a weekend near Santa Cruz."

"Monterey Bay?"

"Yes, that's it."

"Well, it has changed a bit, but never mind." Martha turned back to the man in the doorway. "We are going to need timetables of buses from San Francisco airport to the CalTrain, for the CalTrain itself, and for buses from San José to Santa Cruz." The man turned to leave, but Martha called after him. "And could you see if Mr. Andrews's passport is ready."

Mike realised that Martha was trying to bring their conversation about Passmore to close. "Are you saying that you talked to Passmore and found out that he was involved in some sort of massive conspiracy?" he asked.

Martha remained evasive. "There are no 'massive conspiracies'. What happened is what always happens when governments subcontract the running of their countries to global corporations."

Mike saw that Martha was determined not to return to the issue. "Why are you sending me to Silicon Valley?" he asked.

"We are both going. Clifford Passmore lives, or lived, in a place called Miramar, just down the coast from San Francisco." Martha grinned. "He owned — and you're going to love this — an organic vegetable farm."

Mike smiled. "But what's this 'Silicon Valley' stuff?"

"In San Francisco we will probably be followed by local security guys. They are usually pretty lightweight stuff, but we will split up in order to thin them out, and you are going to lose yours by pretending to be looking up an old friend in the valley. I'll leave the details to you. Just remember, don't get heavy with them or they will start making a real effort. Once they think you look genuine, they'll disappear and we can meet up again. Do you know anywhere in Santa Cruz?"

"Capitola was nice."

"Sounds *fine*."

Mike smiled again. "So when was the last time you spoke to Passmore?"

The question came as a surprise to Martha, who now realised she had underestimated Mike. "This is a bit embarrassing. Well, it's *very* embarrassing. I've interviewed Passmore twice in the last ten years. When Ivan ran into problems, I put a person on to Passmore full-time — just in case he made a move. We even ran checks to make sure he didn't try to leave the US as Troxley. We thought he would need a visa to get into Europe and that we could move in on him when he applied for one."

"But he got away."

"We think that one of the customers visiting his farm collected his passport and got the visa for him."

"Have you got photos of the visitors?"

"Most of them. We set up a camera in a deserted building opposite the access to Passmore's farm. Anyone visiting during daylight got snapped."

"And I thought you were short of people."

"It's a web cam. We get a constant feed from it and take out the stills. The quality isn't great but you can average and enhance them." Martha sighed heavily. "But still, the upshot of it is that he got away. Next thing, Passmore's ashes turn up at our embassy in London." She smiled to herself. "You didn't bring them with you by any chance?"

The assistant returned with a holdall containing a change of clothes. He put it on the table, together with what seemed like a well-used passport and several sheets of paper listing train and bus times. The letterhead was that of the Ritz-Carlton Hotel.

Martha pushed the passport across the polished table. "You're Mike Andrews. You're in Washington as part of the team negotiating the next grain contract. You are staying at the Ritz-Carlton and thought you would take a couple of days off to look up someone you used to know in Silicon Valley. I'm sure you can improvise around that. I will meet you at Capitola on Tuesday morning. If you have lost your tail, wear a cap — if not, don't."

"How about a pink carnation and a copy of the *Wall Street Journal*?"

Martha did not smile. She looked distracted. "It won't go with the clothes."

"Can I ask something?"

"Shoot."

"What's your interest in this? Why should the CIA worry about Ivan Vlachos or David Fairchild?"

"The truth? Well, we don't. A lot of people around here find

Ivan a real pain in the ass. Every time we talk about a deal, he starts preaching to us about the environment, about how we should cut energy use." Martha threw up her hands. "I mean, what energy, for heaven's sake? Then he uses his media exposure to promote his Ivan's restaurants."

"Some states actually have them?"

"Oh yes. Where people were relying on soup kitchens, they have caught on fast. What we don't want is Ivan using them to screw *us* like he screwed you Brits."

"I see your point. You don't want the country to be covered with McIvan's, do you?"

Martha tipped her chair back and gave Mike a quizzical look.

Realising he had touched a nerve, Mike changed the subject. "So why not leave Ivan hung out to dry?"

"Because Ivan is a known quantity and he deals with us as the *United* States."

"What do you mean?"

"Africa, the Arabs and the Chinese don't talk to Washington. They make different deals with each state. Some states they won't deal with at all. Worst of all, some countries don't even deal with the state governor; they do deals with special-interest groups. So we get migration from states which haven't got trade deals to states which have. Then we get ethnic groups trying to oust the state governor by saying they can do a deal with the Africans, or the Koreans. The foreign policy of some of these countries is based on keeping the US as weak and fractious as possible."

Mike raised his eyebrows and rubbed his hand up and down the side of his face. "Who on earth did they borrow a foreign policy like that from?"

"Quit that, Mr. Allchurch!" It was a mild rebuke, but a rebuke nonetheless, and Mike realised that Martha probably had a short fuse. "Another coffee?" she asked. Mike nodded. "I take that as meaning *fine*," she said.

*

"You stupid, stupid bitch!" Brian shouted. Hildee knelt over him laughing, and dangling the fish in front of his face.

"Your problem is, you watch too many films."

Brian was going to shout at her again, but could not catch his breath.

Hildee stood up and put on her skirt and tee-shirt. Taking a bottle of wine and two glasses out of the basket, she waited until Brian had put on his trousers and sat down. "Antique cut glass. Try not to break it," she said, carefully handing him one of the glasses. "And this," she added, pulling the cork out of the bottle, "is vintage wine."

Brian took a large mouthful of red wine.

"Careful," Hildee warned. "Empty stomach, remember." She ran a finger down the frown line on Brian's forehead. "Make that go away, please," she said gently, pushing him down onto the blanket.

As soon as Brian's head touched the ground, he felt drowsy. He then remembered what he had shouted when the fish hit his back. "I'm sorry..."

Pressing her finger on Brian's lips, Hildee shook her head and smiled at him again. "Save your strength," she whispered.

Hildee watched Brian drift in and out of sleep. Sometimes, when a fish bit, he would stir, but would become still again as it was reeled in. There was a smell of coal smoke on the warm breeze long before the steam-powered boat came into view. Reeling in the line, Hildee dismantled the fishing rods and tied them to her bicycle.

The small family-sized pleasure boat passed, its wash lapping against the bank. A young girl sitting in the bow of the boat saw Hildee. "Look!" she cried out. "It's Miss Parks and her man!" An older woman, embarrassed by her daughter's remark, waved and silently mouthed the word 'hello'.

'Her man,' Hildee thought, as she looked down at Brian. Things were definitely not going to plan.

*

Refilling Mike's coffee cup had been a convenient excuse for Martha to leave the room and calm down. Returning, she put the cup in front of Mike and sat beside him. She spoke in a quiet voice, as though confiding in him. "Ivan was our best bet. Annoying, yes — but a known quantity and, on the whole, straight. Fairchild?" Martha shrugged. "Well, we don't know him so well. As he has been Ivan's best buddy for nearly half a century, we could probably do business with him too. But Simitovich we don't know. We hear stories of liberalisation. That will mean a departure from planned production and consumption. While the in-fighting continues, Simitovich is likely to concentrate on domestic consumption rather than exports. What the US doesn't want, or rather what we couldn't cope with, is any disruption to this year's grain supply. Simitovich could cut the grain shipments in half; supply some states and not others, then watch the smoke come up over the horizon."

Mike bit his tongue and refrained from asking if that was what the CIA would advise if the US was the one with a grain surplus.

Martha drummed her fingers on the table while she thought. Standing up, she returned to her seat at the head of the table. "So what we will do is search through Passmore's house for any evidence of collusion with Fairchild. My guess is, there isn't any — but it's hard to prove a negative."

"What makes you so sure there wasn't any collusion?"

"Two things. First, Passmore was totally money-motivated. He didn't have any strong moral convictions and didn't make a move until large sums of money hit his bank account." Martha opened one of the filing cabinets. She returned to the desk with a folder that she pushed across the table towards Mike. "There's a list of payments the CIA made to Passmore over and above his salary. There are also suspect payments Genesis made for things like hospitality, which could have found their way to Fairchild via Troxley. Then there are a few statements from Fairchild's and the Greens' UK bank accounts, as well as Passmore's US and Swiss accounts, from around the period of the attack."

Mike opened the folder. "Doesn't seem to be much here."

"What you've got there is hard-copy evidence from computer runs we did to see if any amounts passing between us and Passmore, or payoffs from Genesis, matched any money that turned up in the accounts of Fairchild or the Green Party."

"And?"

"Nothing matches, and I'm damn sure that Passmore didn't part with any of his own money."

"And second? You said there were two things."

"Yes. Passmore hasn't been short of money, but his accounts have been running a bit low over the past couple of years. We know he received a substantial amount of money, around 100,000 dollars, three months ago. We now assume that was the first instalment for his trip to the UK. But even if you triple it, that's not enough to risk your neck for. He must have had a pretty cast-iron guarantee that he wasn't in any sort of danger. If he did know something embarrassing about Fairchild, he wouldn't have gone at all."

"Why not?"

"Because the invite might have been from Fairchild's people — and he would be dead as soon as the plane landed."

"Which he was, as it turned out."

"But Fairchild wouldn't have dragged Passmore to Britain to kill him. He would have arranged for it to be done here."

"So what are you saying?"

"My guess is it was the same people who fitted up the Greens and Fairchild forty years ago who invited Passmore to travel to Britain. They were the ones who got him out last time, and they were the only ones Passmore trusted."

Mike looked at the folder again. "You've been keeping a close eye on him — a lot of work."

"Like I said, he was a potential threat to Fairchild and indirectly to our grain deal."

Mike decided not to point out the obvious: why hadn't the CIA arranged an 'expedient demise', or whatever the current euphemism was for murder? That would have saved everyone a lot of trouble. But then again, if Vlachos or Fairchild had started to squeeze the US, perhaps Passmore's story would have been a helpful bargaining counter. Was this what was happening now? Again, Ivan would not have sent him over here if that was the case. "So, basically what you're saying is that the person Passmore trusted, and who helped him out of Britain forty years ago, is still in a position of influence. They could still guarantee that he could enter and leave Britain safely. But why did he go? Or, more to the point, what was he being paid to do when he got there?"

"Well, it's pretty obvious he wasn't planning on being killed. Knowing Passmore, I think he would have taken out some insurance. My guess is, he would have left something that would tip us off if he was betrayed."

"But if he wanted that to work as an insurance, he would have dropped a heavy hint to whoever hired him."

"Yes, we could be a bit late. But I still think it's worth a look around his farm."

*

Brian opened his eyes. "What was that?" he said.

"A boat."

He sat up, as if surprised. "Where?"

Hildee got to her feet and picked up one of the blankets.

"Nothing to worry about. Just a family from Downham out for the day."

Brian, not taking the hint that it was time to pack up and go, lay down again. He listened to Hildee killing the fish, counting each thud as they were dropped into the basket. "Sixteen," he said "We didn't do too badly after all."

"We? *I* 'didn't do too badly', but then *I* didn't throw mine back." She tugged Brian's blanket. "Come on, Mr. Tyler. Time to go."

Brian stood up, grabbed Hildee, and carried her to the edge of the river, where he held her out over the water. "What did you call me?"

"Put me down, *Mr. Tyler*!" Hildee shouted.

"We've just made love and you call me 'Mr. Tyler'?

If things had gone to plan, she would have pointed out that they had not made love — merely had sex. But she could not bring herself to say it, or even to look Brian in the face. "You may be reading too much into things," she said, giggling. "Now put me down, *Mr. Tyler*."

Releasing his grip, Brian let Hildee fall backwards before catching her again. She stifled a scream and looked down the river to see if the passengers on the boat had heard her.

"Who am I, *Hildegard*?" Brian said. Hildee laughed uncontrollably. He let go and caught her again.

"Brian!" Hildee screamed. "Brian! Brian! Brian!" Pulling her back onto the bank, Brian put his arms around her. He stroked the back of her head and gently kissed her neck. Hildee sighed and rested her head on Brian's shoulder. "Oh, Brian," she whispered.

Surveying the flat landscape, Brian looked around at the rows of stubble, the rows of vegetables, and the river: lines drawn across a blank canvas on which he and Hildee were the only features. The lines, which started on the horizon, converged at the point where both of them stood.

Losing track of time, he could have been holding on to Hildee for just a few minutes or for a whole hour, watching the water as it flowed past, running his hand gently up and down her back and across her shoulders. He felt her stir and gently ease herself out of his arms. Her eyes sparkled and Brian ran his fingers along her smile lines — lines which had been absent until today.

"Hello! Wake up!" Hildee said, waving her hand in front of Brian's face. "Nice as this is, we have to go."

"Sorry."

"I think my tame policeman's mind has just gone back on duty."

"Far from it."

They rode their bicycles to the sluice gates, then dismounted and stopped to look at the steamboat, which was now moored at the edge of the river. The woman was passing boxes to a man on the bank. "A good day, was it?" she said.

"Sixteen fish," Brian replied, before Hildee could speak.

Hildee reached out and grabbed Brian's arm. "What sort of day have you had?" she asked the woman.

"Only six trout, but over twenty eels," the woman replied.

Hildee, seeing a girl hanging on to her man's arm the way she was holding on to Brian's, would have recognised the telltale signs of possessiveness. It was a way of saying 'you can talk to him, but this man is mine'. Hildee, however, did not realise what she was doing. Nor did she see herself lean into Brian, then tilt her head back to speak to him, as they queued for food in the restaurant. The betrayal of their intimacy continued even when they sat down to eat. Words were missing from sentences as they began to speak the special language common to lovers. Brian poked his fried trout with a fork and asked if it really had been cooked in butter. Even if they had not been lovers, Hildee might have laughed. But if they had not been lovers, she would have answered — not remained silent and merely touched Brian's arm. Matt, who looked as though he had been in the restaurant all day, noticed the change in the way the couple behaved. So did the soldier, who had entered just after they sat down and was now seated in the corner, pretending to read a book.

Hildee and Brian had been ignoring the television. "Reports are coming in of a fire and explosion in London. A number of fireman are feared dead or injured." Brian looked up briefly, then continued his conversation with Hildee. It was the mention of Simitovich that finally captured his full attention. "Lex Simitovich, acting head of the Ukraine Green Alliance, will be visiting London this Friday."

"Today is Sunday, isn't it?" Brian asked.

"Yes. Why?"

"No reason," he replied, mentally counting off the days until Friday. Brian wished he had not heard the broadcast. He resented the intrusion. Looking across the restaurant, he saw the soldier sitting in the corner. Five minutes ago he had been able to ignore him. Hours, which had dragged by earlier in the day, were now evaporating before he could count them.

Hildee sensed that Brian was ill at ease, and she noticed that he glanced over his shoulder several times during the ride back to Nordelph. She too was aware of the short time they had left together.

"Tea in the garden," Hildee said, leading Brian through the house and out onto a paved terrace. On the way, she had collected a small table from the dining room that she now placed in front of a metal bench. "Take a seat. I'll be back in a moment."

Brian looked out across the open fields — featureless except for the occasional tree and clumps of bushes. It was next to one of these bushes that the sun reflected on something. Wandering casually to the end of the garden, Brian crouched by a flowerbed and pretended to examine the flowers. The reflection came and went. He observed a shape, the size of a person. Brian looked at his watch. Had there been enough time for the soldier to make his way from the restaurant to Nordelph? He had seen no-one on the road behind them. Had the soldier used a Jeep? There was nowhere to hide a vehicle out in the fields. Was it a single reflection from a gun site, or the double reflection from binoculars? What did he look like to the person out there? Was there enough sun in this garden to light up a target?

"Tea, Brian." Hildee's voice came from close behind him.

Brian pulled one of the plants out of the flowerbed. Standing up, he walked towards Hildee. There was a heavy feeling in his stomach and a dryness in his throat. He attempted to keep himself between Hildee and the point where he had seen the reflection.

"What's this called?" Brian showed the plant to Hildee.

"Do you want the Latin name?"

Brian threw his arms around her and carried her back towards the terrace.

"Are you all right?" Hildee asked. "You look pale."

"I think the fish upset me."

"Mine was fine."

"The other fish." Brian said as he put her on the seat and dropped the flowers into her lap.

Hildee looked up at him thoughtfully. Brian felt she was about to say something profound. Instead she closed her eyes. "Is it true that in London you are not allowed to put flowers on graves?" she asked, taking his hand and pulling him closer.

"Yes, that's right." Brian refused to be distracted. He turned and looked back down the garden. The clump of bushes was only just visible over a slight rise in the land, and the terrace was shaded. If they were being stalked by a gunman, he would either have to stand up or he would have to come a lot closer to get a clear shot. Brian could suggest that they went into the house, but Hildee already suspected that something was wrong. There was no point in scaring her unnecessarily.

"Sit down. You are making me nervous," Hildee said, tugging at Brian's hand. "Is anything the matter?"

Brian sat down. "No. Just that I was supposed to be back in the office tomorrow and there was something I had to do before I got back."

"Oh, a girl!" Hildee said. "Well, today you are mine. She can have you back next weekend."

"There's no girl..."

"Milk and sugar?" Hildee interrupted, passing him a cup.

"Milk?" Brian exclaimed with mock horror. "You do realise I'm a policeman?"

"Oh yes, I am very well aware of that, *PC Tyler*." Hildee rested her head on Brian's shoulder and stroked his arm. "If you had not been a policeman, you would have had biscuits as well."

Brian laughed and slid his arm around her waist.

Hildee put her feet up on the seat and rested her head in his lap. "If you were in London, what would you be doing now?"

Brian described a typical evening out with Trevor, Stef and the girls in Hyde Park.

"Sounds a bit dull, compared with *this* weekend."

"Yes, it does."

"What about the girls? What are they like?"

"Just girls. Typical party workers, most of them."

"So at the end of the evening you just go home and" — Hildee looked up at Brian — "sew up your old jackets? Are you really happy with all of that?"

"It'll do me."

"'It will do me.'" Hildee shrieked. "Brian, you sound like an old man!" She slipped her arms around his waist and squeezed him. "Sorry. I must stop making fun of you."

"Don't worry about it, *Hildegard*."

Hildee bit him playfully on the arm, and Brian rested his hand on her head, then looked out across the fields. Many of the emotions he had experienced that weekend were either new to him or had been suppressed for many years. Most telling was the way he had felt a few minutes earlier, when he thought Hildee was in danger. There were many things he wanted to tell her. He wanted to ask her to come to London with him, but it was obvious she would never leave here. He wanted to stay here with her, but that was even more absurd. He had never told anyone he loved them. He was on the verge of saying it now.

"Come on. Early start tomorrow," Hildee said, getting to her feet. "Time for bed. I will take the tray — you bring the chairs."

They walked up the stairs, not hand in hand but with Hildee following Brian. He stopped by his bedroom door. "Goodnight then!" she called out as she walked past.

"Goodnight," Brian muttered and pushed open the door. The bed had been stripped and the rucksack had gone. He turned and walked along the corridor to Hildee's room.

Hildee was already naked, standing next to her bed. Brian's rucksack was propped up against the cupboard; his shaving soap and razor were on the shelf over the basin and his book lay on the bedside cupboard. "When did you move all my things?"

Hildee pulled back the sheet and slid into the bed. "While you were down at the end of the garden watching whoever is skulking around in the fields."

"Unbelievable."

"Well, come on then — or are you going to stand there all night?"

Brian undressed and got into bed. Hildee propped herself up on one elbow and ran her hand down the side of Brian's face. "Do you know that if a man spends time with a girl he finds sexually attractive his facial hair grows faster than usual?" She rubbed his chin hard. "Something worth bearing in mind when you get married, and spend an afternoon with another lady."

Brian rubbed his hand across his chin. "It has grown."

"Yes, and you had better get rid of it, or I will look as though I spent all last winter hoeing sugar beet in an easterly wind."

"Do I have to?"

Hildee started to get out of bed. "No. I'll do it."

Brian leapt out of bed and strode to the basin.

"Ah! Do I take it that you still do not entirely trust me?"

Brian dragged the cut-throat razor across his face. "There are limits."

For a time, they just lay next to each other. Neither spoke. Hildee ran her hand over Brian's freshly shaved face and he stroked her hair.

Hildee smiled. "Sorry about this afternoon. You know, the

fish."

"I was jumpy."

"Yes. I should have realised." Hildee's hand made its way around Brian's neck, and then across his chest. "Something like that could have terrible consequences. Give someone an awful hang-up. Put them off sex for life." She moved her hand down his stomach and onto his thigh, then gently massaged him. "Perhaps you will never... No, wait a minute. This is a good sign."

Brian found Hildee's performance amusing, but did not laugh. Instead, he moaned softly and stroked her breasts.

Hildee swung herself onto Brian and teased him until he could stand it no more. Forcing her back down onto the bed, he grabbed her thigh. But Hildee had pulled the bed sheet tightly between her legs. She kissed him on the mouth, then on the neck, gently biting and sucking his flesh. Brian became frantic, lost control and tore the sheet out of her hand.

*

"That was lovely," Hildee said, using the end of the sheet to wipe the sweat from Brian's forehead and from under his arms. "Do you often lose control like that?"

"Never," Brian gasped, and fell back onto the bed. He felt himself drifting off to sleep, but forced himself to stay awake. "Are you...? I mean, do you always...?"

"Do I what?" Hildee asked.

"Always come on so quickly?"

"Well, given that my experience of such things is rather limited, I would say 'no'." Hildee smiled and put her mouth close to Brian's ear. "I take it that your criticism relates to the lack of foreplay."

"Not exactly. I think there may have been a lot of foreplay — a whole weekend of it."

"Ahah," Hildee murmured. "But you think it was unconventional."

"A bit."

"Perhaps you were expecting soft music and poetry." Hildee turned over and lay with her back to Brian. She pulled his arm around her waist. "No music," she said sleepily, "but if you have a poem, feel free."

Brian kissed the back of Hildee's neck and pulled her tightly to him. He could hear her breathing becoming heavier. She too was drifting into sleep. "Deep, mysterious and bright," Brian whispered. "As a river reflecting clear summer skies. If I could choose how I should die, It would be drowning in your eyes."

"Very nice. Who wrote it?"

"No-one."

"Someone must have."

"I made it up."

"You mean as you went along?"

"No. When we were standing by the river."

Hildee felt Brian's breath on the back of her neck becoming stronger as he fell asleep. This had all gone so terribly wrong. She hated this man — for his stupid poem; for ruining her plan. She hated herself — for being so naive; for wanting a baby so badly; for not realising, from the start, that she had fallen in love with him. She hated Brian for having caught her crying over Gerald Whiteside; for having caught her off guard. And she hated him for seeming so vulnerable.

A tear dripped from the end of Hildee's nose. Tomorrow he would be gone and that would be that. What else could she expect — to find him sitting on the terrace saying 'This'll do me'? He had used her and would forget her. She had used him and would probably *never* forget him. Her eyes felt heavier, but the tears still ran down her face. What would happen if she had a child? What if it grew up to look like Brian?

At one in the morning, Brian called out softly in his sleep. It woke Hildee. She listened, bracing herself, expecting him to shout, as he had done the night before. But he continued to speak softly. "Wait," he said. "Stop." The voice became weaker. "I love you." Hildee stretched, and pushed her feet to the bottom of the bed. She felt Brian's grip on her tighten. "I love you, Hildee," he said softly, then drifted off again.

"Well, I love you too, *Mr. Tyler*," Hildee whispered.

They slept together in a position called 'spoons', Brian facing Hildee's back. Spoons is an ever-changing and ambiguous position. The woman can be curled up, protected by the man, who wraps himself around her. Or, if the woman lies stretched out, the man hangs on to her the way a child hangs on to its mother. Throughout the night, Brian and Hildee curled and straightened themselves as their bodies negotiated the true nature of their relationship. By the morning, negotiations were complete. But the outcome would remain a mystery to Brian. He woke alone, naked, on a bare mattress with no sheet. His book and razor had been packed into his rucksack, and his clothes had been neatly folded and placed on a chair beside the bed.

7

Monday 26th August 2041

The terrace was shaded and cool, just as it had been the previous evening. Once again, the garden was bathed in sunlight and the horizon was a pale reddish blue. But yesterday the distant glow had been the sunset reflected on a late-evening mist; today it was the sunrise refracted through the dust from the combine harvesters that were crawling through fields of wheat. When he first sat on the bench, Brian had been wide awake and alert. Now his eyelids felt heavy. The drooping branches of a weeping willow floated in the breeze, gentle and sensual — the movement of a woman's dress as she dances.

"What are you doing here?" The voice shrieked behind him. Brian jumped to his feet. "Sorry." Hildee touched him gently on the arm. "Sorry, Brian. I did not see you there."

Brian looked around the terrace in amazement. "I wasn't exactly hiding."

Hildee blushed. "Expect," she stuttered. "I did not *expect* to see you there. That is what I meant."

This was the first time he had seen Hildee flustered. He put his hand on her shoulder and pulled her towards him, kissing her firmly on the lips. She slid her arms around his waist. A door slammed somewhere in the house and she pushed him away then tugged at his collar. "You really ought to dress yourself properly." A young soldier appeared at the door. "Well, Mr. Tyler," Hildee said, raising her voice, "we must get you to the station."

As Brian and Hildee went back indoors, the soldier held out a tube of glue. "It's all I could find in town, Miss Parks."

"A bit late now. Put it on the desk in the office, please."

The soldier examined the tube. "It should do the job. Says it..."

"Yes, I am sure it will," Hildee snapped, "although some things are very difficult to repair." She brushed past the soldier. "Did you see Captain Hutley in town?"

"No, Miss Parks. I don't think he's back from his weekend leave yet."

"Well, if he does turn up here, tell him to meet me in town. I will be having breakfast with Mr. Tyler."

*

"Are you safe?"

"That's an odd question." Hildee smiled at Brian. "Of course I am, surrounded by soldiers in one of the most highly guarded areas of the country. If you are worried about whoever it was creeping about in the fields, he was probably more interested in you than me."

"Do you think you will get pregnant?"

Hildee did not answer straight away. She looked around. They were at the same point on the road to Downham where Brian had mentioned children on two previous occasions. She recalled something she had read, about a man on a journey being a computer and the landscape being the data that fed its program. Every thought the man had was influenced by the landscape. She wondered what memories lurked in Brian's subconscious and what had caused that particular memory to surface in this apparently featureless countryside. "Probably. One day," she said.

Brian sighed with exasperation. "Do you think I've made you pregnant?"

"Probably."

Brian thought for a moment before speaking again. "If you are, I'll come back. I mean..."

"I hardly think that a shared interest in Marx Brothers' films is a good basis for a long-term relationship." Hildee began laughing, but stopped when she realised Brian was not amused. "Sorry, Brian, but somehow I do not see myself as Mrs. Tyler."

Brian felt hurt and annoyed by the thought that he might have been used as an unwitting sperm donor. This blinded him to the fact that Hildee was now as determined to refer to him as 'Brian' as she had been determined not to only twenty-four hours before. And that when referring to 'Mrs. Tyler' she had steered her bicycle so close to his that Brian had had to swerve to prevent a collision.

But he was not the only one who was confused. To Hildee it had seemed so simple. She would get pregnant and have a child. The father would be gone. She had lost three men from her life. Men were unreliable; they left just when you needed them most. It was better they went before you became too attached to them. This one was perfect, because he would never come back. She would never go to London and give up all this to be a spare part in his life. True, they say ''Tis better to have loved and lost, than never to have loved at all', but in that case why had her mother died just a week after her father? Nevertheless, saying goodbye to Brian was not going to be as easy as she had originally thought.

*

"As much as possible for me but nothing for my friend." Once again, Hildee leaned back against Brian. "He is feeling a bit delicate this morning." She rubbed the back of her hand on his shoulder.

At first, Brian was puzzled. Then he realised why Hildee had cancelled his breakfast.

The waitress smiled and pushed the tray across the counter. "Enjoy yourselves this weekend?" she asked. Brian recognised her as one of the girls Hildee had been talking to at the dance on Saturday.

On the way to their table, they passed the mechanic and his wife. "Don't say I didn't warn you," the mechanic muttered. Brian felt compelled to explain the remark to Hildee, for fear of a repeat of the misunderstanding about Matt's wager.

Hildee looked embarrassed. She pushed her breakfast towards Brian. "Take whatever you want, then stop off at a station on the way and get your own breakfast. If anyone checks, you can say you overslept."

Brian slapped his forehead with the palm of his hand. "Damn! I forgot to move last night's dinner to Cromer."

"I did it. First thing this morning, before the soldier turned up." Hildee smiled and ran her finger across the back of Brian's hand. "While you were fast asleep."

"But you haven't got my S-Card number."

"You would be surprised just how sophisticated that program is — Brian James Tyler."

"What else did you find out?"

"You would be surprised, BJ. Do people call you 'BJ'?"

"No, they don't. No-one knows."

*

The television news reporter was standing in front of a burnt-out building. "A dust explosion is now thought to have been responsible for the deaths of a London fire crew at this warehouse. The warehouse, used to store flour, caught fire on Saturday. The deputy commissioner of the Metropolitan Police, Mr. Stephen Langford, said, this morning, that it was too early to rule out arson and that his department would be carrying out a full investigation."

*

Brian turned to look at the television and sighed. "Well, as I make up a significant part of his department at the moment, that puts paid to the idea that I won't be missed today."

"Especially as you are a fireman." Hildee shrugged when she saw Brian's look of surprise. "Dispensation for fire fighter — eating off the premises." She folded both hands under her chin and tilted her head. "My hero." Brian took a playful swipe at her.

Hildee stopped smiling. "I am really sorry if I have caused you trouble."

Brian looked into Hildee's eyes, reached across the table and squeezed her hand. "I'm not. I wouldn't have missed yesterday for..." he whispered.

Hildee took a deep breath. "That is all very well, but you had better get your story straight. What was Cromer like, Brian?" she said, mimicking how she imagined Langford would speak.

"Golden beaches, cliffs with small cafés, and dusty cobbled streets."

"Very much like Camus's Oran? Have you ever been to Cromer?"

"No. In fact, I've never been to the seaside."

"It has a stony beach. The tide goes out a long way. What else? Oh yes! There is a promenade, one Ivan's and a couple of hotels." Hildee stopped to think for a moment. "You were going to stay in a hotel, but met this girl and stayed with her instead." She mimicked Langford again. "So what was this girl like, Brian?"

Brian stuttered. "Well, well, she was... She was a bit like you."

Hildee laughed. "You spent the weekend with a girl who looked like your boss?"

"No, that's not..."

"Let me see. She was tall, with long legs; blonde, with large breasts..."

"No!" Brian snapped.

"OK. I'm not jealous." But Hildee was and did not continue with the description. She straightened Brian's collar. "You probably will not need to describe that part of the weekend. It's pretty obvious."

Brian looked at his watch. "Time to go, I'm afraid." Hildee carried his rucksack as they walked to the station.

"Good day fishing, was it?" the stationmaster called out, as Brian pushed his bicycle onto the platform.

Hildee handed Brian his rucksack, then slipped her arm around his waist. "You certainly seem to have made a few friends."

Brian looked along the platform. The soldier from Military Intelligence was leaning against the station name board. "Looks like I will be taking some with me."

Hildee looked at the soldier. "Oh, him."

"And him." Brian gestured in the direction of a man carrying a large rucksack who had followed them onto the platform. Strapped to the rucksack was a pair of binoculars and a folding chair.

"That's a bird-watcher. He has probably been to Welney Marshes."

"No. He was in the restaurant on Saturday morning. He was probably the one in the fields on Sunday evening. And dressed like that he could sit by the river and no-one would take any notice of him."

Hildee could feel the rage welling up inside her. "Do you think he was watching while we...? God! You wait until I get hold of Hutley!"

"Hutley won't know anything about it. These people are from the other side of London. They can move into the East Anglian Regiment's patch or Hertfordshire's without authorisation. It's all done on a 'need-to-know' basis."

The train rounded the bend and drew into the station.

"That is why you pretended to be drunk on Saturday, because you wanted them out of the way." Hildee released her grip on Brian's waist. "I am very sorry. It must have been a horrible weekend for you."

"No, not at all. I really..."

The train doors opened.

Hildee put her finger on his lips. "Brian, I know you are not coming back. I am really sorry. Please be careful. Promise?"

"I will come back. I promise."

Hildee grabbed Brian's arms and whispered in his ear. "Twenty euros says you will not." She pushed him away again. "You will miss your train."

Brian picked up his bicycle and put it in the doorway as the doors closed. The doors opened again and he stepped on board.

Hildee held up her hand and gave a little wave with her fingers. "Wasn't that where you should have said 'you're on'?" The train doors slammed shut. She turned and walked back to the station entrance. As the train pulled away, Brian watched Hildee climb into an army Jeep. Her face was red with rage. She was shouting so furiously that Captain Hutley had jumped out of the driver's seat and was standing in the road.

What little respect Brian had for Military Intelligence evaporated as he stood on the deserted platform of Cambridge station. His two followers had stayed on the train, having assumed that he was returning to London, and would probably be at King's Cross before they noticed he was missing.

Two heavily armed guards stood outside the booking hall. One thought the quickest route to the police station was via the Mill Road residential area; the other suggested heading for the city centre along the road, then following the signs. On each side of the main road there were deserted shops and offices. One displayed a sign announcing that all county council departments had been transferred to the GA offices in the Old Guildhall. A spire that Brian thought was something to do with the university turned out to be the Catholic cathedral, which was on a crossroads at what was now the southern edge of the city. On the opposite side of the road, shrubs sprouted from the windows of a crumbling office block. The remains of a metal sculpture hung at an angle from the building's facade. A large rectangular sign indicated that the city centre was straight ahead and the university to the left. The road to Brian's right apparently led to 'The Anglian Regiment — Agricultural Training Centre, Married Quarters, Transport Depot and Swimming Pool'. A piece of wood had been attached to the sign as an afterthought. It had 'Fire and Police Station' scrawled on it.

Cheered by his success in losing the two intelligence officers, Brian was tempted to take a tour of the university. Noting the time, however, he thought better of it. The road to the police station ran along the edge of a large meadow being grazed by sheep. Two tracks cut corner to corner across the meadow, and a rusty lamppost stood at the point in the centre where they met. A number of people, mostly soldiers, were either walking or cycling to the city centre along one of the tracks. On his right, Brian heard lorries revving in the converted multi-storey car park which now served as an army transport depot. Ahead, also on the right, was the turning into Mill Road. It led to the civilian residential area and the army swimming pool ('Open to non-army personnel on Monday, Wednesday and Saturday morning').

Mill Road was shut off to vehicles by a barrier manned by two soldiers. One soldier was sitting in a guard hut; the second was standing on the edge of the pavement. Brian turned left into the police station and wedged the front wheel of his bicycle in the cycle rack. In the distance, on the opposite side of the meadow, was a large building with square turrets, each one decorated with an 'Ivan's' flag that flapped lazily in the warm breeze. Brian looked at his watch again. If he finished his business here in half an hour, he would have time to do some sightseeing, have another breakfast — and still get back to the office by late afternoon.

"Troxley, you said." The desk sergeant wrote the name on a slip of paper. "April 2001? That goes back a bit. Take a seat." He grabbed the phone and keyed in a number. "I've got a Mr. ..." — he picked up Brian's ID card — "a Mr. Tyler from the Met. He's looking for an arrest record from 2001." Pushing the ID card across the counter, he smiled at Brian. "No! 2001," he said, raising his voice. "OK, yes, OK." Replacing the handset, the desk sergeant shook his head slowly and walked away from the counter almost as if he had forgotten Brian was still there. "Someone's coming up from Records," he muttered to the world in general.

The records clerk, whom Brian reckoned was no more than nineteen years old, spoke nervously. Short bursts of speech were delivered in a near-whisper. After leading the way to a small office overlooking the meadow, he pulled a metal-legged chair with a frayed seat out from under a badly chipped table and gestured to Brian to sit down. "I'm afraid all records over twenty-five years old have been archived onto tape. We haven't got the resources to restore them. Even if we had, there's no guarantee that the tapes are any good."

"Have you got the desk sergeant's diary for that month? Or even the arresting officer's notebook?" Brian asked, as he took in the view of the meadow.

"There's a thought! Back in a moment!" The records clerk skipped out of the room like an excited child.

Brian rested his elbows on the table and stared at the stream of cyclists making their way into the city.

*

When the clerk returned, he was carrying a stack of faded blue A4-sized hardback books. The first two he rejected after examining the first page. The third book he thumbed through slowly after opening it in the middle. "There you are! 16th April 2001, 9 p.m. 'Toby

Troxley, Interview Room 2 — charged — detained — re Whiteside Farm.' That's it, I'm afraid."

"So there must be a charge sheet."

"Yes, but that would have been archived. It might even have been destroyed."

"I doubt it in this case." Brian buried his face in his hands and thought for a moment. "Look, if it was archived, all the papers relating to the arrest would have been filed together. There must be an index of cases or investigations. Wouldn't it be filed under 'Whiteside Farm'?"

The clerk looked down at the open book. He tapped his pencil on his teeth. "Yes, maybe. Hang on again."

*

"Got it!" The clerk put a filing cabinet pocket on the table. "Bit thin, I'm afraid."

Opening up the pocket, Brian took out the top sheet of paper. It read: 'All original documents transferred to Norwich 17th April 2001.' He put the page on one side. "Damn! Why did they do that?"

The clerk pulled out the second chair and sat down. "Maybe this man Troxley was sent for trial at Norwich crown court. Where is Whiteside Farm?"

"Downham."

"Norfolk. Well yes, then he would have been sent to Norwich."

"A wasted journey then," Brian said, picking up the next sheet of paper, which was a copy of the charge sheet. Suddenly his mind began to race. A single name stood out: 'PC Stephen Langford.' He looked at the top of the page: 'Charge Sheet' it read. Calmly scanning through it, he eventually came to the sentence containing the name: 'Arresting officers PC James Hendry and PC Stephen Langford.'

Brian placed the charge sheet on the table and slowly worked his way through the rest of the papers: a prisoner transfer sheet, a detention record and a short inventory of Troxley's possessions. Brian looked down the list. "'Passport' — where do you think that went?" he asked the clerk.

"To Norwich, with the rest of his things."

Although it was the passport that Brian had hoped to find in Cambridge, all he could think of now was Langford. If this was the same Langford, why hadn't he told Mike that he was the arresting officer? Brian began to wonder if there was any way Langford could work out that Brian was sitting here now reading this file. Had Hildee really transferred the last record to Cromer? Would anyone here remember Langford — and if they did, were they still in contact with him? Brian stood up. "Well, a bit of a wild-goose chase really. Still, thanks very much for all your help." He turned to leave the room, then stopped. "Would the arresting officer's notebooks still be in the archive?" he asked, trying to make the question sound like a mere afterthought.

The clerk left the room, taking the charge sheet with him. He returned with two box files: one labelled 'Hendry.J', the other 'Langford.S'. Brian grabbed Hendry's box and left Langford's file to the clerk. The clerk was the first to find a notebook. "There you go!" he said, pointing to one of the entries in it.

6 p.m. Radio message. Minibus, registration J930 PBM, spotted by static patrol at junction of A11 and M11. Confirmed we would intercept.

6.15 p.m. Minibus, registration J930 PBM, intercepted. Driver, Toby Troxley, arrested.

The clerk read the entry again. "That was quick. They must have been driving right behind him."

Brian found the corresponding page in Hendry's notebook. The entry was identical. He would have liked to examine the rest of the notebook, but threw it down on the table as if it was of no interest to him. "Well, that's that then."

"Unless you want to go to Norwich?" the clerk suggested.

Again Brian looked at his watch. "Might be time."

"You'll need some paperwork. I'll take you up to the Super. He'll sign something for you."

The clerk led Brian up three flights of stairs to the top floor of the police offices. The chief superintendent of Cambridgeshire Police looked about the same age as Mike Allchurch, and spoke with the same sneering cynicism. "So this man wants to go to Norwich," he said to the clerk as he looked Brian up and down. "Why does he want to do that then?"

"We've come across someone passing themselves off as Toby Troxley." Brian omitted to say that the person in question was dead. "I've just come up here to check through some old records."

"Wish *we* had time for such luxuries." The Superintendent

sighed. "Well, I suppose you'd better have some authorisation or the pongos won't let you in."

"Pongos?" Brian asked.

"Squaddies. Soldiers. The army who guard this prison camp which was once the English countryside." He took a pad from his desk drawer. "Let's have your ID." Brian handed over his card and the Superintendent copied the details onto the form, which he then turned towards Brian. Pointing to the bottom of it, he said, "Sign here. I take it you're not carrying a gun."

"No, sir." Brian signed.

"Good." The Superintendent took the form back. "So I sign here and we're done," he said. "I hope you catch your man."

"Super's not keen on the army," the clerk said, as he walked back down the stairs with Brian. "Our patch is cut in half by the rural no-go area. That's why there are so many soldiers in Cambridge. We've a long-running turf war with the military police. Lots of brawls, a few killings, and obstructions of investigations." The clerk held the main door open for Brian. "Anything else you need, just drop me an e-mail."

Brian was still thinking about Langford. He had wanted to ask the clerk for more information, but feared that his interest would alert someone else in the station — someone old enough to remember Langford. Looking across the meadow towards the Ivan's, Brian wondered if now was the time to have something to eat and reappear on the S-Card database. But that would be a mistake. If Langford found out that Brian was in Cambridge — the city where Langford had once been based — alarm bells would start ringing.

*

"I'm expecting a call from London. If anyone phones, put them through."

The desk sergeant leaned back and looked down his nose at Brian. "And you are?"

"Tyler. Brian Tyler. Metropolitan Police." Brian took the authorisation out of his rucksack and put it, with his ID card, on the counter.

"And where will you be then?" The desk sergeant picked up the authorisation. "This is from Cambridge, not London."

"I'm looking for some archived information."

The sergeant scribbled a note, then reached for the phone.

"Take a seat. I'll see if I can find someone."

Brian wandered over to the large map of East Anglia on the wall opposite. At lunch, he had tried to work out what would happen if his visit to the Central Norwich Ivan's was discovered by someone in London. Would they call here and ask the local police to track him down? It was then that he had thought of trying to intercept the call, so he could offer some plausible excuse for being here. As yet, no plausible excuse had come to mind.

In theory, Norfolk Police were only responsible for the policing in the county itself. However, the map on the wall marked stations in towns and villages right up to the outskirts of Cambridge in the west and as far as the coast to the east. Brian stared at Downham, tracing the road out of the town to Nordelph Manor.

"Mr. Tyler, come to look at our archives?" The young woman holding the door to the main corridor open for Brian wore jeans, a tank top and sandals. She had close-cropped red hair and was tilting her head forward to look at Brian over her blue-tinted glasses. "Exactly what is it you're looking for?"

"Information on a person called Toby Troxley," Brian replied.

"Ah yes," the girl responded. "Follow me, please." She led Brian not into a reading room but into the archive itself. "You can sit over there," she said, pointing to a desk at the far end of the room as she took a box file from one of the shelves.

"That wasn't hard to find." Brian opened the file that had been dropped on the desk in front of him.

"It's suddenly become very popular," The girl said as she returned to her own desk.

The box contained a map of Whiteside Farm, copies of the charge sheet, and the relevant pages from the two arresting policemen's notebooks. Brian went through the box slowly, one page at a time. The passport was not there. He got up and walked over to the girl's desk. "Excuse me, but there appears to be something missing from the file."

"Missing?"

"Yes. I thought you were holding Toby Troxley's passport."

"Yes, but I think it's been transferred to London." The girl opened the file drawer of her desk and took out one of the pockets. "Yes. Two weeks ago a PC Elroy collected it."

"He was authorised to take it?"

"She. PC Elroy was a she. I remember her." The girl handed Brian a sheet of paper that looked similar to the authorisation the superintendent at Cambridge had signed for him. The signature of PC Elroy was almost indecipherable, but the authorising signature was that of the Home Secretary himself. The difference between this authorisation and the one Brian had been given was the telephone number to call in case of queries. It was the number of the telephone Johnny Coates had recovered the previous Friday.

"Can I take a copy of this?" Brian asked. "It's just that I think there has been some sort of mix-up."

"Be my guest. There's a machine outside in the corridor."

Brian laid the sheet of paper face down on the copier, closed the lid and pressed the start button. As soon as the original had been scanned, he lifted the lid again and grabbed it. It had been signed in black ink. 'Perfect,' he thought. When the copy appeared, he took it, folded it twice and rubbed it between the palms of his hands. After flattening it again, he placed it under the lid of the copier. The original he folded and placed in his pocket.

"So, Mr. Tyler, a cock-up on the administrative front." The man sitting at the desk dropped the copy of the charge sheet he had been reading back into the box file. Although he was ten years older than Brian, he had the same youthful appearance. Taking Brian's letter of authorisation from his inside pocket, the Superintendent studied the signature. "How is the miserable old bastard? Still moaning about the army, I suppose." Tossing the letter aside and not waiting for an answer, he dragged the box file towards him and peered inside. "So this must be a real flap, judging by the number of people who've been going through this file." He extended his hand to Brian. "I'm Superintendent Christopher Dickerson, by the way."

Brian shook Christopher's hand and sat down. "How many people have accessed it?"

"You're the third. Your lot from London and then the army both had a poke around."

"When?"

"The army?" Christopher scratched the side of his nose. "Oh, let me think. Last Thursday? Friday?"

"Friday," the girl called out. She stood up and crossed the room. "Sorry to interrupt," she said softly, "but have you still got that authorisation?"

Brian pretended to search for it on the desk, then started to get to his feet. "Oh, damn! I think left it on the photocopier."

The girl gestured to Brian to stay seated. "Don't worry. I'll get it."

Christopher waited for the girl to leave the room. "I had a call from the chief constable of Downham this morning. Apparently a policeman from London by the name of Tyler spent the weekend in the town. Is that a coincidence?"

"No. That was me."

"Part of an investigation I should know about?" Christopher put his hand on the box file.

"It was a social visit. I was visiting a friend." Brian hoped he would not have to mention Hildee, even though Christopher probably already knew about his stay at Nordelph Manor.

Christopher looked at Brian and smiled. "Very sociable, I see." The remark puzzled Brian. The Superintendent took the charge sheet out of the file again and pretended to read it. "You lot get all the best investigations, all the glory stuff — and all the promotions."

"The grass always looks greener..., so they say."

Christopher scoffed and closed the box file slowly. "So they say. Well, any time you feel like swapping jobs just let me know."

"I'm afraid I'm only a humble assistant."

"At the moment." Christopher eased himself out of the chair. "Take care, Mr. Tyler."

*

The Great North Eastern Railway serves Cambridge, Norwich and King's Lynn, with two interleaved services. The London-to-King's Lynn train calls at Cambridge, Ely, Downham and King's Lynn. The Cambridge-to-Norwich train stops at all stations between the two towns, including Ely. Brian could have changed at Ely and caught the London train. However, the platform was teeming with the guards who rode the trains between Cambridge and Ely — the only passenger route into the East Anglian agricultural zone.

Brian was reluctant to leave the train for another reason. On the other side of the station, the King's Lynn train was waiting to leave. He did not trust himself not to get on it. On Friday he had been travelling into the unknown; further and further away from the safety and security of London and home. But the return journey did not feel like a homecoming. Someone had turned the map around. He felt disoriented, not unlike the way he had felt when arriving in Downham by train instead of by car. This disorientation, however, was not down to the means of transport. He had developed an attachment to the place — or rather, to a person. Moreover, he knew that if this investigation turned out badly for him, London would no longer offer either security or protection.

"How was the weather in Cromer then?" The guard looked down at the ID card, then leaned forward to take a closer look at Brian's face.

Brian cursed his luck that he should run into the guard who had interrogated him on Friday evening, but it could have been worse — he could have met him after catching the train at Downham, or on his way from Cambridge to Norwich. At least being on the Norwich train supported his claim to have spent the weekend in Cromer. The question about the weather, which he perceived as some sort of trick, threw Brian. The guard was looking down his nose at him rather than making eye contact. The second guard was also waiting, expectantly, for his answer. Then Brian recalled the weekend of cloudless skies that must have spread across most of eastern England. "Fine. Sunny, thanks," he said.

The guard turned to his colleague as he handed back Brian's ID card. "What do you think; looked out of the window — or a lucky guess?" He asked.

"Lucky sod, you mean." the second guard muttered as both soldiers moved on.

*

The train pulled into Cambridge station. Brian pushed his bicycle the length of the platform, and past the guards, to catch the London train. Settling back in his seat, he felt relieved, but not elated, that he was now outside the agricultural zone. He knew that the place he now regarded as a refuge was the other side of the guards; and that Hildee was still inside the prison from which he had just escaped.

This had all been too easy. Brian could imagine the instructions Langford had passed on to the superintendent at Norwich and to the guards on the train: 'Don't detain Tyler, arouse his suspicions or impede his journey back to London. We will deal with him here.' It was not until the train was well under way that he felt relaxed enough to read his notes.

Whichever way Brian assembled the fragments of information he had collected over the past three days, Langford figured prominently in the final picture. But was he the prime mover, or was he being used by someone else? The American company Rebafing Technology came to mind. It was something the programmer Adam had said — Brian flicked through the pages of his notebook — and obviously something Brian had thought unimportant at the time, because he had not written it down.

If Langford was playing a key role, how did Mike fit into the picture? He must have been briefed. He was dining with Langford just after the investigation began. Is that why he was so keen to wrap up the investigation as soon as possible? But Mike was constantly changing his mind about who was responsible for Troxley's death, and that was likely to drag the investigation out rather than put it to bed.

Motive? Simitovich came to the top of the list. He was in line for the top party, hence government, job. Only Fairchild stood in his way. If Fairchild was implicated in the Troxley affair, if he was shown to have destroyed crop trials — an event that precipitated an ecological disaster — he would be finished. But there was a flaw in that argument.

Rebafing, the Americans, were trying to discredit Fairchild. With Simitovich in power, they would gain. Gain what? Something Adam had said. If Rebafing's programmer had accessed the Internet by using an on-line service, he would never have been tracked down from Britain. On-line services, however, were government-controlled in the US. As he used the Rebafing address it was likely the hacker was not only reasonably sure the UK end was secure but was also acting independently of the US government. Brian was sure Rebafing was the key. Understand what Rebafing was and he would understand everything.

And Langford's role? Langford was in a position to guarantee that the hacker was not detected. He knew where the passport was — *and* he was able to retrieve it. Troxley's S-Card? It was on this side of the Atlantic that a government-controlled computer system was used. Langford had moved Troxley's body onto Mike's patch so he could keep a close eye on the investigation. He had sent the girl up to Norwich to get the passport. He had used Mike to lead him to all the loose ends, to tidy up perhaps. Maybe Mike did kill the two assassins after all.

Brian closed his notebook. He should have shown the girl in the archive the photofit picture. No. That might have prompted her to call London. He looked out of the window. This was all academic, he thought. Mike would be waiting for him at King's Cross. How would Mike handle it? Arrest him, or try to talk him out of continuing the investigation? He remembered the two bodies lying in Hutch's laboratory. Had he now become another loose end to be tidied up? And what would happen to Hildee?

There was no-one to meet Brian at King's Cross. The streets were deserted and he was confident that no-one followed him to Kensington. As usual on a Monday evening, there were few diners in the Ivan's at Prince's Gardens. Once again, Brian sat thinking. He should have been scared, or at least worried, but merely felt lonely and alienated, for no obvious reason. After bolting his dessert, he rushed home to Queen's Gate.

*

The blonde girl shouted into her mobile phone. "Yes, I'm on the bus now. I should be at the CalTrain station in five minutes. Sure. Yes. Sure. I'll call you later. Bye." Mike had already identified her as one of his tails. She had been on the shuttle bus from the airport to the centre of San Francisco, and she had followed him onto the bus to the CalTrain — the train that ran south from San Francisco to San José. She was probably talking to the driver of a car that was shadowing the bus. Mike resisted the temptation to look for it in the near-deserted streets.

The car turned out to be a blue Buick. It would have been hard for Mike to miss it as he waited for the train — it was parked just across the street from the station. The girl could have telephoned the driver after Mike brought a ticket to San José, then the car could have waited somewhere out of sight, but they were afraid they might lose him. As he had only seen two shadows, Mike was naturally more worried about losing *them*. In a city with traffic and crowds, you need at least twelve people to follow someone without being detected. In this ghost town, the number was probably higher.

Mike remembered the CalTrain as being slow, with numerous stops. It was no faster now, and there were a lot fewer stops — Millbrae station, which once provided a link to San Francisco airport was in ruins. When he was last here, the towns along the route had been bustling centres of high technology. Today they were knots of buildings huddled around crumbling stations. There were no high-tech companies, just street markets and a few machinery-repair centres. In Mountain View itself, a tower block, its windows shaken out long ago during an earth tremor, threatened to tumble into the woodland that isolated it from the rest of the town. Rows of empty railway wagons stood rusting in the sidings at Santa Clara. Amongst the trees, the undergrowth was slowly strangling the homes of long-gone entrepreneurs and the apartment buildings of their cleaners and gardeners.

After getting off the airport shuttle, Martha had disappeared into the city. Mike had not spoken to her on the flight; they had not sat together. She was wearing a business suit, had her hair pulled back tightly over her head and carried the sort of large folder that advertising executives used to have. Mike, remembering her advice, bought a newspaper at the airport so that he had plenty of change for the bus and train. To remind him actually to buy a ticket, he fumbled every now and then with the coins in his pocket.

*

It was only when Brian walked into the hallway that he began to feel tired. His legs ached and his arms were heavy. Stef called out from the front room. "Brian! There you are! Someone from your office phoned this morning." She turned to look at Brian, who was leaning against the doorframe. "I told them you had been away all weekend — at the seaside." She stood up and gave him a hug. "I hope I did the right thing. It was about the fire."

"Yes, that's fine. I'll just drop my things into my room."

Stef released her grip, then laughed. "Hey! A new jacket and a new girlfriend. So that's why you're late back!"

"I didn't take a girl," Brian retorted.

Stef ran her finger across Brian's neck. "Well, where did that come from then?"

Brian ran his hand over a day's growth of stubble. Perhaps Stef was referring to the same old wives' tale Hildee had mentioned — the one about a man's facial hair growing faster when he was with a woman he felt attracted to.

It was only when he was in his room, standing in front of the basin and washing away the dust, dirt and smell of his rail journey, that Brian noticed the two bruises on his neck. Now he remembered Hildee gently biting and sucking his neck the previous night. Then, this morning, she had suggested that everyone would know he had been with a woman.

At the bottom of his rucksack, under his clothes, papers, book, Harry's glasses and the two phones, Brian found a neatly folded white cloth. Lifting it out, he realised it was the sheet from Hildee's bed. Wrapped in the sheet were the pieces of the broken ornament and a slip of paper.

> *Brian*
> *This was unforgivable and I am truly sorry.*
> *Loving and thinking of you.*
> *Hildee.*
> *PS. Somewhere for both of us to drown tonight.*

To begin with, the note made as little sense as anything else he had discovered that day. Brian continued to unfold what turned out to be just one half of the sheet he and Hildee had slept on the night before. It was stained and, holding it to his face, Brian could smell the scent of Hildee's body. Wrapping the sheet around his pillow, he lay on the bed. Sleep came quickly. Just before it did, Brian noticed the broken porcelain figure on the bedside table. Tomorrow, he thought, he would ask Stef for some glue. Had he remained conscious any longer, he might have remembered that earlier that morning the soldier at Nordelph Manor had been sent out to get glue. But now he felt Hildee's back against his chest. He could hear her breathing. The room was filled with the smell of her body. There came a deep and dreamless sleep, free from thoughts of soldiers, police, violence or conspiracies.

*

The bus from San José railway station to Santa Cruz stopped at Los Gatos. In 1999 Mike had stayed at the Toll House Hotel while visiting a company which supplied internet security software. The export sales director had recommended the Toll House as it was within walking distance of both his house and the company's offices. Mike was desperately trying to remember the man's name. 'El' something: Elmore, Ellis or Albright. No. There was no 'b' in the name. He could remember where Mr. El-something lived. His first name was French. Pierre, definitely Pierre. The bus turned off the freeway and strained up the ramp. He saw the Toll House, then the road to Pierre El-something's house just past it, on the left. The bus turned right and crossed the bridge over the freeway. The bridge was new and single-lane. It was now also the only bridge that joined the two halves of the town. The remains of the old two-lane bridge, shaken down during an earthquake in 2035, were piled up on either side of the freeway.

The community centre, where the bus came to a halt, was in a part of Los Gatos Mike did not recognise. "I'm taking a look around, then going on to Santa Cruz," he said to the driver, in a voice loud enough for the blonde girl to hear. "When does the next bus leave?"

"On the hour," the driver replied, without looking up.

Mike retraced the bus's route back towards the Toll House, coming eventually to a track which used to lead to a reservoir up in the hills. He remembered walking along it once to get a good view of San José. The track was now overgrown, but Mike could hear, in the gully below, the rush of water which drained down from the reservoir. From here, he knew the way to Pierre's house: left at the crossroads next to the town square, where, the last time he was here, there had been an open-air market; then right, into a small road that led up into the woods. He remembered the house was green, or possibly blue. It really did not matter; the paint would have peeled off years ago. All the buildings around him were pale grey — the colour of weathered wood.

Mike stepped over a gaping crack in the dust-covered pavement. He recognised the house, but not the telegraph pole leaning against the veranda. Climbing through the tangle of wires that covered the garden, he eventually reached the steps that led to the front door. The wooden veranda creaked beneath his feet. Looking for the nail marks which would identify the supporting beams, he tiptoed like a tightrope walker to the door. A small, oxidised brass plate read 'Pierre Elgin. Marketing Consultant'. Things must have got bad before they got worse, Mike thought. 'Elgin.' Of course. 'The man with all his marbles,' his father used to say. After peering through the cracked and grime-covered windows at the bare floorboards in the living room, Mike decided that there was no point in ringing the doorbell.

The sound of a car's engine echoed through the town. It was the only car Mike had heard since getting off the bus. The blue Buick appeared at the end of the street, stopped briefly while the driver looked at Mike, then continued on its way. He first heard the footsteps behind him when he was about fifty metres from Pierre's house. There was no need to look around — he knew it was the blonde girl. A gentle breeze lifted dust from the road in swirling clouds. He fancied that at any moment tumbleweed would blow along what was left of Main Street. The stark afternoon sunlight reflected on the drifts of grey sand that poked, like fingers, from under broken picket fences and spread themselves across the pavement. Accompanied by the haunting sound of the girl's footsteps and, in the distance, the rumbling of the car engine, Mike felt as if he was walking through a surrealist painting or film set. Perhaps it was the onset of jet lag, or even the first hint of alienation, but suddenly he felt in need of the company of other people.

Had he not stumbled across the small coffee bar, Mike might have given in and struck up a conversation with the blonde girl, who was now watching him from the other side of the road. Maybe he was merely suffering from the combination of hunger and thirst. He asked for a coffee. 'Remember to pay,' he said to himself as he picked up a cheese roll.

"That's American cheese," the waitress said.

"That's fine," Mike replied, now conscious, thanks to Martha, of how often he used the word 'fine'.

"Are you sure?"

"Yes, that'll be... just great." Mike sipped the coffee slowly. A fan turned lazily above his head. The room was filled with the aroma of fresh coffee and the sound of twentieth-century rock music. The cheese in the roll was like chewing gum. The waitress smiled to herself as she watched him breaking the strings of cheese with his fingers.

Still clutching half the roll, Mike strolled back to the bus stop. There was twenty minutes to wait and he sat on a low wall next to the steps leading to the community centre. The blonde girl sat on a seat about a hundred metres away. She made a call on her mobile, then folded her arms and tilted her head forward.

*

"You need to pay!" the driver's voice boomed. Fumbling in his pocket, Mike eventually found the right coins. He then walked back up the aisle of the bus and dropped money into the machine. "Ticket! Take your ticket!" the driver shouted. Once more, Mike returned to the front of the bus. The Afro-American driver stared up at him as he leaned back in his seat. "Something tells me you're not from around here."

Mike smiled. "Damn! And I was trying to be so cool."

The driver laughed and shook his head slowly as he rammed the gear lever forward. There was a hiss of air as the doors closed. As the bus pulled away, Mike noticed the blonde girl still asleep on the seat. He walked to the front of the bus for a third time.

"No, you've got it now: money, ticket. There's nothing else."

The driver exclaimed.

"That girl." Mike pointed out of the window.

"Pretty, ain't she?"

"I think she wants this bus."

The driver braked, brought the bus to a halt and turned to face Mike. "Just exactly where are you from?" he asked pressing the horn and opened the door again. He learned towards the door "Lady! You going to Santa Cruz?" he bellowed. The blonde girl leaped up from the seat and sprinted towards the bus. She got there just in time to see Mike returning to his seat.

*

As he waited in Santa Cruz bus station, Mike tried to work out whether the blonde girl was angry with him or just embarrassed. He intended to strike up a conversation with her when the bus arrived at Capitola. However, he did not get the chance — she took out her mobile phone and walked out onto the beach. Mike strolled down to the water's edge. Pelicans circled overhead, their calls drowned out periodically by the sound of waves crashing onto the sand. The Buick failed to appear. Looking up at the cliffs that rose above the beach, Mike assumed that the driver had found a vantage point where he could observe Mike and the girl without being spotted. He took off his jacket, folded it into a pillow, lay down on the sand and slept.

The blood-red evening sun was low in the sky when Mike woke. His lips tasted salty and his face was burning. Rolling onto his side, he could see the girl sitting just a few metres away, her hair and face bathed in the same orange light that lit up the beach and the wooden buildings along the promenade. Shaking the sand off his jacket, Mike staggered towards the small restaurant further along the beach. It took time for his eyes to adjust to the darkness. When they had, he noticed that the girl had followed him into the room. Walking over to a table piled high with tee-shirts and beachwear, he optimistically picked out a hat, took it to the bar and paid for it. By now the girl had chosen a table, so Mike walked over to it and sat opposite her.

"So what sort of day have you had?" As far as chat-up lines go, Mike thought, that one must sound dire, especially as her day had been pretty awful — mostly on *his* account. The girl did not speak. She tried, but seemed to be in a panic. She moved her mouth in an attempt to form words, at the same time trying to hide behind the hand which she brought up to her face.

"I've had a dreadful day," Mike said, ignoring the girl's discomfort. "Came all the way from Washington to find an old friend and discovered he had moved away." The girl began to relax. He wanted to continue with his story, but Mike knew he now had to wait until the girl started to probe. He picked up the menu. "You probably know this area better than I do. What do you recommend?" Although the girl was still shaking her head and making nervous gestures with her hand, Mike realised she was coming to terms with his company.

"Try the prawns," she said. "I never eat anything too heavy after travelling on a hot day."

Half way through the meal, the girl began to steer the conversation away from comparisons between life in America and Europe and towards the reason for Mike's visit to California. She learned about Pierre Elgin and the high-tech company he used to work for, and about Mike's plans to catch a bus back to San José the next day. She noted the Ritz-Carlton letterhead on the printed bus timetable. Mike learned that the girl was from southern California; she was on vacation from university and just 'drifting'.

After dinner, Mike and the girl returned to the beach. A large group of people were seated in a circle next to rocks at the far end of the beach. Varying in age from teenagers to middle-aged couples most had been swimming in the sea — one had a surfboard. "Mind if we join you?" Mike asked.

One of the older men shrugged. "Go ahead."

A man and woman moved to one side to give Mike and the blonde girl room to sit down. "I'll be with you in a moment. I've just got to buy a postcard," the blonde girl said. Mike thought this was probably just an excuse to make another phone call, but in a few moments she was back, carrying a postcard and a pen. Mike noticed her glance up at the cliffs as she sat down.

Introductions over, most of the group started grilling Mike about life in Europe, which none of them had ever visited. Most were casual workers travelling up and down the west coast, picking up jobs on farms and sleeping rough on the beach. When winter came, they would travel inland and work for one of the municipal authorities, as linemen, road repairers, or building workers. Mike realised this was the ideal opportunity to tell his cover story.

"Ever been to the States before, Mike?" one of the men asked.

"Forty years ago," Mike replied.

The blonde girl was sitting just behind Mike and a little way outside the circle. Breaking off from writing her postcard, she leaned forward and tapped him on the shoulder. "Ask them about the company and that Pierre. What was his name? Perhaps someone knows what happened to him."

So Mike asked if anyone knew Pierre Elgin or his company, and he assumed that the girl wrote everything he said down on her postcard. Then he told them all about his trip from Washington and his hope that he would not be missed during the trade negotiations.

Before it got dark, Mike, the blonde girl and most of the others in the group took a swim in the sea. After walking backwards and forwards along the beach to dry off, Mike made his jacket into a pillow again and pretended to sleep. It was eleven thirty when the blonde girl got to her feet and walked up to the road. Mike could hear her talking on the phone, presumably reading out the information written on the postcard. Thirty minutes later, on a road high up on the cliff, a car engine started. Another five minutes passed before the Buick appeared on the promenade and the girl got in. Mike closed his eyes and listened. The sound of the car's engine grew fainter and was eventually drowned out completely by the roar of the surf.

8

Tuesday 27th August 2041

Johnny Coates appeared in the doorway of Brian's office. "Hello! You're back then," he said. "Langford was looking for you. He wanted to see you in his office." Brian looked up. "Er, sir," Johnny added, as an afterthought.

It was like being sent for by the headmaster. Brian remembered the headmaster at the vast orphanage where he had spent most of his childhood. At that time, having no parents was nothing out of the ordinary. How did the joke go? 'I'm a lemming. I'm an orphan. All lemmings are orphans.' The headmaster used to sit behind his heavy oak desk, with Brian's class teacher standing at his side. "You should look on us as your parents," the headmaster would say.

Brian, however, was not an orphan and never looked on the teachers as his parents. He vaguely remembered his mother. He could recall running after a bus. Breaking free from his sister's grasp, he had run down the road. His feet had pounded on the ground so hard that the air had been forced from his lungs with every step. When he had been able to catch his breath, he had shouted. Eventually he could neither run nor shout any more. The bus had disappeared and his mother hadn't looked around once. Only a few hours before, he had been walking with her in the meadows behind his sister's house. "You'll be happy here," she had said, holding his hands and dancing. "You'll be very happy here."

"This'll do me," Brian whispered.

"Sir?"

"Sorry, Johnny. Miles away." Brian got up from his desk. "And I'm still called Brian. Probably 'mud' after Langford's finished with me."

"Oh, he didn't seem in such a bad mood."

'This'll do me.' Brian thought to himself. Was it this investigation or just the visit to the countryside that had made him feel so restless — and had stirred so many memories? A week ago, his life had run like clockwork. It might have been dull, but it was secure. A book a week, collected from the shop in Kensington. A film a week. Saturday night out. Sunday evening in the park. And Stef. However, even before the Troxley case came up things had started to change. Stef's new house. The clearance of undergrowth from the edge of the Serpentine — and the reopening of the café. Would they still bother to take the boats out now that the paths around the edge were clear? Stupid little changes. A man in his mid-twenties should not have been scared of them. But he was.

"So you couldn't be with us yesterday, Brian?" Langford was being every bit as patronising as Brian's teachers used to be.

"I was held up. Well, to tell you the truth, I went to Cromer for the weekend and overslept." Brian tugged his shirt collar, just as Hildee had done.

Langford smiled. "Hope she was worth it." He then narrowed his eyes and frowned. "Bad business, this fire. You heard about it?"

"Yes, sir."

"Want you to get to the bottom of it. See if you can find out who was behind it."

"Aren't we jumping to conclusions? Most fires start on their own — especially at this time of year." The 'we' he had accidentally referred to was Langford himself.

Langford seemed not to notice Brian's implied criticism. "I'm not sure it did. Very serious business. Not just arson — murder."

"But I'm still working on the Troxley case with Mr. Allchurch..." Brian was about to point out that the Troxley case needed wrapping up by the end of the week, but he could not remember if anyone had actually told him that or whether he had merely assumed a result was needed before Simitovich's visit on Friday.

Langford tilted his chair back and stared at Brian. "Mike isn't back from Brussels yet. I should imagine Fairchild is giving him the run-around. If Mike hasn't got anywhere by the end of the week, we will take Fairchild's reluctance to talk as an indication that he was involved in the killing. You've both collected enough evidence to back that up, haven't you?"

The leather chair was making Brian's back sweat. He fidgeted, crossed his legs and pulled himself forward by holding on to his right ankle. "I was thinking of talking to a few of the witnesses again. Just in case we missed something."

"Get one up on your boss, you mean." Langford chuckled and swung his chair around so that he was facing the window. "All right then. But only if you have any time left after sorting out this fire."

As Brian stood up to leave, Langford swung his chair around again and looked up at him. "If you discover anything in the

Troxley investigation which you think I ought to know about, I take it you will talk to me about it first." Suddenly Langford had changed. There was a hint of menace in his voice. He looked Brian up and down, then stared straight into his eyes.

Brian felt uneasy. Should he ask Langford about the arrest of Troxley? Had the Deputy found out about his visits to Cambridge and Norwich police stations? If he had, then how long before he would find out about Downham — and Hildee? How safe was Hildee Parks? As safe as anyone could be in a town patrolled by the army. As safe as Gerald Whiteside? Brian felt his throat dry up. "Of course," he replied, looking down at Langford's trembling hands and trying to convince himself that the Deputy was merely a frail and frightened man. "I'll be at the fire most of the day, I should think," he said, hoping that Langford would be consoled by the fact that Brian would not be digging around on the Troxley case for at least another twenty-four hours.

*

"The wanderer has returned!" Amanda Pearce shouted across to Brian. She picked her way through the piles of charred wood and debris which littered the floor of the burned-out warehouse "And this jacket — cool or what?"

"Very warm actually," Brian said, pulling his shirt away from his neck.

"Oooh! Romance in the air." Amanda took off her glove and prodded the marks on Brian's neck.

Had Hildee's love bites not served him so well over the last two days, Brian might have been annoyed by the constant references to them. "So, any ideas yet?" he asked.

"Not really." Amanda shrugged and looked around the gutted building. "Fire started over there," she said, pointing at a gaping hole at the back of the warehouse.

"Langford seems to think it's arson." Brian started to walk towards the back of the building. "Wants to open a murder enquiry," he called out over his shoulder.

Amanda followed him at a distance. "If anyone is going to be charged with murder, it ought to be the person who sent a bunch of geriatric firemen into this death-trap." She thrust her hands in the pockets of her overalls. "That's off the record, of course."

"Of course."

"I mean, eight people died, and for what?" Amanda kicked a

charred sack of flour. "This! We lost a large part of the North London fire brigade for a few loaves of bread."

It then dawned on Brian that the firemen who had died were the ones who turned up late for the fire in Barnet. He could imagine what Sam would be saying now. "Where are the bodies?" he asked.

"Oh boy! *You* don't want to know. Hutch is crawling up the wall. He's got the bits of eight corpses spread around the lab."

The heat from one of the walls hit Brian in the face. "Must have been some fire."

"And explosion. All the flour was stored on wooden pallets. The first floor was all wood. There must have been a gust of wind. Either that or a window fell out. Anyway, the fire got a shot of oxygen, then there was a dust explosion and the roof caved in. The poor sods didn't stand a chance."

Stepping out into the yard at the back of the warehouse, Amanda picked up a broken bottle and a handful of dried grass. "Ever do this when you were a kid?" she said, using the base of the bottle to focus the sun's rays onto the grass.

Brian watched as a wisp of smoke curled up out of Amanda's hand. "No. I was brought up by the party. We had to recycle everything. Besides, isn't there carbon in that smoke?"

"Well, there you go," Amanda said, dropping the grass and bottle onto the ground. "I'll write a page saying that's what happened, if you do the rest of the report."

"Seems fair enough." Brian took out his mobile phone. "Hello, Hutch. Wanted to be the first to tell you the good news. About those bodies... Yes, the crispy ones." Amanda winced. "Yes, it looks like an accident — so you can dump them." Brian listened for a moment, then added, "Mind you, they are well cooked — seems a pity..." The phone went dead at the other end.

"I wish you wouldn't do that, Brian. I have to work with him." Amanda started to walk back towards the warehouse. "I had a look at the room in Lewisham Street," she said. "Have you had a chance to speak to Johnny yet?"

"No. He was rushing off somewhere and I had to see Langford."

"Yes, Langford seems to have everyone rushing around this week. I'm surprised he didn't nail you to the wall. You must be his blue-eyed boy."

"Did you turn up anything interesting?"

"Two sets of prints — the same ones we found on the

passport."

"Yes. One set belongs to the girl, the other to our mystery man." Brian looked down at his feet. "Can you get me a photo of both sets?"

"No problem. I'll send them up to your office with the report on this lot."

"No!" Brian snapped. Amanda looked shocked. "No," Brian said again, this time in a calmer voice. "The office is such a mess at the moment, I can't find anything. I'll collect them when they're ready."

It was as he walked back to Paddington station that Brian remembered showing Langford the authorisation from the Inland Waterways Security Division — and telling him they were going to raid the address. Perhaps the girl had not seen Johnny after all.

*

The underground train rocked and lurched its way from station to station between Paddington and St. James's Park. For most of the journey, Brian thought of Hildee; for the rest of it, he worried about the investigation. Feeling responsible for someone was a new experience. In fact, it was fair to say that until this week he had never had any responsibilities at all. Now he found himself effectively in charge of one of the hottest investigations in Europe, and even Johnny was calling him 'sir'. Saying he was going to go over the ground Mike had already covered was Brian's way of putting Langford at ease. Nevertheless, he felt trapped and impotent. How could he protect Hildee if Langford did become suspicious?

*

Brian had a plan — or, to be precise, two plans. The second came into being as the train arrived at St. James's. The District and Circle line was rarely crowded, even during what was still referred to as 'the rush hour'. Small groups of office workers, waiting for a train after leaving work together, hardly constituted crowds. In the middle of the day, most stations were deserted. That is why Brian noticed Lenny Drake walking along the westbound platform as the train pulled into St. James's. Suddenly he was conscious of the watch on his wrist and the mobile phone in his jacket pocket. A cloud of foul-smelling dust followed the train out of the station.

266

Brian looked across the tracks — Lenny had disappeared. But Brian knew that as he walked towards the exit Lenny was watching him from one of the dark recesses on the other platform.

*

Mike woke up on a deserted beach, the group of travelling workers having moved on at first light. Unfolding his jacket, he checked the pockets to make sure all his money was still there. The restaurant provided a large bath towel for people washing in the men's room, but five other men had already dried themselves on it that morning. Mike unpacked his small travel bag, which contained a battery razor as well as a hand towel and a bar of soap he had taken from the hotel.

A white van drew up at the door of the restaurant while Mike was finishing his bacon, eggs and hash browns. Martha walked up to the bar and ordered coffee and rolls. She then walked straight past Mike, putting her tray down on a table at the far end of the room. Realising he was not wearing the hat as instructed, Mike took the baseball cap out of his pocket and put it on. Martha giggled. "Bet you're only guessing," she said, sitting down opposite him.

"No. She went last night."

Martha tugged at the peak of Mike's cap, pulling it down over his eyes. "Picked up by some guy in a Buick just before midnight."

Mike looked surprised. "How did you know that?" he asked, taking off the cap and throwing it on the table.

"I was parked behind him up on the cliff." Martha took a sip of coffee and looked out of the window. "Interesting telephone conversation they were having," she said with a smile.

"You overheard them?"

"Listened in. I've got a scanner in the van." She smiled again. "She thought you were cute. Must have been that swim in the sea."

"How long were you up there?"

"Long enough to know you convinced them — or, more to the point, convinced their boss. He told them to give up and go back to San Francisco. Today they're someone else's problem."

*

Some of the lorries that had been used earlier that week to transport grain across East Anglia were now lined up in rows at the Marble

Arch end of Hyde Park. The rest had been retained by the army. Too big to be taken underground, the lorries had been left on what was once Speakers' Corner. There, a team of mechanics decided which vehicles were to be repaired and which were destined for the recycling centre. This tarmacked area, once a popular meeting place and forum for a wide range of political groups, was where the buses that served central London were usually parked. The bus park had been the idea of the first Green Alliance Minister of Transport — a person very close to David Fairchild. The decision to use Speakers' Corner, where individuals could pour scorn on the Greens just metres away from the party headquarters, was no coincidence. Today, however, the mechanics working on the lorries were heaping more scorn on the army, the party and the establishment in general than any of the anarchists who still attempted, from time to time, to use the area for its original purpose.

The buses, having been evicted from the park, were lined up along Park Lane. Double-parked alongside them was a queue of light goods vans waiting to enter the petrol station. The combined noise was deafening and Brian, choking on the fumes, wished he had taken an alternative route to the underground vehicle pound. Once down the ramp and into the old underground car park, the noise evaporated and the air was cool. A number of mechanics were cycling between the stores and repair stations. Each repair station was bathed in sunlight that shone down from the windows above. Skylights had been cut in the roof to save electricity, to make space for repair ramps and to remove the fumes that built up when engines were being tested. From the park above, these skylights looked like rows of greenhouses.

Brian caught up with one of the mechanics and asked them where Sam was working. The mechanic pointed to a General Motors family saloon. The badly corroded front wings had already been stripped from the chassis, and much of the instrumentation had been removed from the dashboard. Sam and the female mechanic were lowering a new power unit into the front of the car.

"Why have you taken the radio out?" Brian said, peering inside the passenger compartment.

"'A car should only be used for a journey along a route where no other form of transport is available. The journey should have a clearly defined purpose and should not be undertaken for its own sake. *A car journey is not a form of entertainment.*'" Sam's quotation from the transport regulations was almost word-perfect.

"Anyway, what do you want?" Sam's voice was harsher than it had been the last time they spoke.

"I need a favour," Brian replied.

"Do you now?" Sam said, without looking up. Brian was taken aback by this response and did not answer. Eventually, Sam stood up and, wiping his hands on a rag, glared at Brian. "The answer's still the same as it was yesterday. There's no way we are going to put our necks on the line while the fire service is run by those idiots. I can't let..."

"It's nothing to do with the fire service."

Sam threw the rag into a metal drum. "Well, what is it then?"

"It's private," said Brian, glancing at Sam's assistant.

"That's all right — no secrets here." Sam smiled, but Brian looked down at the floor and slowly walked away from the car.

"Can you get a length of gas pipe?" Sam asked his assistant.

Brian watched the young mechanic mount her bicycle and set off towards the stores. "Can you telephone your army contact for me?" he said, when the girl was out of earshot.

"And say what?"

"I need a meeting with the commander of the London Regiment — today, if possible."

"Strewth! Tall order, Brian. Patterson is a busy man. Even if he did see you, it wouldn't be today. Probably not this week." Sam frowned. "Don't you have official channels for that sort of thing?"

"It's a question of trust."

"Sounds like you have got yourself into the shit."

"You could say that." Brian walked back to the car and leaned on the door. He looked up at the skylight and the blue sky outside. "How do you stand it, working in here all day?"

"Cool in summer and warm in winter. A few hours outside each day. It's not that bad."

"The fire service coming on heavy, are they?"

"Heavy? They're even talking about sending us to a penal farm if we don't take it up full time." Sam shook his head. "I can't really ask the others to do that, even if *I* wanted to. It's too damn dangerous. I thought you were here playing the soft man. Trevor told me you were on some sort of committee or working party."

"Yes. I volunteered to work on the new fire regulations."

"Well, put in a good word for us."

It was then that Brian realised he was in a position to do just that. "What's your main objection to going full time?"

Sam bristled again. "The same thing that got that crew killed last weekend. The person in charge of the crew at the scene of a fire is not allowed to overrule the commander sitting in the control room."

"That's it?"

"That's enough to get everyone killed."

"I'll make the suggestion."

"And you think they'll take any notice?"

Brian smiled. "My guess is, they haven't had a rush of people to work on the regs. They may not want to discourage me by saying 'no' to my first suggestion."

"Good point. Look, I'll give Ross a call. He may be able to fit you in sometime this week. But don't be surprised if he just tells you to go through official channels."

"Tell him I'm Brian Tyler, that I'm just back from a place called Downham, and want to talk to him about the Troxley investigation. And you'd better tell him that it's important he doesn't mention the meeting to Army Liaison at the Home Office."

"I'll try. Can't promise anything though."

"Today, if possible," Brian called out as Sam rode off on his bicycle.

*

"Well, you've come up in the world," Sam said when he returned. Brian was watching the mechanic wire up the ignition system on the gas-powered engine. Sam was trying to catch his breath. "They want to see you now."

"Thanks. I owe you."

"Just get the fire service off my back."

"I'll see what I can do," Brian shouted as he rode off towards the Marble Arch exit.

*

They drove north out of Santa Cruz. Every few kilometres the coast road narrowed to a single track. After three hours' driving, they were four kilometres from Miramar. During the journey Mike told Martha about the blonde girl, how she had fallen asleep at Los Gatos and transcribed his cover story onto a postcard. Martha found this amusing and explained that the girl probably was, just as she said, a student working her vacation. Pulling off the road and parking behind some tall bushes, Martha placed a magnetic sign on each side of the van.

"'North Bay Computers.' What am I supposed to be, a programmer?" Mike asked.

"Service engineer," Martha replied, throwing a pair of white overalls at him. "We keep this van in a safe house in the city. Mostly it's a parcel-delivery van, but today it belongs to a computer company. Just in case we have to take Passmore's computer to someone who can recover data from a formatted hard drive."

At Miramar beach a sign on the right-hand side of the road marked the entrance to Passmore's farm: 'Organic Food at Ordinary Prices'. Mike wondered what ordinary prices were — the breakfast having cost ninety dollars. Brussels sprouts, cauliflower and cabbage plants were set out in neat rows on either side of the drive. The farmhouse was clad with weatherboarding that had recently received given a fresh coat of white paint.

"So you still haven't got it sorted out then?" A young man dressed in khaki trousers and a short-sleeved denim shirt ran his hand through his thinning sun-bleached hair, then wiped the sweat from his brow. Standing beside the van door, he seemed to be waiting for a response before allowing Mike to get out.

Already out of the van, and half way to the door of the house, Martha called out to the farm hand. "Mr. Passmore called us yesterday and asked us to check it out. Guess his computer must be pretty important to him."

The farm hand followed Martha to the door and Mike climbed out of the van. "Did he say when he's coming back? I haven't heard from him for a week," the farm hand asked.

"Nope. Just said he still had things to do in Europe." Martha stood aside to let the farm hand get to the door. "But he did say he wanted the computer for the weekend."

The farm hand reached up and took a key from the small ledge above the doorjamb. Unlocking the door, he led Martha and Mike inside. "There it is then," he said, pointing to the PC in Passmore's office. "Your colleague said it was the hard disk. He put a new one in and it seemed to work."

"We just want to check," Martha said, then waited until she heard the farm hand close the front door. "Shit! We're too late." She sighed and switched on the computer. "We should have done this as soon as we heard that Passmore was dead." The disk drives whirred and the computer started to boot up.

Mike thought that the disappearance of the data was just a bit too convenient. He was beginning to wonder if this was all an elaborate charade to throw him off the scent. Maybe Martha was co-ordinating some sort of cover-up. Perhaps the other computer engineer, and even the farm hand, were CIA agents as well.

*

"So who is Tyler?" Patterson rolled his chair backwards until it was resting against the window. Staring down at the rooftops of Oxford Street, he waited for Dennis Lummis of Army Intelligence to answer.

Lummis referred to his notes. "According to what we've seen so far, a young lad who likes his drink, who fancies the ladies and who, on the rare occasions when he's sober and out of bed, pokes his nose in where it doesn't belong."

"And his involvement in the Troxley investigation?"

"As from yesterday, he seems to be running it. The other policeman on the case disappeared last Friday." Lummis turned to the next page of his notes and studied it for a while. "According to this," he said eventually, "Mr. Tyler spent an interesting weekend in East Anglia. He made a rather amateurish attempt to fool us into believing he was somewhere else."

"I suppose we'd better find out what he's got to say." Patterson rose from his chair and walked to the door. "Mr. Tyler!" he shouted down the corridor.

Lummis pretended to read his notes, although by now he had absorbed the report from Hereford and the one compiled by his own department. "Army Intelligence," he said, introducing himself to Brian without giving his name. "Now, I know exactly what you are thinking."

Brian gulped, ran his hand over his mouth and turned to Patterson. The Commander, wondering why Brian suddenly had a strained look on his face, pointed to a chair in the corner of the room. He waited until Brian had sat down before returning to his own chair behind the desk.

"What you're thinking is," Lummis continued, "'How am I going to get out of this mess? The party have handed me their dirty washing and I'm going to get hung out to dry with it.'" He flicked through the report from his own department. "Seems Mr. Allchurch had the right idea. After he eliminated the two hit men you were chasing across East Anglia, he did a runner. Wise man." Lummis expected Brian to wither under this attack and was surprised when the young policemen actually appeared to relax.

"Perhaps you've got your own bolt hole lined up," sneered Lummis. "Is that what the little girly in Nordelph Manor is all about? Oh, pardon the pun, by the way." Lummis saw Brian flinch. He turned to Patterson and laughed.

"Look," Patterson said. "why doesn't Mr. Tyler just tell us why he's here?" At first Brian thought that Lummis and the Commander were acting out the roles of hard man and soft man, but Patterson looked irritated and now raised his hand to stop Lummis interrupting.

"I would like some help with the enquiry into the death of Toby Troxley," Brian said.

Patterson sighed. "You'll need to go through your Army Liaison office. We can't talk to you directly."

"There's a reason why I'd rather not do that." Brian shifted in his chair.

"I bet!" snapped Lummis. "The party just want a nice simple story. They don't want any complications. You're just going to have to write your report and take your chances."

Brian could see that Patterson was losing his patience and decided to strike back at Lummis. "It isn't as simple as that. I don't think the party are behind this."

Once again, Patterson raised his hand to silence Lummis. "So you think it was us."

"No," Brian retorted. "I think there may have been a crude attempt to make it look like an army operation. You were first on the scene at the hotel, and Whiteside was killed in an army-controlled area."

Patterson turned to Lummis. "Does anyone know who killed Whiteside?"

Brian did not give him the chance to answer. "Two gunmen, probably the same two who were shot in Turnham Green on Friday night." Brian took a folder out of his rucksack. He handed Patterson a copy of the Inland Waterways Security Division authorisation. "They got into East Anglia along the river system."

Lummis reached across Patterson's desk and took the sheet of paper. "They must have known that we don't patrol waterways. How do you think they found that out?"

"They were probably ex-convicts who had spent time up there. There are enough of them about."

"And all of them are on your files." Lummis dropped the sheet of paper onto the desk. "So it looks like a fabrication by the police on behalf of the party."

"I agree," said Patterson. "Why should this bother us? From what you say, we're in the clear. All we have to do is sit back while the party sort themselves out. The last thing we want to do is get involved in anything political."

"I don't think it is the party," Brian said.

"Who the hell else is there?" snapped Lummis.

Brian shrugged. Patterson leaned forward and picked up the document again. "Looks like the police to me. And the police, as far as we're concerned, are the party. Nothing to do with us."

Taking back the authorisation, Brian folded it in two. "It just strikes me as a funny way to discredit Fairchild, that's all. If I was going to do it, I would choose something he did after the party took control. Anything before that reflects on the party itself. If Simitovich is behind this, what is he going to tell us when he gets the top job? 'Sorry everyone, the whole Green movement is based on a sham. We were the ones who caused the crisis in the first place.'"

Patterson sat back in his chair. He glanced at Lummis, raised his eyebrows, then looked at Brian again. "And so?"

"Well, that's it really," Brian said. "If Fairchild is toppled and the party is tainted — especially the UK branch — then who is going to be in charge in Britain? Will there still be a party in the UK?" He looked at Lummis. "I just thought that you might have thought about that at some point. Especially as the structure and the size of the army depend largely on Green Party policies."

Now both men were looking at Lummis. "Well," said Patterson, "have you considered that?"

Lummis shook his head, then made the mistake of defending himself by attacking Brian. "So this idea of a grand conspiracy is based on that piece of paper and a drunken weekend with your fancy woman, is it?"

"Perhaps if Captain Taylor and Captain Nunn had taken a little more interest in what actually happened at Whiteside Farm and had spent a little less time intruding into my personal life, you would have a better grasp of what was going on. What exactly were they supposed to be doing there anyway?"

Lummis thought the names of the two intelligence officers sounded familiar. He checked his notes again and found Nunn and Taylor mentioned in the report from the Hereford Regiment. "They were there to protect a Miss Hildee Parks from you. We believed that the same people who killed Gerald Whiteside also intended to kill her. And we thought it might have been you and Mr. Allchurch who killed Whiteside."

"So when I was spotted by the guard on the train, your crack team swung into action," Brian said sarcastically. "Pity they didn't bother to follow me out to the manor the night I pretended to be drunk. That's the night I would have..." Brian could not bring himself to say 'killed her'. "They gave me eight hours to get away."

Lummis checked the report again, then looked up to speak, but Brian interrupted. "And who is protecting her now? Not Nunn and Taylor, because they left when I did. You admitted yourself that you don't know where Mike Allchurch is. You think he killed the two hit men. How do you know he's not in Downham right now?"

Patterson smiled to himself. Brian was arguing his case passionately. At least Lummis had been right about one thing: Brian *had* fallen for Miss Parks. "Yes, Mr. Tyler," he said, to save Lummis the embarrassment of trying to answer the question, "we do seem to have made a number of mistakes in the way this case has been handled so far." He looked at Lummis, but spoke to Brian. "Is there anything you think we should be doing at the moment?"

Brian's answer came as no surprise to Patterson, who admired the way he justified the request. "Hildee Parks," Brian blurted out. "I mean, Miss Parks. If I put forward the argument that Troxley and Whiteside were killed in an attempt to discredit Fairchild, then Miss Parks will be a key witness. I don't think it will take long for someone at the Home Office to work that out. I think Miss Parks should have around-the-clock protection until the investigation is complete."

Patterson rubbed his chin. "We can arrange that, can't we?" he said to Lummis.

"Yes. I can't see a problem with that." Lummis wrote in the file.

"Now. Please — or do you want me to arrange it?" Patterson said aggressively, his hand hovering over the telephone.

"No, sir. I'll do it now." Lummis got up and hurriedly left the room.

Patterson sniffed. With Lummis out of the room, he relaxed. "So, Brian, have you discussed this with your boss?"

"My immediate boss is Mike Allchurch."

"Ah, the man on the run. What about his boss? Have you voiced your suspicions to him?"

"No."

Patterson dragged a notebook from the corner of the desk and took a pencil out of a white mug with a broken handle. "So, who is Allchurch's boss?"

"Stephen Langford. Deputy Commissioner."

Without taking his eyes off Brian, Patterson wrote down the name. "I've heard the name. So you don't trust Langford enough to confide in him?"

"No, basically." Brian felt like a traitor. "That's not to say I think he has anything to do with any of this. It could be someone above him." He refrained from telling Patterson about the files in Cambridge and Norwich. Lummis must already know; it was probably mentioned in one of the reports he had been carrying. Nor did Brian say anything about his growing suspicion that Langford had tipped off the girl about the raid on the office.

Patterson doodled on the notepad. "Look for someone with clean hands, Brian."

"Clean hands?"

"Yes. Everyone thinks the army's hands are clean, but we're as tainted as the rest of you. Summary executions, false imprisonment and so on. But your man will never have fired a gun, never have given an order that involved someone being shot or locked up without a trial. He's the sort of person who isn't worried about the return of democracy, or about journalists digging around in his past. That's what keeps the system together: the fear of having to account for the past."

"Everyone did what had to be done. People understand that."

"They did at the time, but now they're not so sure, and tomorrow they'll think we were animals." Patterson stopped doodling and returned the pencil to the broken mug. "I suppose we *were* really, and in ten years' time they'll say we should have arrested looters instead of shooting them on sight. We'll be judged by people with full bellies who never had to fight for the last bottle of antibiotics." He looked away and gazed at the corner of the room. "And when fingers are pointed, the party will conveniently lose the order they gave to have civilians bombed and shelled. That will all be laid at our door. They'll wheel us out one by one, painting us as evil personified so that they can pretend their hands are clean." He turned back to face Brian. "So your man must be sure he's got nothing to hide. Perhaps they're young like you — or just lucky."

Were Langford's hands clean? When Brian came to Centre

Point that afternoon, he had not intended to discuss Langford, or even to let on he suspected that the police were plotting Fairchild's downfall. Once again, he felt he had betrayed his colleagues to an organisation that many in the police regarded as the enemy. He even wondered if he had achieved the primary objective of his visit. "When do you think the bodyguards will be in place?" he asked.

"Don't worry. Your little lady will be safe. I'll organise it myself." Patterson smiled. "Are you aware of any specific threat to her?"

Brian took the photofit of the girl out of his rucksack and placed it on the desk. "This is the girl from the hotel. I doubt if she'll turn up in Downham, but if she does she should be apprehended. So should anyone on the waterways — the gunmen got into the area using Home Office authorisations issued to the so-called 'Inland Waterways Security Division'."

Taking the photofit, Patterson stood up. "Can do. Now, is there anything else you need?"

"Well, it would help if you could send me the fingerprints of the intelligence officers who searched the hotel room where Troxley was found."

"They'll have worn gloves. Anyway, you don't suspect..."

"No, no. It's just in case someone at the Home Office finds out I've been here. I need some sort of cover story. If I could take back some prints, then I can say I was eliminating the army from the investigation."

"Yes. I see." Patterson said. "Very clever. We've got a vacancy in the intelligence section, if you're interested."

"I'll bear that in mind. If all this goes belly up, I might need it."

"I hear you know Trevor Horsfield."

"Yes. We live in the same house."

"Another lad on the fast track. The *young*-boy network."

"I don't understand."

"It's nothing. But if we turn up something, or you need anything, I think Horsfield can be trusted to deliver a message."

"Ah yes, I see." Brian opened the door and stepped out into the corridor.

Patterson followed. "Oxymoron." He murmured.

"Pardon?" Brian looked at Patterson, puzzled.

"Oxymoron. When matey from Army Intelligence said he knew what you were thinking, you were thinking 'oxymoron'.

Everyone does. That's why we took the nameplate off his door. Kept getting defaced." Patterson extended his hand. "Good luck, Brian — and take care."

*

Martha went out to the van and returned with two shoulder bags. The first contained a laptop PC, a modem and an encryption device. In the second bag was the radio scanner for eavesdropping on mobile phones. Martha connected the scanner to a power supply and switched it on. "Just in case your friends in the Buick come back," she said, returning to Passmore's computer and listing the files on the hard drive. She threw the mouse across the desk. "Damn! Well, at least they didn't burn the place down."

"Disks can be recovered after fires. Anyway, this would have survived." Mike pointed to the fireproof safe that stood in a small alcove next to the desk.

Kneeling in front of the safe, Martha turned the dial. "Now all we need is the combination."

The alcove had a frame around it and looked as though it had once been a cupboard. Mike stood on the desk and examined the top of the jamb around the alcove." 32 right, 20 left, 5 right..." Martha was too startled to do anything at first, but then turned the dial on the safe. Mike finished reading the sequence and jumped back down to the floor.

"How did you know they were there?" Martha asked, as she pulled the safe door open.

"Remember where the farm hand got the key from? I think Passmore wanted us to find the key — and the combination."

"Empty." Martha held the safe door open for Mike to see.

This was all too easy. True, Passmore had wanted the information to be accessible if anything should happen to him. Mike was becoming increasingly suspicious of Martha's true role in this affair. "I thought you said you were watching this place?"

"Yes, like I said, a web cam was set up in a building on the other side of the road. Every time someone entered or left the farm, they were snapped." Martha switched on her notebook PC, then connected the modem and the encryption device in a daisy chain between the phone socket in the wall and the computer's serial connector.

Martha rolled the cursor around the screen and clicked one of its buttons. "I'm going to access the database at Langley," she said.

"Let's see if we can identify the 'computer engineer'."

"Why hasn't he been spotted already?"

"Because" — Martha typed in her password — "when Passmore was reported as dead we stopped watching." She moved the cursor onto the menu and clicked. "A bit lax perhaps."

"Very lax."

Martha frowned "I suppose you never cut corners." A long list of dates and times appeared.

Wanting to avoid the argument that was obviously brewing, Mike changed the subject. "How does this camera work then?"

"Well, it's actually like a miniature website." She clicked on an entry in the list and a picture of a bus passing the farm entrance appeared. "Shite! There'll be lots of those. A motion detector triggers a camera if there's any movement near the entrance to the farm. Then the camera takes a series of pictures and sends a message across the Internet to a PC we've set up as a server in Langley. That PC is constantly monitored by another computer behind our firewall. The second PC takes the first frame of a stream of images, adds a date code and puts it in this database."

"Very neat. So there's a picture of us arriving here today on your computer back in Langley?"

"Sure is." Martha scrolled down to the end of the list. "That's odd. There are no entries after the nineteenth. Damn! That PC must have crashed again."

"Perhaps not. The nineteenth was the day we found the body in London." Mike thought for a moment, then fingered the roller ball on the laptop and clicked on the last entry in the list.

"A bus going past." Martha sighed as a new image appeared on the screen. She watched as Mike clicked on the previous entry. "A car passing."

Mike stood back from the desk. "A blue Buick. A bit of a coincidence?"

Martha took control of the PC and recalled the previous image. "Car turning into the farm entrance; bicycle hung on the back obscuring the number plate. It's in a cloud of dust. Seems to have been going at some speed."

"Times?"

"Bus, eleven a.m.; Buick, nine twenty-two a.m.; and the car, nine nineteen a.m."

"Three minutes. Time to get up the drive and round the back of the house. The dust — would it have cleared?"

Martha caught up with him. "Even if it didn't, the Buick

would miss it. Coming from the north, the track to the farm is hidden by trees."

"So what we have is someone being followed by the local security services. They probably shook them off by hiding in here. Then sometime the same day..."

"And before they leave, our camera system dies." Martha placed her finger on her chin and narrowed her eyes. "Still doesn't help us much."

"When was the hard disk installed in Passmore's PC?"

"Good thinking." Martha started listing the files on Passmore's computer. "Well, some temporary and set-up files were created on the nineteenth at around ten in the morning. It does point to the computer engineer."

"So if he knew about your camera, either he was tipped off or he'd been here before. All we have to do now is go back through the images and find him. He might not have covered the number plate on the first visit."

Martha scrolled up through the list of images. Several screenfuls went past before she stopped, turned to Mike and shrugged. "It will take days to search through this lot."

Mike sank down onto the chair. "Why don't you call the local security services and ask them why they were following the computer engineer?"

Martha scoffed. "We're not supposed to be here, remember? The CIA aren't supposed to work on domestic security. Some states don't even let the FBI in."

Pulling the paper tray out of the laser printer, Mike found about twenty sheets of A4 paper. "I thought he was an environment freak? He wasn't using recycled paper."

"It causes a jam in some printers."

"Blank on both sides." Mike muttered to himself as he took the top sheet of paper out of the tray.

"So?"

Something about Passmore's office bothered Mike, something to do with paper. Then he realised what it was. "In our office in London we reuse the paper, print on the back. It's a pain in the arse because you always have to check that you're not printing on the back of something which is classified."

"What are you getting at?"

Mike waved the sheet of paper around the room. "Where's his scrap paper?"

"Worth asking," Martha said, heading for the door.

"We want to check the printer," Martha told the farm hand. "It seems a shame to use good paper. Has Mr. Passmore got any scrap paper lying around?" The farm hand led them to an outbuilding and to two piles of newspapers. Mike grabbed a handful. Amongst them were several sheets of printed A4. It took just over half an hour to extract all the computer printouts from the newspapers.

Martha and Mike divided the printouts between them and began examining each sheet in turn. Most of them were from websites offering advice on organic growing and were discarded on the floor. Web pages relating to Europe were put in a neat pile on the desk. A particularly scruffy sheet of paper Mike picked up had handwriting on the back. "Better look at both sides — he's been using some of these for rough notes."

Martha looked down at the papers on the floor. "So that means we've got to go through that lot again." She sighed. "Let's break for lunch."

It took time for Mike to get used to the daylight. The trees along the drive provided some shade, but at the top of the farm track he had to shield his eyes from the sun. "I should have bought some sunglasses at the airport," he said to Martha.

Martha took off her glasses and offered them to Mike. "Borrow these, if you like."

"No, it's all right — I'll manage," said Mike, taking his hand away from his eyes to look up at the building on the opposite side of the road.

*

In the corner of a small apartment overlooking San Francisco's Bay Bridge a computer bleeped. A programmer, who was struggling with particularly tedious piece of code on another machine, glanced over his shoulder, then looked up at the clock on the wall. He swivelled around and, putting his heels on the floor, dragged the chair and himself towards the other desk. Glad of the distraction, he clicked on the last entry in the list of images and watched as the picture of Mike and Martha filled the screen.

He was about to propel himself back to his other desk when something in the picture caught the programmer's eye. In the background, he saw the word 'Computers'. Closer inspection revealed a white van belonging to North Bay Computers parked in front of Passmore's house. The woman in the picture wore a large pair of dark glasses. The man had his hand over his eyes. When the programmer clicked on the top of the screen, a 'utilities' menu appeared. He selected 'frames' and the two people appeared in postage-stamp-sized image. He selected '+' and the couple stepped forward, the woman taking off her sun glasses; '+' again and the man started to lift his hand from his eyes; '+' once more and the man was staring straight into the camera. "Perfect." The programmer selected the 'fetch' option on the menu and slowly the full-sized image appeared.

'Picture This' was the title of the e-mail sent to a Hotmail subscriber who could have been anywhere in the world but was, as the programmer knew full well, sitting in an office in London. 'Is there anything in this picture which you feel could pose a problem?' the message read. After attaching the image to the e-mail, the programmer selected 'send'.

*

'The committee should examine the way Earl's Court fire brigade operates. It is made up of independent volunteer crews who decide on strategies at the scene of the fire without reference to a central control. This has proved effective in avoiding incidents such as the one that claimed the lives of a fire crew this weekend.'

Brian had not intended this to be the first suggestion he made, but he owed Sam a favour. After reading the paragraph again, and with the cursor hovering over the 'send' command, he remembered something that had occurred to him after speaking to Langford.

'There is still far too much dry vegetation surrounding buildings that are inhabited or used for storage. Posters should be placed in all the Ivan's restaurants to explain the dangers of fire and the importance of keeping inhabited areas free of combustible material. These posters should be printed in full colour to ensure that they attract the diners' attention.'

Lucky Dip would provide the stick and this would provide the carrot. Perhaps Brian could succeed where Mike had failed after all.

"This is a strange one." Johnny had settled into the office, clearing Mike's desk of its ornaments and replacing them with an assortment of electronic gadgets and a laptop PC. "The last call to the machine in the girl's office was from a mobile."

"So? There are a lot of them about," Brian said, without looking up from his own computer screen.

"But this one is supposed to be in our recovered property store."

"You've made a mistake."

"No. I checked. It was confiscated from a black marketeer two years ago."

"It could have been issued to someone without any paperwork. They could have lost it, or it was stolen."

"Bit of a coincidence." Johnny tapped his notebook's screen with a pencil. He seemed nervous. "There's something else. That office belongs to the Home Office. We used it when this place was being renovated."

"When was the last time it was used?"

Johnny shrugged. "Twenty–thirty years ago."

"Well, perhaps someone just noticed it was empty."

Johnny reached across the desk and picked up the phone. "I'll dial the mobile. Maybe we'll hear it ringing," he said with a smile.

"Don't do that. Not yet anyway."

Johnny replaced the phone and stared at Brian. "You'd tell me if I was wasting my time with this, wouldn't you?"

"What do you mean?"

"Well, if this is a police operation and all we're doing is going through the motions. You know, tidying up."

Now Brian appreciated how Mike Allchurch had felt when the investigation into Troxley's murder got too close to the truth. Brian found himself in the same position — and was even beginning to sound like his boss. "Look, there's something you can do. Go down to Records and see if there's anything on Lenny Drake. It might be filed under 'Lucky Dip'. Bring back whatever you find."

"Won't it be on the computer?"

"Some of it, but there should be a hard-copy file as well. I saw him operating in St. James's Park underground station."

"You think he stole the phone from someone who works here?"

"Possibly." Brian saw Johnny's enthusiasm return. "Oh, and when you bring the file back, don't leave it laying around. Put it in Mike's drawer."

Johnny smiled, relieved that he was not alone in suspecting that the culprit was close at hand.

*

"Tyler. Brian Tyler — Mike Allchurch's assistant. I need to see you tomorrow sometime." Brian explained, then listened as Harry pointed out that he knew exactly who he was, then moaned about his missing glasses, made excuses, and eventually issued various threats. "No, I'm not coming mob-handed. I just want a chat." Brian said; trying to undo some of the damage Mike had done to community relations in the East End.

Realising Harry was on the point of hanging up, Brian blurted out. "There might be something in it for you," He waited until the laughter stopped, then added, "Eleven thirty in the waiting room of Waterloo." Without waiting for an answer, Brian put the phone down and studied the screen of information in front of him: Harry Robinson, as he was known the last time the police found any ID on him — an ID which was probably forged. The phone number had been correct, so perhaps the photograph was up to date as well. Brian doubted his plan would work; it was complicated and, according to Mike, complicated plans never worked.

*

"That's a seriously long time ago, Brian. I mean, sir."

The number of people referring to him as 'sir' was on the increase. Brian had grown used to Johnny doing it, but now the habit was spreading through the rest of the department. The archivist keyed in the request. The message 'No Data Available' appeared on the screen. The short, balding youth drummed his fingers on the edge of the keyboard. He picked up a bottle of water and took a swig, waiting for Brian either to suggest another name or to leave him to get on with his work.

"Is it on tape?" Brian asked.

"You're out of luck if it is. Even if the data is still there, we probably won't be able to find a tape streamer which will read it back — or software which recognises the format."

"So what's next?"

The archivist pushed his chair away from the desk. "Leave it with me. I'll see if I can log into a server in Cambridge or Bedford. What name did you say?"

"James Hendry. Special Branch at Cambridge."

"Special Branch?"

Brian shrugged. "It seems to have been a separate police division."

"I'll see what I can dig up."

"Thanks. I'll drop by tomorrow and pick it up."

As he reached the door of the Home Office internal library, Brian remembered that the computerised lending system could be accessed by anyone in the building. This was not the place to borrow a book about the Special Branch.

*

Brian knew he was being watched. Lucky was standing in the shadows on the opposite platform, studying his every move. Brian took his mobile phone from his pocket and pretended to make a call. He had already taken his watch from his wrist and placed it in his pocket. Retrieving the watch, he studied it for a moment, as though making an appointment with the person on the other end of the phone. The train arrived; he finished the call, and returned both the phone and the watch to his pocket.

Thirty minutes later, Brian left the bookshop outside South Kensington station clutching faded copies of 'The British Police' and 'A Guide to Norfolk'. He had just remembered that the archive department worked late, and wondered whether he should return to the office in case the archivist had already found Hendry's details. After considering how long it took just to log on to the Cambridge server, he decided to take the risk and continue on his way home.

*

The programmer propelled his chair across the room the moment the computer beeped. He clicked on the flashing e-mail icon and read the message.

'Re: Picture This. Important you remove the gentleman from the picture. Usual terms.'

The programmer restarted the camera-control software and retrieved another picture from the web cam. Despite the failing light, the North Bay Computers van was still clearly visible.

*

Even if he *had* returned to the office, Brian would have been too late. The archivist had already placed two sheets of paper on his desk. One was the personnel record of James Hendry, stamped 'deceased'. The other was a list, dated April 2001, of all the serving members of the Special Branch who were based in Cambridge. The archivist had circled Hendry's name, as well as one other he thought he recognised. Even if his name had not been circled, Stephen Langford, making his late-evening search of Brian's desk, could not have failed to notice the list.

*

"Sorry to bother you with this, but I'm just sorting out some paperwork. One of my officers claims he visited you on Monday. Yes, I'll hang on." Langford scrolled down Brian's S-Card records while he waited for the desk sergeant at Cambridge to put him through to the duty officer. There had been enough time for Brian to call in at Cambridge before he got back to London. "Tyler," he told the duty officer. "Really? Are you sure it wasn't in the afternoon? Oh, right. Well, thank you." Langford put down the phone and stared at the computer screen.

It took him just a few seconds to work out what Brian had done. Picking up the phone again, he called Norwich police station. "Sorry to bother you with this, but one of my officers, a Brian Tyler, was in your area on Monday. Yes. Thank you." Once again, he waited to be put through. This time it was Christopher Dickerson, the chief superintendent, who came on the line. "Glad to see I'm not the only one working late," Langford said. "I wonder if you can help with this. I'm trying to sort out the authorisation for Brian Tyler's visit to you. It's just that the silly sod tagged it on to the end of his weekend in Cromer." Langford listened while Dickerson recounted the story of Brian's weekend in Downham. "Really? Is she one of *the* Parks family?" He started to scribble some notes on a piece of paper. "Well, he really is a dark horse, isn't he?" By now, Langford had heard enough. Thanking Dickerson, he replaced the receiver, switched off Brian's computer and returned to his own office.

Taking a mobile phone out of his desk drawer, Langford dialled and waited. "There's a problem. Yes, yes, another one. I'll meet you about ten thirty in the usual place."

*

Like Brian, Stephen Langford lived in a building occupied by other people. What had once been a five-star hotel was now home to several families, as well as a number of single men and women. The ground floor housed the Grosvenor Square Ivan's Restaurant. A separate entrance, used by Langford and the other residents, was guarded by two soldiers. Another two soldiers manned the reception desk. Upstairs, groups of rooms had been combined to form flats. The in-house dining smacked of privilege, and party members frowned on the arrangement. The occupants, most of them senior civil servants, claimed that it was the only way to guarantee their security.

Usually Langford would have caught the bus from Victoria to Marble Arch and walked the short distance from Park Lane. Recently, however, he had been staying late at the office in order to monitor Mike and Brian's progress on the Troxley case. By the time he finished work, most of the buses had stopped running. Langford leaned his bicycle against the railings and, taking a handkerchief from his pocket, wiped the sweat from his face. Despite the shade provided by tall buildings and trees, the overgrown square was still sweltering in the evening heat. Warm air from the park drifted down the side streets, and it was not until he was standing in the marble-floored reception area that Langford was able to breathe normally again.

Those diners who were not eating with their friends or family distracted themselves by watching television or reading. Langford was deep in thought and spent most of the meal staring out of the window. He was still weary, although he had slept for over an hour when he got to his room. Noticing that the light was failing, he checked his watch. Without finishing his meal, he stood up and, rather than returning to his room, walked out into Grosvenor Square. "Nice evening for a walk," said the soldier on guard outside.

"Yes," replied Langford. "Thought I might take a little stroll before turning in."

Other than tall grass and bushes growing where there had once been neatly mown lawns, Grosvenor Square still looked much as it had done at the turn of the century. The facades of many of the buildings — with the principal exception of the American Embassy — were well weathered, but only one large house had its windows boarded up.

A few streets away, however, Berkeley Square had not fared so well. Lush green vegetation grew on the ashes of the previous autumn's fire, and the trees were no more than charred black stumps. Ivy choked the railings. In some places, it had spread across the road and up the moss-covered facades of the surrounding town houses. Broken glass, decaying branches, ash and earth covered the pavements around the perimeter of the square. Rioting and looting had reduced many areas of London to this sorry state, but in other cases Nature had managed to do the job on its own. Langford had often thought it was folly to let people remain in the suburbs while the centre of London decayed through neglect. But many people still associated the inner city with mayhem and violence and a three-bedroom semi-detached was easier to maintain than a crumbling town house. Given the choice of living in a cosy house with a garden or having to walk these ghostly, blackened streets, most people chose the airy village-like communities that lined the underground railway.

The singing of blackbirds and thrushes faded as Langford entered the house. The door was already open. Inside, all he could hear was the sound of his own footsteps on the stone floor. Someone struck a match and lit the candle that was standing on a black marble mantelpiece. The flickering light filled the room. Broken furniture was stacked in one corner. Smaller pieces of wood had been piled up near the fireplace. Strips of paper and wires hung from the bulging ceiling and cast shadows on the water-stained walls.

"Another problem?" Miranda Lyndon made no effort to hide her mid-Atlantic accent. The pretence of being East-End born and bred ended when she stopped being Caroline Tate. "I suppose it's Tyler, your clown of a policeman." She screwed up her eyes and tilted her head to one side. "Now, what was it you said about him? 'Got into the gene pool while the lifeguard was at lunch.' Didn't seem to have much trouble tracking me down this morning."

"Well, I..."

"And, as he tricked me into giving a sample of my fingerprint, he now knows exactly who he is looking for."

Langford raised his voice. "Allchurch's absence has given him more scope to interfere." Having got Miranda's attention, he calmed down again and walked over to the window. For the first time that day, the breeze felt cool. The candle flickered and almost went out. When the flame recovered, Langford could see that Miranda looked more worried than angry. He breathed in a lungful of evening air. "Tyler has got to be got rid of. He's right on your tail. He might even be on to your house in Chelsea."

"We can't get rid of Tyler."

"We've got to." Langford held his hand in front of his face, with the thumb and finger almost touching. "He's this close to getting me. And he's spoken to that girl Parks at Downham."

"Well she would have been dealt with already if your dumb coppers hadn't interfered. Thanks to them, we didn't get to finish the job." She sighed. "At least we got the farmer. The girl probably isn't that much of a problem anyway."

"I think she is. If there's a trial, she could be a witness for the defence. Who knows what she told Tyler? He's got to go. We'll let Allchurch write the report. With Tyler dead, he'll be too scared to go digging around."

"You'd better take a look at this." Miranda took a sheet of paper from her pocket and handed it to Langford. "This was taken just a few hours ago."

Langford held the computer printout in front of the candle. "Isn't that a palm tree in the background?" he said, pointing at the picture of Mike Allchurch and Martha Snyder.

"Yes. There are a lot of palm trees in California. That one is in front of Passmore's farm. By now, your dumb cop 'who just wants an easy life' will have realised that Passmore and Troxley are one and the same. With the help of his girlfriend there, who is probably CIA, he will soon be able to place me at the farm. If he does that, the game's over — for all of us."

"So what are we going to do?"

"Done. What I've already done is ask our man Monk to get rid of Allchurch." Even in the candlelight, she could see the colour drain from Langford's face. "Tyler I can cope with. I can move over the river tonight, and anyway I've got a couple more ID's and S-Card numbers left yet. You don't need me to finish this. Just make sure you get Tyler to write the report implicating Fairchild in Troxley's murder — and in the Whiteside Farm cover-up. You can do that, can't you?"

"But what about the girl?" Langford sounded as though he was being strangled.

"She'll be got rid of," Miranda said coolly

"How can you? Both the gunmen are dead."

"Yes. Unfortunate, that. I'll be glad to see the back of your Mr. Allchurch — if it really was him who did it. Luckily, they weren't the last two gunmen in the East End. In fact, when they died we saved ourselves half a million dollars, and two US passports."

"I can't see Tyler co-operating if we shoot his girl."

"His girl." Miranda laughed. "Young Plod and frightfully, frightfully Miss Parks," she said, in a mock-English accent. "He just stumbled on a frustrated spinster and had some fun. When she gets wasted, Mr. Tyler is going to go very quiet. He won't want anyone to know about his dirty weekend. There would be too many questions. I take it you would ask him some very serious questions about his involvement with Miss Parks?"

"Yes. I see what you mean," Langford said nervously.

"Just give the boy a big bag of sweets. Give him Allchurch's job."

"I still think it would be better to get rid of him."

"Look, if you're worried about your own neck, I should keep him alive." Miranda held her arm up in front of the candle so she could read her watch. "Allchurch will be dead in an hour or so. If Tyler goes too, you won't have anyone investigating the Troxley case. The party will use that as an excuse to put in their own men. Then you'll have real problems." She flicked the top of the candle and the room was plunged into darkness. Glass crunched as she walked towards the door. "It's been fun working with you, Stephen. If we don't see each other again, good luck with the promotion. Oh, and my regards to Simitovich, if you see him."

*

"What do you think 'Rebafing' is?" Martha asked. Mike shrugged his shoulders and shook his head slowly. He was still sorting his papers into separate piles and had not yet examined any of them closely. The only thing he had noticed was that Passmore had collected a lot of information on European crop production — the sort of thing the CIA itself was interested in. "It's just that I've seen the word a couple of times already," Martha said, this time turning to Mike and expecting a response, which didn't come. "At first I thought it was something to do with food processing, but here he has written 'Rebafing transfer $100,000'." Having said it out loud, she remembered something. "Wait a minute," she said, grabbing her laptop PC and hammering away on the keyboard. "Yep! That's it! Rebafing must be a person or a company. I think we're getting there."

The pile of papers Martha had been balancing on her lap was thrown onto the desk. Starting a web browser, she clicked on the address of a search engine. The search engine could not find 'Rebafing'. "Well, that's another dead end then."

"Not necessarily." Mike leaned across and looked at the screen. They may not want to be found. If they've got a 'no robot' meta instruction on all their pages, they will stay invisible."

"So?"

"Just type in 'www.rebafing.com' and see what happens."

"Of course! I must be losing it." Martha typed in the address and Rebafing Inc.'s home page appeared. "Right now, we are getting somewhere." She opened up a new window to the database at Langley and entered 'Rebafing' as a search key. Nothing. Entering the address, the zip code, the phone and the fax numbers failed to produce a single record.

"Try the employees," Mike suggested.

Martha progressed through the list, starting with the CEO and working down. "None of these people fit. There are only three people in the US with the same name as the CEO. One is a seventy-year-old retired train driver, the second is in prison and the third is an army sergeant. None of them live anywhere near Boston, where the company is based." She tried a few more names. "Well, at least this one is a programmer."

"Edwin Monk, San Francisco." Mike read the name from the screen. "Long way to travel into work each day."

"Yes, but then we're assuming that the company really is based in Boston. As there isn't any record of it, and most of the employees seem to be bogus, it could be anywhere. Time to start looking at that web address in more detail." Martha opened a window to a route-tracing program and entered Rebafing's address. A list of numbers scrolled down the screen. She copied the last one into another window and pressed the return key. "Yep, it's on a server in San Francisco. My guess is, the server is in the same building as Edwin Monk — and we know where he lives."

"But where does that get us?"

"Well, it might help us prove that Fairchild never received money, via Passmore, from us at the CIA or from Genesis. Unfortunately, that leaves open the possibility that he was naive enough to allow himself and the Green Party to be used by Genesis. But at least we have evidence that an individual or organisation is trying to implicate Fairchild in the death of Passmore."

Mike rubbed the back of his neck. "We still don't know who."

"We probably never will. There will be a whole series of cut-outs. Why not just submit a report giving Fairchild a clean bill of health, with a recommendation that this Rebafing organisation should be investigated further. I can start trickling information across to you as we find out more about the company. If Simitovich is behind this, he'll want your findings buried a.s.a.p."

"And if it isn't him, but some other organisation, what then?"

"He'll still back off. As soon as you mention a possible conspiracy against Fairchild, people will assume that Simitovich is behind it. Who else has anything to gain? People may even start to wonder if Simitovich stabbed Ivan in the back. That would be a disaster for him."

"It's still not the answer."

Martha smiled. "There isn't an answer. All I can offer you is a solution." She stood up and stretched her arms, then turned off the computers. "I'll type all this up when we are on the plane back to Washington. Someone at the office will put together all the financial stuff and you can collect it at the airport." She picked up her shoulder bag. "But that's it for today. Dinner and then the beach for us, I think."

*

Between 2020 and 2030, inflation in the US reached as high as twenty per cent per annum. That is why Martha had to hand over three hundred dollars for a meal Mike could have got for thirty-five dollars when he visited California as a student. When Mike and Martha had finished dinner, they wandered along a near-deserted Miramar beach — shouting to make themselves heard above the sound of the surf. After two or three hundred metres, they sat down on the sand. Mike turned his face towards the sea. The evening sun was still warm.

"So, anything else you want to do?" Martha asked.

"What do you mean?"

"Well, yesterday you were swimming in the sea with a real southern California 'gal'. Hanging out with the hippies. Perhaps you want to go up to Frisco, join a rock-and-roll band..." Her voice trailed away, then she giggled.

Mike lay on his back, listening to the waves booming and the seagulls shrieking. "Sometimes I wonder. If things had been different," he muttered.

"Things couldn't have carried on the way they were. If GM crops or swine flu hadn't got us, something else would have," Martha said, pushing her heels down into the sand. "Nuked ourselves probably."

292

Mike, however, was thinking of the grey, monotonous existence he had endured since the crisis, rather than of the pandemics and famines themselves. No cars, no money, no freedom — three things people here in the US still had. He could not help feeling that he had been robbed. "It's not just that. I suppose it's this place. The way that the US handled it." He sighed. "And there's something about California."

"Of course, *you* were here when Silicon Valley was booming. What was it like?"

"Like Hollywood really. Every waiter in Hollywood had a film script in their pocket. In Silicon Valley they all had a business plan. My father said as American settlers moved west building cities got into their blood. When they arrived here, they just carried on building, even though there was no more land. Dreams and castles in the air. First Hollywood, then Silicon Valley. And now all the high-tech companies have gone."

"Most of it was just froth. Buying groceries on-line went out of fashion when looters ambushed the delivery vans. I suppose downloading a book into your hand-held computer could have made queuing for bread less tedious, but it never caught on." Martha lay down next to Mike. "From what I've read about it, I'm not sure I'm missing much. You all lived so fast. You even abbreviated July to J-u-l." She turned to look at Mike and smiled. "You must have been in a hell of a hurry."

For the first time, Mike realised that *he* was the odd one out. Here, in Martha, he had found the female version of Brian. He clung to ideals and dreams that had no meaning whatsoever in the eyes of the younger generation. Although money and the consumer society had disappeared years ago, he still confused value and price. Even if there had never been a collapse — even if he had lived here in California — freedom would have eluded him. He was destined always to be a prisoner, locked behind walls he never realised were there. He would never have been anyone in his own right; his identity was bound up in his house, car and clothes. Fulfilment and success were proportional to the amount of rubbish he put out for collection each week. His freedom was measured by the number of litres of petrol he burned. Even before the pandemics, people were turning their backs on materialism. With the benefit of hindsight, materialism was a bankrupt religion — no wonder Martha and Brian thought it absurd.

Propping herself up on one elbow, Martha studied Mike's face. He was frowning and seemed troubled. There was sadness in his eyes that she had not noticed before. Feeling bad about teasing him, she reached inside her shoulder bag and pulled out a small tin box.

Mike opened his eyes when he heard the match strike. A hand-rolled cigarette was placed between his lips. "Thought you might need cheering up," Martha said. "I hear that no-one smokes in Europe."

"People do smoke." Mike coughed as he drew on the joint. "It's just that heavy smokers are refused medical treatment."

"What if you get lung cancer?"

"There just aren't the resources available to treat it. Of course, no-one's allowed to suffer. Mike did not elaborate and Martha was familiar with euthanasia. After all, two states in the US practised it officially and most of the others had an unofficial system in operation.

Closing his eyes, Mike drew again. The cannabis was taking effect. The sound of the waves seemed clearer, but more distant. Suddenly, for some unknown reason he found himself telling Martha about the girl in Ruislip. Then he realised that he had never talked to anyone, including Linda, about his fear that someone had probably died, alone, while waiting for the girl to return. He could hear his own voice. It was as though he was listening to someone else telling the story for the first time.

It was not long before they were both laughing. "Where the hell did all the cars go?" Mike giggled. "When I was here last time there were millions of them."

"They're like birds," Martha said, her speech slurred. "You never see dead birds. Where do birds go when they die?" She sat up. "No, no. I've got it. There was a guy in Milwaukee who ate a whole car. Perhaps he's moved to California. Perhaps his whole family moved to California."

The light began to fade. Mike took off his shoes and walked in the surf. "Looking forward to getting back?" Martha asked.

"I'm a bit worried about my wife, Linda. She wasn't well when I left." Mike then remembered that he had met his first wife a week after returning from America. "Are you married?" he asked.

Martha looked out to sea and there was a long pause before she answered. She was trying to decide whether she still considered herself married. "I lost my husband," she said eventually, realising immediately that this sounded as though she had merely misplaced him. "He was with a team of agents who went into New York. They were trying to recover something from a building in Wall Street. Whatever it was, someone on the Hill thought it was worth risking ten lives for. Anyway, no-one ever saw them again."

"When did..."

"Ten years ago," Martha interrupted. She could have said 'Quit that, Mr. Allchurch'. It would have meant the same thing. She didn't want to talk about it any more. Mike, perhaps still under the influence of the cannabis, surprised himself — and Martha — by running his hand down her back, then slipping his arm around her waist. Martha, without looking at him, put *her* arm around *his* waist.

*

Closing down the software, the programmer stood up and walked through to his bedroom. He took a revolver and a box of ammunition from the drawer of his bedside cabinet. While placing six shells in the chamber of the handgun, he ran through the list of precautions he took when driving down to Passmore's farm. Usually a bicycle was strapped to the back of his Ford 4 x 4 in order to obscure the number plate, but since he had modified the web cam that was no longer necessary.

*

"The camera," Martha said, when they reached the road. "I'm supposed to get it back." Mike let go of her waist, relieved that a slightly embarrassing episode was now over. The back door of the abandoned house was secured with a padlock, even though most of the windows were missing. Martha took a key out of her shoulder bag. "Can't be too careful." She laughed.

The house was built of stone and had marble floors. Its south-facing wall had tall, narrow windows and the air inside the room was cool, despite the August heat. On the landing, at the top of a dust-covered spiral staircase, three windows overlooked Passmore's farm. The web cam and proximity sensor had been fixed to the sill of the right-hand window. A solar panel and battery, disguised as a ceramic and metal sculpture, were wired to the camera. On the back of the camera itself, a small green indicator shone brightly in the rapidly failing light. Martha took a screwdriver from her shoulder bag, then, as an afterthought, ran her hand in front of the proximity sensor. The green light was now accompanied by red and yellow indicators. The yellow one flickered for a while, then went out. Shortly afterwards, the red light faded.

*

Outside Bay Bridge apartments the throaty roar of a Ford 4 x 4 was echoing down the street. If the programmer had waited another five minutes, he would have heard the computer beep as another incoming image was received.

*

"Funny. I thought our friend had trashed this thing," Martha said, removing the crocodile clips connecting the output of the web cam to the stripped telephone wires.

"Perhaps they've cut the phone."

Martha shook her head slowly as she undid the screws fixing the web cam and the positioning wedges to the windowsill. "If the wire had been cut, the red light would have stayed on. The guy's a programmer. He probably hacked into the image-collection server."

"But then you would still be getting images."

"Hardly worth worrying about," Martha said, handing the camera, sensor and power pack to Mike. "Let's get back and see what else we can find out about our Mr. Monk."

*

Three seats back from a group of Japanese businessmen, the blonde girl was pretending to read a magazine. The next flight to Tokyo left in two hours. There could be little doubt that the delegation was returning to the airport. Her mobile phone rang. There was a short exchange before she got up, walked to the front of the bus, and asked the driver to stop.

"So what's the panic?" she said, getting into the car.

The driver squealed the tyres of the Buick as he swung it across the road. "Our old friend has surfaced again," he said.

"Who?"

"The guy from Miramar."

"What?" The blonde girl shrieked. "Do you realise we'd have been finished in half an hour? I suppose you volunteered us —

without asking me."

The driver ignored her protests. "He was spotted about five minutes ago, heading for the coast road. He's going to Miramar again."

"And we're going to lose him again — or is it third time lucky?"

"I've got a plan."

"Just what I was afraid of."

*

"Come on, Mr. Monk. Tell us something about yourself." Martha stared at the database entry for Edwin Monk.

Mike was only half-listening. He sat with his elbows on the desk, examining the web cam. "If he was being followed by our friends in the Buick, then he must have flown in to San Francisco. How long has this camera been installed?"

"Five years at least."

"Pass me that screwdriver."

Martha took the screwdriver out of her bag and, looking over Mike's shoulder, put it on the desk. "A spot of industrial espionage?"

"There are some scratches on these screws. They look recent."

Mike removed the camera's back panel. "'Beijing Electronic Devices'."

"Very amusing."

"No, that's what it says on this chip. I thought you and the Chinese weren't on speaking terms."

"We're not. What the...?" Martha picked up the web cam and peered inside.

"Seems like your virtual agent may have been turned."

"But why?"

"So they would know when you turned this place over. Monk is probably going underground at this very moment."

*

Four kilometres to the north of Passmore's farm, the programmer checked his mirror. The road behind was clear. The security services, he thought, must have given up, or it had been too late in the day to follow him out of the city.

Three kilometres further south, a blue Buick was reversing

into a side road, the driver carefully positioning the car so that it was at an angle of forty-five degrees to the coast road. He had taken the freeway south from the airport, cut across to Half Moon Bay, then driven up along the coast to Miramar. The blonde girl fidgeted in the seat next to him. She bemoaned this harebrained scheme and stared northwards down the deserted coast road.

*

"This is strange." Martha scrolled through the data. "He's never flown into San Francisco — or anywhere else, for that matter. He hasn't got a car. Perhaps it wasn't Monk after all."

"Or perhaps he's deleted all the records from the databases."

"The car registration perhaps, but not the flight records. That would mean getting inside our own database."

"And that's difficult, is it?" Mike smiled.

Suddenly the phone scanner, which had lain silent on the desk all day, crackled into life. "Brown Ford 4 x 4 intercepted. We are now in pursuit. Out."

"Our friend with the Buick." Martha leapt to her feet and ran to the window. "It seems he's on his way here with our mysterious Mr. Monk."

"What would Monk be coming here for?"

"I'm not sure, but I think I'd rather meet him on our terms." Martha searched around the room. She picked up a baseball bat and handed it to Mike. "You take this. I'll get the gun out of the van." She was just opening the front door when the Ford slid sideways into the farm entrance, closely followed by the Buick. "Out the back!" Martha shouted, slamming the door.

Once outside, Martha and Mike split up. Mike edged around the south side of the house. In the near-darkness, he was able to get to the van without being seen. A cloud of dust raised by the two vehicles swirled in front of the house. There was the sound of angry voices, and Martha emerged from the north side.

"He's got a gun!" the blonde girl shouted.

Mike thought the girl had spotted *him* and mistaken the baseball bat for a gun. He stepped out from behind the van. Martha frantically signalled to him, but stopped when she realised Mike was taking no notice. The blonde stood paralysed by fear as Monk pointed his revolver at her head. Mike swung the baseball bat awkwardly towards Monk, who jumped as it entered his peripheral vision. The gun went off and the blonde girl let out a scream as the bullet flew past her head and into the trees behind her.

Monk buckled at the knees as the clumsy left-handed swing hit him on the right temple. He moaned and staggered forward, then seemed to regain his balance. Raising the bat, Mike waited for Monk to drop the gun. The girl screamed again. Mike wanted her to stop. The programmer held on to the gun, and the bat came down on Monk's head with a thud, sending him sprawling. The girl stopped screaming, but her mouth remained wide open.

The young man put his arm around the blonde girl. "I'd better call an ambulance."

"No-one calls anyone until I say so!" Martha shouted, as she picked up the revolver. The youth was going to argue, but Martha took her ID and thrust it into his face. "You've just wandered into a CIA operation and I suggest you stand back."

Mike bent down and rolled Monk over so that he could see his face. "He won't need an ambulance anyway."

"You mean, he'll be OK?" The youth seemed relieved, until he noticed Mike glaring at him. "Jeez. You've killed him."

Martha picked up the baseball bat and turned it around in her hands, as if preparing to swing it. She then passed it, handle first, to the youth and began to walk away. Mike looked up, hardly believing what Martha had done. He did not even lift his arm to defend himself when the youth raised the bat.

"Your brains, sonny. Use them or lose them." Martha pressed the revolver against the side of the youth's head. "Our story is that we had a bit of trouble fixing a computer and phoned for help. When our friend here arrived, Bonnie and Clyde crashed in and clubbed him to death. All anyone has to do to prove it is to check whose prints are on that bat you're holding." The youth let the bat fall to the ground. "Now, it doesn't matter to me if you're dead or alive when the police turn up. In fact, on balance..."

"OK. What do you want?" the youth blurted out.

"That's better. First, you are going to call your controller and tell them you lost the Ford again. Then my colleague here is going to ask you and your lady friend a bunch of questions. I'm going to get someone here to clean up, and tomorrow morning we are all going back to San Francisco and will forget that any of this ever happened. Won't we?" The youth nodded, and Martha took the revolver away from his head.

*

There were howls of derision from the other end of the phone when the youth told his controller that he had lost the Ford for a third time. Folding the mobile, he returned it to his pocket, then sat down next to the blonde girl, who was looking nervously around Passmore's office.

"You're the guy who was at Los Gatos and Santa Cruz," the blonde girl said.

"Were you following Monk on the nineteenth of this month?" Mike asked, trying to assert his authority by ignoring her observation.

The girl recognised Mike's English accent. "We don't have to answer any of *your* questions."

Turning to Martha's laptop, Mike clicked on the entry for the nineteenth in the web cam database. The picture of the blue Buick appeared. "There you are, outside the farm. And Clifford Passmore, the farmer who lives here, hasn't been seen since. Did you kill Passmore as well?"

The blonde girl looked at the picture on the laptop, then at the youth. "That was the second time we followed the Ford. We didn't know it was, whoever you said, er, Monk." She snivelled. "We followed him a couple of months ago, but we lost him."

Martha was in the hall, speaking on the phone. "If you could. We need the placed cleaned up." She listened for a while, then added, "Yeah, sorry, the van's been blown and we've got company, so park your car away from the farm." She listened again. "Thanks. You're a pal." She returned to the office and sat on the desk.

"Why did you follow him?" The girl did not answer, so Mike prompted her. "He wasn't from outside the state. He hasn't even flown anywhere."

The blonde girl glanced at the youth again. Mike decided that silence would undermine her resolve. When it had, she sniffed. "He picked someone up at the airport."

"Who?" Mike snapped, seizing the moment.

"A woman. Girl."

"Name?"

The girl turned to the youth. "Did you write it down?" The youth shook his head. "No, neither did I."

Martha eased herself off the desk. "But if we looked at the flight for that day, you'd recognise the name."

"No." The girl shook her head. "There's a problem." She could see that both Mike and Martha were growing impatient. "But we do know what date it was."

Martha frowned. "Well?"

"It was the fourth of July." She waited for a response, but both Mike and Martha remained silent. "Monk, I mean the guy in the Ford, picked the woman up from the airport. We followed but lost them just north of here."

"Didn't you ask for backup from San Francisco?" Mike asked.

Martha and the girl answered together. "Fourth of July." "Very clever. Everyone was on holiday," Martha added.

Mike half-turned in his chair and scrolled through the list entries in the image database. "Morning or afternoon?"

"Afternoon."

"Time?"

The youth shrugged. "About four, half past perhaps," he said.

On the fourth of July, the closest entry was twenty to five. Mike clicked on it. A picture of the Ford 4 x 4 sweeping into the farm entrance appeared. Stepping forward through the images retrieved the blue Buick, a bus, another bus, and the farm hand going home. The next picture showed three people leaving the farm entrance: Monk, Passmore and a girl. Mike felt a strange sensation. The last time he had seen Passmore, his head had been spread around a hotel room. The last time he had seen the girl, she had been sitting on the edge of the bed in the same hotel room — explaining how difficult everything was for her 'father'.

"Well, that explains everything." Mike looked up at Martha. "Can you get me a copy of this picture?"

"Sure." Martha turned to the blonde girl. "So why didn't you stop her at the airport when she left?"

The girl seemed to be recovering from her ordeal. She threw open her arms. "She just disappeared."

"What do you mean 'disappeared'?"

The youth sighed. "Someone got into our database and deleted her record."

Mike laughed. "Don't you write anything down?"

The youth took out his mobile and waved it at Mike. "All done with these..."

"Anyway," the girl interrupted, "we didn't realise she wasn't on the database. If she had still been there, the airport would have been alerted when she checked in for her flight."

"I've got all I need now," Mike said to Martha, without realising how the blonde girl would interpret the remark.

"What will happen to us?" the girl asked nervously.

"It's OK." The harsh edge had gone from Martha's voice. "Someone will come and sort out the body and baby-sit you until we are out of the city. Then you're free to go."

Wednesday 28th August 2041

Brian was brooding over something. Stef had noticed the way he distanced himself from the others by pretending to read. The previous evening he had appeared to be engrossed in his book on farming, but Stef had soon realised Brian was merely turning the pages without reading the text. "Do you know what's wrong with Brian?" she asked Trevor, when he carried his laundry basket into the kitchen.

"Seems OK. A bit quiet." Trevor searched through his pockets and dropped a handkerchief into the basket. "Mind you, I haven't heard him shout out in his sleep since he's been back."

"Calling out during the day instead. I'll go and get him up."

Stef met Brian on the stairs. "Thought you'd overslept," she said, taking the book out of his hand. "Bringing your work home with you again?"

"No. I picked it up by mistake." Brian was not sure why he lied about the book on the British police system. Perhaps he was anxious after discovering the true role of the Special Branch and the likely nature of Langford's role within it. The Special Branch had been disbanded in 2010, but at the turn of the century it was supposed to liase with MI5, Britain's domestic security agency. However, the two groups had spent most of the time competing with each other. Both had been eager to please the government of the day and demonstrate their usefulness. They did this by cracking down on real or perceived terrorism and making highly publicised drugs busts. If the Socialist government of the time had a hidden agenda on GM technology, there were two organisations who would have been only too willing to implement it. Langford appeared to have been acting as an escort for Troxley, making sure he got out of the country. What else had the Special Branch done for the government? Discredit the Green Alliance? Smooth the way for Genesis Natural Products Inc.? Compromise Fairchild? Surely Langford was not making a move against Fairchild after all this time — not on his own.

"Your book!" Stef called out.

Brian had continued walking down the stairs, leaving Stef

holding the book. When he returned to get it, Stef hit him on the head with it.

"Wake up!" She hung on to the book when Brian grabbed it. Lowering her voice to a whisper, she said, "There's something I meant to ask you. Not that I mind if you did, of course, but did your girlfriend come back here with you on Monday?"

"No. Why?"

"It's just... Nothing really." She seemed embarrassed and quickly changed the subject. "Oh, I mended that ornament. The glue may go a bit yellow after a while. You might be able to get some ceramic paint to cover it."

Only after he had left the house did Brian realise why Stef had asked about the girl. The scent of Hildee's body had still been present in the room when he returned the previous evening.

*

Had he not been expecting it, Brian would have hardly noticed being jostled on the stairs leading out of the underground station. He had deliberately joined the small group of people leaving the platform. Some were making their way to the Home Office; others were heading to Ivan's for a late breakfast.

*

"Right!" said Brian, throwing Lucky's file down on the desk. "I'm off to get my man. What are you doing?"

Johnny was reassembling a telephone receiver, having wired a small box to the circuit board inside it. "There you go! A phone with a built-in microphone and a permanent connection to the main PBX. Dial the right number and you can listen in to the office."

"How many phones have you done that to?"

"Enough to get a good idea of what's going on."

"Well, keep it to yourself. For now anyway. While I'm out, see if the girl from the hotel..."

"Caroline Tate."

"Yes. Caroline Tate. See if she has ever used that S-Card number she gave us anywhere in London during the last two years."

"A bit unlikely."

"Very unlikely. Then look for any number that stopped being used..."

"Around the time you and Mr. Allchurch tumbled her," Johnny said enthusiastically. "Then any number which started showing up at the same time. Especially ones used within walking distance of the office we raided yesterday."

"Right, although you can probably rule out Queen Anne's Gate."

"One slight problem, sir." Johnny folded his arms. "We can't get access to the S-Card system."

Taking his rucksack off the coat stand, Brian unzipped the pocket and took out a computer disk containing the software Adam Greer and Tony Cameron had written. "There!" said Brian, tossing the disk to Johnny. "Careful how you use it and don't leave it on the hard drive." Brian waited while Johnny installed the software, then he took the disk back, knowing full well a second copy would be made as soon as his back was turned.

*

"Mind if I take a look in your locker?" Brian held his ID card up so that Lenny Drake could get a good look at it.

"I'm a bit busy at the moment, Mr. Tyler. Train due in a few minutes."

"I'm sure the passengers won't miss you as much as I miss my watch and mobile, Lenny." Brian started to walk towards the guards' locker room, without waiting to see if Drake was following. "Sorry, Lenny. I would have called you Lucky, only it doesn't seem appropriate today," he shouted over his shoulder.

A single light bulb lit the damp and musty locker room. Patches of rust spattered the grey-painted metal doors of the lockers themselves. Brian found the one labelled 'Drake' and stood in front of it.

"I don't know why you bother. It's not as if you can sell them to anyone."

"It's all right for you. You can have a mobile any time you want. The rest of us have to make do with phones that don't work. A girl will give you a really good night out for a mobile. Know what I mean?" He turned and looked at Brian. "Perhaps you don't."

"Enough of your cheek! Just open it." But Brian knew Lenny was right. Mobiles were usually only issued to the police and army. A thriving black market existed for handsets, SIM cards and imported charging cradles.

Lenny rummaged in his pocket until he found his key, then undid the padlock and slammed the door back. "There! One phone, one watch. Quits! Right?" He locked the door again and started to walk away.

"Not so fast, Lenny." Brian carefully put the watch and phone in his rucksack.

Lenny turned and, noticing Brian was wearing gloves, sighed heavily. "Come on, Mr. Tyler. Give us a break."

"If it was up to me, Lenny, I wouldn't run you in. You see, I was up in East Anglia this weekend and saw fields of cabbages and those other things. You know, the tall plants with funny lumps all the way up them."

"Brussels sprouts." Lenny spat the words out.

"That's them. And I thought, 'pity the poor sod who has to pick those in the winter.' But then you know all about that. How long were you on that penal farm in Lincolnshire?"

"Two years."

"Two years. That's a long time. It'll be four years this time. You probably won't have any fingers left to stick in people's pockets after that. That's why I feel so bad about taking you over the road. If I had my way, I'd make a deal, but — to tell you the truth — you've got so many people's backs up I don't think I could swing it for you."

Lenny leaned against the locker. Thrusting his hands in his pockets, he looked down at the floor. "OK. What sort of deal are you looking for?"

"I just said, I don't know if..."

"Oh, just tell me what you want — and what I get out of it."

"Well, what you get out of it is a new S-Card number, a new name and a new job."

"And what do you want to know?"

"Nothing. I just need you to do a couple of little jobs for me."

"Now, don't tell me. Let me guess." Lenny pushed himself away from the locker with his elbows and walked slowly around the room. "You want an object or a piece of paper to appear mysteriously in someone's pocket. Then you can say to them, 'Gotcha red-handed!'"

"Lucky, you read my mind."

"You people, you really make me..." He stared at Brian. "When?"

Brian took the watch out of his rucksack. "We've got thirty minutes to get to it."

"That him? Old guy, thin on top?" Lucky sniffed and shuffled his feet.

"Yep. That's the one." Brian took Harry the Print's glasses case out of his pocket and handed it to Lucky. The announcement of the imminent departure of the Eurostar to Paris echoed around Waterloo station.

"Then we're quits. New name, new job and my record disappears."

"This, and one other job."

Lucky glared at Brian as he took the glasses case.

"I did say two jobs," Brian said.

Watching from a distance, Brian wondered why Harry had not felt the glasses case drop into his pocket. Lucky did not jostle him. In fact, there was no physical contact at all. For a moment it seemed as though Lucky had been tumbled. Harry turned around with a start, but this was because, with the hand that was not planting the glasses in Harry's pocket, Lucky slammed a baggage trolley into a wastepaper bin with a deafening crash. Lucky apologised, then dragged the trolley away, running one wheel over Harry's foot as he did so.

"Some clumsy bastard ran over my foot," Harry complained, after Brian had introduced himself and sat down. The waiting room was almost deserted and, as food was no longer being served in the café, all the tables were free. Opening a battered leather briefcase, Harry took out a flask and placed it in front of him. When he had poured some tea into a cup, he added milk from a small bottle and stirred it with a pencil. From his pocket he took a paper bag containing biscuits. "I'd offer you one, but I know how touchy you coppers are about eating without a licence." This trivial action threw Brian. It took him back to the weekend and that evening on the terrace with Hildee. Harry was not the sort of person Brian took a dislike to. He had intended to feign a degree of aggression. Now he realised he couldn't. The meeting was going to be a complete failure. To cap it all, he felt guilty about the trick with the glasses.

"I wanted you to take a look at these for me," Brian said, passing three pieces of paper to Harry. "Please," he added, before realising how pathetic it made him sound. Instinctively reaching into his pocket for his glasses, Harry took the Inland Waterways Security Division authorisation, the document-release authorisation from Norwich and an authorisation Brian knew to be genuine.

"So what's this all about?" Harry asked, opening the case and examining the glasses. "I suppose what you're telling me is that this could have been anything. A plate for an S-Card or a hundred-dollar bill. Some sort of threat, is it?" He put the glasses on and gave the papers a cursory examination. "What am I supposed to be looking for?"

"Are they all genuine?" Brian could see Harry's hand shaking with rage.

"Genuine! Genuine! Genuine!" He threw each page on the table in turn. "Anything else?"

Brian put a copy of the photofit on top of the other pages. "Ever seen her?"

"Nope!" Harry snapped, without even picking up the photofit. "You said there was something in this for me."

All Brian wanted to do now was get the meeting over with as quickly as possible. His confidence shattered, he felt cheap and inadequate. "There could be a big printing contact coming up. Posters in Ivan's up and down Britain."

"The government's got plenty people who can do that without having to come over the river to me."

"This will be full-colour. I thought you were the only printer who can still do that." Brian did not wait for an answer. "Here's the person to contact." He was irritated and threw the card on the table. "I don't know what arrangements they make with people from this side of the river, but I'm sure they'll make it worth your while. Anyway, you could always come across to our side."

"It's not that simple," Harry said, as Brian picked up the picture and documents. "Me and the wife lived in the same house since we married. She's buried over this side. But you wouldn't understand that."

"No. I wouldn't." Brian stood up and returned the papers to his rucksack.

Brian had almost reached the stairs leading down to the station concourse, when Harry called out to him. "Over a month ago."

"What?" Brian returned to Harry's table, sat down and rested his rucksack on his knee.

"About a month ago, the girl came to me." Even though the waiting room was deserted, Harry spoke softly. "Said she wanted some S-Cards printed. I told her I didn't touch them. Then she said, right out of the blue, that there's trouble with numbers above fifty — especially the seventh number. Said it was used by the police to track people. 'Why tell me?' I thought. I'd already told her I didn't print cards."

"She didn't believe you."

"Maybe. Anyway, I was talking to another printer, from abroad. Now, he *does* print S-Cards. He said he got a call, around the same time as the girl visited me. He was given the same story. Make any sense to you?"

"Some."

"Well, there you are then, for what it's worth." He waited for Brian to ask another question, but then realised he was deep in thought. "Come on then," he said, slapping his hand down on the table.

Brian jumped. "What?"

"The papers. Let's have a look your documents again." This time Harry studied each piece of paper carefully, murmuring to himself as he did so. "That one seems OK," he said, giving the genuine authorisation back to Brian. "These two have identical signatures on them."

"Well, they're both signed by the Home Secretary."

"No, no." Harry took an eyeglass out of his briefcase. "Traced. These signatures have been traced by two different people." He handed the Inland Waterways Security Division authorisation back to Brian. "The person who did this one had a shaky hand, but there's no doubt they were both traced."

"How do you know?"

"Line thickness doesn't vary and both signatures are identical. You sign your name twice and see how different the signatures are. My guess is, they did this with some sort of stencil or a trepanning device."

"What's that?"

"A pen on a link mechanism."

"Yes. We found something like that."

"Dirty deeds in high places, eh?"

Brian realised that Harry had heard the rumours. "Looks that way."

"Not all it's cracked up to be over there, is it?"

"It's all I know, Harry. Party school, party college, and now a party job. It's a bit of a shock to find out that something's gone rotten inside it. Still, perhaps things will sort themselves out."

"Well, I'm past worrying." Harry stood up to leave. "Thanks for the name, by the way. Perhaps you can give your boss a few lessons in man management."

Mike was deep in thought as the car headed north along the freeway to San Francisco. The clean-up had been handled efficiently by the local CIA agent. The body had been buried, and the van had been driven away while Martha distracted the youth and the blonde girl. Even Mike did not get to see the driver. The local agent was never referred to by name and he never used Martha's name. Nevertheless, there had been a lot of talk about cover and discussion about replacements. Mike guessed that this was aimed at misleading the two 'prisoners' the local agent was to baby-sit. After these amateur sleuths were released from Passmore's farm, the local CIA man would discard his brightly coloured clothes, rinse the black dye out of his hair, and wash the make-up from his face. Then he would join the farm workers drifting along the coast road.

It was Martha who broke the silence. "So why did you hit Monk twice? You wasted your key witness" — although she was not sorry. Alive, the programmer would have posed a number of logistical problems.

Mike shrugged and shook his head. "I don't know."

"It was the girl, wasn't it? You just couldn't bear to watch your southern California girl get wasted."

Although Martha was laughing, and humming the Beachboys' 'California Girls', she had got close to the truth. When the programmer pointed the gun at the girl, Mike had felt an anger well up in him, a rage that had been simmering for years. The car bumped and rocked along the uneven highway. "What was he doing with a gun anyway? I thought computer programmers were nerds."

They left the car in a run-down multi-storey car park, and its key on top of a steel roof girder nearby. They took different tram routes to the bus station and separate shuttle buses to the airport. Once the Airbus to Washington was airborne, Mike walked to the front of the plane and sat next to Martha. They spent the flight huddled over the laptop, finishing the report Mike would take back to London.

*

Despite Harry's compliment, the interview had left a bad taste in

Brian's mouth. He now realised he could never be the hard-nosed policeman Mike had become. After copying Lucky's S-Card number onto a piece of paper, Brian gave the file to Johnny to take back to Central Records. While returning the authorisations and the photofit picture of the girl to the Troxley file, he noticed the photograph of the unidentified fingerprint — a piece of evidence that still needed to be checked.

As it was lunchtime, Brian thought he would have Hutch's lab to himself. One by one, he opened each drawer until he found a body that looked about the same height and build as Lucky. Taking a blank toe tag, he wrote Lucky's S-Card number on it and exchanged it for the one already attached to the cadaver. When Hutch started the autopsy, he would request the file. It would be Lucky's file that would turn up and be stamped 'deceased'. There would be some minor confusion about personal effects, but Hutch would assume that Amanda, or someone else upstairs, had lost them.

"Easy, isn't it?" Brian swung around to find Dr. Hutchinson standing behind him. "What is it? Someone who has grassed up his mates for a new identity? Or someone who is going to eliminate a villain you can't bring to book?" Hutch felt the cuff of Brian's jacket with his thumb and finger. "Very nice. You can't get these in London. Been on a trip? I do hope you're not doing this for material gain. You're not, are you?"

"No, sir," Brian answered nervously.

"'Sir.' Now that's what I hear they're calling *you* these days." Hutch pushed the drawer shut. You're not the first to take a few short cuts to close a case. You lot upstairs think we're all asleep down here. We put a body in a drawer and, hey presto, the next morning she's got a different S-Card number."

Brian registered that Hutch said 'she'. He wanted to press him on this point, but could he be trusted?

Hutch's mood changed. "I'm going to lunch. Please don't interfere with anything else," he said sharply. Before leaving the lab he went into his office and turned the key in the filing cabinet.

As he walked past the office, Brian noticed that the top drawer of the filing cabinet was not quite shut. He pulled at the drawer, then realised Hutch had unlocked rather than locked the cabinet. In the daybook there were four entries for females in the week following Troxley's death. Brian copied the names, cause of death and dates onto a piece of paper, then replaced the book and pushed the drawer shut again.

With Hutch out of the way, Brian realised he had access to a computer that Langford was unlikely to search after office hours. Opening up *The Guardian*'s website, he entered '+simitovich', '+official' and '+visit' in the search field. Fifty-eight entries appeared. Limiting the search to the last year reduced the number to nineteen. Some were duplications of the same news report. Eventually Brian was left with a list of four countries and nine separate visits.

*

Amanda's lab seemed to be deserted, but Brian was taking no chances after his encounter with Hutch. In fact, Amanda was hunched over a microscope at the end of the lab. "Just come to check some fingerprints," Brian called out as he waved the photograph. "I think that Mike has been pawing things without gloves on again."

"Help yourself. All your prints are stored alphabetically in the drawer labelled 'Home Office'."

There were only five photographs in the 'L' section. The one marked 'Langford. S' was a perfect match for the print found on Troxley's passport and the fax machine. The fact that Langford was heavily involved was now beyond doubt. Whether Brian could do anything about it was less clear. However, with the information from Hutch's daybook, it might be possible to catch the girl.

*

As Brian had hoped, most of the personnel department went for lunch at the same time. The one clerk who remained behind claimed she was too busy to look for any files. Anyway, she seemed to be unhappy about leaving the front desk. Officially, personnel records were out of bounds to anyone other than members of the personnel department, but Brian explained that he was not going to remove anything, and made his offer to look for the information himself sound as though he was doing the clerk a favour.

Copies of all travel authorisations were added to personnel files. Langford's file contained only one: a visit to Brussels two years ago. This did not tie up with either of Simitovich's visits to the EU headquarters. Brian had wondered if Langford's excessive periods of sick leave might have been a cover for clandestine meetings, but none of these tied up with Simitovich's trips to Britain either. The discovery was both disappointing and worrying. Now it was more important than ever to catch the girl.

*

With the S-Card database access software, Brian was able to put a name to the S-Card number taken from the body in the lab. Next he called Padreep Kumar and explained that someone he knew was looking for a job at Heathrow.

Padreep provided a contact in personnel, then asked if Mike had been in touch. He became agitated when Brian said he had not, explaining that Mike's wife was seriously ill.

After checking that Lucky's new identity had never been convicted of a serious offence, Brian typed up a letter of recommendation addressed to the personnel manager at Heathrow. He then typed a second letter, explaining that there had been a mistake at the Home Office and that the records of the person he had previously recommended had been confused with those of a notorious pickpocket. Brian printed a copy of both letters.

After lunch, Brian paid his second, and last, visit to Lenny 'Lucky Dip' Drake. "This will get you the job, Lucky," he said, handing over the letter. "And a copy of this letter will be sent if you let me down. Is that clear?"

Lucky read the letter. "Seems fair enough. And you're sure my file will be deleted?"

"Marked 'deceased' as soon as they finish cutting you up."

Lucky gulped and rubbed his neck. "Don't say things like that. I've just had my lunch."

*

"This is all very well, but it still doesn't tell us what number she is using now." Johnny examined the list of names he had compiled from S-Card data.

"No. It won't. What you need to do is check the people, females, who disappeared from the database for a few days during the week after the murder."

*

"Right. I've got twenty-eight in Central London, but..."

"Now plug those into the police 'Holmes' database to see if there are any matches."

Johnny typed one number after another into the database. "Hey! Spooky! Look at this, sir." He leaned back so that Brian could see the screen.

"Right. That's the one," Brian said calmly. "'Found in Goodge Street — multiple stab wounds — died before ambulance arrived.'"

"Got better two days later." Johnny whispered. "Eating in Ivan's in Chelsea every evening since."

*

It was nine thirty when Brian and Johnny gave up and left the Chelsea Ivan's in King's Road. Brian had taken advantage of Johnny's optimism and won five euros from him. Deep down, he had known that the girl would be one step ahead of them. It had even crossed his mind that Hutch had tipped her off. But he knew it was more likely that, after coming so close to being caught the day before, she had put yet another identity between herself and her hunters.

The guards and the waiters at the Ivan's remembered seeing the girl, but no-one could recall which direction she walked in after leaving the restaurant. "She's over the river," Brian said to Johnny as they rode their bicycles towards South Kensington — keeping to the main roads in order to avoid the rubble-strewn side streets.

Catching the girl was important. Brian had to know if she was the link with Simitovich. If neither she nor Langford were in contact with the Ukrainian deputy, it meant that a third person was involved. That person could be working in the Home Office. With them still in place, Brian could not move against Langford without being ambushed by his accomplice.

From Brian's point of view, the evening had not been a complete waste of time. He discovered that he was not the only disillusioned and frustrated young man in the police force. Johnny, a trained electronics and computer engineer, regarded the Home Office as prehistoric. Brian even suspected that he was one of the contributors to the Ivan's Killer network. Johnny lived in Knightsbridge, in a flat stacked high with computer equipment. His brother imported power supplies — the first component to fail if a computer is left unused for a long period. As the two parted company at Brompton Road, Brian insisted that Johnny ate at

Prince's Gardens in future.

The streets seemed even more silent than usual. For the first time since moving to London, Brian felt totally alone. He thought of Hildee and wanted to continue riding until he reached King's Cross. In his mind, he reconstructed the previous Friday's train ride and daydreamed about the cycle ride from Downham to Nordelph.

*

It sounded as though someone answered the phone, but then the line crackled and went dead. Brian tried twice more without success. He even tried his mobile, in case there was a fault at the London exchange. He wished now he had sent her an e-mail before leaving the office — damn the risk. What could Langford or anyone else do, even if they did find out?

*

John Campbell had been lucky. Had he taken the later train, the guard would have recognised the Inland Waterways Security Division document as a forgery. It was only after his train had reached King's Lynn that all guards were briefed to stop and detain anyone carrying Home Office papers. If the guard who had given Brian the third degree the previous week had checked Campbell's papers, the police and army in King's Lynn would have been on full alert by now. Campbell's guard, however, had a short memory. He also forgot the long wooden box, marked 'Pumping Equipment', which in fact contained a high-powered rifle and ammunition. Had he searched Campbell's rucksack, he would have found enough food and water to keep the man going for three days.

Campbell was no stranger to East Anglia, and had even spent time in Downham. For him, this was a return journey. Two years ago he had escaped from a penal farm and made his way north through Black Fen to the coast. Now he was retracing his footsteps. The chance to earn American dollars, and get a passport and visa so he could spend them, had been too tempting. In the year and a half he had been hiding in the East End, this was the first serious job to come his way — one that used the skills he had learned in the army.

In a King's Lynn back street, Campbell found a small motorcycle. Strapping the wooden box to its frame, he pushed the machine a hundred metres down the road. It was out of the owner's earshot when he pushed down on the starter pedal. The machine burst into life and within the hour Campbell had passed through the abandoned hamlet of Terrington St. Clements and was heading south through Black Fen. He remembered the route well enough not to need a map until he reached Downham itself.

Hildee woke with a start. As a rule, she was not a light sleeper and could not understand why the sound of the motorcycle had woken her. Half an hour later, she was still trying to get to sleep. She heard footsteps outside, crunching on the gravel drive. The doors downstairs creaked as though someone was trying the locks. She thought it must be her imagination. Opening the curtains slightly, she could make out the shapes of the bushes where Brian had spotted the gunman. At first, nothing moved. Then Hildee saw him. A man with a gun on his shoulder, making no attempt to hide himself, was strolling across the garden. She ran downstairs to the study to get the revolver. She toyed with the idea of calling the police, but worried about appearing stupid if it was only Morris Haswell checking that the house was secure.

It was several years since Hildee had slept with a gun beside her bed. She lay awake, waiting for the sound of breaking glass. Eventually she convinced herself it was only Morris outside — or, at worst, a poacher. Brian's visit had made her nervous. She stroked her arm, then gripped it tightly, imagining he was still there. A stupid thing to do, she thought, and then she fell asleep.

9

Thursday 29th August 2041

Hildee woke suddenly and, hearing the commotion outside, feared she had overslept. But it was too early for the army. Hutley was always late, and even the guards and office workers did not arrive until 9 a.m.

Two Jeeps were parked in the drive. Around one of them stood a group of soldiers who were receiving instructions from their commanding officer. Eventually the soldiers dispersed. Half the group climbed into one of the Jeeps, which then sped off down the drive. The remaining soldiers fanned out across the grounds. Hildee, who had been watching all this through a gap in the curtains, pushed back one of the faded velvet drapes. The officer glanced up at the window, as if he had been taken by surprise. He climbed out of the Jeep. At first, Hildee thought he was about to approach the house, but he didn't. Instead, he sat on the seat at the edge of the drive and unfolded a map he had taken from his pocket. A second soldier joined him. Together they surveyed the grounds and surrounding fields as if they were planning a campaign.

There were raised voices when the first of the regular soldiers arrived. The officer sitting on the bench insisted the regulars hand over their guns. Hutley made matters worse by asking the officer who the hell he thought he was. Hildee suspected she was about to be arrested. Perhaps this was why she had not heard from Brian.

*

Too angry to be frightened, Hildee unlocked the front door and strode towards the tree where she had left her bicycle. The arguing stopped, and all the soldiers watched as she grabbed the bicycle, then turned to face them. "I am going into town for breakfast. I assume you will have sorted yourselves out by the time I get back."

Hildee had only ridden a few metres when the officer called out to the driver of the Jeep and pointed down the drive. The Jeep's engine roared into life and, scattering gravel, the vehicle raced down the drive ahead of Hildee's bicycle.

When the Jeep stopped, a heavily built sergeant got out and blocked Hildee's path. "We're going into town. You can have a lift."

"Do I have any choice?" Hildee was already resigned to the

situation and was dismounting.

"It's for your own good, Miss Parks," the sergeant replied, wheeling the bicycle back to the house. He stood talking to the officer, nodding agreement, referring to the map, and occasionally looking back towards the Jeep. Hildee noticed that the sergeant did not salute when he had finished talking; he merely turned and ran back down the drive. Meanwhile, the driver had picked up a small machine gun and was scanning the grounds and the main gate continually, glancing nervously at everything that moved but avoiding any eye contact with Hildee. When the sergeant returned, the driver handed the machine gun to him. On the journey into Downham, neither soldier spoke to the other, nor to Hildee.

There was an air of quiet determination about the sergeant. Hildee thought he was a lot like Brian — not as handsome, and lacking the vulnerability and charm, but nevertheless determined to remain in control of the situation. He queued at the counter with her while the driver waited outside the Ivan's. The sergeant studied everyone who approached Hildee, staring at them with the same humourless expression on his face. Only when they reached the head of the queue did his mood change.

"'Standard' for me, and here's a dispensation for me mate outside." Suddenly he had acquired a London accent, his eyes had softened and he smiled. Hildee's friend Tilly, who had already taken a shine to her Brian, blushed when the sergeant leaned across the counter.

"What's *your* name then?" he whispered to her.

"Tilly," the waitress replied.

"Na," he said, with a smile. "No-one's called Tilly. You just made it up."

"Did not," she retorted. "It's short for Matilda."

"Prove it," he said, picking up his tray of food and the box of sandwiches for the driver.

Just as Hildee and the sergeant were finishing their meal, Tilly approached the table. "There you are, you see. 'Matilda.'" She handed over her ID.

"Yes, so you are." The sergeant studied the card, then looked up at her and smiled. "Perhaps I'll see you around."

"Perhaps you'll see my boyfriend around as well." Said Tilly.

It was back at Nordelph that Hildee discovered why the sergeant had acted out of character. To Hutley's annoyance, a desk in the main office had been commandeered by the new arrivals. The officer and the sergeant were both out of the room, and Hildee decided to use the opportunity to find out what these uninvited guests were up to. In an unmarked folder, there were a number of small maps showing the river and drainage systems. There was also a list of all the regular soldiers and workers who visited the manor and, at the back of the folder, a photofit of a girl. The girl bore a strong resemblance to Hildee's friend Tilly. The sergeant had tricked Tilly into showing her ID, checking her identity without her realising what he was doing. Again Hildee thought of the way Brian had behaved at the weekend. Had she been as gullible as Tilly?

"Excuse me, Miss Parks." The sergeant stood in the doorway. Hildee made no attempt to hide the fact that she was studying the folder, but the sergeant did not ask her what she was doing at the desk. "Have you got a gun?"

"Yes," she replied, with some apprehension.

"Can I have a look at it for a moment?"

Hildee fetched the revolver from her bedroom and passed it to the sergeant, handle first. Lifting the gun to his nose, he sniffed the end of the barrel. "I'd better take this," he said.

Hildee felt a sinking feeling in her stomach and her resolve weakened. So this was it, she thought. Perhaps Brian had been arrested, or — more likely, considering the timing — he had implicated her in the killing of Gerald Whiteside. "Look," she said, "I usually inspect the farms about now. I take it you have no objections to that." She realised she was in denial of her imminent arrest.

"Certainly. I'll take you myself." The sergeant led her out to the Jeep. Beckoning one of the two soldiers stationed at the front door, he handed over the revolver. "Sort this out, quick as you can."

The chill had gone from the morning air. Dust swirled behind the Jeep and the breeze tugged at Hildee's hair. This might be the last time she ever travelled along these lanes, Hildee thought. Imagining what Brian was doing at this moment made her head spin. Which would be worse? Being deceived by someone who had pretended to love her? Or someone she cared about deeply being thrown into jail?

*

Careful to avoid letting the morning sun reflect on the binoculars, Campbell continued surveying Nordelph Manor. He had spent the night hidden under trees beside a field where, forty years before, Green activists had attacked Sergeant Bryant. The previous evening he had kicked the motorcycle out of gear and let the engine die away slowly. From a distance, it sounded as though he had ridden off into the night along the Littleport road. In fact, he had freewheeled the motorcycle down the track leading off West Farm Way. A group of trees surrounded by tall grass and bushes provided adequate cover for anyone who wanted to watch the manor house without being seen. The fields around him had already been harvested, so there was little chance of being disturbed by farm workers. Campbell used bales of straw to hide the motorcycle. After unpacking the gun and eating a supper of bread and cheese, he had settled into his temporary home and slept.

Now, within the space of twenty minutes, three vehicles had entered and left the grounds of Nordelph Manor. Furthermore, one guard was posted at the main gate and a second one was patrolling the perimeter fence. Campbell had been led to believe that the house was only lightly guarded during the day and not guarded at all at night, but there had already been one change of guard and it was obvious he could not approach the manor without being challenged.

Then another Jeep emerged from the drive. This one, however, was not heading towards the town. Instead, it drove down the dirt track to Whiteside Farm. Through the binoculars, Campbell could see three passengers: Hildee Parks and the driver sitting in front, with a guard in the back. The telescopic site confirmed what he had already guessed. The Jeep was too far away and the road it was travelling on too rough for a decent shot. Before it reached the farm, the Jeep disappeared behind a row of trees, re-emerging in the farmyard itself. The Jeep was now even further away. Campbell watched as the driver parked it in front of the corn-drying shed. Hildee Parks and the soldier climbed out and walked into the shed. The driver waited in the Jeep.

There was no cover between Campbell and the farm, only open fields. Wanting to live to spend his dollars, he was not interested in a suicidal attempt on Miss Parks's life.

Fifteen minutes elapsed before Hildee and the soldier came out of the corn dryer. The driver must have started the engine immediately he saw them, because the Jeep pulled away as soon as the pair had climbed in. Campbell watched the trail of dust moving along the farm track. Instead of returning to the manor house, however, the driver turned towards Downham. Half a minute later, dust was rising from another farm track. Campbell guessed, correctly, that Miss Parks was on a tour of Nordelph's farms. He assumed, again correctly, that she did this every day. He looked at his watch.

The next vehicle to arrive at Whiteside Farm was a grain lorry loaded with wheat from one of the surrounding fields. Campbell watched the lorry tip its load into the dryer's inlet pit. Ten minutes had elapsed since the Jeep had left. Although the exact timing might be different the following day, the outline of a plan took shape in his mind. All he had to do now was stay where he was until dark.

*

"Yes, I'll be right along." Brian put down the phone. "The big boss calls," he said to Johnny. "Give it five minutes, then call that mobile number."

Johnny rummaged through the papers on his desk. "Right! Got it!" he said, taking his watch in his hand.

"It doesn't have to be exact. Just give me time to get in there."

Langford was pretending to read the report lying on the desk in front of him. When Brian entered the room, he pushed it to one side. "Ah, Brian. Take a seat. Things going well?"

"Fair. Making some progress," Brian said. The thought of where that progress might lead turned his stomach.

"Hmm." Langford stared at Brian. "Will you get the Troxley report finished by Friday?"

"I had assumed that Mike, I mean Mr. Allchurch, would be doing that when he gets back."

"I'm afraid Mr. Allchurch won't be coming back. It seems he is detained abroad, indefinitely."

"Sorry?"

"Mike has disappeared. It seems that the last anyone heard of him he was in America. It's fairly safe to assume he won't be returning."

"Emigrated?"

"No-one knows for sure. Seems likely though." He studied Brian for a while, wondering if he really was as surprised as he looked. "I take it you haven't heard from him?"

"No. Nothing."

Folding his arms, Langford glared at Brian "Any developments I should know about?" He spoke slowly and deliberately. "Anything come out of your trip at the weekend?"

Brian was lost for an answer but, in the event, did not need to provide one. A mobile phone rang. Langford picked it up and pressed the answer button. Even Brian could hear the howl of feedback.

The feedback grew louder as Langford moved the mobile closer to the phone on the desk. Then he pulled the plug from the telephone and switched off the mobile. "You're a very clever young man," he said, smiling at Brian. "You should go a long way in this department — if you play your cards right."

"Meaning?" Brian knew exactly what he meant and could feel himself becoming increasingly angry.

"Well, for a start, Mike isn't coming back. There's an opening there. There's a chance you can make a name for yourself with the Troxley case. Your report should demonstrate you're commander material."

"Wouldn't the report be better coming from you? After all, your involvement with Troxley is greater than mine — and it goes back further."

"No need for sarcasm, Brian. Things are changing. We either go with the flow or drown. You think it over. It's a big opportunity. A year as a commander and you'll be on your way." He stood up and walked to the door. "Get that report to me by tomorrow afternoon."

Brian stood up to leave. "But there's still..."

"You've got all the information you need. You know Fairchild is up to his neck in all of this. There's nothing you can do to save him. Try to defend him and *you'll* sink with him. And *you* haven't got a plane ticket to America, have you?"

*

Johnny was jubilant "Got him then!" He exclaimed. Brian stood staring out of the window. He was furious with Mike and annoyed with Johnny. Mike had run off and left him to carry the can. Now, because he was listening when the mobile was picked up, Johnny knew that it was Langford who had tipped off the girl.

"Johnny, I want you to keep your head down for a couple of days. There's a party boss flying in at the weekend..."

"Simitovich."

"That's the kiddie. Anyway, you go over and help Padreep Kumar with security at Heathrow."

"But what about...?"

"Just do it!" Brian snapped.

"Yes, sir." Johnny's face flushed.

"Just *do* it. All right?" Brian pointed to the phone on the desk, then raised his finger to his mouth. He took a piece of paper and wrote on it. 'Ivan's, Prince's Gardens, 9 p.m.' Johnny took the note and without saying another word left the office.

Brian returned to Langford's office. "OK, I'll do it," he said, leaning against the doorjamb. "But I'm sending Johnny Coates over to West London Division. I don't want him involved in any of this."

"Good. Well done, Brian." Langford smiled. "You won't regret it."

"I hope not." Brian sighed, realising he probably wouldn't live long enough to regret it.

*

Padreep could not decide which piece of bad news to give Mike first. He watched the passengers coming down the steps of the 747 from Washington, parked on the apron in front of Terminal Three. Perhaps it was a mistake and Mike was not on the plane. After all, there were rumours flying around that Mike had asked for asylum in the US. But his name was definitely on the passenger list. Then Padreep saw him, walking, head bowed, towards the arrivals hall.

*

Weariness seemed to come in waves. One minute he felt wide awake, the next his eyes grew heavy. Padreep had to tell him twice before it sank in that Linda was seriously ill in the West Middlesex Hospital. Padreep could not bring himself to say that she had died during the night — and Mike ran off before Padreep could tell him that Brian Tyler was sitting in his desk at the Home Office.

*

"I'm here to see Linda Allchurch," Mike told the receptionist, for the third time. Again she prevaricated. "Now!" Mike shouted.

"The doctor is on his way," she said, putting down the phone.

The doctor, who had started work at ten the previous evening, looked as tired as Mike felt. "Mike, I'm sorry about this, but I'm afraid it's bad news." He had known Mike for several years, and Linda for a lot longer. That was the only reason it was difficult to explain that Linda had died at three o'clock that morning. Breaking news of the death of a loved one to waiting relatives was a daily chore. He *tried* to look genuinely concerned, even though he usually wasn't. The infection had not spread to other patients, or the staff, and the body had been disposed of quickly, with the minimum risk of contamination. That was all he really cared about. A person was treated like a diseased limb: once it became irreparable, the best thing to do was to remove it as quickly as possible.

"But how? When I left, all she had was toothache." Mike slumped into a chair and buried his face in his hands. He felt he should cry, but couldn't.

"It was an abscess. We tried antibiotics, but nothing worked."

All Mike felt was guilt. While he had been lying on a beach in California, Linda had been writhing with pain. But there was more to it than that. He had been out of the country when his parents died. He had been unable to do anything to save his first wife and child. He was still mourning *their* loss, and there was simply not enough grief left over for Linda. If he was honest, the only person he felt sorry for was himself. "But you *knew* Linda." He stood up and moved closer to the doctor. Lowering his voice, he said, "You've got access to antibiotics that work on *anything*."

The doctor had heard this argument before. Everyone agrees with the policy that the most advanced antibiotics should be held in reserve. The trouble is, everyone knows a special case — usually a member of their own family. "Look, Mike, let's get some fresh air."

"Sod the fresh air! I want to see her body." Even Mike knew this was absurd. Linda had already been cremated. He followed the doctor out of the main entrance.

Looking up at the sky, the doctor sighed. "I've known Linda for longer than you have."

"So you just stood by and let her die?"

"No. That's just it. I didn't. We've got the latest antibiotics from Switzerland. It's illegal to use them without special permission, but I did." He looked down at the ground and drew a breath. "They didn't work. By rights, I'm supposed to report that. I won't though, because if I did they would lock me up. Judging by how ineffective it was, I imagine people have been using it illegally for some time." He felt sorry for Mike's generation, who

323

could remember the days when antibiotics were the answer to everything.

"Do you think there is anything that would have worked?"

"To be honest, no. Those pig farms in Holland and Germany put the bugs decades ahead. Even if we still had all those pharmaceutical companies, I don't think we would ever catch up again. Bacteria only have to be lucky once; we have to be lucky every time. The pig industry gave the bugs an infinite number of throws of the dice."

"Doesn't sound very encouraging."

"See it as an adjustment. We've just downsized to cope in a world where we can't control disease. No more package holidays or living in crowded cities. Too much contact, and disease slaps us down again." The doctor shrugged and walked back towards the main doors. "We may get ahead again, but if we don't, what the heck! This is how it was for thousands of years. Antibiotics are probably more trouble than they're worth."

"If you're not the one who's dying."

"Yes. Sorry." The doctor realised he had already forgotten about Linda.

"Was she alone when she went?" Mike saw from the look on the doctor's face that she was.

"Sorry, Mike. You know the rules about bacterial infections."

*

Mike slept until lunchtime. On waking, he went with the children to the Rayners Lane Ivan's. In view of their mother's death and their father's absence, both had been given the day off school. Linda's daughter had already cancelled her mother's S-Card. She announced that she was moving out of the house to live with relatives in Ealing. Mike's son seemed to be more edgy than upset. Mike wondered whether the boy blamed him for Linda's death, but it was said that children these days didn't carry as much emotional baggage. Mike was probably reading too much into his son's mood.

"Dad, I'm thinking of joining up."

For a moment, Mike thought he had misheard. "Joining up?"

"Yes, as an engineer. Not a pongo or anything like that. You know, jump before I'm pushed."

Mike imagined coming home to an empty house. On the walk back from the restaurant, he noticed every overgrown garden and derelict house. He could not decide whether he was angry, scared or both. Suddenly he felt helpless and impotent, unable to defend himself. Even if he found the strength to fight, it was not clear who he should be fighting. Who was to blame for all of this?

*

"Your gun, Miss Parks. Mind if we go out the back and try it?" The sergeant led Hildee through the house and out onto the terrace, where he handed her the revolver. She noticed it had been cleaned and oiled. "Three shots at one tree, and a second three shots at the other one." The sergeant said.

She looked at the sergeant, hoping for some clue to his intentions. As usual, he refused to make eye contact with her.

"In your own time, Miss Parks."

Hildee raised the gun and fired two bursts. Her ears were still ringing when the guards came rushing into the garden. The sergeant ignored the two soldiers and walked over to inspect the two patterns of bullet marks.

The sergeant took the gun from Hildee, and reloaded it. "Remember, lads, if you want to hide from Miss Parks don't disguise yourselves as trees." He said as he returned the revolver. At first, Hildee was unsure whether to take it. After doing so, she stared at it, waiting for the sergeant to say something. But he merely walked back into the house. Suddenly the sergeant stopped in his tracks, hesitated, and then continued walking, at a pace, to the front door and out onto the drive.

Hildee was just about to enter the office when the front door burst open. The officer took his cap off and strode across the reception area to where she was standing. "Miss Parks, I'm terribly sorry about this. My sergeant has just informed me that you probably don't know why we're here." He explained their role as bodyguards and the urgency with which they had been deployed.

For the first time, the officer smiled. "We assumed you must have been told. The orders came right from the top in London." Hildee knew that this must have something to do with Brian.

Hildee's belief that she was under arrest amused the sergeant. He laughed at the idea as he climbed into the Jeep to escort her into town for lunch, thus defusing the tense atmosphere between Hildee and the soldiers. And as everyone relaxed, slightly less attention was paid to minor details — minor details that might have frustrated the plans of the gunman hiding in the fields opposite.

All the notes on the Troxley case lay in a pile on Brian's desk. The draft report was ready and two copies had been printed. Brian put the first copy in his rucksack to work on at home; the second copy he took down the corridor to Langford's office. "If you want to change anything, let me know tomorrow morning. You should have the real thing before Simitovich arrives."

"Good lad, Brian." Langford dropped the report on his desk and tapped it with his finger. "I'll read it tomorrow morning. Think I'll have an early night — long day tomorrow." At first, Brian was puzzled that he did not read the report, or at least take it home with him. Then he realised that Langford had probably logged into the network and read it as Brian was typing it.

Returning to his office, Brian copied the report from the network onto the hard disk of Johnny's laptop. After packing all the notes and forensic reports into his rucksack, he emptied the drawers of Mike's desk. Some items he threw into the wastepaper bin; others he put in his rucksack. With the laptop disconnected, he printed off another copy of the letter countermanding his recommendation of Lucky Dip, and wrote a covering note addressed to Lucky himself. He then slid both into an unsealed envelope, which he put in his jacket pocket. Deep down, Brian knew that what he was doing was basically dishonest. He should have felt some remorse, but Langford had left him with little choice. If Mike had been here, he would probably have done the same. Was there anything else? Brian decided that was it, and headed for home.

*

Brian could not be persuaded to go to dinner. Trevor tried but Brian insisted he was going later. Before everyone left, Stef came up to his room to make sure he was not sulking. As they all trooped off down the road, Brian, who was sitting near his bedroom window, heard someone say the word 'lovesick'.

It was twenty five past eight when Brian finally finished work on the report, and ten to nine when he arrived at the Prince's Gardens Ivan's. Johnny was sitting on his own in the middle of the dining room. Stef and her boys were on a table in the corner. After collecting his food, Brian went and sat down opposite Johnny.

Trevor assumed that Brian had not seen the rest of the group and started to walk towards his table. He stopped in his tracks when he saw Brian take an envelope out of his pocket and slide it across to his companion.

"Can you get this to Lenny Drake — or whoever he is now — first thing tomorrow morning?" Brian watched as Johnny felt the envelope. "Tell him 'Now we're quits'. He'll know what that means."

Johnny put the letter in his pocket. "Your name's mud in Western Division."

Brian shrugged. "It's going to be mud whatever I do. By the way, I've borrowed your laptop. I'll bring it up to Heathrow tomorrow."

"There's no need. I think Padreep Kumar has got everything under control for the Simitovich visit."

"Langford will be happier if someone from Central is there as well. Apparently, Simitovich might be making some announcement about the Troxley case. If he does, it makes sense to have someone on hand who can comment on the investigation."

"So it's true what they say? You really are..." Johnny stopped when he realised Brian was glaring at him.

"Really are what?"

"Nothing." Johnny shifted nervously in his chair. "Look, I've got to go. I'll see you tomorrow."

"Don't forget the letter. I promised Lenny I'd make it quits." Brian watched Johnny leave. He wondered how people like Langford lived with themselves. Perhaps they never had to think about it. Perhaps there was always someone willing to do the dirty work for them. Was all this worth it? When it was over, could he just walk away? Would this ensure Hildee was left in peace and that he would be free to return to her?

*

Campbell would have been happier if there had been less light, but this was probably as dark as it was going to get. He slung the rucksack over his back and carried the gun with its butt under his armpit and the barrel pointing towards the ground. This, he hoped, would make him look less like a poacher and more like a worker returning from the fields.

The last grain lorry had visited Whiteside Farm two hours earlier. Campbell assumed that there would be no more harvesting until the dew lifted the next morning. Two deep ditches cut across the fields, so there was no direct route to Whiteside Farm. Campbell was forced to walk due south until he reached the main Bedford Drain. Eventually, after following the riverbank towards Downham, he arrived at the front of the farm. Here he sat and waited. There was a light in the window of one of the farm cottages. He had been told the farm was deserted — but then he had also been told that Nordelph Manor was practically unguarded.

*

Morris Haswell knew he should have been asleep in bed rather than slumped in an armchair. The harvest seemed to be dragging on this year. Despite Miss Parks's insistence that he only carried out light duties in the dryer, he still felt weary by the end of the day. The radio play had been a detective story. Morris had stayed up to listen to it, but fell asleep before the end. Switching off the light, he carried the radio upstairs to listen to the news. Perversely, once he was in bed he could not sleep. Then he heard it — a metallic rattling noise. From the window at the front of his cottage, he looked across the farmyard. The noise seemed to come from the tractor shed.

Wearing a jacket over his pyjamas, Morris eased open the back door of his cottage and stepped into the garden. Slowly he made his way along the path that lead to the drying shed and the yard. Putting his hand into his jacket pocket he gripped the revolver he had picked up before leaving the house. After he had stood for about a minute, staring across the yard, a gust of wind rattled the large metal door of the tractor shed. Morris cursed and, returning to his bed, wondered if the detective story on the radio had put ideas into his head.

*

Inside the tractor shed, Campbell was unaware of Morris Haswell's late-night stroll. He stacked wooden vegetable boxes in front of the window overlooking the yard. The window itself swung. Leaving it open would attract the attention of anyone in the yard outside. Carefully undoing the screws that fixed the hinges to the frame, he removed the entire window. Now, lying flat on his stomach on the wooden boxes, Campbell had a clear line of fire into the yard. All that remained was to get a few hours' sleep, then wait for Miss

Parks to arrive.

10

Friday 30th August 2041

"What do you mean, 'not conclusive'?" Mike folded back the report so that the picture of the girl was at the front, and pushed it across the desk. "There's the girl from the hotel, with Troxley, in California."

Langford didn't pick up the report. He remained remarkably calm considering, until ten minutes ago, he had thought Mike was dead. "So what does that tell us? That Fairchild sent her there to lure him to Britain."

"That makes no sense at all. Fairchild would have told her to kill him in America — not drag him over here where there would be an investigation."

Langford leaned forward and pushed the report back across the desk. "Look, Mike, the report's written. Brian's done a damn good job..."

"Oh yes, I notice he's sitting at my desk. His prize for the cock-and-bull story he's dreamed up, I suppose."

"We thought you'd run off to America. There are a lot of people around here who thought you were staying there. You've got to convince people upstairs you're still reliable."

"How do I do that? Put my name to the bullshit in Tyler's report?"

"I really didn't expect this from you, Mike. You, of all people, know there's got to be a change. Fairchild has got to go."

"And it doesn't matter what we have to do to get rid of him. Is that what you're saying?"

"Well, we can hardly vote him out of power, can we?" Langford took a deep breath and shook his head. "We're both old enough to remember what this country was like before Fairchild and his mob took charge."

"I seem to remember we were piling up bodies and trying to stop food riots."

"Before that," said Langford, becoming increasingly agitated. "We had freedom, democracy and a decent standard of living."

"Well, it wasn't the Greens who put an end to that. Perhaps if there'd been a little more control over those companies who were providing everyone with that 'decent standard of living', we wouldn't be in this mess. Perhaps if we'd had a Green government ten years earlier, toothache and appendicitis wouldn't be so lethal."

"Yes. I'm sorry to hear about Linda."

"Sorry!" Mike shouted. "What the hell do you care?"

Brian had been listening in to the conversation using the phone tap Johnny had set up in Langford's office. When he heard the door slam, he knew that Mike was on his way back.

Mike burst into the office shortly after Brian had replaced the receiver. "This takes some beating! It hasn't taken you long, has it?" He pushed against Brian's shoulder as he pulled open the drawers of what had once been his desk. "Where's all my stuff?" Brian pointed to a cardboard box in the corner of the room. Mike rummaged through the papers and water bottles. When he stood up, he was holding a revolver.

"No, look Mike, don't..."

"Don't do anything silly? That's a bit rich coming from you." He pointed the gun at Brian, but then raised his hand with the gun lying flat on it. He was merely presenting the weapon as a warning to Brian not to follow him. "If *you* haven't the guts to write a report that will stop Simitovich, perhaps I can find another way."

"Out of my way!" Mike shouted, when he met Langford half way down the corridor.

"Mike seemed a bit upset." Langford looked calm for a man who had just had a gun thrust in his face. "Do you think he'll do anything silly?" he asked, as he sat down opposite Brian.

"It *is* his speciality."

"Is there any way of stopping him?"

"Well, I was going to go up to Heathrow later to check on the security for the Deputy's visit." Brian looked at his watch. "I'll bring the visit forward," he said, disconnecting the laptop from the network. "It just means I'll have to finish the report on the train."

"Ah yes. There was something I meant to ask you about your report."

"I won't be long. Mike will probably calm down by the time he gets there. If I'm quick, I might even catch him before the next train leaves."

*

"Quits! Call *this* quits? The devious bastard!" Lucky stood reading Brian's letter. Johnny had spent almost an hour tracking him down. Brian had forgotten to give him Lenny Drake's new name so Johnny had to tour both terminals asking the supervisors if anyone new had started that week. "Well, thanks anyway, mate." Lucky folded the letter and pushed it into his top pocket, then slowly screwed the envelope into a ball.

"I think there was something else in the envelope."

"Just your boss's idea of a joke," Lucky muttered under his breath as he walked away.

*

Campbell woke when he heard the corn dryer start. The grain elevator squeaked and rattled as Morris tested it. A few minutes later a large grain lorry swung around in the yard and tipped its load into the inlet pit. Once again, the elevator burst into life. When the lorry had left the yard, Campbell collected sacks from around the shed and laid them on top of the boxes. This was day three. The bread he had brought with him was stale and there was only a small piece of cheese left. The remaining water was warm and he wished he had refilled the bottle the previous night. If Miss Parks kept to her schedule, however, this job would be finished in another two hours. Then, assuming that a grain lorry turned up on time, he would be eating lunch in King's Lynn by two o'clock.

*

The westbound platform of St. James's Park underground station was deserted. Brian studied the timetable. It would be another hour before Mike reached Heathrow. He tapped out a number on his mobile. "Trevor, Brian here. Got a spot of bother and need some help. Any chance of a vehicle — something fast, a driver and a couple of men?" He could just hear Trevor, who had put his hand over the receiver, shouting to someone.

"Can do," Trevor said when he came back on line. "Where are you?"

"St. James's Park underground."

"On our way!" Trevor shouted, over the sound of a diesel engine being gunned into life.

*

The Land Rover slowed to a crawl on the M4 motorway. They were still four miles from Heathrow and Brian realised Mike's train would arrive at the airport before they did. He noticed, after he had been hurled against the door twice, that the other passengers were holding on to handles suspended from the roof. Cracks in the road reduced their top speed to sixty-five kilometres an hour, and collapsed bridges forced the Land Rover to use slip roads and roundabouts. Brian took out his mobile, but the Land Rover ran into another pothole before he could dial and, once again, his head and shoulder banged against the door. "Can we stop? I need to call the airport."

*

The train stopped at Hounslow West. Only two more stations to go. The girl sitting opposite Mike stood up and got off. She walked down the platform and then stepped through a gap in the fence. After a few seconds, she had disappeared into the trees surrounding the station. The train creaked and groaned as it gathered speed. The carriage grew darker as the undergrowth on either side of the track became thicker. Then the train plunged into a tunnel. There was a delay before the lights came on. Even when they did, the few remaining bulbs generated little more than a dull yellow glow. Mike felt in his pocket for the gun. Someone had to pay.

*

Padreep took some convincing, but eventually agreed to detain Mike when he arrived at the airport. Brian explained that holding him would be in everyone's best interest.

*

Sitting on a creaking wooden chair, Mike rested his elbows on the metal-topped table and stared into space. He did not turn around when Brian and the soldiers entered the detention room. Johnny, who was leaning against the wall, handed Brian the revolver.

"What were you going to do with this? *Club* him to death?" Brian asked, as he inspected the grime-covered weapon.

"So am I under arrest, sir? I take it I'm supposed to call you 'sir' now," Mike sneered.

Brian pointed to the door, then looked around the room. When Johnny, Trevor and the soldiers had left, he sat down at the table. "Look, Mike..."

"Don't patronise *me*, you two-faced sod," snapped Mike.

Brian stood up, pushing the chair away so violently that it

tilted backwards and fell to the floor. "I haven't got time for this," he said, striding to the door and snatching it open. "Trevor, in here please."

Brian pushed the revolver into Trevor's hand. "Take Mr. Allchurch into town. Park up in Victoria, somewhere quiet, and wait for further instructions." Then, without looking at Mike, he pushed past the soldiers and stormed out of the room.

*

The Jeep roared into Whiteside Farm and parked in front of the grain dryer. Campbell could not believe his luck. The last grain lorry had only just left and he would have at least fifteen minutes to clear up. When the next lorry arrived, he would get rid of the driver and the operator of the dryer; empty the lorry himself and drive it back to the field at the end of West Farm Way. After picking up the motorbike, he would take the lorry north to Black Fen, from there it would be just a short motorcycle ride to King's Lynn.

Meanwhile, the driver of the Jeep had presented Campbell with the easiest target imaginable. Hildee Parks, the sergeant and the driver were all sitting with their backs to the window of the tractor shed. With such a target, he hardly needed the telescopic sight. Six shots — two for each person — should finish the job. All he had to do was wait until they stood up, then fire.

*

Air travel was an embarrassing necessity for the Green Party. Although there were no domestic flights, aircraft were used on routes between a number of European states. European Airlines provided a service that was as basic as possible and, like the stripped-down cars, was not a means of transport that anyone used for pleasure. The seating was not divided into classes. Even when Ivan flew, he sat with the other passengers. As the flight from Kiev to London touched down at Heathrow, Lex Simitovich vowed that all this would change when he gained power. His days of spending four hours sitting in a cramped seat next to a screaming child would end as soon as he became the European Leader of the Green Party.

Like all other passengers, Simitovich had to pass through customs control. Ivan loved doing this. Man of the people that he was, he would laugh and joke with other passengers as an embarrassed official checked his papers and hand luggage. Simitovich was a sour man, not given to smiling. To his way of thinking, being too familiar with the man in the street lost a politician the respect he needed to govern effectively.

*

"I'm Brian Tyler of the Metropolitan Police." Brian could see that this meant nothing to Simitovich. "I've been working with Stephen Langford." Still there was no response. "On the Troxley case."

"Ah yes. This I have heard of," Simitovich sneered.

The customs officer glanced at Brian, waiting for confirmation that he should challenge Simitovich. Brian nodded and stepped back from the counter.

"Anything to declare, sir?" the officer asked. Simitovich never carried hand luggage for the very reason that it only prolonged this humiliating process.

The customs officer steeled himself. "Turn out your pockets, please, sir."

"Oh really!" Simitovich sighed and thrust both hands into his pockets. A bunch of keys, some coins and other assorted objects clattered onto the metal-topped counter. On top of these, he dropped his passport and a handkerchief. "That's the lot," he hissed.

"That's fine, sir. You can..." The customs officer was not expecting to find anything out of the ordinary and was just as keen as Simitovich to end this embarrassing confrontation. However, his eye had caught something strange. Before the handkerchief landed, he thought he had seen a small bottle of pills. It was possible, but highly unlikely, that Simitovich had some rare complaint that justified the possession of medication. He glanced at Brian, and took his cue from the fact that the young policeman was staring in disbelief at the contents of Simitovich's pockets. "Have you a permit for this medication, sir?" he asked, pushing the handkerchief to one side and picking up the bottle.

"I've never seen those before," Simitovich said dismissively.

The shock of finding the word 'Chitosan' on the label almost made the officer drop the bottle. The words spewed out of his mouth before he realised what he was saying. "I'm afraid I must caution you that it is illegal to import Chitosan into the UK and I am therefore arresting..."

"Arrest!" Simitovich exploded with rage. He turned to Brian. "Could you please explain to this man just who I am?"

Brian leaned forward and spoke softly. "This will be better dealt with out of public view. Let's talk about this somewhere more private," he said to the customs officer.

"Thank you very much, Mr. Tyler." Simitovich was visibly more relaxed as Brian led him and the customs officer to the detention room.

*

The cross hairs of the telescopic sight moved up Hildee Parks's back. She was the first to get out of the Jeep. Campbell knew that in a few seconds the sergeant would climb out and stand behind her. The cross hairs were now over her heart. At this range, Campbell could have gone for a head shot, but there were two other targets and he could not afford to miss. The sound of six shots echoed around the farmyard. A cloud of dust rose up around the Jeep. The driver lay on his side with one foot still in the vehicle. Hildee Parks, blood dripping from her nose and mouth, was sprawled face down under the sergeant. The driver was the only one who cried out. The only sound Hildee made was a low moan as the air was squashed out of her lungs by the sergeant falling on top of her.

*

Padreep looked through the glass panel in the door of the detention room. "That's Simitovich," he said turning to Brian, who was standing beside him. "First you arrest Mike and now you want to arrest Simitovich. It's a bit of a jump, isn't it? Why not try a few people in between? Just tell me you're not serious."

"Deadly serious."

"But you can't."

"No, *I* can't. I haven't got the rank, but *you* have."

"*Me*? No, wait a minute."

"Look," said Brian, "all you have to do is sit in while the charge is read out. Chitosan trafficking is a serious offence. There's no way he can come back at you for arresting him."

"It's not him I'm worried about." Padreep fixed Brian with a stare.

"Don't worry. *You* sort out Simitovich. *I'll* deal with the rest. Just point me to an office with a decent phone line in it — and tell me where I can find Johnny Coates."

"Upstairs in the Transport Police office." Padreep scratched his head and looked into the detention room again.

"Oh, and one other thing. I didn't arrest Mike."

Padreep seemed both relieved and puzzled. However, this piece of news seemed to reassure him. "Come on. Let's do it," he said to the customs officer.

Brian watched as Padreep and the customs officer sat down opposite Simitovich. Through the door, he saw Simitovich becoming increasingly agitated.

*

"Sir, have you heard?" Johnny leaped out of his chair as soon as Brian walked into the Transport Police Department's office.

"Heard what? And stop all this 'sir' business." Brian slipped the laptop computer off his shoulder.

"About Simitovich. They say he's been arrested."

"And I thought you were supposed to be looking after him."

Johnny was about to offer an excuse. Then he noticed that Brian was smiling. The laptop was dropped on the desk in front of him. "E-mail the report in the directory called 'Report' to this address," Brian said, handing Johnny a page from his notebook.

"*The Guardian*. But why...?"

"Just *do* it, and then forget you ever saw it." Brian grabbed his mobile and punched in Trevor's number again.

Johnny plugged a phone lead into the laptop's modem and attached the report to an e-mail. Clicking on the attachment displayed the report itself. He read a few lines and was about to ask Brian how he knew that Simitovich was using Chitosan to bribe members of the police. Then he recalled the events of the previous evening and decided to take Brian's advice and forget he saw anything.

*

The two soldiers sitting in the back of the Land Rover had taken all the shells out of Mike's revolver. They took it in turns to squeeze the trigger. "No," one said.

"Yes it did." The other soldier laughed.

"No way. There's no way this thing would ever fire."

"Ten euros?"

"You're on."

Mike looked at his watch. It felt as if he had been sitting there for more than an hour and a half. Perhaps the two soldiers' gallows humour was making time drag. At first, they had been quite talkative. He had described his trip to the Ukraine and America. However, they soon became bored, or perhaps realised that bonding with him would make their job more difficult.

Mike jumped when the mobile rang. It was Trevor who answered it. He listened without responding, then turned the ignition key. "We're going, lads!" he shouted over his shoulder, as he slammed the Land Rover into gear and pushed the accelerator pedal to the floor.

Trevor passed the phone to Mike. "Brian wants a word, sir."

Puzzled, Mike took the phone. Brian's request confused him even more. "Sorry, Brian. Did you say 'arrest Langford'? What the hell for?" He listened again. "Well, if you think you can make it stick."

During the journey, the soldier sitting opposite Mike replaced the shells in the revolver. As the Land Rover pulled up outside the Home Office, the gun was thrust back into Mike's hand. "You'll have to make the actual arrest. It's outside our jurisdiction, apparently." The soldier explained.

*

Stephen Langford slowly turned the pages of Brian's report. In an hour's time he would be releasing it to the press and handing a copy to Simitovich. Tomorrow, he and Simitovich would present their findings on the early evening news. Next week, he would talk to Mike and get him to see sense before doing something about Tyler. That was it, of course. That was what had been puzzling him about this report. He turned to the front page, which listed the main findings of the investigation. Then he turned to the back page, which listed the conclusions. Tyler had not put his name to the report. The implications of this had just sunk in when the door burst open. "Mike..." Langford was about to stand up and had already extended his hand.

Mike thought that this display of friendliness was absurd, considering he was carrying a gun and had two soldiers with him. "Stephen Langford, I am arresting you on suspicion of colluding with a person or persons unknown to fabricate evidence implicating leading politicians in the murder of Toby Troxley. I must warn you..."

"Mike, this is most irregular. The army have no power of arrest in the Home Office."

"*I'm* arresting you."

"But you've been suspended." Langford reached down and pulled open the top drawer of his desk. Mike squeezed the trigger of his gun twice. Langford staggered backwards. The first shot tore a hole in the back of his chair, but the second entered his lung and lodged next to his spine.

"Shit!" the soldier shouted. "You've just cost me ten euros."

*

The door to the corn dryer creaked open. The sergeant raised the machine gun and pointed it at Morris Haswell. "Friend!" the driver shouted. He had been in a better position to see what had happened.

Hildee leaped to her feet as soon as she saw the gun in Morris's hand. "Just what the hell do you think you're doing?"

"Saw a rat, Miss Parks," he said, handing her his dust-covered handkerchief. "A really big one."

Pleased that Morris had distracted Hildee, the driver tapped the sergeant on the shoulder and pointed to the tractor shed. There was a splash of blood around the window frame, and the muzzle of a rifle protruding from the opening.

"So you decide to start firing at it just as we arrive. Not very clever really." She pointed to her tee-shirt. Look at the mess my clothes are in!"

Morris seemed oblivious to her ranting. "Think you'd better get Miss Parks back to the house," he said to the sergeant.

After helping her into the Jeep the sergeant, using Morris's handkerchief, attempted to staunch the flow of blood from Hildee's nose. But Hildee snatched the handkerchief, tilted her head back and glared, first at the soldier and then Morris.

The grain lorry in which Campbell had intended to escape arrived. Morris started the elevator. It was not until he had climbed the wooden steps inside the dryer that he felt faint. It was nothing to do with having killed a man — he had done that before. His mind was full of 'what ifs?'. What if he had not put the revolver in his jacket pocket the previous night? What if he had returned to the house when he realised he was still carrying it that morning? What if he had not looked out of the corn dryer's hatch when he heard the Jeep arrive? Luck. It was all a matter of luck.

Hildee Parks escaped because Campbell's luck had run out. He knew Morris was there but had dismissed him as a doddering old man. As killers went, Campbell was not in Morris's league. True, Morris had cried himself to sleep the day he had to kill one of his dogs, but he had not thought twice about executing the people who killed Hildee's uncle. Lying flat and framed by the open window, Campbell had been an even easier target than Hildee and the soldiers. Morris was no novice. There was no hesitation. His hand did not shake. In his mind, he had become the gun — a mechanism without a conscience. The first shot disabled Campbell; the second shot killed him. There were four more shots, and only one of them missed the target. It had only done so because Campbell's body went into a spasm.

11

Saturday 31st August 2041

Hildee was getting used to sharing Brian. He was still 'her Brian'. "It's your Brian," Tilly said, taking time off from clearing the breakfast tables to sit down next to her. Smoothing out the newspaper with her hand, she drooled over the picture on the front page. "You lucky devil," she said.

By the evening, others had joined the queue. Tony Cameron and Adam Greer, even Peter Pardoe from the police station (who, apparently, had played a key role in the investigation), they all claimed a piece of 'her' Brian. Hildee knew that the other diners in the restaurant were watching her, waiting to see her reaction when Brian spoke. A woman who had been regarded just two weeks ago as cold and unapproachable had suddenly become warm, friendly and the centre of attention.

*

When the television broadcast started, however, the person speaking did not seem like 'her' Brian at all. He had become distant and spoke in a strange language Hildee had not heard before. Not 'spin speak'; there was no 'moving on' or 'putting this behind us'. Instead, the newly appointed commander hinted that there was still a great deal of work to do. They were nowhere near discovering the whole truth. There was need for further investigation and an overhaul of the Metropolitan Police.

The first question appeared to throw him. Just how had he discovered the connection between the fat-busting drugs ring and the conspiracy against David Fairchild? Brian hesitated before answering. He changed the subject and described the report that Mike Allchurch had found on Langford's desk. He explained the anomalies, the misleading statements and the omission of the evidence collected in America. Then, without making a specific allegation, Brian expressed his strong belief that someone with access to Chitosan was using the drug to buy influence within the Home Office.

Would Langford be put on trial? Brian was confident that he would be. Although Langford had been badly wounded, the doctors believed that the former deputy commissioner would be well enough to be interviewed on Monday. Why was Langford shot and why had Allchurch been suspended? Hildee studied Brian's face. She wondered whether his boss had been suspended in order to make way for him. Was this part of Fairchild's attempt to purge the police of dissident elements? Brian's face gave nothing away as he spoke in a matter-of-fact voice. "The suspension is only temporarily while we hold an internal inquiry." And those were the only questions he had time for. Confident and self-assured, he was everything Hildee wanted 'her' Brian to be — except here and with her.

Sunday 1st September 2041

Stephen Langford died in his sleep sometime in the early hours of Sunday morning. Brian was not told until seven a.m. The bullet that hit Langford ensured he would never walk again. However, apart from the risk of peritonitis, the doctors had expected him to live. The prospect of spending his day off performing an autopsy did nothing for Hutch's temper. In the event, he was home again before lunch. Once it was realised that Langford had died of a morphine overdose, it only took Hutch and Brian an hour to follow the paper trail back to the Euthanasia Unit.

The manager of the Euthanasia Unit remembered the girl who delivered the letter. Long black hair, blue eyes and very well spoken. She had seemed upset, but not distraught. Stephen Langford had signed the letter itself. The signature compared well with the one on his police ID card. A bit too well, Brian thought, remembering his conversation with Harry the Print.

Other than in cases of lung cancer and some forms of mental illness, the decision to terminate was made either by the patient themselves or by an immediate relative. Although it was unusual, it was not the first time the doctor had seen a letter from someone stating that they were unwilling to spend the rest of an already austere life as a cripple. He merely checked the signature and passed the S-Card number on to the Pharmacy Department. The pharmacist added a fatal dose of morphine to the painkillers Langford was being given to help him sleep. The nurse who administered the injection would have paid little attention to the dose or what was in the syringe. The system was designed to protect the sensibilities of all those involved in its implementation. So efficient was the process that the guards outside Langford's room did not realise it was under way.

Friday 20th September 2041

"It was a clever move, but you didn't think it would keep them off your back for ever?" Hutch had his feet up on the end of Brian's desk. "People have short memories. Everyone has forgotten about Langford and the Chitosan." He let his feet drop to the floor and stood up. "Blaming Mike is a convenient way to clear the decks."

"But there's no way Mike was involved." Brian folded his arms, leaned back against the windowsill and, tilting his head, looked up at the sky.

"He shot Langford and they say he killed another witness in the US. It looks as though he was tidying up."

"He thought Langford was going for his gun. Mike was going to kill *someone*. After his wife died, he went on some sort of guilt trip — looking for someone to blame, I suppose." Brian looked back into the office. "I thought he was going to shoot me."

"No-one's going to be interested in that. They'll crucify Mike, then start on you."

"Who are 'they'?"

"Someone in the party and their friends in here."

"Johnny, can you take an early lunch?" Brian asked, without looking at him.

When Johnny had left the office, Hutch transferred to his chair. He was about to speak, but Brian interrupted. "I was talking to Mike just a couple of days ago. Clearing up a few points." Brian returned to his desk and pulled open the top drawer, without looking for anything in particular. "He told me something interesting about his trip to Brussels. Apparently, he got the impression that Fairchild's people have someone inside the Home Office. Someone was keeping them pretty much up to speed on the Troxley case." With his head bowed, as though he was still searching the drawer, he looked across the room at Hutch. "Any idea who it could be?"

Raising one eyebrow, Hutch shook his head. "No idea at all."

"Because if I was talking to him now, I would ask him to go back to Fairchild and tell him to shake this place up and then let go of it."

"What do you mean?"

"What I said. If the police continue to be an extension of the party, they are always going to be used to resolve political differences. They should tell Fairchild to move the Met. back to New Scotland Yard where it belongs, drop the commissioner and put Padreep in charge. Am I making myself clear?" A hint of aggression had entered Brian's voice. "Padreep can reform the Met, I will reform the Home Office, and regional commissioners should be appointed to reform all the other forces."

"And who will run the Home Office?" Hutch smiled. "Lining up a nice little job for yourself, are you?"

"The party can appoint whoever they want."

"Whoever gets the job will face the same old problem."

"No they won't, from now on each regional force, and the Met., will include representatives from the local councils."

Hutch sucked air through his teeth. "Sounds dangerously like democracy, Brian. Didn't realise you were a fan of universal suffrage."

"Hardly." Brian slammed the desk drawer shut. "Perhaps Fairchild's friend could get in touch with me sometime before the end of the week. If Fairchild agrees, I'll set up a press conference."

Hutch stood up to leave. "And what about Mike?"

"Perhaps someone could find him a job that keeps him out of the way for a while. Something simple that doesn't involve more than two things happening at once." Brian handed Hutch a computer disk.

"What's this?"

"Everything I just explained to you."

This was not what Brian wanted. After spending two months designing a program of reforms, he had thought that would be the end of it. The report would be handed to the Commissioner and then life would return to normal. He had even planned the trip to Downham and hinted to Hildee that he would be with her before the end of the month. Dragging the computer keyboard across his desk, Brian recalled Hildee's S-Card record. This was the closest he got to her — monitoring her visits to the restaurant and the medical centre. Closing down the window, he opened up his e-mail software and composed a message.

Saturday 21st September 2041

Tony and Adam were fooling around with their mobile phones. "Look! Our website!" Adam called to Hildee. "Mr. Tyler sent us these," he said enthusiastically.

Hildee had also been given a mobile phone, but it was at home, switched off and shut away in her desk drawer. That would have made things too easy for Brian. So would the internet phone

Tony had installed for her. She did not want a disjointed conversation with someone who sounded as though they were gargling in a dustbin. Hildee wanted Brian here with her, and he had promised to come — that weekend.

The televised press conference was sombre and Brian spoke without interruption. At first, Hildee did not realise that she was crying. She probably started when Brian said what a long haul the reforms would be. It was then she realised that the e-mail was not just postponing his visit for yet another week; it was telling her that he was never coming back. Perhaps he had never intended to return. His eye was set on a top job at the Home Office — which, according to the television interviewer, was within his grasp. By the end of the broadcast, Hildee was sobbing. It was as though someone inside her, over whom she had no control, was releasing all the tears that had been bottled up over the years.

The other diners became concerned. Tilly telephoned Matt and helped Hildee to the car when he arrived.

*

"He is not coming back, is he?" Her sobbing echoed in the entrance hall of Nordelph Manor. "I have made such a fool of myself. People must think I have been very silly."

People did not. They had seen a young woman suddenly bloom after years of imprisonment in her own personal winter. Seeing her wither just as quickly reminded them that autumn was over and that the hardest part of the year was upon them. Matt put his arm around her. "If it's any consolation, *I* always thought he'd come back," Matt said.

Sunday 8th December 2041

"It doesn't make any sense and this is the last time we do it," Stef said. Trevor and the others jeered from the bank. It did seem pointless to row the boat down the Serpentine now that the path around the edge was clear, but Brian was growing weary of change. The café at the end of the lake had been renovated and there was dancing until late into the evening. Stef tried to get Brian to join in, but he had stubbornly refused to have fun.

"Did I ever tell you about that lodger we had?" she asked, without expecting a reply. "His wife had died and he came to stay for a while. I suppose his house was more than he could cope with on his own. Anyway, he never said much, very quiet. I thought that after a while he would get over it, but six months went by and he was still the same. Then one day he just went — disappeared. So I was clearing out his room, and in the wardrobe were all his wife's clothes. You could even smell her perfume. I suppose he just got over her, made a clean break"

"Tragic," Brian replied, in a sulk.

"No. Just a bit sad. 'Tragic' is when your life stops while you pine for someone who is still alive."

Friday 20th December 2041

Stef's words came into his mind as Brian watched the reflection of the watery early afternoon sun on the Serpentine. A group of party officials were scurrying past with their collars turned up against the bitterly cold breeze that was blowing across Hyde Park. Seeing Brian, one of the officials broke away from the group and entered the restaurant.

Mike Allchurch sat down opposite Brian and glanced out of the window. "Nice view. They've made a good job of the place." Brian did not answer. "All alone then?" Mike persisted.

"Sorry. I was miles away." Brian looked around the restaurant as though he was looking at it for the first time. "Just having a break. Been over at Park Lane all morning."

"That's where we're off to. We'll be there for a couple of days. Big meeting about the euro. How are you going to cope with this new monetary system?"

Brian shrugged. "Not thought about it. How's Frankfurt?"

"Fine. Just right. And I hear you're a busy man these days. 'Onwards and upwards' and all that. Want a coffee?"

Brian shook his head and looked out of the window again.

"I hear I've got you to thank for the Frankfurt job." Mike drummed his fingers on the table. He was on the point of getting up to go, but changed his mind. "Saw something funny today. I just flew in to Heathrow and saw Lucky Dip in the arrivals lounge."

Brian smiled. "Still got your watch?"

"Last time I looked at his file it had 'Deceased' stamped on it."

Brian shrugged. Mike leaned across the table. "And when I cleared out my desk I couldn't find that bottle of Chitosan."

"I thought someone might get the wrong idea after what we found on Simitovich."

346

"I think it disappeared from my desk before Simitovich got here, don't you?"

Brian took a deep breath. "Possibly."

"So why didn't you let me shoot him?"

"Because if you had, we would have been buried out on some penal farm by now. Langford didn't act alone and Simitovich isn't the only dissident voice in the party, but I guessed that no-one would throw in their lot with a drug runner. If Fairchild can get the reforms through, in time the whole ugly gang will fade into the shadows."

"And if it hadn't worked, was there a plan B? Is that why the army were holding me until Simitovich was arrested?" Mike realised Brian was not going to answer, and he was not sure he wanted to know anyway. Outside, the other officials were banging on the window and pointing at their watches. "Still, we all got what we wanted, didn't we?" said Mike as he stood up.

"Oh yes. Didn't we just?! Take care, sir," Brian muttered under his breath. He was staring out of the window again, so did not see Mike's mock salute. The still, grey water of the Serpentine stretched into the distance. Maybe Mike was mistaking movement for progress, but he, at least, believed that he had found what he was looking for.

*

Brian finally made up his mind. Meeting Mike had helped. "That's the end of that," he said, removing the software from his computer. He had looked at Hildee's S-Card record for the last time, noticing as he did so that she had missed five meals that week. She had already been on medical rations for two months. He watched Johnny, frantically typing on his keyboard. That was him, three months ago. And he had become Mike — or how Mike used to be. Staring morosely at the computer screen, watching someone dying alone. He could not let his obsession with Hildee drag him down, the way the woman in Ruislip had crippled Mike. Taking the computer disk from the drawer, he deleted the last copy of Tony Cameron's software. "Sentimentality is an expensive luxury."

"Sorry, sir?" Johnny looked up. "You said something?"

"Oh, it was nothing." Brian switched off the computer. "Onwards and upwards."

*

Hildee would have stayed downstairs, listening to music, but the fire died down and she could not be bothered to make it up. There was no wood or coal left in the study, and the central-heating boiler struggled to keep the temperature above fifteen degrees. So she retreated upstairs and took to her bed. Outside, an icy drizzle was drifting across the fields, and water dripped from the bare branches of the trees in the gardens. The wind from the coast was not as strong as usual, but it did force the cold into the house, and it brought with it the sound of the trains travelling through Downham station. Hildee liked to play music or listen to the radio. The sound of the trains made her feel lonely — especially lonely tonight.

She turned off the radio when the newsreader started to talk about reforms. There had been enough talk of reforms for one day. The soldiers mentioned them while they were loading the last of their filing cabinets onto the lorry. "All part of a reorganisation," the young guard had said. He was rather sweet and had thanked her for making his stay so pleasant. He had said she made a better commander than Hutley. Hutley had never returned. Matt had talked of seeing him living wild near the coast. The truth was far less exciting. Hildee had received a letter from Hutley's mother, in which she thanked Hildee for looking after her son and explained that he had suffered a breakdown and was resigning his commission.

Now the rest of the soldiers had gone. Reforms made her think of Brian. Was he thinking of her? Probably not. Definitely not. On Fridays the doctor usually called. At first, Hildee had thought this was odd. Then it became obvious that Brian was in contact with him. Feeling guilty because he too busy, or just plain unwilling, to drag himself away from London, he had asked the doctor to check up on her. Then, later in the evening, the e-mail would arrive. 'Are you sure you are OK? Switch on your mobile. Thinking of you.' He never mentioned it, but he must have realised she was pregnant.

Today the doctor did not come, and there was no e-mail. Obviously three months had been long enough to get over her. He had a guilt-free weekend ahead of him. Hildee was too tired and drained to feel bitter. Turning out the light, she wrapped the covers around her aching body. In the distance, another train set off from Downham on its lonely journey to the coast. Sleep — a lonely journey into darkness — came only too easily.

Wednesday 10th May 2051

On the platform of Downham station, Billy Spencer was waiting for his school friends to arrive on the Ely-bound train. His mother had died in childbirth and he had been adopted by Matt Spencer and his wife. Billy had never been hungry, never seen a dead body and cared little who his real father was. When he grew up, there would be no question of his being forced to join the army. There were no armed guards outside the station where he now waited and, by the time he married, dying in childbirth would be an extremely rare event.

The train arrived and within moments the platform was filled with children. Billy shouted to his father, who was standing on the platform opposite. Matt was preoccupied with a pile of wooden crates that had just been unloaded from the London-to-King's Lynn train. The young apprentice from Cameron Electronics drew Matt's attention to his son. "Kids," Matt said as he waved, "don't know they're alive."

The apprentice was not much more than a kid himself. He worked for Tony Cameron, who had taken over the instrument-repair company when Andrew Cameron died. With the apprentice's help, Matt threw the crates into the back of his van. "So we're ready for the off then," he said.

Matt knew it was only a matter of time before the apprentice started ribbing him, teasing him about the old days. Perhaps this one was old enough to have played in one of the abandoned housing estates, raking over the evidence of a way of life he would only read about in books. He was from the generation who had the luxury of history lessons, but never listened to the teacher. But then why should *they* care what all this cost? Matt's generation had made a point of drawing a line under all the pain and had erased from their collective memory all those who had died. Today all the old housing estates were gone and the reclaimed materials had been stockpiled in vast goods yards. The new houses being built were clustered around railway stations.

"They say there used to be wolves out here," the apprentice piped up, after they had been driving for forty minutes.

"Really? And who said that?"

"They say you were the only one who dared travel out here." The apprentice surveyed the bleak fen landscape. "So what will you do when the new railway is finished?"

"People will always want things in a hurry."

"I reckon you'll have to retire."

Matt reached behind his seat and picked up a small box. "Seen one of these before?"

Fumbling with the carton, the apprentice eventually got it open. "An MPEG player! They're like hens' teeth!" He studied it for a moment, then put it back in the box. "Can you get me one?"

"Waiting list, I'm afraid. Three months at least."

"Oh. That's a shame." He handed the box back to Matt.

"Keep it."

"Really?"

"Yeah. Thirty pounds and it's yours."

The apprentice took out his wallet and had passed Matt two notes before he realised. "Sorry, Matt. It's all I've got."

"Bloody euros."

"Sorry. I've got some pound coins at home."

Matt stopped the van. The apprentice stared at him apprehensively. "Wait a minute," said Matt, taking the twenty-euro note. "This is a new one. I'll take this off your hands." He released his grip on the player. "Now, enough messing about. Where's this mobile-phone base station of yours?"

But the apprentice was not listening. He opened the door of the van and climbed out. "Is that Black Fen?" he asked, pointing to the two parallel barbed-wire fences in the distance.

"Yep. That's it all right." Matt got out of the van for a better look.

"You knew the people who lived there?"

"Yes. *When* people lived there."

"Tony says they killed Mr. Andrew."

Matt could not get used to the younger generation's habit of calling everyone by their first name. "Mr. Cameron's father died of a disease caught from people living in Black Fen. They didn't kill him on purpose." Matt remembered it well: Cameron dying after coming out here to look at an old telephone exchange. Then the quarantine and the men in white body suits and masks. The convoys of ambulances travelling through Downham and the field hospitals that had been set up outside Black Fen itself. The smoke that rose from the fen during the day and the gunfire at night."

"Where did they all go?"

"Died, some of them. The rest moved away or were resettled somewhere else." He became irritated. "I don't really know, and this won't get your mobile-phone system up and running, will it?"

*

"I really would like a photograph."

"Well, the fire's out. What do you want me to do? Set the house on fire again?" The fireman shook his head and walked away from the young photojournalist.

The girl followed the fireman back towards the fire engine. "Well, perhaps in that case, if I could have a few comments from you, we could use the photo we have on file."

"Fine by me, love. Fire away — pardon the pun." The fireman turned to his colleagues and grinned.

"Now that you are head of the London fire service, will you stop attending fires?"

"The London fire service is made up of autonomous units. If a large fire breaks out I will, of course, step back and concentrate on co-ordination. But let's hope the days of the big fires are over."

"But it's been suggested that your desire to lead from the front is an attempt to overcome your own fear of fire."

"What sort of nonsense is that?"

"Is it true that your own parents were killed in a house fire?"

The fireman leaned into the cab of the tender and grabbed a metal tube. He lit the smoke canister and threw it into the remains of the house. "Come on, lads. Let's give the lady her photograph."

While she was taking the photograph, the journalist's mobile phone rang. She was wanted back at Farringdon Road straight away.

*

"How long will it take you to finish the fire-chief story?" Gerald Petrie asked, without looking up from his desk. Eventually he found the piece of paper he was searching for. "Vlachos has died in his sleep." He pushed it across the desk to the girl. "There you go. Write it up for tomorrow's issue. Get copy over to the BBC and they will put it out at six this evening."

'During my lifetime Europe, and the rest of the world, has suffered as never before. See my death as the end of an era. Do not mourn my passing. Celebrate the beginning of a new age.'

The journalist looked puzzled. "This is serious?"

"What he said when he knew he was dying, apparently. I *have* checked it out." Gerald smiled. "Probably gains something in translation."

351

The journalist looked at the sheet of paper again. "Wasn't there something about ten years ago? Some attempt to oust him?"

"Just concentrate on the profile. I'll include all the rest in my piece."

But the girl would not leave it alone. "There was a policeman, here in London. He had something to do with it. A big scandal..."

"Or perhaps you'd rather do a profile on the new director of the UK Ivan's chain?"

"OK, OK. I get the message."

*

The housing officer, who had already given up trying to hurry the pair of students along, became exasperated when he was asked to look at yet another interesting 'find.'

The officer had been asked to carry out an inventory of houses in South Ruislip. If enough houses were habitable the western section of the Central underground line would be re-opened. The task was slow and laborious, because the students helping him were supposed to take detailed notes as part of their third-year projects. Moreover, they were frequently distracted by various remnants of the twentieth century.

This time, however, it was not a wide-screen television, or an invalid lift. The students had discovered human remains on the floor of an upstairs bathroom. The housing officer chastised the students for touching the remains and forgetting to put on their facemasks. Ushering the pair out of the house, he called the local health centre and asked for a body-collection team.

The students expected that the team, comprising an elderly man and a young woman, would merely bury the remains and disinfect the house. They were surprised when the woman produced a digital camera and began making copies of the faded photographs she found pasted in an album. While the old man was in the bathroom, shovelling the bones and cloth into a wooden box, the girl broke open an old bureau and typed any names she found on documents into a portable computer.

The whole process took an hour and a half. The engineer complained about the delay. "Nearly two hours," he said. "They must have a lot of time on their hands."

The students merely shrugged. One tapped the other on the shoulder and showed him a page from a magazine. "Look at all those television programmes! Unbelievable!"

"Working late again," Padreep said. It was only when the phone rang that Brian looked at the clock.

"Damn! I'm going to get shot! It's these light evenings."

"It's overwork. It's about time you took a holiday. Which, in a way, is why I've called."

"I'll take a break in August."

"Next week actually. You've heard that Vlachos is dead?"

"Yes, I've heard. So?" Brian had already guessed what Padreep was about to say.

"So you're going to the funeral. Representing the force."

"I'm sure they wouldn't miss us. Anyway, someone else can do it."

"I can order you to do it."

"Yes, I suppose you can," Brian said, with a hint of resignation in his voice. Today had not gone well and he had found it increasingly difficult to concentrate after hearing of Vlachos's death. The events of ten years ago still played on his mind from time to time. He still had feelings of guilt, regrets and nagging doubts about what he had done. Usually, after spending an evening brooding, his wife would talk him around and the next day he would bury himself in his work again. This time the funeral would drag things out for a fortnight. "I'll do it." He sighed.

"Take the family, stop off in Paris and Vienna. Make a holiday out of it."

"OK, I said I'd do it." Brian began to sound irritable. Early evening sunlight streamed through the office window. He slid some papers into his briefcase and sat quietly for a moment. Most people's lives were made up of thousands of small decisions. Most people never bothered to consider how things would have turned out if they had acted differently, or chosen a different path. Brian, however, could clearly identify the moment he decided to change his life — and perhaps many other people's lives. A 'social mutation' someone once called it.

Thursday 18th May 2051

The picture of the girl with the squint, sitting between her mother and father on a garden bench, appeared on the London missing persons' database at ten thirty in the morning. Two people who could have identified the girl immediately had not touched a computer for over five years.

Padreep Kumar was in a meeting at the Home Office. Having resigned as commissioner of the Metropolitan police in 2047, he had stood as a Democratic Green Alliance Party representative in Britain's first election. He won the West London seat in the newly formed House of Commons — since renamed the House of Representatives. The following year he had been appointed Home Secretary.

Mike Allchurch was taking a late morning coffee break. Maria, his wife, was always telling him to be positive. 'Don't act like a cynical old man,' she would say. So he tried to sound like one of the bright young things from the European Central Economics Unit who were seated around the conference table.

"These have been tried out in Britain." The young man passed a number of twenty-euro notes around the table.

Picking up one of the notes, Mike walked across to the window. For a moment, he stood gazing out at the river Main. He lived in a small flat on the other side of the river. It was surrounded by pine trees and had a small garden. Last weekend, his son — now an engineering manager on the railways — had come out to visit them.

"Mr. Allchurch?"

"Sorry. Miles away." Mike rubbed the note between his fingers, then held it up to the light. "Printed in the UK?"

"Yes. What do you think?"

"Very good." He looked at it again. Would asking if Ivan Vlachos had ever worn a pair of glasses with Silhouette frames make him sound cynical? Probably it would. "Excellent," he said, as he handed the note back to the young man.

*

"Dad, why did you call that man 'Lucky'?" the girl asked. Her father never got the chance to answer.

"He was the magician. The one in the story," her brother said.

"Was he the magician?" The girl sought confirmation from her father. "Was he the one that made the wicked witch fly away?"

"Of course he was." Her brother was astonished by her ignorance. "He made Mum's watch appear from behind your ear."

"Why is a magician working at a railway station?"

Brian tried to change the subject. "Did you know that the next bridge is so strong that if two trains travelling at a hundred and twenty kilometres an hour put their brakes on, at the same time, it wouldn't fall down?" They were half an hour from St. Pancras, recently renamed Fairchild station after the former European president, and gliding through the Kent countryside. Mrs. Tyler had been less than amused by the encounter with Lucky Dip.

The children, however, would not be distracted. "He called you 'Brian'. He should have called you 'Mr. Tyler', shouldn't he, Dad?"

Brian heard his wife sigh. Opening *The Guardian* magazine, he read the profile of the new head of the London fire service and the tribute to Ivan Vlachos. He recognised Gerald Petrie's prose papering over the controversial period when Ivan had been forced to resign from the party:

'Ten years ago Ivan stepped down as Leader of the Ukrainian Green Party to take up the post of Chairman of the European Green Party. Working alongside European President David Fairchild, Ivan guided Europe back to democracy and drafted Europe's Green constitution.'

Putting the newspaper down on the table, Brian looked out of the window again. His wife did not like secrets popping up from Brian's past. Until today, she had thought Lucky Dip was no more than a character in one of Brian's silly bedtime stories. Now she realised that he was just as real, and as annoying, as Aunty Stef. And Aunty Stef could be very annoying — especially when her theatrical hugs and kisses were aimed at Brian, rather than the children. Stef would start talking about the past and Brian would lapse into some sort of dreamlike state. His wife was the first to admit this made her jealous. Maybe Brian had another life somewhere else. Perhaps he spent time with another woman when work took him away from home. Who knew? But when he *was* with her, she really would have liked his full attention.

"What were you thinking?" she would ask.

"Just things," he would reply, although recently "This'll do me" had come back into fashion.

The river Medway stretched into the distance, a gleaming silver ribbon laid across the rolling Kent countryside. The late morning sun glinted on the water, but now Brian was standing on the bank of another river — gazing across the fields around Nordelph Manor.

Perhaps Mike was right. Perhaps there *was* a plan B. Even a plan C, D or E, for that matter. Or perhaps no real plan at all. Inside us there is an elementary desire that determines how we interpret the world and build our lives. Every decision we make is based on a dataset that is beyond our comprehension. People claimed that Brian had acted for the good of the party, had risked everything for some higher ideal. In truth, all he had done was to seek the safety and security that had eluded him as a child. Every decision is a personal decision; every act is a selfish act. Everything is decided by our genes' desire to survive. The interaction of our elementary desires is what passes for society. It comes into being without our knowledge and evolves outside our control. It is us, it is the meta man. It alone decides when it is born, how it lives, and when it dies.

And Mother Nature danced, raised her skirts and teased him. For one brief moment, Brian not only saw, but understood. And Nature *can* be a loving mother, a beautiful temptress, or an exciting lover. It is not until you try to dominate her that you find out what a tough bitch she really is.

"What were you thinking?" she asked.

Friday 20th December 2041

"What were you thinking?" Hildee looked down at the shivering body slumped in front of the last remnants of the fire. She paced the room for a while and then returned to his side. She wanted to shout at him but was unsure where to start. So she started with his decision to walk, without a coat, the three kilometres from the station. For not finding out if there was a connecting bus before he left London. For not finding Matt and getting a lift, or staying in the Swan until the next day.

"Whatever were you thinking?" She moved on to broader issues. Why give up a perfectly good job? Would he be happy spending the rest of his life as a provincial police chief? And anyway, why had *she* not been consulted before this momentous decision was made?

Brian had stopped listening. During the walk from the station, the cold had got into his bones. He began to shake uncontrollably. Helping him up to her room, Hildee undressed him and put him into her bed. Then she sat in a chair and watched him. She considered sleeping in the next room. After all, sleeping *with* him would send out all the wrong signals. It would confirm her acceptance of this situation. Eventually, she slid between the sheets and lay next to his cold body — holding him until he stopped shivering.

Saturday 21st December 2041

The atmosphere was tense but not strained. Both were wary of each other. After breakfast, Brian spent the morning first in Downham library and then in the police station. He met up with Hildee in the Ivan's after she had finished her community service at Downham school. Brian said little during lunch and spent most of the time reading. Had he wanted to talk to Hildee, it would not have been possible. Wherever they went, someone wanted to talk to Brian. She listened carefully, in case he gave some hint of his intentions. She did not realise that Brian was studiously avoiding the subject — especially after the lecture Hildee had delivered the previous evening. Back at Nordelph, he took his books into the office and continued his studies. The door was left open and Hildee wandered in from time to time. On each occasion, Brian made a point of asking a question about some farm or other, or whether this or that village was still inhabited.

Once, she found him taking papers from the library and, later, using the computer. She wondered if he was covering his tracks. Perhaps he had lied about his new job and was just making sure he would not be compromised after his next promotion. He certainly seemed more relaxed after he had used the computer. He must have found the software Hildee had used to alter her S-Card records, deleting the odd meal here and there. But Brian had already realised what she had done. For a woman nearly four months pregnant she looked remarkably healthy — radiant even.

"I thought, tomorrow, we might have a quiet day together," Hildee whispered, as Brian drifted off to sleep.

"Sorry," he murmured. "Matt's giving me a tour of the county. Plenty of time. We'll have plenty of time..."

"What?" Hildee tugged his arm but he was already sleeping, or at least pretending to sleep. She now realised why Brian and Matt had been deep in conversation during the dance that evening, leaving her to fend off the barrage of questions: 'Has he asked you yet?' 'Is he staying?' "Are you staying, Brian?" she whispered. His breath was heavy on her neck. Perhaps she imagined it, but his arms did seem to tighten around her.

Sunday 22nd December 2041

"So where else will you want to be going, sir?" Matt tugged his forelock and laughed. "Bloody freezing, isn't it?" He pulled his coat tight around his body and held the collar up against his face.

"Amazing." Brian stood at the edge of the cliff, watching the waves crash down on the beach below. "This is the North Sea?"

"The Wash. The North Sea is out that way." Matt pointed east and the wind caught his coat. "That's where this wind is coming from. You must be frozen to the bone."

"Just a bit."

Back in the Land Rover, Matt tried to get the heater working. "You're not really dressed for these parts. Haven't you got a coat?"

"Wore out last year. Just never got around to replacing it. Anyway, we're heading back now, aren't we?"

"We'd better. Looks like snow is on the way." Large grey clouds had formed on the horizon, boiling up and into the sky and reducing the sun to a dirty yellow disk.

Brian expected Matt to turn south at King's Lynn and take the direct route back to Downham. However, they turned west, drove through the town and did not turn south again until they reached Terrington St. Clements. Eventually leaving the road, the Land Rover bumped along a track for half a kilometre. Parking under a tree, Matt grabbed a rifle and jumped out. He led Brian through the trees until they came to a wide expanse of frost-covered farmland. "Quiet! Stay back a bit." Matt raised the gun. In the failing light, Brian could just make out shapes moving across the field. Three shots rang out, then one more. Two of the shapes faltered, fell and skidded across the frozen ground. "Come on!" Matt grabbed Brian's arm and they ran across to where the two roe deer lay.

Dragging the animals back to the tree, Matt took a rope and strung them up by their front legs. With a long-bladed knife he slit their stomachs, watching Brian's face to see how he would react. Brian half turned away as the innards fell, in a steaming pile, on the ground. "So you're staying then?"

"I'm not sure."

"Not sure?" Matt shouted.

"It's up to Hildee really."

"I'll tell you something!" Matt waved the bloodied knife at Brian. "Cousin Hildee loves you like crazy. You'll break her heart if you leave her again."

"Not the impression I get. She seems pretty cold towards me at the moment."

"Scared, you mean."

"Scared of what?"

"Scared you'll end up dying on her." Matt untied the animals, then rummaged around in the offal, putting the hearts, livers and kidneys into a small sack. "You see, it's an investment, isn't it? A woman invests in a man she thinks will last the course. Give her lots of healthy kids." He grinned as he dragged the animals back towards the Land Rover. "Of course, clever people like you and cousin Hildee dress it all up as love and romance. You dance around each other even after you've made the decision."

Brian helped Matt lift the deer. "You could be right."

"Don't let me interfere. I just wanted to know if you're staying. I wouldn't like to think I'm wasting my time with all this."

Brian was not sure what he meant. He got into the passenger seat and closed the door. Climbing into the driving seat, Matt looked across at Brian. "My guess is, you'll stay. Just try not to get yourself killed. Can't stand weepy women."

"I'll bear that in mind." Looking up he saw that the clouds were now rolling overhead. "Venison tomorrow, is it?"

"For someone." Matt slammed the Land Rover into reverse and spun it around.

They had only travelled another two kilometres when Matt turned off the main road again. Soon the Land Rover was crawling down the main street of a darkened village. When they reached the centre, Brian could make out the shapes of people walking along the pavements: parents and children dressed in torn clothes. Everyone looked malnourished. Brian felt disoriented. It was if they had driven into a bad dream.

"Where the hell are we?" he asked.

"Not a bad guess. This is Black Fen. This is where all the survivalists and dropouts live. Some of them escaped from penal farms, but most of them just thought they could make a better go of it on their own." Matt brought the vehicle to rest outside a small village shop with oil lamps burning in the window.

When he stepped out onto the pavement, a group of people gathered around Brian. One pushed a gun into his ribs. Even after he had seen and recognised Matt, the man still kept his gun pointed at Brian. "There you go!" Matt threw open the back door of the Land Rover. "Two gutted deer, seventy-five litres of oil, spades, forks, saws and a couple of axes."

"For what?" the man sneered.

"A coat, hat and gloves for my friend here."

"Fair enough." The man muttered. "Care to step into the fitting room?"

Brian was glad to get out of the foul-smelling shop and back into the Land Rover. After only fifteen minutes his head and hands were so warm that he had to remove the fox-fur hat and goatskin gloves. The deerskin coat he left on. "What a place! I really didn't realise..."

"Better get a move on. We're late." Matt seemed reluctant to talk about what they had just seen. He drove in silence until the lights of Downham came into view. "You know I'm not a great fan of Ivan and your Green friends, but if someone hadn't done something, we'd all have ended up living like that." He looked out of the side window rather than make eye contact with Brian. "And there are still greedy bastards out there who would poison us all back into the Stone Age for a quick buck."

Brian wondered if Matt was trying to tell him something; letting him know that people here would accept him; that, in their eyes, what Brian had done was right, not just for the party but for everyone. Perhaps he was, but in all the years Brian knew him Matt never mentioned these things again.

There were few diners in the restaurant. Brian had hoped to meet Hildee there. He felt guilty about leaving her on her own, but Matt had insisted they went out alone. Tilly told Brian that Hildee had been in earlier; she had wanted to get back to Nordelph before dark, but had asked after him.

*

The curtain in the study moved when the Land Rover arrived in front of the house. Although Hildee opened the front door as soon as Brian had climbed the steps, she was cool towards him.

Hildee could feel herself trembling with rage. She ran her finger over the stitching in the fox-fur hat. There was no doubt in her mind where it came from — or how Brian had got blood on the bottom of his trousers. "Look, Brian, I do not know whether you will stay or not. That is up to you." It was almost as if she was fighting back tears. "But, if you do stay, never, *ever* do anything this stupid again." She threw the hat at Brian and stormed out of the room.

Leaving the coat, gloves and hat in the office in order to avoid another outburst, Brian climbed the stairs to Hildee's room. The light was already off and he thought she was asleep. As he got into bed, she sighed and pulled his arms around her. "Sorry," he said, and gently kissed her neck.

"I was just..."

"I understand," Brian whispered. "Now I understand."

*

Rather than face another farewell on the platform of Downham station, Hildee said goodbye to Brian in the restaurant. She still doubted he would return. Back at Nordelph, she pulled his suitcase out from under her bed. He would hardly miss two changes of clothes and a couple of old books. Could he be that cruel? She laughed out loud at the thought of Brian arriving in London wearing a deerskin coat and fox-fur hat. Then her doubts dragged her down again. Why would a man who was heading for the top of the police force swap his job with a commissioner in some rural backwater like Norwich?

Where was the china ornament? Perhaps he could not repair it. Perhaps it was still in his room in London. Late in the afternoon, she was sitting alone in the office. A light dusting of snow outside reflected the sunlight into the room. It had the effect of turning her perception of the room through 180 degrees — or exchanging afternoon and morning. If the snow lay for a few days, she would get used to it, but at the moment she felt disoriented. It was almost a relief when the light faded. It was then, while drawing the curtains in the study, that she discovered the figurine. Brian had put it behind the photographs on the table in front of the window.

*

The snowfall became heavy: ten centimetres fell in two hours. There was a commotion at the main gate. Lights swept across the garden as a vehicle turned around. Brian stumbled up the drive like small boy. "The road is blocked," he said, trying to catch his breath. "Morris was in the restaurant. Gave me a ride back on his tractor." His arms gripped Hildee tighter than they had before. She realised that Morris had told Brian about the gunman at the farm.

That night, while Hildee lay in bed, Brian stood looking out of the window. The moon was lighting up the snow-covered fields for miles around. "We could be the only two people in the world," he whispered, as he climbed into bed. Hildee took hold of his hand

and pressed it against her abdomen.

Thursday 18th May 2051

In time, their two very different ways of life became one. They would breakfast together, then meet up again for dinner in the evening. Brian tried to make time in the winter when the farm was quiet, and only travel to London in the summer when Hildee was busy. His career took off again when Padreep was appointed Home Secretary, although it was quite clear that he would never leave Nordelph. As head of the Reform and Oversight Committee, he was regarded one of Britain's most important policemen. Hildee knew that if he had stayed in London he would have been one of *Europe's* most important policemen. If this bothered him, he never let it show.

For her part, any regrets she had were hardly worth mentioning. She wished she could control her temper. She wished she had never called Brian 'BJ' in front of his colleagues. The nickname had stuck and now even people in Downham used it. Then she had told Brian, a long time ago, that she would never want to be Mrs. Tyler. So she was still 'Miss Parks', even though they had married, on the beach at Hunstanton, in a ceremony conducted by an army padre Matt had invited onto Downham social club's trip to the seaside. She had given birth to four children, three of whom had survived. No, there were few regrets.

"Will she ever come back, Dad?"

"Who?"

"The wicked witch. Will she ever come back?"

Brian ruffled his daughter's hair. "No, she's gone. She can't hurt us now."

*

The A340 Airbus circled over Long Island. Martha Snyder watched Manhattan slide under the wing. She found the ending of direct flights from Europe to Washington inconvenient. On the other hand, the reopening of New York had ended her quest to find out what really had happened to her husband. Once the city had lost its air of mystery, it had become easier for Martha to put him to rest.

The aircraft levelled out. Martha rested her head on the back of the seat for a while, then saved the biography of the new EU president to disk and closed down the screen of her laptop.

Below, in the Seventh Avenue offices of New Century Bio-Ag Inc., the annual board meeting was just getting under way. "I'd like to introduce Miranda Lyndon. As you all know, Miranda has done some marvellous work for the company over the last ten years." Brushing her black hair from her face and tucking it behind her ears, Miranda waited for the applause to die down. She fixed her audience with her clear blue eyes. Her accent was mid-Atlantic — not as refined as the one that had convinced the doctor she was Langford's daughter, but not as coarse as the one she had used in the hotel where Troxley's body was found.

"Ladies and gentlemen, the populations and economies of Europe and the US are growing rapidly. The return of democracy, liberalisation and free-market economics has generated a strong demand for basic commodities. Year-on-year consumption of oil, copper, tin and zinc are on the increase. This is also true of coffee, tea, and even cocoa. Soon the governments of the US and Europe will be forced to secure reliable supplies of commodities from third-world producers — or risk losing elections. Our company is well placed. We have the experience gained during the Rebafing project and the technology we inherited from Genesis Natural Products Inc. So armed, we can help government agencies consolidate their positions in third-world countries. Even if governments are not interested, there are corporations who appreciate that creating a technology dependence in third-world food markets is an efficient way of holding down commodity prices."